NOT
FAMOUS

This is a work of fiction. Names, characters, organizations, places, events, and incidents are either products of the author's imagination or are used fictitiously.

Independently published by Matthew Hanover

matthewhanover.com

Contact: me@matthewhanover.com

ISBN-13: 978-1729166215

NOT FAMOUS

MATTHEW HANOVER

PROLOGUE

I SHOULD BE planning a wedding right now, but I'm not. Instead, I'm just a guy who proposed to his girlfriend and ended up humiliated and alone.

I'd done everything right. I'd even asked Lauren's parents for their blessing in advance. They were thrilled when we spoke and excited about me *officially* becoming a part of their family. All I had to do was pop the question.

Lauren and I were together for nearly five years and living together for two. I had no reason to believe she'd say no. We'd talked about marriage in terms of "when" not "if" for some time, and especially after she finished graduate school earlier this year. Even so, I was nervous and kept putting off my proposal until the right time. I'd considered proposing on her birthday in November but chickened out and decided to wait until New Year's Eve.

What could be more romantic? Right? I didn't know it at the time but waiting that one month changed everything.

I had a simple plan: A fancy dinner out, propose after the meal and before dessert. *Voila!* We'd be engaged. We'd get married. We'd live happily ever after.

Before dinner I suddenly got nervous about a public marriage proposal. It had seemed like a good idea at first, but on the way to the restaurant I suddenly felt weird about proposing around a bunch of strangers. So, I decided to wait until we got home to propose. In retrospect, this was probably for the best, because there's a good chance witnesses could have documented the whole disaster. I can just imagine some well-intentioned diner realizing I was in the middle of a marriage proposal and deciding to capture the moment on their phone for us so we could preserve the memory. After it took the ugly turn that it did, the video instead would have been posted on YouTube and Facebook and gone viral.

So, back at our apartment would have to do. Sure, the setting wasn't as romantic, but I knew I still wanted to do it that night. We'd get to celebrate a new year and a new chapter of our lives together—the setting didn't matter one bit.

We were watching the *Times Square New Year's Eve* celebration on TV and I quickly planned the perfect moment to ask: approximately fifteen seconds before midnight I'd ask, she'd say yes, a few 'OMGs' and tears, and then we'd kiss right at the stroke of midnight.

Except when I got on my knee and asked her to marry me she didn't say anything. As the seconds passed and I wasn't getting an answer, I started to panic.

Then the countdown started.

"10-9-8..."

"Now would be a good time to say yes or no," I said.

I tried to force a laugh to take away some of the pressure, but nothing came out.

"... 6-5-4..."

And *still* there was no response.

"Lauren?"

"... 3-2-1... *Happy New Year!!!*"

She just sat there. 2014 was officially over. 2015 had begun, but my marriage proposal was still in limbo. Something was horribly wrong. Finally, I asked, "Are you okay?"

She shook her head. "Does that mean you're not okay or does it mean you don't want to marry me?"

"I want to marry you," she said finally, but her tone of voice made it clear I shouldn't celebrate yet. "I want to say yes more than anything, but I need to tell you something first."

"Okaaay."

At this point, I couldn't imagine what it was she wanted to tell me, but knowing she had some epic revelation made me sick to my stomach. My first guess was she was going to tell me she was pregnant, but that didn't make sense. That's usually something girls will tell a guy to get them to propose, and I had just done that. Plus, she was on birth control and we were always careful. Always.

"I can't say yes until you know this because..." She took a deep breath. "I—I slept with someone else."

She couldn't look at me when she told me. I had no idea what to say to this, so I just sat there, dumbfounded. The celebratory sounds of people in New York City cheering the new year serving as the worst possible backdrop for this horrible, horrible moment.

"When?" I managed to ask. I'm not sure why this made a difference, or even if I really wanted to know. It was just the first question to pop out.

"A month ago. It only happened once I promise. It was when I was on that business trip in Nashville."

I was supposed to go on that trip with her, but I'd bought the ring a few weeks before that and was low on cash and couldn't afford to go. Lauren kept explaining herself as I processed this. "...I was drunk. Otherwise it would have never happened. I know being drunk isn't an excuse but that's why I needed to tell you. I've been so afraid to tell you the truth, but the moment you asked me to marry you, I knew I couldn't keep it secret anymore and you deserved to know the truth before I—and it hasn't happened since."

"What do you mean it hasn't happened since?" I asked. "Wait, it's someone from your office, isn't it?"

Lauren nodded, her eyes full of tears. "I'm so sorry."

The whole evening had just blown up in my face. I tried to be calm, to make sense of everything. I just couldn't. I yelled and said some things I probably shouldn't have. She apologized endlessly. I couldn't listen to any of it, though. I left the apartment just to get away from her. Away from the girl who had broken my heart. I just wanted to walk away from what happened and clear my mind.

I never cheated on Lauren. I used to wonder if I had, maybe I would have been okay with her bombshell to say "well, I had mine, she had hers, so we're even," or something stupid like that. All sorts of things go through your head when you find out your girlfriend and would-be fiancée cheated on you. Mostly they come in the form of questions:

Who is he?
Do I know him?
Have I met him?

Do I really want to know?
Who's better in bed?
What does he look like?
Could I kick his ass?
Who's better in bed?

The usual stuff. As much as you want to ask the questions you don't necessarily want to hear the answers because in the end, the more you know the more it hurts. The weight of everything just crushed me. I had to come to terms with the fact that my life had significantly changed, and not in the way I had planned it to.

Lauren sent me a bunch of texts while I was out walking. There were sixteen by the time I checked my phone. I couldn't deal with her texting me all night, so I turned off my phone and crashed at my friend Jay's place.

The following afternoon I came back to the apartment and she was waiting for me, still upset and hoping there was a way to salvage our relationship. Honestly, part of me wanted to. We'd been together for so long and I wanted to spend the rest of my life with her. I knew she was sorry, but one trip without me and she makes such a huge mistake? With a coworker she would still see all the time? I never for a second worried she'd cheat on me, but now I'd always worry. I'd always have a nagging suspicion. There was no way to fix this. There was nothing she could say or do to make this right. Deep down, she knew it too, and agreed to move out by the end of the week.

Considering how things turned out, I'm glad I never told anyone (except her parents) that I was planning to propose. It was the worst and most humiliating moment of my life. So, when people found out we were no longer together, I said things like, "She wasn't the one," and "We just drifted apart," or "It was no one's fault really, just one of those things." It hurt to make such lame excuses and protect Lauren, but I didn't want people to know or talk about it behind my back. I just had to figure out how to get over it and move on with my life.

It's been two and a half months since that fateful night, and I'm still trying.

PART I

CHAPTER I

"NICK, WAKE UP," says a female voice in a British accent.

Her name is Emma. I'm surprised to hear her at all because I was hoping she'd have simply woken up and left without waking me so I could pretend like last night didn't happen.

"Uh-huh," I mumble.

"What time is it?"

I sit on the edge of the bed there isn't much light, but I find my boxer shorts on the floor and put them on before getting up to find my phone.

"It's almost eight," I tell her, before getting back under the covers.

"Fuck. I'm going to be late for work," she says. She whips the covers off her and rushes out of my bed. She runs over to the door and flips the light switch and starts looking for her clothes, which, along with mine, are in a mess on the floor from last night. "Don't you have to be somewhere?" she asks.

"I mostly work from home. Me and my friend Jay have our own business."

"Right. Well, I work for an architect who will go mental if I'm even a minute late for work."

"That really sucks."

"It gets worse, I also wait tables on the weekends and the nights I don't have class. I pretty much have no life at the moment. Fuck, where are my knickers?" She lifts the comforter at the foot of the bed. "Ah found'em!"

She dresses in front of me like it's no big deal, like we are a couple and this kind of thing is common for us. Sorry Emma, it's never going to happen. I didn't like her much when I asked her to come back here, but loneliness got the better of me. *What kind of girl goes home with a guy after what was only a thirty-minute conversation?* Not only do I feel no better now than I felt before last night, I'm now thinking I may need to get a blood test after she leaves.

She picks up her jeans and sits on my side of the bed to put them on.

"We should do this again soon," she says buttoning up her shirt. She will be disappointed if she's waiting for me to agree with her. But Emma doesn't wait for a response. "Anyway, say hello to Devon for me." She gets up and glances down at the floor. "Where's my other sock?" She looks around, then discovers it by the door. "Speaking of Devon, I was wondering, isn't it weird sharing a flat with a girl you're not shagging?"

"It was better than moving out because I couldn't afford the place on my own."

Devon was not my first choice to move in after Lauren and I broke up. I'd originally asked Jay if he'd consider moving in with me. I'd been staying at his place while Lauren moved out, and I knew I needed a roommate fast. It made a lot sense since we run a business together, and he was interested until I told him what his half of the rent would be. Dan (one of Jay's roommates) and his sister Devon happened to be listening to our conversation and Devon mentioned she was looking for a place to live. Even though I wasn't exactly thrilled with the idea of living with girl after just ending a relationship with one, I'd known Devon for a while, and she seemed pretty cool. It was certainly better than having a stranger move in. So, Devon moved into the bedroom I shared with Lauren, and I moved my stuff into the smaller second bedroom.

Emma puts her jacket on, picks up her purse and smooths her clothes with her hands, like that will help. "It's a good thing no one at work saw me in this outfit yesterday." She looks at me like she's expecting something. "You know, the dreaded walk of shame?"

I don't know what to say.

"Right, well, I'd better be off," she says. "Look, I know last night was no-strings-attached, but are you going to walk me out?"

"Oh, yeah, sure," I say, and get out bed. I dress quickly and walk her out of my room and lead her to the door. She leans in and kisses me.

"Next time you want to have some fun, let me know."

"I will," I lie.

I've never been a one-night-stand kinda guy. Remember, I wanted commitment with Lauren. I bought the ring. I got down on one knee. I did all of that shit. As thrilled as I should be that I've just had sex for the first time in two and a half months all I can see is that my situation hasn't improved. My life right now is not what it was supposed to be. I should be with the girl I was supposed to spend the rest of my life with. I should not be sleeping with some random chick.

I blame Devon for the whole thing. Devon had grown tired of my moping around, and insisted for weeks that I needed to get laid to get out my funk. She got tired of me refusing and finally resorted to pinning me down on the couch until I agreed to meet her friend Emma. Devon is small but surprisingly strong.

"Let me explain something to you, Nicholas Forrester, your depression is annoying the shit out of me! She's single, horny, and perfect for you. You may be an average looking guy, but you're her type. And she doesn't want a boyfriend, she just wants to get laid. You need this!"

"Just get off of me!"

She let me go.

"Trust me dude, you'll like her. She's hot and she's got a sexy British accent."

"British accents are sexy?"

"Come on. This is practically guaranteed sex."

"I'd rather find someone myself."

"But you're not even trying right now! Seriously, don't you think your ex is getting laid right now?"

She had a point. The mental image of Lauren having sex with someone else stung my eyes and hit me in the chest, hard. If she was having sex with other people, then so was I.

"Make the call."

That's how I ended up with Emma.

CHAPTER 2

Devon comes out of her room while I'm making breakfast. She's just woken up, and her eyes are barely open. She's wearing a t-shirt with the name of a band on it and gym shorts. I'm pretty sure I've never seen her wear the shirt before, so I'm thinking it doesn't belong to her. I suspect she wasn't alone in her room.

"Way to go, Nick!" she says.

"What?"

"Emma! You nailed her last night, didn't you?"

"Yeah."

"I was right, wasn't I?"

"About?"

"The best way to get over someone is to get under someone else, right?"

I don't know what to say and so I say the first thing that comes to mind.

"You were right."

"Yes! I knew it! This is good. Now you'll have more confidence to get out there again."

"Maybe. Hey, where did you end up last night?"

"I dunno. A few places on Union Street. Saw a band at the Tap," she says pulling down her shirt taut so I can read it. "Ever heard of Candlepin? They're pretty awesome. Fuck, I wish I had brought my camera—I'd say you and Emma should have come with me, but I met this guy and we..."

"Came back here," I say, finishing her sentence. "And I'm assuming he's still here?"

"He'll leave when he wakes up. Don't worry. Anyway, he's the lead singer's cousin."

"Cousin? You didn't even hook up with someone in the band?"

"He's *managing* the band right now, and he may get me to do some photography for their new album. And you are banned from giving me shit today. You, my friend had sex last night thanks to me."

"Fine, whatever. So the band was good?"

"They were incredible. You should come with us tonight. They have a gig at Revolution."

"I don't know. Maybe another time."

"You got other plans?"

She knows I don't have any plans.

"Fine. Sure. I'll go."

Just then a shirtless guy comes out of her room.

"Where the fuck is my shirt?" he says.

"I'm wearing it," Devon says. "Nick, this Justin. Justin, my roommate, Nick."

"What's up?" I say.

"Hey," he says to me, then looks at Devon. "Am I going to get that back?"

"Maybe," Devon says, and laughs. "Nick's going to come tonight."

Justin looks at me and says, "Nice."

"You heading out?" Devon asks Justin.

"Yeah. The band's rehearsing this morning, and I gotta get stuff ready for tonight. So, I do need my shirt back."

Without warning, Devon lifts up the shirt, pulls it over her head and hands it to Justin with a smile. She's wearing a bra underneath, but I feel awkward and look away. This is the problem with having a girl for a roommate.

* * *

Mom calls an hour later. She calls regularly to keep track of me because, according to her, I don't fill her in on my life unless she asks. She didn't find out about Lauren and me breaking up until a week and a half after it had happened. Mainly because I made a point of not calling her. I know I probably should have told her within a day or so because we'd been together for a long time, and I'm sure everyone assumed that getting engaged was inevitable. When I did finally tell her I gave her the same boilerplate excuses I gave to everyone else. I'm sure mom figured out there was more to it than that, but thankfully she didn't press me for details. She was disappointed though. She always liked Lauren. Lauren was very helpful a few years ago when my mom's second husband Glen died. She stayed with us at the house and helped out with the wake. I thought my younger sister Lacy (half-sister, actually) never seemed to like her.

Today, instead of the usual mundane questions, Mom has a different agenda.

"Lacy says she's been trying to call you," she says.

Mom has always wanted me to take more of an interest in Lacy, and I always tried, but between her animosity towards my girlfriend and the twelve years that separate us, finding common ground was difficult. Lauren may not be in the picture anymore, but the age difference is still an issue. I've been hoping this would just resolve itself over time when she is older and more mature, when the difference won't seem so large.

"I've been a bit busy," I say, which is true, but Mom isn't convinced.

"Really Nick, you could make some time for her."

"She's fourteen, we don't have—"

"Almost fifteen."

"We have nothing in common."

"She's your sister, she doesn't have her father anymore and she needs her older brother."

The mere mention of Lacy's dad is enough to get me to surrender.

"I'll call her sometime this week."

"You mean it?"

"I'll try."

"Her birthday is coming up soon, and I want you to be there. In fact, I want you to spend the night here with us. I'm not going to ask you to spend a whole day with her, but one night with the family isn't much to ask."

"Don't worry, I'll be there."

"Thank you."

"Look, mom, I have to go. I'll talk to you later," I say and hang up. I do have to get work done and working in the apartment is too distracting right now, so I pack up my laptop and go to Starbucks.

CHAPTER 3

"A DOUBLE-TALL NO whip mocha," says the old man in front me in line at Starbucks to the barista.

He always gets the same drink every day, and he always has exact change. All of the baristas and regulars here know him. I started coming here on a regular basis after getting laid off last year, and when he discovered I was new he started talking to me when he'd see me come in.

The barista at the register, Jess, looks happy to see me.

"Hey Nick. What can I get for you? The usual?" They know my name here, too. And what I drink.

I did get laid last night for the first time in months, so I'm thinking I deserve more than a regular coffee today.

"I'll have a grande Americano. Thanks."

"No worries," she says, and grabs a cup and writes my drink order on it and my name.

I wait by the espresso machine for my drink. There's a barista I don't know very well working the machine. She's short with a slim figure like the lead girl from the *Harry Potter* movies. I don't think most guys would say she's smokin' hot, but she's pretty and cute in a way that really works for me. She's got long, light brown hair, with a few light freckles on her face and these amazing bluish-green eyes that made an impression on me the first time I noticed her here a few weeks ago. Despite finding her attractive, I've never said anything to her beyond giving her my order when she works the register or saying thank you when she hands my drink. I've never tried flirting with her before, but today I feel like giving it a try. I guess there's some truth to Devon's theory that getting laid would give me more confidence to "get out there." Of course, as I'm about to open my mouth to say something she calls out a drink she just made.

"Caramel Macchiato for Melissa," she says, and puts the drink out, which is then swiftly taken by the woman standing behind me.

"Wow, you got some skill," I say to her when she starts making her next drink. Dumb, I know, but I couldn't think of anything else. "You're kinda new here, right?"

"I am. I moved here a couple months ago from Connecticut. I worked at a Starbucks there, too."

"Good to know."

"You're in here a lot."

"Yeah, I work here."

"At Starbucks? You sure about that?"

Boy, I'm an idiot.

"I mean, I have a web design business. I usually come here to work. On my laptop."

She laughs. "Oh, I see." She puts a lid on the drink and eyes Double-Tall No Whip Mocha Man. "Here's your Double-Tall No Whip Mocha." She smiles, and he takes his drink, thanks her, and pats me on the shoulder before taking a seat near the window where he's greeted by another customer. They immediately begin talking up a storm like old friends.

I turn back to the cute barista. "And you know Mr. Double-Tall No Whip Mocha, already. That's good."

"Oh yes. I know him."

"It's probably a requirement to work at this Starbucks."

She laughs again. "It definitely should be!" She makes two espresso shots, pours them in my grande cup, and fills the cup with hot water.

"You must be Mr. Grande Americano?"

"Yes, that's me."

She puts the cup down for me to take. I grab it fast, and a bit too forcefully, and the lid pops off, causing much of the drink to spill all over.

"Oh shit, I'm sorry I—"

I fumble for some napkins hoping to contain the spill, but she whips out a towel and cleans up everything effortlessly. She smiles at me.

"I'm sorry, I must not have put the lid on tight enough."

"No, I—"

"I'll make you another one."

She can't possibly believe this was her fault, but I'm relieved she's acting so nice about it to spare me some embarrassment.

"Thanks. I'm sorry about—"

"Don't worry about it," she says with another smile. She rapidly prepares me a new drink, and when it's done I carefully reach for it, handling the drink like a bomb. She notices and laughs.

"Thanks so much," I tell her.

"Any time," she says, and starts working on the next drink.

"Well, see you later," I say as I walk towards an open table.

"Have a good one," she says.

It's been a long time since I've flirted with anyone, so, of course I'm a bit rusty. Did she know I was flirting? Do I want her to know I was flirting? I have no idea, but I think I'll want to try again.

Back at my table, I put my earbuds on and get some music playing, log on to the free Wi-Fi, and try to concentrate on working. But I can't stop thinking about that girl. I even take my earbuds out so I can hear what she says too. Not that it's anything all that important. She mostly calls out drinks or makes small talk with other baristas or customers. Occasionally she laughs this sweet, adorable laugh that I find really attractive.

Later, she comes out to wipe down tables and when she does the table next to mine we make eye contact. She smiles. I smile back. And before I can even think about what I should do next, she's on to the next table. I keep watching though, trying to at the least catch a glimpse of her name tag so I will know her name. But I never see it long enough to read it. I should think of something to say, but my mind goes blank. It's only after she leaves that I come up with a great line. Before long I realize she's no longer here. Her shift must have ended and I didn't catch her leave. I guess I'll just have to come back tomorrow.

CHAPTER 4

JAY IS ON my couch with Devon when I get back to my apartment. She's watching the TV, but his eyes are barely open.

"You look like hell," I tell him. "Another late-night gaming session?" I ask.

He nods.

Jay is tall and lean, and you would think that someone with his kind of height might play basketball or some other sport. But no, he's a video gamer—as are his roommates. They love it all, including retro games from the 70s and 80s (they even have a retro gaming night), and they obsessively read comic books, go to Comic Cons and all that science fiction and fantasy stuff. Of course, they have a huge flat screen TV, and a sweet sound system to enhance their obsessions. They also each own a wide variety of t-shirts that proudly display their geeky habits. Like today, Jay's wearing a vintage style Pong shirt.

Jay's roommates can be fun to hang out with. I've been over there to play retro video games a couple times and that can be fun—but that seems to be extent of their social repertoire. Even Devon likes to hang out with them, which is really strange. They're not really her crowd, but she hangs out with her brother Dan and she's also friends with Dan's girlfriend, who is really into all that stuff too. They got Devon to go with them to Boston Comic Con last year and complete a group X-Men cosplay. She went as Mystique and got to spend the day barely dressed and painted blue and she had a blast. Then her picture showed up on some list called *The 12 Sexiest Cosplays From Boston Comic Con* on some popular blog (she ranked #3) that went viral, and *voila!* she found herself a new hobby.

"So, I hear we're going to Revolution tonight," Jay says. Apparently, Devon has invited him to join us. Not that I mind since I was going to ask him to come anyway. "I hope this band doesn't suck."

"They don't suck!" Devon says, hitting him in the arm. "I saw them last night. They're awesome."

Candlepin, she explains, is well known in the Boston music scene. A few years ago they put out an album that got some national publicity and they ended up doing a national tour (and when I say national tour I mean small clubs in select cities, not big venues, and mostly on the eastern seaboard) and one of their songs ended up on the soundtrack to some independent movie that Devon couldn't remember the name of. They were never nationally famous, and even in Boston you had to be into the local independent music scene to know of them. Still, most local bands would love to have the success they had. They've put out five albums and sold something like 70,000 CDs in their ten-year history. Then about six months ago the lead singer Cassandra Rogers got married and decided she wanted to start a family and left the band. If they were close to a major label record deal, the departure of Cassandra derailed them a bit. Still, they were quite successful for a local Boston Band. They were never as big as, say, the Dropkick Murphys, but they've done well for not being on a major label. Now that they've recruited a new lead singer and keyboardist they are working on a comeback.

"—trust me, they are really good," Devon adds. "I know you'll like them."

"What kind of music is it again?"

"Oh, they're a mix of jazz, folk and rock. I'm telling you that you'll like them, and if you don't it will only reflect poorly on your taste."

* * *

We get to Revolution at 6:30, only to discover the show starts at eight, according to the chalkboard sign outside. We're so early that the band hasn't even started setting up yet. If fact, they're not even here yet.

I haven't been to Revolution Public House (which we just call Revolution) in years. It is pretty much the way I remembered it. The building is deep and narrow. It's old, but it has character. At the far end there's a small stage which was recently built, and a door to a back area. There's a mezzanine level that overlooks the stage so patrons on both floors can enjoy the live entertainment. The wait staff have classy black uniforms.

The band arrives a half hour after us through the exit off the alley. Candlepin is a five-piece band, and they're all lugging in equipment, except the new lead singer Nava, who is chatting people up. Eventually she recognizes Devon and says hello to all of us. She acts like we are all her best friends and is all excited that Jay and I have never seen Candlepin before. Most of the people who come their shows are people who have been fans for a while, she explains, so she's thrilled to see some new blood. She introduces us to the rest of the band, who are now setting up on stage.

"That's Hank," she says pointing to the drummer. "That's Blake," she points to the guy setting up his keyboards. "He just joined the band, too. And those are the two Andys," she says referring to the guitarist and bassist. They're all too busy to shake hands, but they each greet us with a "Hey!" or a "What's up?"

Nava leaves us only when she sees someone else she knows coming in and goes to talk to them. Devon leaves us too in order to talk to Justin.

"Who's that?" Jay asks.

"That is Devon's connection."

"Connection or *connection*?" Jay asks.

"*Connection*," I say.

"So, he's not even in the band?"

"I asked her the same question. Nope. He's their manager or something."

"Whatever. I guess it's time for a real drink," he says.

"Agreed."

* * *

Up on the stage now is the opening act, a cute girl in a white sundress. She's tuning her acoustic guitar and talking with the sound guy. All of a sudden, I recognize her. It's the girl who made my drink at Starbucks this morning. She nods at the sound guy and steps up to the microphone. "Check, check, check... a little more. Check. Good." She looks out at the crowd, "Hey everyone. My name is Alli Conwell. Thanks for coming out tonight—"

"Justin says she's really good too," says Devon, who has rejoined us. I look at her and mouth the word "quiet." Devon sticks her tongue out at me then walks off to take a few pictures from different positions in the room.

You always hear "good things" about an opening act, but most of the time you find out very quickly why they are just an opener. Usually their songs all sound alike, they have a cheesy stage presence, or are just plain forgettable. But Alli The Starbucks Girl's singing is amazing. She's got a beautiful voice and she's incredibly talented on the guitar. After only a couple songs I am beyond impressed. I notice that most other people are similarly enchanted by her performance. I've never seen anything like it. I almost feel bad for Candlepin, who have to go on after she's already blown the audience away. Everyone claps and cheers at the end of each song, and they're not just humoring her, they really like her. I do too. After several songs Alli seems taken aback by the response she's getting and thanks the crowd repeatedly.

I look around for signs of a guy she might be with. There's a table with a bunch of her CDs on it, but no one is there. And that is the spot you'd expect the boyfriend or girlfriend of a musician to be during a show, right? This assessment may not be the most scientific since she could have a boyfriend who didn't make it to the show tonight for any number of reasons. I do hear occasional comments from guys in the crowd about how hot Alli is. And I agree, but I can't help being just as taken, if not more, with her performance.

"This is a new song," Alli says about midway through the set. "It's called 'Someday,' and I—" Nava screams approval, interrupting Alli mid-sentence. Alli just laughs at Nava's outburst and thanks her, and just starts playing. I am not one to respond to music emotionally, but this song gets to me. The lyrics suggest it's a song about loneliness. It's kind of sad and beautiful. I'm not the only one moved by the song either, I see people around listen intently as she sings, as if we're all in a bizarre group paralysis. I even notice Devon, who is now towards the end of stage taking side view shots of Alli, appears awestruck.

When the song is finished the crowd goes wild, and Alli is visibly moved by the intensity of our approval. Even in my admiration of her talent, I'm very much aware of the fact that she said it's a *new* song, and if she's recently written a song about being lonely that probably means she's single.

Alli follows that with a couple covers: "Yellow" by Coldplay, and "If I Die Young" by The Band Perry. The songs are instantly recognized by the crowd and bring on loud cheers as well. She finishes her set with a couple of her own songs. She blushes at cheers and hoots. "Thank you all so much. I'll be selling CDs right over there if you want one." She points to the front of the room. She puts her guitar in her case and carries a box of CDs to the front of the room where's there's a table set up for her to sell them. A small line starts to form in front of her.

"I'm gonna have a quick smoke," Devon says.

"I'm getting a CD," I tell Jay.

"Grab one for me," Devon says, fishing a ten-dollar bill from her purse. She finds Justin and they go outside. Jay and I head to the back of the line.

The line takes a long time to move. We can hear each person buying their CD rave about her performance and ask her questions. When it's finally my turn I try to play it cool. "Great set," I tell her.

"Thanks. You want a CD?"

"Definitely," I say, a little too enthusiastically. She looks at Jay, who is standing next to me, not behind me. "You too?"

"Are you on iTunes?" he asks, like a jackass.

"Yes, actually. I am."

"Really?" Jay asks surprised.

"Uh-huh, it's pretty easy to do, even for independent musicians not with a label."

"Oh. Cool. Well, I'll find your stuff on iTunes later."

"Okay," she says.

"I'll make sure he does," I assure her, then turn to Jay. "Why don't you just go if you're not gonna buy a disc."

"Okay, okay. Chill out. I'll be outside." He leaves, not soon enough.

"Sorry about him," I tell her. "I'll make sure he downloads your album from iTunes."

She laughs. "It's okay. Really."

I give her Devon's ten-dollar bill and a ten of my own. "I really do need two CDs though. I have to buy one for my roommate."

"Really? And where is this roommate you speak of?" she asks, mockingly suspicious.

"Oh, outside. Having a smoke," I explain. She hands me two from the box. The disc comes in a cardboard sleeve that shows a tight shot of her holding her guitar. The back shows a wider shot of her sitting on a floor holding the guitar, smiling, but not looking at the camera. It looks really good. I take out the CD and even that looks legit, with the photo from the back cover printed directly on the disc.

"Wow, this looks really good for not being with a label." I tell her, hoping she'll appreciate the compliment. I probably shouldn't have sounded so surprised. "I mean, it looks awesome. You wouldn't have guessed just by looking at it that you self-published it." Except that it was just a sleeve with no liner notes.

She laughs at my bumbling awkwardness. "Thanks. I wish I didn't look so stupid in the picture though."

"You don't look stupid. You look amaz—it all looks great." I nearly stumble on my words, trying not to sound like I'm flirting, which I am, a little bit, anyway. Not that I want to be too obvious about it. She seems to have noticed, so I quickly change gears. "Thanks again for making me another Americano this morning."

She laughs. "I didn't think you recognized me."

"How could I forget? I mean... you... anyway, never mind... I'm Nick, by the way"

She laughs. "Hi, Nick. I'm Alli." She holds her hand out for me to shake. The formality of handshaking seems awkward and impersonal in this context, but I shake her hand anyway, because not shaking her hand would seem like an insult. The trick here is to keep talking, even though I am stumbling on my words. I just gotta keep this conversation going.

"Is Alli short for Allison?" A stupid thing to ask, I know, but I need something to buy me a few crucial seconds to think of something better.

"Nope."

"Oh, so what does it—"

"Hey Alli, good set," interrupts Blake, Candlepin's keyboard player. He's walking passed us towards the bar with Andy the guitarist.

"Yeah, awesome job," says Andy.

"Thanks, guys!" she says, waving to them as they approach a couple girls at the bar.

"So," Alli says, returning to our conversation. "Are you interested in coming to another show?"

"Of course."

"I'm playing at Scollay's at Faneuil Hall every Friday night for the next few weeks. You should come. And, here—" She hands me a small postcard that has her album cover on it. "This is a list of other shows I have coming up." I flip the card over to see the list.

"Awesome, thanks."

There's a girl behind me waiting to buy a CD so I step aside to let Alli do her thing. She smiles at me and gives me one of those short "see you later" waves. I find Jay outside with Devon. A bunch of people are out here getting in a quick cigarette before Candlepin play. There's even a homeless guy dancing and singing around for change.

"Did you really have to be such a dick in there?" I ask him.

"Why the hell am I going to buy a CD when I can copy the songs off of yours? Or Devon's? Besides, she isn't even who we came to see."

"So you'll buy a Candlepin CD if you like them?"

"Maybe," he says, unconvincingly.

"You ought to support local bands by buying their albums. Don't be so cheap," Devon says, putting her cigarette into one of those plastic cigarette butt receptacles.

"Like you should talk," Jay says.

"Hey, I don't like paying *taxes*; I have no problem spending money on a good band. And neither should you."

When people start to head back inside *en masse* we follow them in. Candlepin are on stage now. No sign of Alli anywhere. I stop looking when the band starts playing. Once again it seems she has disappeared on me. Devon spends most of the first set taking pictures. Then, too cool to be mixed in with the crowd, hangs out with Justin at Candlepin's merch table.

Candlepin are a great band, and I can tell why they've enjoyed the success they've had. They know lots of people at the show tonight, and Nava makes regular shout outs during their performance. Jay uses a break between songs to tell me he's gotta take a leak and heads off towards the bathrooms. I keep an eye out for Alli, I even move around to check every possible place, but can't seem to find her. I just have to accept the fact she's left.

I don't see Jay again until just after Candlepin's first set. "I got some good news," he tells me.

"What's that?"

"I've been talking to the owner of Revolution. We're gonna meet tomorrow to discuss redesigning their website."

"Nice. When?"

"Tomorrow morning."

"Oh, okay," I say, disappointed. I was gonna go to Starbucks early tomorrow and hopefully see Alli again. He doesn't seem to notice my lack of enthusiasm.

At the end of the show I buy Candlepin's last album and the five-song EP they recorded soon after Nava joined the band and they wrote some new songs. I'm told a new album is currently in the works. Devon tells us she's going with Justin to an after party. I won't be waiting up for her tonight. On the train back towards home I double check my pocket to make sure I still have the card with Alli's upcoming gigs listed on it. I do.

I'm not sure what it is about this girl, but I want to make time to go to her shows and get to know her better. I guess I am ready to get back out there.

Well, Devon, I guess you were right.

CHAPTER 5

THE NEXT MORNING Jay and I meet up by Hynes Convention Center T stop and walk down Newbury Street towards Revolution. It's an unusually warm day for the month of March, and when a couple of girls walk by Jay can't help but ogle them.

"I can't wait for the summer, dude," he says. "Those girls will be wearing practically nothing then."

"Should we discuss anything before we meet with Keith?" I ask. Considering we're on the way to a meeting with a potential client and haven't discussed things in advance, this seems like a good idea.

"Nah, we'll be fine. Just let me do most of the talking."

"Is that supposed to make me feel better?"

"Hey, you know I'm good at reeling them in."

"Yes, you are, but—"

"Hey, I got us this gig, so I get to—"

"*Potential* gig."

"Potential gig. I got this meeting set up. I spoke to him before. I know what I am doing. Trust me."

"Okay, if you're willing to take responsibility." Our company has been doing well for a while now, but every potential gig is important, and I don't want to screw this up.

"Of course."

Jay and I rarely agree about business decisions. It's a problem that became clear early on when we were trying to come up with a name for our web design company. We didn't like either combination of our last names (Forrester & Wright Design or Wright & Forrester Design) because it didn't sound fresh or contemporary, but we couldn't think of a name we both liked. It was Lauren who picked out a name we could both agree on: Wicked Creative Design Group. She even designed a logo for us. Shortly after things ended with Lauren I floated the idea of changing the name but Jay he put his foot down and said it was too late. All the paperwork had been done, and the website, business cards and such. He was right; I knew it even then, but that doesn't mean it doesn't fill me with disgust knowing it was her idea.

Revolution feels different in the daytime. It's mostly empty now, with just a few people minding their own business. Keith, the owner, is excited about the idea of a new website and is surprisingly aware of how inferior the current one is. We sit at a table in the corner, away from the cappuccino machine, and the small handful of customers scattered throughout drinking their coffees and working on their laptops.

Keith is quick to note that the website that is up now is the site the previous owner had, with only minor updates to the information since he bought the business. He thinks big about the potential a new website can have. Clients like this are a rare find. Most don't understand the value of a decent website, or how having a proper one can boost business. And Jay, doing what he does best, excites Keith by pointing out all the things he could and should have on the Revolution website but doesn't, and things we can do that those DIY web design sites can't. I sketch out some potential layouts, illustrating to him how a responsive site would work, so that the site looks good whether you are on a computer, a tablet or a smartphone. The meeting goes on for about an hour before Keith wants to start asking about price. Before Jay can give him a ridiculously large price that might make Keith think twice about working with us, I say that we'll put together a proposal and email it to him in a couple days.

"We should have given him a price right then and there," Jay says after we've left. "I want to get to work on this thing right away."

"You've blown two potential projects in the past month by overcharging. We're gonna think this through and give him a good price."

"He's excited *and* has money," he tells me, like I don't know. "He'll pay whatever we ask."

"Not necessarily. Remember our proposal for Burnham & Modine?" Burnham & Modine is an architecture firm that Devon does all their project photography for. Not long after she moved into the apartment she told them about us and we got to submit a proposal for redesigning their incredibly shitty website. That was over a month ago. Jay convinced me to quote them a price I was not convinced they'd pay and it turns out I was right.

"It could still happen."

"It's dead. Face it."

"Whatever. Sometimes you have to take risks. Like asking to be paid what you're really worth. You never want to take risks anymore."

"It wasn't a risk, according to you," I remind him. "You said it was a sure thing."

"Well, sometimes sure things don't work out."

Yeah, like me proposing to Lauren. That was supposed to be a sure thing. I guess technically it was, since she didn't say no, but it still ended with both of us hurt. Maybe that's a bad analogy, but Jay's comment has me wondering if maybe I haven't been willing to take some risks lately. Especially since the Lauren debacle.

"Okay, fine," I say. "Just don't fleece him. Quote what we're worth. Be fair."

"Of course."

Jay and I part ways on the subway. He invited me to work on the proposal at his place, so I have to explain to him my plan to see Alli at Starbucks.

"See, you're getting back out there. Taking risks again," he says.

"Very funny."

* * *

Alli is not at Starbucks when I arrive. I order a drink and sit, hoping she'll make an appearance from the back, or come in for a shift. An hour later she still hasn't shown up, and since I didn't bring my laptop to do any work I decide to go home.

Devon is at the apartment when I get back.

"Have fun with *Justin* last night?" I ask.

"Justin? Oh, I ditched him at the after party. Let's just say we're not politically compatible."

Devon doesn't come across as someone who would be political, but she's a hardcore libertarian. She's very passionate about it, which can sometimes make her as annoying about politics as some vegans are around people who eat meat.

"You were compatible two nights ago," I remind her.

"I didn't *know* two nights ago. Anyway, we got into a huge argument at the party. Let's just say neither of us were interested anymore after that. Enough about him, did you find that singer chick?"

"How'd you know I was looking for her?"

"Jay texted me. You are such a stalker."

"Excuse me? You're the one who has been telling me to get out there. That getting laid would restore my confidence and shit. So, I'm getting out there."

"What about Emma?"

"She's—"

"You'll have a better shot at regular sex with Emma than you will with that other girl."

"Why do you say that?"

"Do you know how many guys must hit on her every night she plays?"

She has point. Sure, Alli was friendly to me, but that still didn't mean she didn't already have a boyfriend or had been just as friendly with other guys when I wasn't around. I can't be the only guy interested. "Beats me."

"I'm telling you. I've spoken with Emma. She said you're good in the sack. Who knew, right?"

"Thanks."

"Seriously, you've got a sure thing with Emma. But that singer chick... it ain't gonna happen."

* * *

Alli isn't at Starbucks the next morning either. I briefly consider asking the barista Jess if she knows if Alli is working today. But the last thing I want is for Alli to know I've been looking around for her. So, I work on a web design project and listen to some music to kill some time.

The music collection on my laptop is quite small. I'd converted most of my CDs to MP3 years ago, but after a hard drive crash last year (and the painful realization that I wasn't backing up my music collection) I've really only got the small handful of songs I purchased digitally and could restore, and a few songs I've found on lurking on my hard drive since. My CD collection is in my old room at my mother's house, and I always forget to bring them back with me to remake the MP3s. So, I use various streaming services mostly, even though I find myself skipping over most of the songs, even newer stuff. It's not that I don't like the stuff I skip over, but I have different musical moods that makes it hard to know at any given time what I'll be in the mood to listen too.

It's funny how you can buy an album, even one by your favorite band, and still only really love maybe three or four songs on it. A couple more you might like, but the rest you listen to only rarely. They don't make it onto your playlists because you know that those will be skipped over regardless of the mood you are in.

Don't believe me? Take a random Beatles album. *Rubber Soul,* for example. How many songs can you name off top of your head that you *really* liked off that album? "In My Life," of course. "Norwegian Wood." "Girl." I guess the last one is "Michelle." That's only four of twelve songs. But I'm loving Alli's *entire* album. When they come up at random on my computer or iPod, or car stereo, I don't skip over any of them. Sure, her album has only nine songs, so the odds are slightly in her favor, but really, her songs just speak to me. It's not just because it's new and fresh music to me either. I've added all the Candlepin songs from the 5 song EP but only a few from their previous album that I've taken a liking to. I should probably listen to the whole album again at least one more time, but I'm pretty sure I've gleaned the best songs from it already. Besides, they'll have a new album soon, which I'm sure I'll like even more.

I work well while listening to music but find myself distracted when Alli's songs come up. Her voice sends chills up my spine, and certain lyrics send the hairs on my arms on end. And there were definitely original songs she played the other night that aren't on her album that I want to hear again. Her next show is tomorrow night. I know I'll be there, and I know I'll want to ask her out.

CHAPTER 6

Jay calls me later to discuss our proposal for Keith—specifically, how much we want to charge him for our services. Before Jay even tells me what he's thinking of charging he goes into a spiel about why he thinks his number is spot on. He's convinced that because Keith has a lot of money and is excited about the project that we don't need to low-ball our proposal. I know he's got a point. When we first started we low-balled our prices a lot in order to snag much needed clients. Now that we've been at this on our own for a while, Jay wants to make up for our past underselling of our work. Still, I'm a bit concerned that if we charge more than he thinks we are worth he might take his money elsewhere.

"If we get the job, you'll wish we charged more," Jay counters.

"Probably, but is it worth the risk? I mean, have you noticed that clients haven't been coming to us as quickly as they used to? We *need* the job. We can't afford to lose a potential client because they think we're ripping them off." This happens all too often. People understand the value of having a website, but they don't get the value of a web designer's services. Jay gets this, but he still gets greedy sometimes. "Keith may be that one-in-a-million client that seems really excited and anxious to pay us big bucks, but really, do you think a guy who buys an independent coffeehouse when there's enough competition from bigger, corporate chains—"

"Exactly, he's a bit of a sucker," Jay says.

"Or he's a really good businessman, with a plan and a brain, who will know right away when if we're overcharging him."

"I'm not saying we should overcharge him. I'm saying we should quote him what we're worth."

"That's fine, if your quote is realistic."

"It's more realistic than you getting with that singer chick."

"What do you mean?"

"Dude, you haven't got a chance."

What the fuck is this about? First Devon, now Jay? Shit, it hasn't been that long since the whole Lauren thing blew up, I thought they'd still be trying to boost my confidence.

"Thanks, man. I appreciate your vote of confidence."

"I'm not trying to be a dick or anything. Just think about it. Do you think you were the only guy with a hard on for her last night? Trust me, you weren't. And how many gigs does she have a week? She must have guys all over her. Or a boyfriend. Probably both."

"I think I need some new, supportive friends."

"I *am* being supportive. All I'm saying is there are plenty of guys trying to get in her pants, so, why set yourself up for potential disappointment when you just got yourself a fuck buddy who will let you in her pants anytime you want?"

"I'd rather find someone to be in a relationship with and, I don't want a relationship with *her*. So, what's the harm in trying with Alli? If I'm ever really horny and really desperate, I got Emma's number."

"Okay, fair enough. I was just trying to bring you down to earth."

"And I'm trying to bring *you* down to earth about how much we should charge in our proposal," I say, trying to change the subject back before I get any more pissed off at him. So we go back and forth for a while before we settle on how much to quote Keith for the new website. It's more than I would have quoted, but definitely fair and in both of our comfort zones. I am not, however, about to agree with his and Devon's position that I have no shot with Alli. Instead of trying to catch her at Starbucks again I'll just wait for her gig Friday night and make a move.

I know it's a long shot, but it won't hurt to try. What's the worst that could happen? She could have a boyfriend, which would suck for me, but it wouldn't be the end of the world. I'd just be *another* guy who saw her sing who hit on her and she'd forget about me quickly and I'd just move on with my life. After what happened with Lauren a simple rejection would be cake by comparison.

CHAPTER 7

BY FRIDAY AFTERNOON all the confidence I had while talking to Jay is gone. I discovered Alli's fan page on Facebook, and saw she's got 59 fans on there already. Not a lot, but the page looks to be only a few months old. Still, she's got a few people who are really into her music. They're mostly girls, but there were a few guys who had posted comments on there saying they liked her stuff. Nava was all over it telling Alli and everyone else how awesome Alli is and to go to her shows. Nava appears to be Alli's biggest fan. Although she now has some competition.

I spent quite a long time looking around, scrolling down to the earliest days of the page's existence a few months ago. There wasn't much activity by fans though until last month. Nava was the first one. I suspect most of the initial wave of fans on her page were also Candlepin fans who either were invited by Nava or discovered Alli at a Candlepin show.

Even if I assume that she doesn't have a boyfriend yet since she is new to Boston that doesn't mean others haven't had an eye on her since she started playing gigs locally. So, I'm starting weeks if not months behind. She could have guys following her at all or most of her shows. Not that I saw any guys lingering around her at Revolution but still, it's possible.

Instead of dwelling on it all day I head down to the show early. Three hours early. There's a Starbucks at Faneuil Hall, and I brought my laptop, so I could try to do some work, but I feel too nervous to give any of my projects my full attention. So, yeah, this was pretty stupid especially since most people with an agenda like mine would arrive "fashionably late." But, the last thing I want is for someone else with similar intentions to see Alli first. So, here I am.

After an hour and a half of wasting time I'm more than ready for a beer. So, I head over Scollay's and take a seat at the bar, which still has a decent number of free stools available.

Alli arrives a few minutes later, and I can tell by the look on her face she recognizes me from the other night and is happy to see me, which is awesome.

"Hey! Nick, right?" Remembering my name, another good sign.

"Yup. Nick. And you're Alli. *Not* short for Allison." She laughs. Another point scored by me. I'm on a roll. "I haven't seen you at Starbucks all week."

"No, I've been on a few later shifts this week. I'm working tomorrow morning though." She picks up her cell phone and checks the time, "Excuse me one second, I need to put my stuff down." She puts down her guitar and equipment in the corner and comes back to me at the bar. "You're here kinda early, aren't you?"

Great, now she thinks I'm a stalker. Not good.

"Well, I was getting some work done." I tap my attaché, hoping that's enough to indicate that there's a laptop in there on which I was doing work. "Thought I'd just check things out here."

"Oh, well, I'm just setting up now. If you need to get back to your work won't be on until eight. Nothing really to see now."

Is she telling me I should go? Shit. Another bad sign.

"I'm good. I got a bit bored working. Do you need any help?" I ask.

"Nope, they have someone here to help me with the speakers and the sound. Thanks though."

I'm not sure if I scored any points with that or not.

"But thanks so much for coming. I'm glad someone I know is here," she adds.

A good sign. She's glad I'm here. Even if I'm only "someone."

"Good. I'll just take a seat and get a drink then."

"If you want to leave your bag with my stuff in the corner here you can."

Nice. I wasn't expecting that.

"Thanks. That'd be great. It was starting to take its toll on my shoulder." I lift the strap over my head and she takes it before I have a chance to figure out where to place it amongst her things.

"My pleasure," she says. She hides it behind her guitar case, shielding it from potential thieves I assume. I sit at the corner with a direct view of her setting up. I want her to know where I am, and to appreciate that I am the only person (as of now) who has come out to see her play tonight. I leave my jacket on the stool next to mine, so no one tries to take it for themselves. I know that sounds a bit pathetic, but aren't all crushes like this? Even when you are closer to thirty than to twenty?

They have a few games on the various TVs, but I'm not here to watch them. Still, I'm careful not to stare at Alli as she finishes setting up. I even check my email on my phone so I don't appear as though I'm here to hang out with her, as opposed to just to see her play.

Should I be this pathetic at my age? I have no idea. Some girls are worth the effort, and I know this girl is worth the effort.

I'm thrilled when she comes to sit next me after she's done setting up. Of course, there aren't that many free seats at the bar, and I am the only person there she knows, as far as I am aware.

"So, you want a beer or something?"

"I can't... I'm not twenty-one yet."

"You're not?" I'm surprised. She looks young, but I figured she was probably Devon's age.

"Nope, sorry. Nineteen. You?"

Nineteen? Crap, she's going to think I'm a dirty old man. I think briefly of lying about my age, but nothing good would come out of that, so I tell her the truth. "Twenty... six."

She orders a water from the bartender and sits down next to me.

"So, we're basically the same age," I say.

"Is that so? How did you figure that out?"

"See, I'm told I'm immature for my age." I explain, and I'm trying too hard to prove it as well. Still, she laughs, a good sign that she is not put off by the seven years between us.

The bartender comes back with Alli's water, and I order a Guinness.

"And can I have a menu, please?" Alli asks.

"How about you, boss?" the bartender asks me.

"Oh, I'm sorry, have you not eaten yet?" Alli asks me.

"I haven't. I was kind of hoping you hadn't eaten yet either and we could... eat together."

I can see by the look on her face she's surprised by my suggestion and not sure what to do.

"Oh, wow. Umm..."

"I mean, if you don't want to that's fine. I'll just—"

"I'd love to. I just... never mind. Yes," she says this with an embarrassed sort of smile, which I can't help but find incredibly sexy.

And so Alli and I have dinner together at the bar, and it's a real good time. She tells me what it is like working at Starbucks and earning her living singing and playing music gigs.

When it gets close to eight, I decide to make my move.

"We should do this again."

"I have another gig in—"

"I meant just the dinner part. Not at a gig."

"Oh, wow. I dunno, I..." She thinks for a bit. "Can I give you answer after my last set?"

"You're really going to make me wait that long to tell me?"

"Yep." She laughs. "I figure it gives you a reason to stay until the end."

"Trust me; I'll be here until then anyway."

"That's good. Now I won't feel so bad for making you wait." She smiles, gets up, then goes to the corner where her equipment is set up. I watch her, and she can't stop smiling like she knows she's driving me crazy and is enjoying it.

This must be a good sign. If she intended to say no, she'd have been quick to tell me to avoid an awkward moment later. Right? I'm pretty sure she wouldn't give a guy false hope.

It's now that I notice that she's left cash on the bar to pay for her dinner. I was hoping I'd get to pay and then at least I'd feel like this was our first date. How do I interpret this? Is it a bad sign? No sign at all?

Alli opens up with a cover of "Into The Great Wide Open" by Tom Petty and the Heartbreakers. It receives a respectable amount of applause from an audience that's not entirely paying attention to her yet.

"Thanks," she tells the audience shyly. "My name is Alli Conwell, I'm here tonight until eleven. I hope you enjoy the set."

All the songs Alli plays are cover songs. Most of them I have heard before, but when she plays a song I like that I don't know I keep note of the lyrics in my head to Google them later so I can figure out what they are and download them from iTunes.

She occasionally speaks to the audience, who are mostly watching one or more of the games playing on the televisions but are still half paying attention to her. They turn to her when she speaks, and you can see them move slightly to the music that they know and cheer when she plays songs they really love when they recognize them. Some songs she announces to grab their attention. Other times, she'll let the audience detect the song on their own. She looks thrilled when a few people sing along to her selections.

At the end of her first set she comes to the bar and sits next to me.

"How'd I do?" she asks.

"Awesome. Loved it," I tell her.

"Thanks."

"Are you going to play any of your songs?"

"They want me to play stuff people here will know. That's kind of a condition."

"I'd still like to hear your stuff."

"Well, you're probably the only one here who has even heard my stuff before. I prefer playing my stuff, but gigs like this pay well, so I need them. And I make a good amount in tips, too."

I'm sure that's true. I saw a lot of people toss a bill or two in the jar she's put on top of the stool in her corner as they left. And I heard quite a few people talk about how good they thought she was. I have no idea if it is typical of this crowd or not, but I'm impressed nonetheless. Not only that, our conversation is often interrupted by people asking her where she's playing next, or give her a song request, or if she has a CD they can buy. She sells three CDs while she's on break.

"I'm impressed," I tell her.

"Thanks."

"It's too bad you can't play your own stuff tonight."

"If they want to hear my stuff, they'll buy a CD or go to a show where I can play my own songs. I need gigs, whatever they are... I need money to buy food and pay the rent. So, every gig is a good one."

"How do you pick what songs you play?"

"Gigs like this I'll need to play songs that are proven crowd pleasers. I do like to play stuff by artists that I like, or songs that have some meaning for me, but there is stuff they expect to hear, and I need to oblige them. I'm paid to entertain."

"Well, you're doing a good job."

She blushes and excuses herself to start her second set. Back at the mic she asks for some requests, and people shout out song suggestions. She plays most of them and her tip jar fills up with change and bills.

* * *

When her third set is over she starts packing up her stuff, not even acting like she's leaving me hanging for an answer to my pathetic attempt earlier this evening in asking her out. So I figure I've got nothing to lose and ask what her answer is outright.

"Answer to what?" she asks, smiling.

She's still playing with me. I'm guessing she knows the power she has over guys and has pulled this routine before. I bet it works every time.

"I asked you out a few hours ago."

"Oh, right," she says, pretending to remember something she'd forgotten. "You did, didn't you? What did I say?"

I figure two can play at this game. "You said yes."

"Really? I did? I guess I better give you my number then." She takes my iPhone from my shirt pocket and puts her number in my contacts. When she gives it back to me I pull her number up and call her. We both hear her phone vibrate in her purse.

"What are you doing?" she asks.

"Giving you my number, too."

A successful evening, indeed.

CHAPTER 8

I'VE PROMISED MYSELF not to call Alli for three days and challenged myself not to go to her Starbucks either... and I'm making good on that promise two days in, but it's difficult. Right now I'm trying to keep busy on some work projects at home while Devon is out shooting photos for one of her clients so I won't obsess about calling Alli, but it's not been easy.

In fact, it's been so difficult not to call or visit her at work that when my mom calls I actually welcome the distraction. When she asks if there is anyone new in my life, I'm in a good enough mood that I tell her I am "sort of seeing someone," that we kind of went on a date the other night. This is a bit of a stretch, but I know that it's the version of events she'd like to hear. Except, of course, that I'm engaged, soon to be married, and will soon be giving her grandchildren. She'll have to wait a long time before that's a likely announcement, and who knows if this thing with Alli will become a relationship at all, let alone a serious long-term one.

But, mom is happy, and even surprised. Of course, she asks for details and I offer only a few nuggets of information, because I've already exaggerated things enough. Mom decides that she'll like Alli and suggests I should bring her up to the house sometimes.

"We're so not even close to that point yet, mom."

"I know, I know. But I had to ask. Just, keep me posted on how things are going."

"I will." I probably won't.

To avoid more grilling on the subject of Alli, I tell her I have to go get some work done and she lets me go without any more harassment. Of course, talking with my mom about Alli has me thinking about her again and now I can't wait anymore. So, I head over to Starbucks. Yes, I'm pathetic and weak, but I take my laptop with me, so I can have an excuse for being there in case she's not there, but mostly in case she's there and I need an excuse to hang out there for a while so Alli doesn't think I'm going just to see her. I know that sounds pathetic, but hey, you do what you gotta do.

* * *

Alli is sitting by herself at a table when I arrive, writing in a notebook, and drinking an iced coffee. She must be on a break.

"Hey there," I say.

She looks up and smiles. "Oh, I'm glad you're here. I have something for you."

"You do?"

She reaches in her bag. She hands me a CD-R with *Alli Conwell - Live @ Revolution 3/6/2015* written on it with marker.

"It's a recording of the show from the other night. Candlepin let me use their equipment to record my set."

"Seriously? Thanks! This is awesome!" Alli blushes. "Mind if I sit here?"

"You're welcome. And, of course you can," she says. She moves her chair a few inches closer to the empty chair at the table, where I sit.

I take my laptop out and open it up. "Do you have any music on that?" she asks.

"A bit."

"May I take a look?"

"Sure. I don't have much on my laptop right now, but..." I open up iTunes and turn my laptop towards her. Then she looks through my music and occasionally jots down the name of a song in her notebook. She tells me she's looking for songs to play at her next gig.

She's going to customize her setlist for me. How cool is that?

She won't show me her list though. I have to find out at the gig. Then she asks me if I can bring some people. As much as I'd love for it to just be me that shows up to see her play I know it's better for her if I bring people, so, I tell her I'll make some calls. She's overwhelmed with gratitude. I figure this is my chance to make a move.

"Would you like to do dinner somewhere before the show?"

"With your friends?"

"Well, I was kinda thinking just us."

"Like a date?"

"Yeah. I did ask you out the other night, remember."

Alli suddenly looks nervous, which worries me. "I know... I would, it's just... I'm taking care of my landlord's dog this weekend, and I hate to leave him alone too long, I—" she looks at me, and seems to notice the disappointed look on my face. "But he should be fine if I take him for a good walk before I go." She mulls it over in her head, "Yeah, that sounds like fun."

"Great. Good. I'm looking forward to it."

She smiles. "Me too."

We sit in an awkward silence when a quiet alarm goes off. She pulls a small white timer out of her pocket.

"I'm sorry, my break is over."

"That's okay, I got work I can do anyway."

"I'll see you later, then?"

"For sure."

She smiles again and goes back behind the coffee bar. Of course, I can't get my head into work now But, I got the live CD to listen to. She even taped a track listing on the back of the case. So I put the disc in, name the tracks, and import the disc into my library. The quality of the recording is phenomenal, and I can't believe she thought enough of me to make me a copy.

Double-Tall No Whip Mocha Man comes to chat with me after Alli goes back to work, he's noticed that she and I were sitting and talking to each other. I tell him that I'd just asked her on a date and she said yes. He offers me his congratulations and goes back to chat up other people he knows. So, I listen to Alli's live recording, focusing mostly on that instead of my work. I'm about ready to give up and just go home so Alli doesn't suspect I'm here only to be around her. Just as I'm about to pack up my stuff Devon texts me advising me that she's got "company" over and I shouldn't come back anytime soon.

Great.

* * *

"You're still here?" Alli asks me while she's wiping down table an hour later. She looks surprised to see me.

"Yeah, but I think I'm all done working. That recording was great, by the way. Thanks for the copy."

"No problem. I'll have more in the future if you want them."

"Absolutely."

"So, what are you up to now?" she asks.

"I don't really want to go back home. My roommate has... company."

"You can't go home when he has friends over?"

"It's not that kind of company."

"Oh. I'm sorry," she says, understanding. "I guess I can't blame you. I wouldn't want to be around that either."

"So, umm, since I'm kinda stuck here... if you'd like to get dinner *tonight*, too, I can stay here until the end of your shift."

"Are you asking me out on another date *before* our first date?"

"Well, I just thought—"

"I am free tonight," she says. "So, I guess you're in luck."

How about that? Am I good or what? Double-Tall No Whip Mocha Man would be proud.

* * *

So, we go out to dinner after her shift. I have to say I'm proud of myself for managing to turn one future date into two. Maybe that's not much of an accomplishment, but it's been a while since I've been on an actual date, and I know this is going well. We talk more about what it's like being a musician and I find myself asking her a lot of questions about it, and she tells me about what it's like for her to perform on stage and about songwriting.

"I know I probably come across as shy in person, and I am, but for some reason I don't feel so shy when I sing. And my songs, some are really personal stories that I would only be able to share through music," she explains.

"So what are your songs generally about?" I ask.

"If you can't figure that out, then I'm not gonna tell you. That's where that whole shy thing comes in."

"Oh, right. Good point. Sorry."

"It's okay. Lots of people ask me about what my songs mean, or who I'm talking about. I think the nice thing about being a songwriter is that it doesn't necessarily matter what the story behind my song is. I just want people to react and feel whatever they feel from listening to it. I don't think it's all that hard to figure out what my songs are about, but what does it matter, really? We all respond to songs we enjoy differently. Two people can get something totally different from the same song and that's okay. I just want people to enjoy and emotionally respond to my music. That's all I can ask for."

"They do. I could tell at the Revolution show."

"How about you?"

"I was really moved by your songs."

She covers her mouth like she's trying not to laugh. "I'm sorry, I'm not laughing. Really. I'm not. That's very sweet of you say, and that really, really means so much to hear you say that. I'm just, I'm sorry. I'm sorry. Even when someone is giving me a compliment, I feel embarrassed and—"

"It's cool. I totally get."

"I'm not really good at one-to-one connections. I'm super-shy and awkward. I try not to be, but it's kind of a difficult thing to get over."

"I'm sure it is."

"I try to make up for that by trying to connect with an audience through my songs. So, thank you for telling me."

"You're welcome. And believe me, you're really talented, and you're going to do really well."

She blushes. "I'm glad you think so."

I do think so. I'm not just saying so to flirt with her. It really is one of the main reasons I like her. Okay, I liked her before I even knew how talented she was or that she was a singer. I was attracted to her first, sure, but seeing her singing on stage was pretty amazing. I want whatever this is between us to become something significant. I know that must seem silly to say while on my first date with a girl since I broke up with Lauren—and I'm not counting Emma for obvious reasons—but there's something interesting and unique and captivating about Alli. The fact that I've just used the word "captivating" ought to be proof enough there is something about this girl that just gets to me.

We sit in an awkward silence for a while, neither of us sure what to say next, until I ask her how she got hooked up with Candlepin and she tells me about how she met Nava at one of her first gigs at a coffeehouse when she came to Boston, and that Nava gave her contacts at bigger venues and with other bands that would be interested in having her as a support act, and of course, Nava got Candlepin to agree to have her open for them the other night. Blake also recommended her to the guy who handles booking at Scollay's. Apparently, she's impressed a lot of people already, myself included. This is one of the most interesting dates I've been on.

When the waitress drops off our check I put my credit card on top. When the waitress comes back Alli picks up the check and card and hands them to her.

The waitress comes back with *two* checks. Hands me one, hands Alli the other. It appears that Alli slipped her own card with mine to split the bill.

"You didn't have to do that," I say, trying to mask my irritation.

Girls often offer to pay for themselves on a first date, as if they really expect you to split the bill with them. I've never let them. It's a test. They know it. We know it. And they always back down after the first time I tell them it's on me. It's a game, sure, but it's one that we know we have to play. This, however has *never* happened. I've never known a girl to covertly put their credit card with the bill. I'm shocked, and concerned I've done something wrong tonight.

"I'm sorry," she says. "I just thought I should pay for myself."

Have I misinterpreted the evening? Is that possible? There was no way she could have thought this was just a friendly dinner. She *knew* it was a date. Why would she pay for herself? Now what do I say? She's already made it impossible for me to even try to pay the whole bill, so what can I do now? What did I do wrong? Is this her way of saying this is our first and last date? If she made the effort to pay her half, then obviously she had some reason for it. But I can't think of any misstep this entire evening.

"This was fun!" Alli says with a big smile. "Thank you so much for asking me."

"I—I'm glad. I had a lot of fun, too."

She smiles.

"We're still on for dinner Friday, right?" I ask, trying to hide my nervousness.

"Of course," she says. "I can't wait."

So, I didn't screw things up tonight. Maybe she just has a hang up about guys paying for her on a first date? That could be it. Well, I guess I don't need to dwell on it. We're still on for Friday night, and that's the important thing.

CHAPTER 9

I FEEL GOOD back at home. Devon isn't here, so I sit back and look for a movie to watch. I can't find anything on Netflix, but I remember that in the DVD player is *The Usual Suspects*—I'd planned to watch it about a month ago but only got as far as putting the disc in the player. That goes to show you how little I watch movies on disc anymore. I've already seen it many times, but it's still a great movie with a phenomenal plot twist that blew me away when I first saw it several years ago. Tonight, I feel like finishing it.

At 11:30 I hear multiple voices at the door as it opens. It's Devon and she's brought back people. Great. So much for solitude. I can tell from the voices that Devon has brought back a guy and a girl. It's only when they come into the living area I notice the girl is Emma.

"Don't you ever answer your texts?" Devon asks.

"I didn't feel my phone go off," I say, pausing the movie.

I look up and make eye contact with Emma, who appears slightly drunk. I make out like I only just realized it was her who came in with Devon. "Hey," I say.

"Hey Nick," she says laughing, "long time no see."

I look over at the guy Devon brought back here. He's kissing her neck in a way that nonverbally tells her that they need to get started with what they came back here to do.

"Nick, this is Dean. Dean, this is Nick. See you crazy kids in the morning," Devon says, pulling the guy in the direction of her room. The door closes tight, and there is a short burst of laughter from Devon.

Emma and I don't say anything. She takes a seat on the couch and gives me a closed-mouth smile and a well-here-we-are shrug. I'm not sure what I'm supposed to do. Devon must have brought her back here for us to hookup. I grab my phone and look at Devon's text messages that I missed:

Hey, I ran into Emma.

Dude. She wants to get laid!!!!

You better be home.

Looks like I was right. I thought I'd made it clear to Devon that I didn't want to pursue anything with Emma. But Devon was under the impression at the time that I had no chance with Alli, which clearly isn't the case. Is this thing with Alli going to go anywhere? I don't know. Do I really want to sleep with Emma tonight? Honestly, there's a part of me that does—and I'm doing my best to ignore it. I resolved the other day that what happened with Emma was just going to be a one-time thing. If things didn't look promising with Alli, I'd probably just cave, but there is potential there, and I'm sure sleeping with Emma again would screw that up somehow.

"So?" Emma says, with an air of impatience.

"So..."

"Bloody hell, Nick. Do fancy having it off again, or what?"

"Having it off?"

"Oh, for fuck's sake. Do you want to shag?" With a look of extreme impatience she straddles me on the couch. I know my window for being able to say no is closing fast.

"See, the thing is—"

"Are you about to turn me down? Did I mention I'm not wearing any knickers?"

"Seriously?"

"Why don't you find out?"

"Yeah, well, the thing is... I was on... a date earlier."

"So what? Is she your girlfriend or something?"

"Well, no. But—"

"Then I reckon we can still shag," she says.

"Really... Emma... I... can't..."

"Have you gone mental?"

"Apparently I have."

"You *really* want me to stop?"

I do and I don't. The effort she just put in has definitely reconfigured my blood flow, but the guilty feeling is far more persistent. "I'm sorry."

She resignedly moves off of me, and sits on the opposite side of the couch, annoyed. At that moment, we can hear the unambiguous noises of sex from Devon's room.

"Well, I'm gonna fuck off out of here," she says to me.

"You could watch the rest of the movie with me," I say.

"Are you taking the piss? No, I don't watch to watch a stupid movie."

"It's not stupid!"

"Sure it is, my ex made me watch it once."

"Seriously? You've seen it and you still think it's stupid? Come on! The whole time they're looking for Keyser Söze, and he's been talking to him the entire movie, hiding in plain sight! It's gotta be one of the best plot twists ever."

"Look, I came here to bonk your brains out. So, unless you've changed your mind I'm going home for a strum."

I shake my head, indicating my mind is set. "Sorry."

"Unbelievable," she says.

"I'm more surprised than you are," I say, which is an understatement.

* * *

Devon rips into me the next morning. "What the fuck is a fuck buddy for if you don't fuck her? What the fuck, dude?" It's an impressive number of times to say fuck in such a short sentence, even for Devon.

"What?"

"Dude! You made me look like an asshole. Do you think I suggested she come back here with me last night because I thought she just wanted a chat or watch a stupid movie?"

"*The Usual Suspects* is not a stupid—"

"You think you have a shot with that singer chick, don't you?"

"Her name is Alli. And yeah, actually, I think I do."

"Nick, I hate to disappoint you, but—"

I'm not about to hear any more of her bullshit. "For your information, we went on a date last night."

Devon looks surprised. "Oh really? Then what were you doing at home, by *yourself*?"

"Well, the date was over, and—"

"She had to get home before curfew, huh?" Devon laughs. "Did she have to get in her jammies and have her mommy tuck her in?"

"Shut up."

"I'm serious. So, you went on *one date* with her, didn't even fuck, and what, you're like in a serious relationship or something?

"Not yet. But maybe. We have another—"

"Whatever," she says, interrupting me, "at least one of us got laid last night."

"Yeah, *we* heard."

CHAPTER 10

I'M FEELING PRESSURE to find people to bring to Alli's next Scollay's gig. I'm just not sure who to ask. I'm hoping I won't have to ask Devon and Jay. Of course, they haven't exactly been the most supportive friends lately so it's not like they'd come anyway. Going through the contact list on my iPhone I see the names of a lot people I used to hang out with but haven't seen in ages. For the past few years Lauren was the one who was primarily responsible for our social calendar, and the further along we were in our relationship the further away we went from my circle of friends in favor of her circle of friends. I still kept in touch with my friends, of course. There's the occasional email or message on Facebook, or a text, but never any phone calls.

The first person I call is Daniella, an old friend from college. She married another friend of mine from college, Mike, a year after graduation. I was pretty close with both of them in school, but we grew apart. I've lost touch with quite a few friends who either live far away or have gotten married since college, but I was really disappointed that I lost touch with Daniella and Mike. I certainly tried to keep things up, but I haven't seen them in almost three years, which is right around the time they had their kid. Sure, we're friends on Facebook and still have windows into each other's lives, but that's not enough to maintain a real friendship. Once you start having kids you have bigger things on your mind than friends who aren't "real adults" with mortgages and parental responsibilities. Still it would be nice to see them again and hopefully rekindle the friendship.

She sounds excited when she picks up the phone. "Hey, Nick!" This is a good sign. She knew it was me when she picked up, so she still has me in her contact list.

"Hey, how are you?"

"I'm good. I'm good. How are you? It's been, like, forever since I've heard from you."

"Well, you know, busy times." I could point out that that she and Mike were equally capable of contacting me, but my goal here is to get them to come out and see Alli play, not point fingers at each other over who's to blame for our falling out of touch.

"Totally. How's... Laura?"

"Lauren," I correct her. "We broke up. A few months ago."

"Oh, I'm sorry. What happened?"

This really isn't what I want to be talking about. "It's complicated," I say, hoping she won't press me on the subject.

"I see," she says. "But you're okay, right?"

"Yeah, you know, moving on."

"Well, that's good."

"Yeah." I know I should ask about what's new with her and Mike, but I don't have a lot of time so I just ask her about coming to the show. "So, anyway, I was wondering... this Friday, this... friend... of mine is doing an acoustic show at Scollay's. She's really good, the kind of stuff you used to like. I thought maybe you and Mike would be interested in coming."

"*This* Friday?" she asks, and I know she's already thinking of reasons to pass.

"Yeah, this Friday. Two days from now."

"Where is Scollay's?"

"Faneuil Hall."

"Oh, okay." She pauses. "What kind of music again?"

"Well, she'll be playing cover songs, so, you know, pretty much anything, I guess. You can make requests if you want. At the very least we can just hang out, have a drink, enjoy the music—" She doesn't respond immediately, like she's coming up with an excuse.

"I actually can't drink right now," she says.

"Why not?"

"We haven't posted about this on Facebook yet, but, we're expecting again. I'm due in October."

"That's great, congratulations."

"Thanks, we're really excited."

"We could still celebrate." I suggest, in the hopes of making this still happen. "I mean, you two probably don't get many nights out these days, right?"

She laughs. "That's for sure. And I'd love to hang out and catch up some time. But I don't think we can make it this Friday."

"Oh, okay," I say. I'm disappointed that they won't come to Alli's show, but I'm also disappointed that we won't get to hang out after all these years. I wish I'd tried harder to stay close friends with them.

"Some other time? Okay?"

"Sure," I say.

She's sensed the awkward turn this conversation has taken and makes an excuse to get off the phone. Which is fine because I still have to get some bodies to Alli's gig.

Next, I try a guy I used to work with named Garrett. He's a safer bet (I think) seeing as we used to hang out a lot. Sure, it was after work and with other work people, but that must count for something—even if we haven't hung out since I lost that job. He likes to go out and drink, and that is what I am asking him to do now. He sounds genuinely interested.

"Is she hot?" he asks.

"Seriously?"

"I'm just asking..."

"She's cute."

"Cute, or hot?"

"Is there a difference?"

"Of course," he says, as if I'm an idiot for asking.

"What difference does it make? I'm not asking you to come to check out her looks. I'm asking you to hear her play."

"It's nice to know," he explains. Garrett was obviously the wrong person to ask. "What kind of music?"

"Well, she'll play cover songs mostly. You can request stuff if you'd like."

"Can I think about it?"

This is what he says when he really means "If I can't find anything better to do, I'll go."

"Yeah, sure think about it," I say. "I'll text you the details, and if you can make it, great."

He's not going to make it, I know he isn't.

"Yeah, cool," he says.

We shoot the shit for a while until I realize I still got to find *someone* to come to the show. Once he's gone, I start scrolling through my contacts again. I pick out potential candidates, but I give up trying to recruit people after four more failed attempts. Friendships are fragile things that need regular care to survive, just like a house plant. If you forget to water it consistently it starts to wither away and die. Sometimes you think after a long lapse that you can just dump a whole lot of water on it and it will come back to life. Maybe, if it was strong enough to begin with you can revive it. But let's face it, college friends move on, get married, start families, and need other married couples with children to form their new social circles. Then you're left with work friends. But all you have in common with them is work, and that's hardly the strongest foundation for a friendship. I may see Garrett again, but now that we don't work together the friendship is most certainly doomed. He said he'll call me some time, but I doubt he will.

So I have to accept the fact that Devon and Jay are my only options. I suppose I could just not invite anyone to come, but I told Alli I would, and if I don't bring at least one person, preferably two, then she'll think I'm an asshole for saying I'd bring people but didn't, or she'll think I'm a loser with not a enough friends to ask. Either scenario doesn't bode well for me.

I have to beg Devon to go. She's moderately interested because she did enjoy hearing Alli last week, but it takes a while to convince her to come anyways. I tell her that if she and Jay come I'll score some significant points with Alli. Devon can't hide her skepticism that I have a shot anyways, so I tell her that not only did Alli go on a date last night, but we're having dinner together before the show Friday.

"Ooooh... dinner! Mr. Stud! The real question is: who is she going home with?"

"With any luck, me."

"Fine, I'll come for a little while. But after what you did to Emma I promise this is the last time I'm helping you get laid."

So that's one person.

Next, I call Jay. He's reluctant until I offer to buy him *two* beers. You'd think he'd be willing to help me without any sort of bribe.

* * *

Two hours before Alli and I are supposed to meet at Faneuil Hall I text her to make sure we're still on. Twenty minutes later with no reply has me worried that Devon and Jay were right, maybe I was fooling myself into thinking I had a shot. Maybe she's sitting there trying to come up with an ironclad excuse to back out of the date without hurting my feelings too much.

She does reply in the end. After apologizing for not replying sooner because she was doing laundry and playing with her landlord's dog she says she "can't wait" for dinner. This is good. I'm so excited that I head down a little early. Thankfully, I only have to wait twenty minutes before Alli arrives in her Uber with her stuff. After I help her unload the car she thanks the driver, I help her bring her guitar and equipment in Scollay's, and we walk over to the Asian fusion restaurant nearby.

Last time we talked mostly about what it is like for her being a musician, so tonight she wants to hear more about me and what I do. She seems very interested in how Jay and I ended up starting our own business. She finds this fascinating, expresses her admiration for our taking matters into our hands by starting our business after losing our jobs. I think she gives us too much credit, but I'm not about to argue with her when it's obvious she likes the fact that I have an entrepreneurial spark in me. She gets really excited when I tell her how we're talking with Keith about redoing the Revolution website. Web design, while it sounds exciting and interesting, is hard to talk about to people who don't know about it. I can't imagine that talking about the client who wants three different versions of flowcharts for their new website could be interesting to her.

"That's great that you are able to support yourself with your own business. I hope I can completely support myself soon," she says.

"Aren't you?"

"Well, I mean, with just singing. Without Starbucks or some other job."

"You'll get there."

"I hope so."

"You're incredibly talented."

"Thanks, but there are a lot of talented musicians who struggle."

"I believe in you." I know I'm laying it on thick, but I'm telling her the truth. It's working too. She blushes and averts her eyes, like she's overwhelmed by the compliment.

"That's really sweet of you to say."

"I mean it."

"I know you do. And it's really sweet."

It's at this point that Alli decides that she wants to know more about my family.

I try to just give her the highlights, but she asks loads of questions (some asked carefully or qualified by assurances that I don't have to answer them if I don't want to) so I tell her about my parents' divorce, my mom getting remarried, Lacy's dad dying a few years back. She's curious about the relationship I have with my mom and sister. I explain that my relationship with my mother is fine, but my sister and I don't really relate to each other because of the difference in our ages. Alli finds this sad, because she says as only child she feels if she had a sister or a brother they'd have been the best of friends.

When I ask her about her family, she's instantly more reserved. She had explained she came here from Connecticut, so I asked her how her parents felt about her moving away and pursuing a music career instead of college. After a long pause she tells me she doesn't live with her parents. "My dad's cousin and his wife are... or were my legal guardians until I turned eighteen," she explains.

"Oh," I say, a bit surprised. "How come?"

"It's not something I really want to talk about."

"Oh, I'm sorry," I say, though my curiosity is piqued.

"It's okay. I'm not trying to be rude or anything. It's just... it's just my family situation is complicated and not easy for me to talk about. I'm sorry."

"No, I'm sorry," I tell her again. "Can you tell me how they felt about you moving away?"

"Sure. They understood. They knew I wanted to make a living with my music, and that nothing was going to get in the way of that. I used to just sing at church on Sundays and some local open mics, and I loved it, but I knew I needed to go to a bigger city with a good independent music scene to, I guess you can say, start my career in."

"So, why Boston?" I ask. "Not that I mind that you came here. I'm glad you did, I'm just curious."

Alli smiles. "Well, Boston has always appealed to me, and it's not too far away from home. We visited here once with when I was fifteen and I really was fascinated by the history. It's also not as intimidating as New York City."

"You made a good choice," I say.

"Thanks. I've been lucky so far with the opportunities I've had here, and Dave and Christine are very proud of me."

"That's good. I suppose you talk with them a lot about how things are going out here?"

"Yup, all the time, I—" Alli stops abruptly as the waiter comes with our check.

"Looks like we're out of time," she says, almost sounding relieved. Then she looks at her phone, "Oops, I better start getting set up."

"Go ahead, I'll finish here."

"Thanks," she says, getting up, "I'll see you over there." She pulls out a twenty from her pocket and puts it on top of the check, and briskly walks down towards Scollay's.

Son of a bitch, she did it again. What is going on here?

I try not to panic. I'll just pay with my credit card and put the twenty bucks into her tip jar tonight.

Alli is still setting up when I get to Scollay's. I don't see Jay or Devon yet, so I make a quick run to the bathroom downstairs. When I walk in I see Jay washing up. He breaks the news that Devon won't be showing up tonight because some photographer's assistant got sick and she was available to fill in taking photos at a wedding at the Omni Parker House.

"But she *wasn't* available. She said she'd be coming. I told Alli I was bringing people."

"I'm people."

"You're a person. One person. Now I feel like an asshole."

"Hey, shit happens. Devon's gonna make a nice chunk of change tonight. That's probably a bit more important to her than helping you score with a girl she thinks you have no chance with. Can you blame her?"

I hate to admit that I can't blame her.

"Listen, I wouldn't worry about it," Jay says. "If you really have a chance with her, then it shouldn't matter if you only got one person to come." His words hardly make me feel better about the situation.

"I do have a chance with her. We just had dinner together. The two of us."

"A date? You guys were on a date earlier?"

"Yeah, and it was our *second* date."

"I thought I was helping you have a chance with her, you said you needed my help to make you look good. If you were just on your *second* date you don't need me third-wheeling tonight. I'm gonna bail."

"You seem to be forgetting that I actually need you here. If I don't bring anyone I'll still look like an asshole. It could be the difference between me going home alone tonight or me going home with her," I say, even though my hopes of hooking up with her tonight vanished when she threw that twenty-dollar bill down at dinner. As a compromise, we agree that he'll stay for one set, then come up with a good excuse to leave.

When I explain to Alli that only Jay could make it she's cool about it and asks Jay to suggest some songs for her to play.

Jay lists off some songs he'd like to hear, and Alli promises to play a few.

"Awesome," he says. "So, how's Boston treatin' ya?"

"Good. I think. I'm happy for the opportunities I've gotten so far to get gigs. I was worried I'd have to busk in T stations just to have the opportunity to play in front of people. I don't think I'd feel safe doing that. Especially being new to the city."

"Cool. Cool."

"Well, I better get started," Alli tells us.

Alli plays "Closer" by Kings of Leon midway through her first set. It's one of Jay's requests, and he enjoys her version of the song, but he doesn't like it when I suggest he give her a tip. I try to explain to him that since she played something he wanted, it would be nice if threw at least a buck into the glass sitting on the stool in her corner. Especially since I've agreed to buy him two beers tonight. He reluctantly agrees and puts a single dollar bill in there as Alli starts another song. She briefly interrupts her singing with a quick "thank you."

"Was that so hard?" I ask.

"Parting with *my* money is always tough."

When Alli finishes her set Jay stands up, indicating he's ready to leave. He tells her he needs to meet up with a potential client who just emailed him. Not the most believable excuse this late on a Friday night, but Alli doesn't seem suspicious, but she looks at me with curiosity.

"Do you have to go too?"

"*I* got to meet him." Jay clarifies his lie, "Nick doesn't. It's like... a preliminary meeting. That's all. Anyway, this was really cool, I'll definitely come again sometime soon."

"Sorry I didn't play more of the songs you requested yet."

"No problem. Next time. You crazy kids have fun," Jay says and heads out. Alli smiles shyly as if she has figured out his excuse is merely a ruse.

Alli sits in the stool next to mine, and I apologize for not doing a better job getting people to show up.

"It's okay. You tried. You're here anyways. So far, you're the only one I know who has come to one of these gigs."

"How could I miss it? You're amazing." Alli smiles and turns away, I can see she's blushing at the compliment. "Sorry, I don't mean to embarrass you."

She makes eye contact again, and I can see she's still blushing. "I better start my next set," she says.

I would normally feel like a loser, sitting here by myself watching her play, but I'm having too good a time to care. And when Alli's last set is over she asks me to help her take her stuff home. I think it safe to say she's making a move since she's certainly managed to bring all her stuff home by herself before. So, I'm feeling pretty confident that something is going to happen tonight.

CHAPTER 11

We Uber back to Alli's place and I help carry her stuff in. She lives in a basement apartment in a house near Coolidge Corner. She tells me how her landlord, Mr. Putnam, gave her a great deal in exchange for her paying rent in cash, and he knocks off a portion of her rent when he needs someone to watch his thirteen-year-old daughter Eden when he's not around, or like this weekend when she watches the dog while they're away.

"She was basically my first friend when I moved here," she explains. "Her parents are in the middle of a divorce, so she splits her time with them, and she comes down to visit me when her parents are fighting on the phone. The whole thing is really tough on her. She and her dad are away for the weekend, and so I'm watching their dog while they're gone."

I'm still amazed that my being here was *her* idea. Even if I had offered to help her bring her stuff home and she took me up on it, it was still likely that she'd just have me help her load her stuff in the Uber car and then we'd go our separate ways for the evening. I certainly didn't think going back to her place and possibly spending the night was going to be her idea, especially after the way she paid for her half of dinner. So, I'm equally excited and strangely nervous about what's about to happen. I'm thinking I have to make the next move. Our two dates have gone well, but I'm thinking sex is not likely to happen tonight. Who knows? We'll see if she gives me any new signals. I didn't bring any condoms with me, but if she did ask me here to spend the night with her she's bound to have her own stash or is on the pill. But I'd be cool with just a little fooling around, too.

We walk down a paved path, Alli opens the gate to the fenced backyard and points towards the door that leads down to her apartment, closing the fence behind me. Her apartment is small, but enough for one person. There's a small kitchenette, a decent-sized living space, a bathroom and a bedroom. Alli puts her stuff down on the floor, then notices a basket of folded laundry on the couch. She excuses herself quickly, grabs the basket and runs it into the bedroom. I hear a dog whine in the corner, and see the little pup looking excited inside his crate.

"This must be your landlord's dog," I say when Alli comes out of the bedroom.

"Yup, that's Derby." She walks up to the crate, "You happy to see me, Derby?" she says in a cutesy voice. She opens up the crate and Derby comes running out. He's small, with short, light brown hair and a black, wrinkled face. He runs for me and then cowers at my feet.

"It's okay, Derby, don't be scared," she says.

I try to pet Derby, but he runs off into her bedroom.

"He'll run around for a bit. He's just excited to be out of the crate. Do you want a drink? I've got water and orange juice."

"Water's good."

Alli opens her refrigerator just as Derby comes running out of her bedroom with something in his mouth.

"Oh shoot, can you try to catch him and grab whatever he's got?"

I go after Derby. There aren't many places to go, but he runs fast, and whatever he has just looks like a multicolored blur to me, but he doesn't want to give it up. I manage to close the door to the bedroom before he decides to escape in there. I finally catch him when he runs past my feet. I scoop him up and grab hold of what's in mouth. "Let go, Derby!"

"Pinch him behind the neck," Alli says. I try it and repeat the command, he opens his mouth and I let him down. "Got it," I say as Derby runs maniacally around the apartment.

"Good," Alli says as she pours us both some water from one of those filtered pitchers, "What did he have?"

That's when I realize I'm holding a pair of Alli's panties in my hands.

"Looks like Derby got into your laundry," I say, holding them up for her to see, and chuckling. But she doesn't find it funny at all. Her face goes white with embarrassment and now I'm standing here like an idiot holding her underwear in my hand. I'm not sure what to do, and she's just standing there mortified. Of course, Derby hasn't given up and tries jump up at me to grab them again.

"No Derby," I say, "these are Alli's." I notice a bright orange ball under the coffee table, grab it and toss it towards the kitchen. But he's far more interested in the panties, and doesn't go after the ball. He stares at them like they're a treat that I'm about to give him.

Alli finally holds her hands out, and I lightly toss the panties to her. Derby goes berserk thinking we're playing a game with him. She stuffs them into the front pocket of her hoodie like she's trying to bury them. Derby sits still, but is ready to pounce the moment he sees them again.

I try to laugh the whole thing off like it's not a big deal.

"This is so embarrassing," she says. If she finds *this* embarrassing, then I'm pretty sure that she didn't ask me over so we could hook up. It's obvious that me seeing her panties was not on her agenda for tonight. I knew sex was unlikely, but that didn't mean we still couldn't make out, and fool around. Instead, I feel like I've violated her privacy in some unforgivable way because she's too embarrassed to even look at me now. She'll probably just thank me for helping her and send me off any minute.

I can't even think of a joke to relieve the tension.

"Don't be embarrassed," I say. This is the best thing I can think of to tell her at the moment.

Alli sits on the couch with a horrified look on her face. Derby comes over to her and puts his paws on her lap. Derby sniffs around the pocket of her hoodie, but Alli shoos him away. "No! Bad!"

So, what do I do now? Do I sit next to her? I can't imagine why a pair of cotton panties would derail all the progress I made tonight, but I have a feeling they have.

Is this my fault? Maybe I need to apologize.

"I'm sorry," I say. "I thought they were... a sock or something. I didn't realize it was—"

"Can we... stop talking about my underwear?"

"Sorry," I say.

Alli sighs. "No. Don't be sorry. I'm sorry. I'm acting stupid, aren't I?"

"Nah," I say reassuringly, even though I think she's overreacting a bit.

"I can't believe this... the first time there's a boy in the apartment... Really, Derby?" She gives Derby an accusatory look. He tilts his head at her, not knowing what he did that was so wrong.

"Bad puppy! I'm sooooo not happy with you right now. In fact, you need to go outside anyway, so here." She walks towards the door and he follows her, she opens it up and runs outside.

"That'll keep him busy for a while," she says closing the door. "It's a big backyard."

I don't think there's anything I can say to ease her embarrassment, so I just need to change the subject.

"This apartment is pretty nice."

Alli composes herself. "Thank you."

I take a seat next to her on the couch. There's no need for a tour because everything there is to see can be seen from the living area, except the bedroom, which I suspect she won't be showing me any time soon.

Alli gradually relaxes and we're eventually, able to talk just like we'd been on our date earlier. Alli lets Derby back in a little while later and puts him in his crate where he curls up to sleep. We continue to chat, and it seems like neither of want to close the book on the evening just yet despite the tiny unpleasantness when we first got here.

Next thing we realize it is nearly two in the morning, and we sit in awkward silence unsure of what to do next. I wait for her to make the next move. I'm hoping she'll offer to let me spend the night here, even though her sheepish demeanor suggests that is highly unlikely.

After the silence starts to get even more uncomfortable, it's clear I'll have to make the next move, or we'll just sit in silence until morning.

"I guess I should get going."

"Yeah, I guess so."

Oh well. So much for that. Looks like I have a long walk ahead of me.

I get up from the couch and start towards the door.

"Listen, I know it's really late—" she's about to tell me I can sleep here, but I don't think she's decided if she really wants me to, "so if you want... need to stay here tonight, you can."

Finally! "Oh, yeah, sure." I try not to sound too thrilled. I don't want her thinking this was my plan all along. "Thanks. That probably would be better than me walking home at this hour."

"As luck would have it, I do have an extra toothbrush."

"Oh, good." I definitely wasn't expecting that.

"Not because I usually have overnight guests or anything. I don't. I haven't. I just bought a new one for myself the other day, and it made sense to buy a double-pack." She's talking so quick like she's worried she said something wrong. "I'm sorry, I don't know why I'm nervous. I just didn't want to you think—you can use the extra one, it's not a problem."

"That be great. Thanks."

She sighs, relieved. "Okay. Great. I'll go get some sheets for you."

"Sheets?"

"For the couch."

"Oh. Right," I say. I must sound disappointed, because Alli frowns.

"Did you think you'd be sleeping somewhere else?" I don't say anything. Have I just lost my invitation to spend the night here? "If you did, then you should know right now I'm not, you know, like that." She looks at Derby who has perked up in his crate at the sound of her voice getting stern. "Right, Derby?" Derby just tilts his head, confused.

"No, of course not. I just—I just figured I'd just sleep on top of the cushions; that's all."

Nice save, I think.

I hope.

"Oh, sorry. I thought maybe you believed when I asked if you wanted to stay... never mind—just figured you should be comfortable. I have extra sheets and a pillow. I don't have anything you could wear to sleep, I—"

"I'll sleep in my clothes, no problem."

"I'm sorry. I didn't realize how late it was."

"Really, don't worry about it. I wouldn't have expected you to. Besides, I've had a great time talking."

"Me too," she says. She stands awkwardly for a few seconds then heads over to her linen closet, which is right next to the door to the bathroom. She comes back with sheets and a pillow. "I apologize for jumping to the wrong conclusion. Anyway, you can brush your teeth and everything first."

"Thanks."

Her bathroom is tiny but it's nice. Recently renovated and very neat. The only addition to the decor she has contributed are the floor mats and the shower curtain, which are dark blue to match the accent tile on the floor. She's left the toothpaste out next to the fresh toothbrush. After I'm done brushing my teeth, I come out to find she's covered the couch with the sheets for me. Then she goes into the bathroom, brushes her teeth, and heads back toward her room.

"Goodnight, Nick," she says to me from her doorway.

"Goodnight," I say.

"Goodnight, Derby," she says. Derby perks up briefly, then rests his head again. "See you boys in the morning."

CHAPTER 12

I WAKE UP to the sound of Alli's shower running through the bathroom door. After about ten minutes she comes out of the bathroom fully dressed, hair still wet. "You can shower now if you like; I'm just gonna let the dog out in the backyard while I'll dry my hair in my room."

I could wait until I get home, but I do feel rather grimy from sleeping in my clothes last night, and part of me hopes we'll do something together today, so even though I'll have to put on the same clothes again a shower can't hurt. There's a fresh towel waiting for me on the counter.

While Alli had a spare toothbrush and sheets for me, I'm stuck using what's available in her shower to get clean. Girly shampoo, conditioner, body wash. Sure, I'll smell a bit feminine afterwards, but hey, when in Rome, I guess.

After my shower I'm careful to be as dry as possible before stepping out onto the floor. I'm normally not so careful at home, much to Devon's annoyance, but as guest here I'm careful not to get her floor wet. Speaking of Devon, she must be wondering where I am. There has not been a time since we've lived together that I've not come home at night, so she must be thinking all sorts of things.

When I get out of the bathroom, dried, dressed and ready for the day, she's playing fetch with Derby. I check my phone. No texts or calls from Devon. I guess she wasn't all that curious... Or was too drunk to notice.

"So," I say, "Would you like to do something? Get breakfast maybe?"

"I was going to ask you the same thing."

Since Alli's shift starts in an hour there's really only enough time to go to her Starbucks for breakfast. The barista Jess takes my order. I order for myself, then when she asks, "Will that be all?" I point to Alli and say, "Whatever she wants." Jess grins when she realizes that Alli and I are here *together*, and when Alli orders there's an unspoken dialogue between the two them through their facial expressions. Once Jess has the whole order rung up I quickly give her my card before Alli attempts to pay, but we do end up getting Alli's employee discount.

By some sort of miracle, a table with some comfortable chairs frees up and we're able to snag it before anyone else does.

I immediately get us back into conversation before she can say something about me paying for her. We don't seem to run out of things to say. We talk about music. She says I should be open to some more genres besides alternative, rock and classic rock, that there's a lot of folk and country, and country pop that I would like as well. Before I can think of a response, our breakfast sandwiches are announced, and I go up to get them. When I get back, Alli reaches for her bag, "Here, I know you got to use my discount, but let me pay you for my half of breakfast—"

"You know, you don't have to keep paying for yourself, Alli."

"It's fine, really. I don't mind."

"I got it, okay?" I say, trying not to sound annoyed.

"Okay, fine. This time." But her concession doesn't satisfy me.

"I think it's okay for me to pay for you more than just this once."

"Why is that?"

"Well—" I say, not exactly sure how to explain, "you know, it's not uncommon for two people who are dating—"

"Oh, are we *dating*?"

"Well, we've gone out a few times now, I really like you. I think—hope you really like me."

"I like you. I guess I just wasn't sure if—" She shifts uncomfortably in her seat. "You really want to date me? Like, be my boyfriend?"

"Absolutely."

"You're sure?"

"How else will you let me pay for you?" I say jokingly.

"Being my boyfriend means you get to pay for me?"

"Yeah, that's usually how it works, isn't it?"

"I have no idea."

"You don't?"

"Well... the thing is..." She looks down at the table, hiding an embarrassed expression on her face. "I've never actually had a boyfriend before. So, I don't really know what they do about paying for meals or anything, really."

Excuse me? Never had a boyfriend? I can't believe that. I mean, I don't know why she would lie about that, but I can't let this go without asking for an explanation. "Really? Never?"

She shakes her head. "There have been *no* boyfriends." She lifts her arm up and makes an O-shape with her hand. "Zero. Not even a date... well, I mean, I guess, before you there weren't."

"How is that possible?"

"Are you making fun of me?"

"No. No... of course not. It's just can't believe—"

"I don't lie," she says. "I hate lies. I don't lie about anything. Not even that."

"Of course not. I didn't mean to suggest you were lying, it's just... hard to believe."

"Why is that?"

"Well, for starters, I can't imagine that no one has ever been attracted to a beautiful girl like you." I'm surprised by my own bluntness and honesty. I've never been so bold in telling any girl I liked how pretty I thought she looked.

She blushes. "Your compliments are appreciated, but physical attractiveness isn't everything."

"Well... no, I wasn't finished. You've also got a tremendous talent, and you are by far the nicest person I've ever met."

"Thank you. It's okay, I know you're not like that."

"You do? How?" I ask.

"You just seem interested in *me*. I never thought that would happen for me."

"Why not?"

"I can't really, I..." She plays with her napkin nervously.

"Well, I like you for you. Absolutely, one hundred percent."

She smiles. "I'm so glad. The other boys... I dunno, I never was sure. Maybe I was too nervous, or didn't feel comfortable, or..." She shifts uncomfortably in her seat, breaking eye contact like she doesn't want to talk about it.

"So, I'm not the first guy to have asked you out?"

"There have been a few since I moved here."

"But not before?"

She shakes her head. "I didn't really even have any friends before I moved here. See, I was homeschooled and..." her voice trails off and I can tell this conversation is making her feel awkward.

"I'm sorry. I'm probably asking too many personal questions. It's just that I was surprised, that's all. I thought I was lucky that you didn't already have a boyfriend, to be honest."

"It's not that I've never wanted a boyfriend, I just... I want a boy to like me for *me,* not because—well, for the wrong reasons."

"Like what?"

"They're hard to explain."

"Do you want to try?" I ask.

"I can't. I'm sorry."

Well, that's a little weird.

"You were also... different," she adds.

"Really, how?"

"I suppose it's because you got to know me first. We got to hang out before you, well, you know. And I knew that you were interested before, you were kinda obvious about it, you put such a huge effort into coming to see me play, trying to get your friends to see me play, and helping me bring my stuff home... and you *talk* to me. You seem interested in me and who I am. It's not like you stare at my boobs the entire time," she glances down at her chest, "not that they're that special but you just seemed genuinely interested in me as a person and what I do. I'm usually really shy with people, especially boys, but, I dunno, I'm not so much with you. Even Nava can be a bit intimidating at times."

"I can see that. She intimidates me too," I say.

Alli laughs and leans in closer to me. "And, you know, you make me laugh, too. I've heard it's important to have a boyfriend who makes you laugh."

"I hope that means you'd like me to be your boyfriend."

She smiles. "If you still want to be."

"Yes, I do." I tell her, and she smiles.

And that's how we make our relationship official.

PART 2

CHAPTER 13

"So, what do we do now?" Alli asks after we finish eating. "I don't mean to sound silly, this is just new territory for me."

"Well, first you'll have to be more open to letting me pay for you," I say.

"I didn't realize how much that bothered you. Sorry."

"Beginner's mistake," I say, so she won't feel bad.

"I have a lot to learn, I guess," she says.

"You'll be fine." I tell her.

"Is there anything else I need to know?"

"Well, I'll probably go to all of your gigs," I say. "I could run your merch table for you. If that's okay with you."

"Of course. That would be really helpful. I probably miss out on sales by not having someone to run the table while I'm playing. And I'm too shy to ask someone."

"Well, problem solved."

"Hmm. I could definitely get used to this 'having a boyfriend' thing."

"And since I have a roommate, we'll probably spend more time hanging out at your place than mine. You know, when we aren't out."

"Oh, why is that?"

I'm surprised the answer isn't obvious, and I try to think of a delicate way to say what I mean. "You, know. For privacy."

She blushes, and we sit there awkwardly until she decides to speak again.

"I have a gig at a bar on Harvard Street from eight to eleven tonight. So, if you meet me at my place at seven, we can carry my stuff over. It's a short walk from my apartment."

"Sounds like a good plan."

She smiles. "Well, I guess I better get to work now."

We both stand up and she waits. She appears unsure of what to do next.

"So, I'll see you later?" she asks.

"Can't wait," I say, and she blushes again.

She looks at me awkwardly, not knowing what move to make next. I move in for a hug, which surprises her a little, but she reciprocates, which feels nice. Then she walks behind the counter and into the back room. There's no line so I get a refill of coffee before I go. Jess is now at the espresso machine, and another barista, whose name I don't know, takes my order. He's got a big smile on her face.

"So," he says, "You and *Alli*, huh?"

"Yup," I say.

"That's awesome. Good for her," he says, and give me my refill for free.

* * *

Alli and I arrive early to the gig, which is at a small hole-in-the-wall bar a short walk away from her apartment. According to Alli, they don't pay well, but it's a fairly steady gig, and a short walk from her apartment. I explained to her on the walk over that in the future I'm more than happy to drive her to and from gigs that are farther away so she won't have to rely on Uber as much.

"It's one of the perks of having a boyfriend with a car." I explained, figuring she'd resist.

Amazingly, she's okay with the offer. "Sounds fair. Because one of the perks of having me as your girlfriend is that I can get you on the guest list so you don't have to pay if there's a cover. Most of the time, anyways."

There is no cover charge tonight, but it's still a nice perk for future reference.

About ten minutes after our arrival Nava shows up with a small group of people, and she is excited when she sees us. She bombards us before we have an opportunity to acknowledge her, and it's clear from her animated conversation—even though I can barely understand her—that she knows the big news already. She hollers to the bartender and orders three shots of tequila. Before Alli can protest, Nava rushes over to the bar, pays for the shots, comes back and offers one to each of us to "toast the new happy couple!" Nava shouts at the other patrons in the bar, and we get a few light claps and a cat call whistle from someone I can't see. Then Alli awkwardly hands her back the shot.

"I'm sorry, I can't—"

"You sure? I won't tell that you are... underage." She whispers the last word as if that will make a difference to

Alli. I haven't known her that long, but I know she's not about to pretend she's of legal drinking age. So, instead, Nava and I toast, and she downs both her shots before I can even get mine down.

After Nava is done embarrassing us, she returns to her friends. Alli apologizes for that brief uncomfortable moment.

"How did she know, you know, about us, already?" I ask.

"Was I not supposed to say anything?" she asks innocently.

"You can tell anyone you want," I tell her.

"Okay. Good. I thought maybe I'd made a *faux pas* or something."

"Nah, I just didn't know you two, you know, were buddies or anything."

"We're not. Not really. I mean, she's nice and has helped me a lot, but we don't hang out or anything. We're... too different, I guess. But she comes to my Starbucks, and she came in while I was on break, and she asked me what was new, and—"

"You don't have to explain. It's cool."

Nava is the only other person here that I know, but she's with her own friends so I decide to stand solo when Alli's set starts. She opens with her song "Seeing Through Me" and immediately follows that with "Wallflower" — two of my favorite songs on her album. The crowd—I say "crowd" loosely since there's really less than thirty people here— seems pleased so far, and clap for her. She smiles bashfully. "Thanks everyone, my name is Alli Conwell, I'll be playing here until midnight. And I'm here every Saturday night the next three weeks."

She adjusts the tuning on her guitar.

"So, as Nava pointed out earlier, I have a boyfriend now, and he's—" Alli gets interrupted by a cacophony of hoots and cheers from the crowd. Alli blushes. "Thanks, thank you. Anyway, he's right over there, helping me sell CDs tonight." She points me out to the crowd, and most people look in my direction. I feel pretty darn cool until one guy shouts out, "You can do better than that!" and laughs.

"Hey! Be nice!" Alli says to him, before addressing the whole crowd again. "Anyway, if you like what you hear tonight, and would like a CD, he'll take care of you." Then she announces that she's gonna play a couple songs for me. She plays a song I recognize. It's not from her album, but I recognize from the first time I saw her perform. Then she plays a cover of Vertical Horizon's "Everything You Want"—one of my favorite songs which she certainly discovered on my laptop the other day. Very cool.

I sell about eight CDs before Alli finishes her last set, and a couple more to Nava's friends afterwards. It's not a lot, but when I tell Alli she looks pleased.

"Usually, I only sell about four." She explains. "A lot of people here are regulars, too. So, this was good night. Maybe you're a good luck charm."

CHAPTER 14

Two weeks into my relationship with Alli I've learned something about dating a musician: It's exhausting.

There's a lot of late nights and lugging equipment to and from gigs and open mics. As exhausting as it can be, it's also extremely cool. I enjoy going to her gigs and have been exposed to some great local bands. I give Alli a lot of credit for the effort she puts into it. She can play a gig that ends at midnight or one in the morning, and still open at Starbucks that morning on just a few hours of sleep. It's rare when that happens, since she can usually negotiate her schedule with her manager. Between Starbucks and performing, she also squeezes in time to write new songs and market herself. Since opening for Candlepin she's gotten some good publicity. She was mentioned when they were written up in the *Boston Globe* about their comeback on the Boston's music scene. The reporter wrote, "Opening for Candlepin was Alli Conwell. She captivated the crowd with her poignant and unpretentious acoustic rock/country pop songs. The young singer-songwriter is sure to make a name for herself on the local music scene." That was enough to get a writer at *The Dig* to do a short profile on her, which was published this week. It wasn't much, but the paper has good circulation and she was proud of it. I snagged a bunch of copies the day it came out.

When Alli has late gigs I usually end up crashing at her place.

On her couch.

Okay, I know she made it very clear to me that being her boyfriend wasn't gonna change where I'd be sleeping right away, but over the course of these nights in our physical relationship has progressed... slowly.

And by slowly, I mean not at all.

With Alli being new to world of relationships I knew things weren't gonna move fast, (which I am okay with since recently relationships that moved fast didn't turn out so well) but it's now been two weeks and we haven't even kissed yet. It seemed like every time I was about to make a move, she'd say she was tired and had to go to bed, or get up off the couch and offer to get us drinks. I knew she was just nervous, so, despite my desire to move things along, I knew the best thing was to wait for her to make the first move. So, I've stopped making obvious moves, and here we are. It's a bit frustrating.

Okay, it's *very* frustrating. But I believe that in the end the reward will be worth it. I just hope it doesn't take too much longer.

Alli doesn't seem to have many luxuries, but she does have a widescreen television (albeit a small one) and gets to use her landlord's Wi-Fi. So, I brought over my Roku and on her free nights when she has no gigs and didn't have work late I've been introducing to her to some of my favorite shows and movies on Netflix and Hulu. It's nice to just stay in and relax since we spend so much time at bars, clubs and coffeehouses. Nights in without loud music or lugging equipment have become kind of a luxury.

Sometimes, if she's in a creative mood, she'll work on songs. This is what dating a musician is about. Anyone can go to a show and enjoy a performance in the company of others willing and able to fork over a small cover charge for the opportunity, but this was like my own private look into her creative process. One time she tried to teach me to play guitar, but I was a hopeless student. No musical talent in me at all.

* * *

Mom calls more often than usual. Since I told her there was a new girl in my life she's been checking in with me two to three times a week, usually with some stupid computer question, but we both know it's really to ask how things are going with the "new girl." I tell her things are fine, and "no, I'm not ready to bring her up to meet you yet," and I promise her that I will bring her up to meet her and Lacy when "the time is right." If she calls when I am with Alli I just let it go to voicemail. One time recently Alli noticed I had refused one of my mom's calls and she told me it was okay if I wanted to take it.

"It's just my mom," I told her, thinking it was no big deal.

"Oh, you can call her back. You shouldn't—"

"It's fine, really. She's just calling to find out when I'm going to bring you up to meet her and Lacy."

"Oh," Alli said, surprised to hear this. "Should I have met them already?"

"There's no standard timeframe," I explained. "But probably not for a while."

"Oh, okay." She almost sounded disappointed.

"Do you want to meet them?"

"I don't know. I mean, yeah, it be nice to meet your family."

"It's probably still a bit early for that."

"When do you think it will be the right time?"

Probably sometime after our first kiss, I thought. "When I'm confident they won't scare you away."

Alli laughed. "I'm not going anywhere," she said. "Your family won't scare me away. I'm sure they're very nice."

I've never been one to rush into bringing a new girlfriend home to meet my family. In fact, it's something I put off as long as possible, and have since high school. My dad lives in Florida with his new wife, so he's not much of a concern (he only met Lauren twice over the entirety of our relationship). But I can't avoid my mom... and she can be embarrassing around a new girlfriend, and I'm pretty sure Lacy has decided never to like *any* of my girlfriends. Plus one little detail I've not mentioned to my mom is the age difference between Alli and me. That's an awkward conversation I've also been avoiding.

I'd also been putting off bringing Alli back to my apartment. It's been easy because it makes sense to go back to her place so she brings her guitar and equipment home, and we usually get back late and end up staying in anyway. Sure, I probably should have offered to take her there, but she also hasn't asked to see it. I didn't offer mostly because I didn't think she was ready to meet Devon. And, I wasn't ready for her to meet Devon.

I just knew the two of them together was just asking for trouble. But when she had a gig close to my place, I—idiot that I am—happened to mention I lived nearby. So, of course, Alli asked if I'd like to show my place to her after the gig was over. I had no excuse to say no that wouldn't have hinted I was hiding something, so I said, "Sure," and hoped she'd forget about it. She didn't of course.

"It's kind of late, did you want to stay over?" I asked, hoping this would change her mind.

"Oh, right. Shoot. I didn't bring a change of clothes or anything." She thought it over. "I guess it's okay. I feel like, as your girlfriend, I should have seen your place by now."

"You can sleep in my room. I'll stay on the couch."

"Thank you. Are you sure?"

"Yeah, of course." Though, I dreaded the barrage of jokes Devon will make at my expense if she notices Alli and I not sharing my room overnight.

We got back to my apartment before midnight. It was right around then I got the feeling this was a worse idea than I expected. I was certain it was a bad idea when we walked in to find Devon sitting on the couch in her Red Sox jersey and, from what I could tell, nothing else. Her long dark brown hair looked a bit sweaty and messy, and I suspected she wasn't alone in the apartment.

"Hey," Devon said. "I didn't think you'd be coming back here tonight." Then she noticed I wasn't alone. "Well, well, well... you must be Alli." Before Alli could respond the door to Devon's room opened and a guy (thankfully dressed) came out. "So, umm, this is Russ."

"What's up?" Russ said, not in the least surprised to see people here.

"He tends bar at—" Devon started to explain, but then turned her focus to Alli, "I'm sorry, I forgot to introduce myself. Alli, I'm Devon."

"Oh, *you're* Devon?" Alli said. There was nothing ambiguous in her tone or her facial expression, she was surprised that Devon was in fact Devon.

That's when it occurred to me that I never actually clarified that Devon is a girl. I should have, but, seeing as Devon is the only Devon I know the ambiguity of her name just didn't dawn on me. In retrospect, did I subconsciously know that Alli would have an issue with my roommate being a girl, and because of that did I not elaborate on that detail? I think maybe I did. So yeah, I'm not totally innocent here. And... as I thought more about it, it occurred to me that there may have been a few times Alli was under the impression that Devon was a guy and I didn't correct her. Stupid. Just stupid. She was bound to find out eventually, and this was hardly the best way for her find out, and it ruined the good mood of the evening.

Russ, either sensing something was awkward or just wanting to bail after getting what he came for, declared his need to leave so Devon escorted him out.

"So, *that's* Devon," Alli said, when Devon and Russ were out of earshot.

"Yep. That is Devon."

Devon returned quicker than expected. Normally I'd expect her to stick around and chat, but even she could sense that I was in deep shit and had worked out an exit strategy. "Well, I'm beat, I'll leave you two alone. I... umm... yeah... goodnight," she said before retreating off to her room.

"So, Devon is a *girl*." Alli said after Devon's door closed. She did not sound happy, and I knew I was in trouble.

"Yeah. Devon is a girl," I repeated, dumbly.

"And you two live... *together*?"

I wasn't really sure what to say. "Yeah. It's not a big deal."

"If it's not a big deal why didn't you tell me before?"

I didn't have a good answer, so I didn't say anything.

She sighed. "Is there anything else I should know?"

"I... don't think so."

"Does she always walk around like that?"

"Like what?"

"Practically naked."

"No, she wears clothes most of the time."

I thought I was being funny, but Alli wasn't laughing.

"I don't know. I guess I just don't understand why you have a girl roommate. You weren't a couple, were you?"

"Oh, no. Definitely not."

"So, you're *just* roommates?"

"Well, friends, too."

"Has she lived here a long time?"

I didn't like where this conversation was going, but I couldn't see any way around the inevitable.

"No, a couple months or so."

"And, you lived alone before that?"

There it was. Shit.

"Well, for a little while. I couldn't afford this place on my own, so that's why Devon lives here." I hoped this was a satisfactory answer.

"Okay." She seemed ready to drop the subject, and as much as that was a relief, I started to feel really guilty. I knew I had to come clean.

"But before that, I had a girlfriend who lived here with me."

"Oh."

"Yeah. She—"

"You don't have to tell me about your—her. I mean, I get that you have a past and stuff. It's not like I didn't assume you had a serious relationship before me. I don't want to be one of those girls who is jealous about her boyfriend's ex-girlfriends. I just—I need you to be honest with me, and to trust me. If you hide stuff from me that means you don't trust me. And then I can't trust you. I mean, I know you're not gonna tell me *everything*, and you don't have to, but I'm pretty sure you having a girl for a roommate was something you should have told your new girlfriend. And that you once lived with an ex-girlfriend. I don't need details. I don't *want* them, really. But important stuff I should probably know about. Okay?"

"Okay," I say. I'm curious if her not wanting to grill me about my past is more about me not grilling her about her past and her situation with her family, a topic she made clear she wants to avoid.

"So, there's nothing else you want to tell me, while we're talking about this?"

Do I really want to tell her everything about Lauren? That I proposed? That had she not cheated on me we'd be planning a wedding a right now? I knew I should have told her, but I'm really hoping I can go to my grave without telling anyone.

"No," I said, which was technically true.

"Okay."

"If you don't want to stay here tonight anymore I can take you—"

"I'll stay," she said unenthusiastically. "It's fine."

As bad as this was, it went better than I expected.

Devon wakes me up early the next morning. I open my eyes to see her above me, pointing her camera at me.

"Let me guess. You slept on the couch last night because you didn't tell her your roommate is a girl?"

"Yeah, apparently I forgot to mention it. Why do you have your camera?"

"I wanted to immortalize your stupidity. I hope you had a nice night on the couch you fucking moron."

CHAPTER 15

I OFFER TO help Alli bring her stuff back to her place so she can shower and go to work. She agrees, but she still sounds a bit upset about the Devon thing. She lets me pay for her ride on the T without protest, but she's unusually quiet, avoiding eye contact. Even after I bring her stuff down the stairs and into her place.

"So," I say. "I'll see you later?"

"Okay," she says. She sounds sad, still angry.

I turn to walk out, figuring there's nothing I can say to make this better and the best course of action is to just let her cool off.

"Nick!" she calls as I'm halfway up the stairs. She races to meet me, and my heart starts racing, anticipating some speech about how things aren't going to work between us and— "I'm sorry. I'm sorry if I'm overreacting. It's just... I'm not used to this, you know? I don't know if I'm acting the right way or the wrong way. I just... I want you to know you can trust me. I *need* you to trust me."

"Don't apologize," I tell her. "It's my fault, one hundred percent. I'm an idiot. A moron. A dumbass."

She smiles. "I won't disagree with you on that."

"I'll do better, I promise," I say.

She squeezes my hand. "Good, because I don't like being mad at you. You're really great, and having a boyfriend has been—I don't know... I thought it would be scary and stressful and, now that I'm with you, I feel... happy. And, I know we'll have fights, I know that's normal, but I don't want those fights to be about big things like, my boyfriend not telling me he lives with a girl, but about, I dunno—"

"Who pays for dinner?"

She laughs. "Yeah. Like that."

"I'm okay with that. And, for the record, I'm really happy, too."

"Really? You are?"

It's then that I lean in and kiss her. I'm not sure what made me think this was the right moment, but I just go for it.

Alli is flustered. "Oh, wow. That was..." She smiles wide giving up on coming up with the words. "Can we... umm... Do that again?"

I kiss her again.

"That was nice. I liked it," she says.

"Good."

"Did you... like it?"

"Of course."

"I'm glad. I've been really nervous about it the past couple weeks."

"I figured," I say.

"I'm sorry it's taken so long. I just wasn't sure if I'd know how or if I'd be any good at it. I didn't want to disappoint you."

"Don't worry, I wasn't disappointed. I just figured it would happen when you were ready, and, I dunno, something told me this was a good time."

She smiles. "It was. I think we both needed it."

"I think so, too."

"Well, I guess we better do it again, tonight," she says.

"It's a date," I tell her.

And that night, sure enough, there's lots of kissing, but *nothing* else. She makes that clear multiple times when, in the heat of the moment I reach for her chest. It's a reflex, I can't help it. Each time I tried she would take my hand before I got anywhere. I apologize after each time, and she whispers, "It's okay." My self-control might be horrible, but she's got some discipline in her.

"Okay, well, I think we better stop now," she says after probably the fifth time she rebuffed my reaching hands.

"I'm sorry, I didn't mean—"

"No, it's okay. I just want to go slow. That's all."

"I understand."

"You're okay with that, right? You look disappointed."

"It's okay. Really," I say.

"You sure? I mean—"

"Yes, I'm sure. I'm sorry. I got to work on my self-control."

"Well," she says, jokingly. "Yeah, maybe a little. But it's okay."

"I don't want to, you know, push you or pressure you or anything."

"And, I just want you to enjoy my company. Are you sure you're not disappointed about taking things slowly?"

"I'm not disappointed at all."

She gives me look as if to say *Seriously, you expect me to believe that?*

"Okay, I'm... a little..." I try to think of different word for disappointed that won't sound so negative, but can't. "See, it can be..." Is *frustrating* a good word to use? Probably not. I'm going nowhere fast trying to explain myself. "I guess what I'm trying to say is, I do enjoy your company. Really. A lot. I'm not disappointed. I look forward to being with you. The last thing I want is to make you feel uncomfortable or anything. I'm sorry if—" I can't exactly explain that I've gone a lot further with other girls at this point in past relationships. That's the last thing she'd want to hear.

"It's okay. I get that you, you know, want to do more than just kiss. And it's not that I don't, I'm just not ready, yet. If anything, I'm the one who should be worried that you'll get frustrated and not want to be with me."

"Trust me," I say. "That will *never* happen. I'll try harder to control myself. I promise. If I mess up, just stop me. I won't complain or hold it against you."

She smiles. "I'm glad to hear that. I'm sorry for being such a prude. I'm just a bit nervous and self-conscious. I promise we won't be stuck, you know, just *kissing* forever, when I'm ready—"

"Let's make a deal," I say.

"Okay?"

"I promise not to break up with you for keeping things slow, and you promise to not break up with me if you have to stop me in the heat of the moment."

I can't even begin to express how surprised at myself I am. I know this sounds bad, but a younger version of myself would have looked for a way out of this. But when

I look at Alli, and how delighted she is after hearing my proposition, I find myself feeling happier than I have in months.

"Deal," she says.

I know it's too early to be talking about our relationship's long-term prospects, but I really am in this for the long haul. Am I sexually frustrated? Sure. But I'm not going to break up with her, and I don't want her to break up with me. Part of me worries she might. Between the slow progress of our physical relationship and how guarded she is about her past, I can't help worrying she's just trying to keep me at a safe distance.

I don't try anything more for a few days, waiting for her to initiate the next level. She said I'd know when she was ready, but it quickly becomes clear that if our physical relationship is going to progress then I'm the one who will have to initiate. It's a full week before I try again, and again she stops me. And then I feel awful. I don't want her to think I am not happy being with her, so I find ways to show her that I really do appreciate her—like bringing her flowers, making her dinner at home, stuff like that— so that she knows that I'm all in with this relationship, that she's not just another notch in my belt.

I've also been helping her as much as can to make it easier for her to balance her day job and her music. I can really only help with the promotional and sales stuff though. I go to every gig and run her merch table. I also help her hang up fliers, and after some resistance, she even let me design some better ones. She's always looking for places to send CDs to, like local music publications, pop culture rags and blogs, and I help her find the right places she should reach out to. Even with my help, she still works incredibly hard to fit everything in. And, for all that work she doesn't make a lot of money, and she could very easily tell me I'm too much of a distraction and break up with me.

CHAPTER 16

I'VE BEEN DESIGNING a website for Alli in my spare time the past three weeks. She doesn't know about it yet, though. Right now she only uses Facebook to connect with her fans because, she explained, she had no idea how to set up a website and Facebook worked well enough and it's free. I haven't devoted a ton of time because Jay and I have been somewhat busy with new work—especially after we got the job to redo Revolution Public House's website—but I've been squeezing in an hour here and there on nights when she has a late shift at Starbucks and I didn't have any work for clients to do, and I'll work on it at her place after a late gig once she's gone to sleep.

Would you believe that she didn't even own alliconwell. com? I discovered this when I first started working on her website and snatched that up for her. Once the site was more or less ready, I linked the domain to it, and even set up a custom email address.

I know she's a bit weird about accepting help like this, but my hope is that she'll love the site so much that she won't be able to refuse it. I plan to show her what I've done before her gig tonight. She's opening for a band called Bullhorne, who are supposed to be really good.

I arrive a Starbucks a couple hours before her shift ends.

"Hey, is Alli here?" I ask the lone barista behind the counter.

"Yeah," he says, and calls out towards the office. "Hey Alli, your boyfriend's here!" Alli emerges a few seconds later.

"Thanks!"

"What'll ya have?" he asks me.

"Just a tall bold." I tell him. He gets my coffee and I hand him a five, but he waves it off. "On the house, man."

"Thanks."

"You didn't have to do that," Alli tells him.

He shakes his head, like he's heard this kind of thing from her before. "Don't worry about it, seriously," he says.

"Thanks, Devon," She tells him. So, she works with a guy named Devon. Great. Barista Devon lets her take over the register while he pours my coffee.

"So," I whisper to her. "That's Devon."

"Yep, that's Devon." She whispers, like she's in on the joke.

"You never told me Devon was a guy," I say jokingly. Thankfully, Alli finds this quip hilarious and laughs like it's the funniest thing she's heard all day.

"You make me laugh," she says, and leans over the counter and kisses me on the cheek. "You gonna do some work for a while?" A couple of teenagers come in and get in line, so I take my free coffee and move out from the line. "Yeah, I'll just be over there," I say, pointing to a chair in the corner.

"Okay, I'll see you soon," she says, and waits for the kids to decide what they want. The first one can't decide if they want a Frappuccino or an iced tea and is vocalizing her decision making process. Alli waits patiently with a smile, and I go take a seat and set up my laptop.

When Alli gets a break she sits down with me and asks me what I'm working on.

"Actually," I start, suddenly nervous about how she'll react, "I've been working on something for you."

I rotate my laptop for her to see the screen. She studies it carefully. First, there's the look of shock when she fully grasps what I've been working on. It's a nice site, if you ask me. She doesn't really need a lot on the site, so it's a one-page design utilizing parallax scrolling. She scrolls down the page, seeing images I've lifted off her Facebook page float in the background between her biography, list of upcoming gigs, contact information and social media links.

"What's this?" she asks, pointing to the row of icons at the bottom.

"Those would be links for your Facebook page, Twitter page, YouTube channel—"

"But I don't have a Twitter page or a YouTube channel," she says.

"Well, I know, but, you know, they're great ways to connect with and expand your audience," I explain, sounding too much like I'm pitching a regular client. More often than not, we float a social media strategy to potential clients and make them pay extra for it. "If you don't want to set one up, that's fine, I can take it out. Any of the icons can be taken out."

She smiles, though it's a small smile. Then, after a bit more scrutiny, she looks down at the table as if to avoid eye contact with me.

"I love it. But really, you shouldn't have taken all that time—"

"I wanted to."

"I know, and really, I appreciate it. It's just, I've looked into this before. I can't afford—"

"You don't have to pay for hosting." I explain. "It's hosted on my webspace. It won't cost you anything. And I'm not charging you for the site design."

"I can't accept this for free. If I'm going to do this, I want to pay a fair price for it, and I can't afford that right now."

"Is it really so terrible to accept something for nothing? From your boyfriend?"

"You don't understand. When I was—" She pauses abruptly, like she's caught herself before telling me something she doesn't want to tell me. "I just need you to respect my decision."

What's the big deal anyway? Everyone has a website these days. Some of the shittiest bands I've ever seen have websites, and decent ones.

"I'm just trying to help you," I explain. "With a good website you can connect better with your fans, reach more. I mean, every little bit will help you out if you want to make it big."

She looks at me shocked, "You know that's not why I'm doing this, right?"

"It's not?"

She sighs. "See, that's the problem with non-musicians. They think we are only doing it because we want to be *famous* musicians."

"So, you're not?" I ask. "And I mean musicians in general, not you specifically.

"No. Most of us aren't... I don't think. *I'm* not for sure. Personally, I think most of us just want to be successful at it."

"Successful doesn't mean famous?"

"Does being a successful web designer mean being a famous one?"

"No."

"So there you go. I just want to be able live and live comfortably doing my music. That's all."

"I see."

"People *think* I want to be famous though. They think all musicians do. Remember that interview I did for *The Dig*? The writer asked me who my influences were? I mentioned Taylor Swift and a few others."

"Ugghh, again with Taylor Swift?"

"What's wrong with Taylor Swift?"

"My *sister* likes Taylor Swift."

"So? You know I've played her songs before, right? Like, last night I played her song 'Mine' and you really seemed to like it. And the other night at Paddy O's I played—"

"I like everything when *you* play it; what's your point?"

"Never mind. Anyway, I forgot about that question afterwards, but when the article came out it made a big thing about that. It was kind of embarrassing. The article was nice, but for some reason she inferred that I want to be famous like Taylor Swift and made that an angle in the article. It was embarrassing. I mean, I'd love to have her success, and to have my music mean so much to so many people. But I don't desire fame. But that's not what this is about. I love singing and writing songs. I just want to be able to do that and support myself doing it. If my music enables me to afford nicer clothes, buy a nice house and see the world, I'd be so grateful, because even just *one* person responding to my music is a gift."

"You *could* make it."

"*You* could win the lottery."

"What's that supposed to mean?"

"I'm just saying you shouldn't count on me becoming a big star. I'm not."

"Well, I—" Alli's phone vibrates, she takes it out. "What's up?"

"Oh, it's my landlord's daughter texting me. She wants to hang out at my place because her dad is fighting with her mom on the phone." She types out a reply.

"Does she hangout at your place a lot?"

"When I'm home, and I don't have uhh... company," she smiles at me and puts down her phone. "Anyway, what were we talking about?"

"I was just saying I think you *could* make it."

Alli thinks for a moment. "What does *make it* mean to you?"

"Well, I don't know... a record deal. Selling records worldwide, umm—"

"So, in your estimation Candlepin hasn't *made it* yet?"

"Well, no, I guess not. Do you think they have?"

She nods. "Kind of. I know they're only big around Boston, but they've played some the best venues here: T.T. The Bears, The Middle East, House of Blues, Brighton Music Hall... and they fill them up each time. Their fans absolutely love them. They know all the words to their songs and sing along. They cheer when they recognize a song because they're so excited to hear it. And when the show is over, they chant 'one more song' over and over because they just have to hear more. That's what I want for myself. One day."

Alli's phone timer goes off, meaning her break is over, as are my hopes she'll use the website I've designed for her. I close my laptop a bit too forcefully out of disappointment, and Alli notices.

"Oh, Nick, I'm sorry about the website. I really appreciate what you did though, maybe..." she starts to say, but doesn't finish. "Are you mad at me?" Alli asks.

"No, I'm fine," I say.

"Please don't lie," she says. "If you're upset, please tell me the truth. I'll always tell you the truth."

"I'm not upset. Just... disappointed, that's all. I'll get over it."

"I'm glad you want to help," she explains. "I just need to do things my way. I'm okay with you buying me dinner or whatever because you're my boyfriend, and apparently that's how it works, but when it comes to my music, I don't want special favors or handouts. I'm sorry. I know you want to help me. But if I ever do become a real success at this, I want to be able to look back at how I got there and not doubt that it was my *talent* got me there. I don't want to feel like I had to take advantage of my boyfriend, or a family connection, or—"

"A website is important, but it's not like it will make or break you. Besides, I do think you're talented. That has to count for something."

"I know you do. But if I get a real website, I want to pay for it like anyone else would. I don't want—can we talk more about this after my shift?"

"Sure."

She leans in and kisses me on the forehead. "You're the best."

So, when Alli returns to work I open my laptop again and look over the website I created once more. Disappointed is definitely an understatement. I redirect alliconwell.com to her fan page on Facebook, thinking that's a reasonable compromise, and the domain name is dirt cheap and she should have that anyway. I also email her the password for the Twitter handle I've snagged for her. Hopefully, she'll use it.

CHAPTER 17

AFTER ALLI'S SHIFT we stop by her apartment to pick up her stuff for her gig and to drop off my laptop. We take the T to Davis Square and find the bar she's playing at. I'm still a bit miffed about her refusing to accept the website I've built for her, so I get a beer and hang out at the bar while Alli sets up. She checks her levels and tunes her guitar. All of a sudden, she has a surprised look on her face.

"Hey!" she says into the microphone, and waves. She's not talking to me, she's looking past me. I turn and see a familiar person. It takes me a few seconds to realize that it is Blake, the keyboard player from Candlepin. He sees me and joins me at the bar.

"Hey, I remember you. Uhhh..."

"Nick," I say.

"Right, you were at the Revolution show. What's up?"

"Not much."

"You here for Bullhorne?"

"No, I'm here to see her," I say, pointing to Alli.

"Cool, man. You a groupie or something?" he asks.

"No. We're dating."

Blake is taken aback. "No shit? Since when?" His reaction is very curious. Like he's shocked and disappointed.

"Yup. For a few weeks now."

Blake flags down the bartender and orders a Harpoon IPA then points to me. "And give him another of whatever he's got."

"Thanks," I say. "Not necessary, but thanks."

"So... things going well with you two?"

"Really well, thanks." I wonder why he cares.

"Well, congrats, buddy." The bartender comes back with our beers. Blake lays down some cash and the bartender takes it.

"You know Bullhorne's stuff?" he asks me.

"No. Alli has a CD, but I've never listened to it."

"They used to open for Candlepin some years ago."

"Yeah? I've heard they're good," I say.

"I've heard that, too."

"I thought you said—"

"I joined Candlepin around the same time Nava did."

"Oh right. So how'd you get hooked up with them?"

"My cousin owns D-Line Records in Sommerville," he explains. "Have you heard of it?"

"No," I say.

"Well, Candlepin recorded their first two albums there. When he heard they were looking for a keyboard player not long after I moved here from Cali he put in a good word for me. And the rest is history."

"Oh, you're from California?"

Blake takes a long sip from his beer. "Yup."

"Why'd you leave?"

"Hey, I'm gonna introduce myself to the guys in the band. Catch ya later."

"Uh, yeah. See ya," I say.

That was weird. I'm not sure what it is, but something just rubs me the wrong way with him. Buying me a beer for no reason, asking about Alli like that. He had to know about us. Why would he pretend not to know? And then the way he just bailed on me. Did he really want to just talk to the band? Did he not like me asking about why he moved here?

A look over towards the stage and Blake is talking to someone in the band, but soon turns his attention to Alli. She's excited to see him. He opens his arms, indicating he wants a hug, and she obliges. I watch dumbfounded, then Blake looks at me and winks. At least I'm pretty sure he did. When Alli continues to set up I can't help noticing that Blake is checking her out as she gets her guitar hooked into the band's sound system. When she bends down to close up her guitar case, he tries to look down her shirt. When she stands up he averts his eyes, and pretends he's paying attention something else entirely. This infuriates me even more.

I watch Blake like a hawk the entire evening. I can tell he's really checking Alli out more than listening to her performance. He looks like a creepy old man. Okay, he's not that old. I'm guessing he's only ten years older than me. But still.

Not much happens during her set, but afterwards Blake brings her a glass of water while she's putting her stuff away. That asshole is trying to show me up, I just know it. Fucking jackass. I resolve not leave Alli's side for the rest of night. Blake doesn't hang out with us the entire time, but when he does I feel like he barely acknowledges I'm there.

He talks to her about recording an album and tells her he plans to give the recording of her show at Revolution to his cousin with the record label and she's really excited at this because if his cousin likes he might be able to squeeze her in his schedule and give her a good deal on studio time and everything else. I'm not a player in this conversation at all and I get the distinct impression that it's intentional. He's definitely trying to impress her.

His whole routine tonight has pissed me off so much that when Alli mentions his name on the train ride back to her apartment I tell her I don't like him, which surprises her.

"What do you have against him?"

Since she's really big on honesty I decide I might as well tell her what I saw, regardless of the risks of doing so.

"He was checking you out tonight."

"He was not," she says, a bit too quickly in my opinion.

"I saw it. He was always looking at your chest or your ass."

I know she doesn't like crude language, but in my anger I couldn't really think of a different word for it. She lets it slide for the moment. "I'm sure he wasn't."

"He was."

"Look, the only important thing here is that I'm *not* interested in him. Never have been. He's not my type. At all," she says.

"You could be *his* type," I say.

"I'm sure I'm not anymore."

"What? What do you mean *anymore*?"

"Well—"

"Was he one of the guys who asked you out before me?" Alli did say there were a few guys who asked her out before me when she moved to Boston, and she must have met Blake before she met me, or at least before we started dating, so he certainly could have been a guy who was interested and missed his chance. But she would have told me that, wouldn't she?

Alli is quiet for a moment. "Well, kinda... he was, but—"

I want to say something, but I'm trying to process this new information in the context of his appearance tonight. He asked her out. She rejected him. He shows up here. What for?

"Are you mad?" Alli asks.

"I—I'm surprised this never came up before."

"Well, I—we haven't seen him since the Revolution show over a month ago. And, it wasn't a big deal so it never occurred to me to mention it. It was before you and I started dating. Before I even met you... he just asked if I wanted to go out sometime and I said no thank you and that I wasn't interested in dating anyone at the time. He was fine about it. He couldn't have been that into me, he had a woman with him at the Revolution show."

Yeah, but he came here alone tonight.

"So really Nick," Alli adds. "I don't even think he was that interested me anyway, and, as I told you already, I'm not at all interested. He's almost twice my age. That's just... eww... I'm interested in you, and only you. If you trust me, that's all that matters."

"I know what I saw. He's trying to make another move on you. Bringing you water, telling you about his studio—"

"It's his *cousin's* studio."

"Whatever."

"Nick," Alli says, her tone suddenly really serious. "He's just trying to be helpful. Just like Nava is. He's new in town, like I am. So, I think he just wants another friend. That's all. Can't you just be happy that I know people who believe in me enough to help me—"

"Why is he able to help you, but not me?"

I think this is a great point. But Alli gives me a frustrated sigh. "Nick, that's different. He didn't offer me something for free that other people would have to pay for. It's no different than how he helped me get the *opportunity* to play at Scollay's—"

"Wait, what? He got you that gig?"

"I told you that."

"Oh, maybe you did." She might have, but it must not have seemed relevant at the time.

"Yeah, well, he gave my CD to the guy who handles their booking—I guess Blake used to do solo gigs there before joining Candlepin—and he offered me the chance to play, so it's different. And Blake knows I'm not interested in him, and that makes a difference."

"Was that before or after he asked you out?"

"Before, I guess."

"Of course."

Alli crosses her arms, looking annoyed. "All Blake did was give the guy a copy of my album, and he liked it enough to offer me a chance to play a few shows. And he's giving his cousin a copy of the recording at Revolution. If he likes it I'll still have to pay for everything, which is what I've been saving up for. I don't want handouts, Nick. Getting the Scollay's gig, or the studio time isn't getting handouts. If I thought he had an ulterior motive, I wouldn't accept his help. He's always acted appropriately around me since I turned him down. Even if he is, you know, interested in me—not that I think he is—well, I told you already I'm *not* interested in him. Not in the least. You don't have to worry."

I didn't think I had to worry about Lauren, either. I know Alli's not Lauren, and I want to trust her, but there's this part of me remembers what it felt like when Lauren told me she cheated, and it's hard to shake the feeling that it could happen again.

The ride back is mostly quiet after that. I am still in a sour mood when we return to her place. She seems annoyed with me, and I don't like it.

"I'm sorry for earlier," I say.

"Thank you. And, I know I've said this already, but I am really sorry about the website stuff. You understand, don't you?"

"Yeah. I guess..."

"It was a really sweet thing to do, and it really means a lot that you want to help me."

She comes close to me and kisses me. It's not like her to initiate, and it's a pleasant surprise.

"I really do appreciate everything, Nick," she says, taking my hand and leading me to the couch. We kiss some more, and then for the first time, guides my hand to her chest. After weeks of nothing but kissing I'm surprised, but hardly disappointed. Alli smiles and closes her eyes again. I know sex is out of the question tonight, and probably for a while, but I feel confident enough to touch her underneath her shirt. When I try she stops me before I get anywhere. She puts her hand on mine and shakes her head sympathetically. "That's too much, okay?"

"Okay." I can't help sounding incredibly disappointed.

"I'm sorry, I'm such a prude, I know—"

"No, listen... This was really nice. I just didn't know how far—"

"And... it's not like I want you to ask my permission every single time you—you know, want to speed things up a little. And it's not like I don't want to... I'm just... I don't want to do stuff I don't feel ready for yet."

"I understand."

"Are you sure? You're not disappointed, or thinking of breaking up with me?"

"Remember our agreement?"

"Yes." She smiles, and puts my hand back on her chest, over her shirt. "You can keep going, if you want."

We pick up where we left off, but before long, my iPhone, which has been sitting on Alli's coffee table, starts vibrating. It vibrates loud enough on the hard surface to make both of us stop suddenly. I tell Alli I'll let it go to voicemail. So, we keep going. Then my phone chimes signaling I've received a text message. I'm inclined to ignore that too, but Alli stops things and says it's time to cool down for the night anyway. So, I pick up the phone and read a series of texts from Jay.

"Holy crap," I say. "I can't believe it."

"What is it? Is everything okay?"

"Jay just texted me. Burnham & Modine finally decided to hire us. They've been silent for months, but we just got the job."

"That's so great! Congratulations," Alli says, hugging me.

I call back Jay. He doesn't even say hello, he just screams and hoots and gloats that he was right, that our price wasn't too high.

"See? I told you they would bite. This is huge!" He says and starts hooting again.

"You are a genius," I say mockingly.

CHAPTER 18

AFTER TWO MONTHS of thinking we'd blown a major opportunity with Burnham & Modine we're now feeling really good about ourselves. In fact, Jay, who's usually pretty cheap, suggested we take Devon out to dinner to thank her for referring us to our new client. The down payment alone provides both of us with some much-needed income that will make the next few months much easier. Jay is willing to splurge tonight because we're—to use his words—"finally being paid what we're worth," and he believes this is a turning point for our business that is worth celebrating. He's right. This could be an opportunity to get more business from other firms in the industry. There are a lot a lot of architectural firms in Boston, and most have shitty websites.

I ask Jay if he minds if Alli join us since she has tonight off. He's cool with it as long it is understood that I, not the company, will be paying for her dinner. I agree, of course.

So, I invite Alli and she agrees to come, though it quickly becomes clear that it would have been better if she had just stayed home. When we order drinks Alli says she's stick with the water, but Devon, who knows Alli is only nineteen, wants her to get a real drink anyway.

"I'll order a glass of wine and give it to you, if you want," Devon suggests.

"No, thank you."

"Seriously, they won't even notice."

"I can't do that."

Devon shakes her head, almost offended that Alli didn't accept her offer. I was hoping this dinner would be the start of Alli and Devon becoming friends. So far, I don't think it's going to happen.

Then, when we order, everyone orders a steak, instead of Alli, who orders salmon.

"Not getting a steak?" Devon asks.

"No, I—"

"Are you like one of those fake vegetarians who will eat fish, or something?"

"No, I just—"

"Who goes to a steakhouse and doesn't get steak?"

Alli just looks at her, wondering why she is giving her a hard time.

"Leave her alone," I say to Devon.

"Hey, was just trying to have a conversation."

"Yeah, well, try harder," I say.

"Okay. *Alli*... how's the music stuff going?"

"Umm, okay, I guess." Normally, Alli would enjoy this line of conversation, but Devon has really intimidated her.

"Just okay, huh? Well, you know what might help?"

"What?" Alli asks.

"Okay, hear me out. You're cute and all, but you got, like, no tits."

"Devon, what the fu—" I start to say.

Devon holds her hand up, silencing me. "I said hear me out. I'm not trying to be a bitch or anything, I'm just saying it's a competitive business, you know, I'm not suggesting you should dress like a slut or anything, but that would—"

"Excuse me, but my... *breasts* shouldn't matter," Alli says, whispering the word breasts like it's a dirty word she doesn't want to be caught saying it out loud. She crosses her arms as if she feels exposed and needs to hide them.

"I'm not saying they *should*. I'm just saying they *do*. Never underestimate the value of sex appeal," she explains, and cites Nava as example. At gigs, Nava wears low cut shirts, dances suggestively, and according to rumors she once flashed the crowd when she was with a different band.

"I'd rather people listen to my songs than look at me," Alli says.

"Yeah, yeah," Devon says, dismissing what Alli said. "I'm just saying... *it helps*. With many things. Trust me. You know how many drinks I've not had to buy, or speeding tickets I've gotten out of because of these?" she says, pointing at her own chest.

"Can we talk about something else?" Alli asks.

"Yeah Devon, I'm sure there's another inappropriate topic we can discuss," Jay says.

And so we move on to something else, and Alli becomes quiet, obviously to avoid being in Devon's crosshairs. When our food comes she quietly eats her meal. I look at her to make sure she's okay, and she smiles awkwardly, and holds my hand under the table. I can tell she's anxious for the night to be over. She only appears relaxed when Devon excuses herself to get herself another drink from the bar after she's decided the waitress is taking too long to check in on us. She comes back with a beer but appears annoyed.

"Can you believe the bartender carded me?"

"You're twenty-four, what did you expect?" I ask.

"The waitress didn't card me. And *you* weren't carded," she says to Jay.

"I'm older... And I *look* older."

"Whatever. It's bullshit. When I was younger I was barely carded. I barely had to use my fake ID." She looks at Alli. "I'm telling you, it's these big tits."

Alli ignores her.

"You know, I got a fake ID when the Red Sox were in the World Series in 2007," Jay says. "I was only nineteen then—I barely ever got carded."

Devon gets all excited by the topic. "Holy shit, I've got a story to tell—"

"We know," Jay and I say together.

"I'm not talking about you two," she looks at Alli, and proceeds to tell her about how she lost her virginity. The only thing that even makes it worth telling is that it happened the same night the Red Sox won the 2004 World Series, breaking their 86-year curse, but that's enough for Devon to consider it worth repeating to friends and strangers alike. Yes, Devon is twenty-four years old and she still brags about it eleven years later. The whole Red Sox World Series thing pretty cool, but you would think at her age this topic would seem just a tad juvenile. Alli is hardly amused by Devon's story, or her enthusiasm for it.

"So, Alli... you're the newbie to our little clique here... What's your story?" Devon asks.

"Devon, stop," I say.

"My story?" Alli asks.

"You know, when you popped your cherry. Punched your V-card. Lost your maiden tag. I bet it's not as good as mine."

Alli is not impressed.

"This is *not* appropriate dinner conversation," she says. "That was a horrible story and I feel sorry for you. You shouldn't act so proud about it!"

"Hey, hey, calm down," Devon says, taken aback. "I was just—"

Alli gets up from her chair. "I need to use the restroom."

Devon says nothing and Alli walks off.

"What... the fuck... was that about?" Devon asks.

"This is just a guess," Jay says. "But I'm thinking she's not as comfortable sharing as you are."

"She didn't have to freak out like that. I don't appreciate being slut-shamed. Nick, what's her deal?"

"I could ask you the same question."

"Of course, now I really have to pee, but I'm afraid to go into the bathroom while she's in there."

"I guess you should have thought about that before you—"

"I was just making conversation." Devon gets up, chugs the rest of her beer, and starts to move in the direction of the bathroom.

"Are you crazy?" I ask. "She'll flip out if you—"

"I'll fix this, don't worry," she says and walks off, leaving me totally unconvinced the situation will improve.

"I hope you've had fun tonight," Jay says, "because this might be your last date with Alli. For a while, anyway."

Jay and I settle the bill when the waitress checks in on us. It was an expensive meal. Not just in terms of price, but the damage done to mine and Alli's relationship, courtesy of Devon.

After about five minutes Devon returns. Jay and I look at her waiting for her to tell us what happened.

Finally, she says. "We had a chat. We're all good."

"What did you say?" I ask.

"None of your business. Rest assured, I apologized."

"That's it?"

"I told you, we had a chat. Everything's cool."

"Then where is she?" I ask.

"She just needed another minute."

"Geez, Devon, what did you say to her?"

"I told you, none of your business. Just trust me, everything is okay now. I might not be her favorite person in the world, but you know, a few minutes of girl talk smoothed things over."

When Alli comes back she apologizes for storming off and we all get up to leave.

"Well, thanks for the dinner guys," Devon says.

"Yes, thank you," Alli says.

"No problem ladies," Jay says.

"So, Alli," Devon adds. "I'll see you Saturday night?"

"Yeah, I'll see you there."

Once Devon and Jay have left us, I ask Alli about what Devon meant about Saturday night.

"My gig."

"You mean you invited her?"

"She offered to come to a show, I dunno, I guess that was her way of apologizing for giving me a hard time earlier, and I mentioned the show in a couple days, and she said she'd be there."

"What else did you two talk about? I mean, how do you go from being so upset with her you have to leave the table to inviting her to your next gig?"

"We, just, you know... girl talk."

The thought of those two having "girl talk" scares me.

* * *

The next day I try to convince Devon not to come to Alli's gig.

"Dude, seriously, I'm doing you a favor by going," she says.

"How do you figure?"

"Trust me. I know you think she sees me as Miss Super Slut who shares an apartment with her boyfriend—and, okay, I don't doubt that's how she sees me—but I put a lot of effort into clearing the air with her last night because I know she means a lot to you. I know I gave her a hard time at first, but I'm like that with everyone. That's like my thing. I didn't realize she'd flip out. So, instead of getting laid tomorrow night, I'll be sitting at a bar *with you*. Don't worry. She and I won't ever be BFFs, but I get her deal now, and I'll act accordingly. Well, to the best of my ability. For what it's worth, I do think she's really talented, and if we can find something to build a bridge over our differences, I'll do that for you."

"Why?"

"Dude, you're my friend. After watching you depressed and alone for two months it's nice to see you happy for a change."

"I still think this is a bad idea."

"Look, trust me when I tell you, if I don't go it will be worse."

"Why?"

"Because I told her I'd go. If I don't show up, she'll get pissed at me again and take it out on you."

"I see your point."

"No shit. Because I'm right."

CHAPTER 19

DEVON ARRIVES LATE to Alli's Saturday night gig, of course. I was hoping she'd seen the faults in her plan and decided not to come, but she walks in just after Alli's first song. She barely acknowledges me before she heads right to the bar to get a drink.

"Thanks for showing up," I say when she joins me at my table.

"Yeah, yeah, I'm late. Shit happens. I'm here. That's the important thing."

"I guess so," I say.

"How much did I miss?"

"This is her first song."

"Really? Then don't give me shit."

I stop giving her shit, and just try to enjoy Alli's performance. She mixes in a few cover songs into her set list. Devon over-animatedly cheers for Alli when she plays "My Happy Ending" by Avril Lavigne.

"Can you dial it back a notch?"

"What? I'm helping. She needs people to cheer. And I love this song."

"Fine, but don't make it so obvious that you know her."

"Oh yeah, good point."

Devon behaves herself through the rest of the set, and things seem to go smoothly even after Alli joins us during her break. I've pre-ordered her dinner for her so she can eat quickly and start her second set in a half hour. Alli and Devon seem fine together tonight. Devon makes a few song requests and Alli promises to play some. Things are going well enough that when I have to take a leak I feel okay leaving the two of them together.

Jay predicted tonight would be a disaster, so I give him an update via text:

So far so good.

He responds a minute later:

Give it time.

When I return all hell has broken loose. Devon has a guy pinned against the wall in a full nelson hold. Alli is looking on, confused and terrified. I don't know what's going on here, but a bunch of people are watching as Devon is yelling in the guy's ear.

"What the hell is going on?" I ask.

"This piece of shit stole Alli's tip money."

Sure enough, the little jar Alli had on top of a barstool while she played is empty. It had several bills in when Alli finished her set.

"I did not!" he protests and struggles futilely to break free. "Get the fuck off me!"

"I saw you, asshole! Don't pull that shit with me." He continues to struggle to get out of Devon's grip, learning the hard way just how deceptively strong she is for her size.

"Devon it's okay don't—" Alli says.

"No. This dipshit took your money and he's going to give it back to you. All of it." She slams him against the wall again, "or I'm gonna call the cops. Your choice."

A bunch of people in the bar start chanting, "Call the cops! Call the cops! Call the cops!"

"Fuck me," the thief says, realizing that he's not about to get any sympathy from anyone in the bar, which may have been his only salvation.

"If you don't give Alli her money back you'll never fuck anything again for the rest of your life. I promise."

"Fine!" he shouts, "Fine. I'll get it out."

"Not a chance. I ain't letting you go. Tell me where it is and my boy Nick will get it."

"Inside my jacket pocket. On the left." He grunts.

As I move in to retrieve the money Devon reminds him what she'll do to him if he tries to resist me. I can feel a bunch of bills in there and pull them out. I reach in again just to make sure I didn't miss any.

"Okay. We're good," I say.

The thief turns his face as far around as he can towards Devon, "Good, now fucking let me go."

"Not yet," Devon says. I wonder what she has in mind for him. "Now, I want you to apologize to Alli."

"What?"

"You heard me. Apologize. Say you're sorry. Prove to me you I shouldn't call the cops."

"But you said—" Bam! Devon pushes his face into the wall again.

"Do you think I give a shit what I said?" Devon pulls him off the wall, still in control of his upper body, and leads him to Alli. She can't believe what is going on and looks on the verge of tears. But I don't think it's because she had money stolen from her, I think she would just rather put all this behind her and move on. Or maybe she's touched at how Devon is taking care of this situation for her. I know I'd be. I kind of wish I was the one pinning the guy to the wall.

"Now say you're sorry to her." Other people in the bar start cheering for Devon and egg the guy on to apologize.

He almost looks he is gonna apologize, but instead spits on the ground in Alli's direction. I'm about to lunge at him myself when Devon goes ballistic. She turns him around and kicks him in the groin. Before he even gets a chance to react he takes another blow to the gut, this one with her fist. Then she puts him in a chokehold and pulls him out the door. The entire bar cheers for Devon.

I give Alli a comforting hug, "You okay?" She nods, though I can tell she's a bit shaken. I hold the money out for her to take.

"Can you hold onto it for now?" she asks.

"Sure."

Everyone claps for Devon when she returns. There are hoots and whistles and even offers to buy her drinks. She takes a bow.

"Sorry about that, Alli. I just couldn't let him steal from you."

"Thank you," Alli says, and gives Devon a hug. Devon is surprised by Alli's gesture, as am I.

"No sweat. I got your back, kid," Devon says.

"Thank you," Alli says again, releasing Devon from the embrace. "I, uh, better start my next set."

"Geez, Devon," I say when Alli is back getting her stuff ready to go. "You were quite a force to be reckoned with."

"You learn a lot about kicking some ass when you grow up with two brothers," she explains.

The audience seems far more interested in Alli's performance after the incident. She gets more tips than usual, and someone even buys her a drink, which she had to refuse, but offers to Devon, who, of course accepts it and then chats up the guy who bought the drink. I also sell an abnormally high number of CDs tonight. Between her tips and CD sales, this was probably one of her best nights.

At the end of the evening Alli's packed up and we look for Devon. We find her outside making out with the guy who bought Alli the drink. When she notices us, she breaks away from the guy to talk to us.

"So, yeah, you guys can go on without me. I'm... probably not coming home tonight."

"Why am I not surprised?" I say.

Devon ignores me and looks at Alli. "So, Alli, I had great time tonight. Great show. Seriously, once people like, decided to notice you were playing, they really dug you."

"Thanks," Alli says.

"Well, anyway, I better get back to, well, you know," she says, gesturing over to her guy.

"We know," I say.

* * *

Mom calls me the next morning while I'm still at Alli's apartment. She asks about work, so I tell her about our big new client, and she's impressed. She also wants an update on Alli—of course—and I just tell her things are good.

"You two have been together almost a month now, right?"

All of a sudden, I panic. It has been about a month. I think. We're due for a one-month anniversary date. Well, crap, what day do we celebrate? When me met at Revolution? Definitely not. Our first date? That was March 15—I remember because I remember thinking of "Beware the Ides of March!" from *Julius Caesar,* which is the only thing I remember from *Julius Caesar.* Today is the 19th of April, so we're passed that. Well, we officially became a couple the night after her second gig at Scollay's. I try to recall an image of Alli's gig flyer with the date on it. I'm fairly confident that gig was March 20, which means we became a couple on the 21st. How did I—

"Nick? You still there?"

"Uhh, yeah. Still here. Sorry."

"So, a month?"

"Yeah, it'll be a month in a couple days."

"That's great. Well, we'd still like to meet her sometime soon, you know?"

"We?"

"Lacy wants to meet her, too."

"You will. Eventually."

"You know—" she starts to say, and I know what's she's going to propose. "You could bring her with you for Lacy's birthday."

"Lacy's birthday? Why would I bring my girlfriend up for my sister's birthday?"

"You promised you'd come up for Lacy's birthday."

"Yeah, but—"

"And you've been with this new girl a month; I think it's about time—"

"But Lacy's birthday?"

"Look, I know you're busy, but the last time we saw you was at Christmas, before that, Thanksgiving."

The mention of Thanksgiving reminds me that that was around the time of Lauren's business trip to Nashville when she cheated on me. It still bothers me to think about it.

"Nick!" Mom shouts, bringing my attention back to the conversation.

"Fine, I'll ask her," I say.

"Ask me what?" Alli says. She's just come out of the shower, hair still wet, but fully dressed.

"Is that her?" Mom asks.

"Yeah."

"Let me talk to her."

"Talk to her? Why?"

"So I can—" I don't hear the rest because Alli takes the phone from me.

"Hello, this is Alli ... Oh, hi! It's nice to finally speak to you! ... Oh yeah, I know ... This Friday? I can't, I— ... Oh next Friday? Yeah, I can do that ... Great! I'd love to ... I don't think that will be a problem either I can change my work schedule if it is ... Oh, no problem at all, I've been wanting to— ... Yeah ... Okay, great, I will see you both then! ... Oh, I'll handle that ... I'm looking forward to it, too! ... Shall I put Nick back on? ... Okay, here he is. It was really nice talking with you." She hands me the phone.

"Hi," I say into my phone.

"She sounds so sweet, Nick."

"Thanks."

"Well, it's all settled. You two will come up for Lacy's birthday."

"Great," I say, without any enthusiasm. Alli gives me a look as she takes a couple bags of garbage to the front door.

She whispers. "Be back in a bit." I nod and Alli walks out, shutting the door behind her.

When I put my ear back to my phone my Mom's already talking again.

"Huh? What was that?" I ask.

"I just said I'll make sure Lacy has her room clean so Alli can stay there with her."

I'd nearly forgotten about this. When Lauren and I would stay over for holidays she always had to bunk with Lacy. Mom was quite clear that even though Lauren and I were adults and shared a bed while we were dating and lived together we weren't married so she didn't want her daughter to think that behavior was okay. There was no debate; that was the rule. Of course, Lauren would always sneak out in the middle of the night to my room and sneak back in early the next morning, anyway.

"Is that really necessary?"

"You know the rule," Mom says, but something in her voice suggests she might be persuaded.

"She's nearly fifteen. I think she's figured out—"

"Nick—"

"I don't want Alli bunking with Lacy."

"Why not?"

I don't really have a good answer for her. "I just don't." The idea of those two sharing a room and talking just seems like something I'd like to avoid. If Lacy decides she doesn't like her then Alli will be crushed. It seems like the best thing is to keep them separated.

"Are you really going to give me a hard time about this?"

"Yeah, I am. It's just one night, Mom." I know this is a weak argument, so add. "Look, Alli and I are both adults, and I think Lacy is mature enough that—"

"Look, I'm too tired to argue about this. Let's make a deal. She can stay in your room with you, but, just don't... you know... No funny business, not with Lacy in the next room."

That won't be a problem.

"Consider it done," I say.

"I'm not happy about this, but I don't want you pouting all night while you're here."

"So, we're good?" I ask. At that moment Alli comes back from outside.

"I guess we are," Mom says. She's not happy about this at all.

After the call, Alli looks at me with excitement. "Well, this is going to be fun."

"Sure, a whole evening with my family sounds like a blast."

"Your mom sounded really nice. I'm sure your sister is, too. *I'm* looking forward to it."

I groan.

"Stop that. It'll be fun. I'll get to meet your mom and sister, celebrate her birthday, see the house you grew up in..."

"Speaking of celebrating, we have something to celebrate."

"We do?"

"Yeah, the 21st is our one-month anniversary."

"Our one-*month* anniversary?" Alli asks, confused.

"Yeah, that's a thing."

"Oh, okay. So, that means... what exactly?"

"It means we get to go out someplace nice for dinner to celebrate."

"Oooh, did you have a place in mind?"

"I was thinking you could pick. Is there someplace you'd like to go?"

She thinks it over. "That restaurant in the castle?"

"You got it," I say.

"Now I'm really excited."

So, a couple days later, we go to the Smith & Wollensky's in The Castle at Park Plaza—which turned out to be the worst place in the entire city for us to go for our one-month-anniversary.

CHAPTER 20

WHEN ALLI SUGGESTED having our anniversary dinner in "the restaurant in the castle," I thought it was a great idea. There was absolutely no reason to believe this was a bad place to go for a nice, romantic dinner.

We arrive and Alli just loves it. She can't get enough of the place. I suspect this is the kind of place she's fantasized about being taken on a date to. I almost feel stupid for not taking her here sooner. When the hostess seats us she looks all around, soaking everything in. I couldn't help looking around either, and then I spot Emma, taking an order at a table close to the one we're seated at. Immediately, this burning sensation in my gut nearly topples me over. This is *not* good.

And that's not the worst of it. She's *our* waitress.

I knew Emma waited tables at a restaurant, I just didn't know *which* restaurant. If she mentioned which one I wasn't paying attention or had simply forgotten. Honestly, it's been weeks since she even crossed my mind. As far as I was concerned our one-night stand was well in the past, virtually forgotten, and she knew I was in a new relationship... sort of. Of course, she wasn't exactly thrilled that I had turned her down that night of mine and Alli's first date, but that doesn't mean she'd do something like sabotage this anniversary dinner, does it? I have no idea, and frankly, I'm not exactly interested in finding out, but there is no way to change our plans.

So, yeah, I'm panicking.

When she comes to our table to deliver bread and take our drink order she has a sinister looking smile on her face, and I know I'm doomed.

"Well, well, well. Look who it is," she says.

I am, of course, too nervous to say anything. Alli looks at me confused.

"I'm Emma," Emma says directly to Alli. "Nick and I know each other well."

"Yeah," I say, before Alli can ask. "She's friends with Devon." It isn't the whole truth, but it isn't a lie. The last thing I needed on this night of all nights was for Alli to find out about Emma. It was in past, sure. It's definitely not ideal on a romantic date with your girlfriend while being waited on by a girl you once slept with. And there is still the question as to whether Emma harbors any ill will after our last encounter.

"Right. I'm friends with Devon," she repeats with that faux cheeriness that I hope to God Alli doesn't pick up on. "And I hear you're doing my company's website?"

"I am?"

"Yes. Burnham & Modine. Devon said—"

"Oh, right. Yeah. I didn't realize that's where you work." Even though Devon referred us to them, it never occurred to me that Emma might work there. Suddenly I'm not so happy about the job.

"Yeah, well, I guess that's another year without getting a bonus."

"I'm... sorry?"

"Come on Nick, I'm just having a laugh. So, what brings you two lovely people here tonight?"

"It's our one-month anniversary," Alli tells her.

"Brilliant!" Emma says. "Well then, I better bring you some drinks so you two can start celebrating. What'll you have?"

"Water will be fine."

"Just a water, dear? No wine? You are celebrating tonight, right?"

"I'll take a cranberry juice, too I guess," Alli says.

Emma smirks at me, like she's just discovered a secret. "Right. And how about you, Nick?"

I somehow manage to order a red wine. I have no idea which I picked out, and I'm sure I'll be too distracted to even be able to taste it.

"I'll be right back, *kids*," Emma says and rushes off.

"Maybe we should leave?" I suggest.

"Why, what's wrong?"

"I... she doesn't want to wait on us, she knows me. That can't be—"

"She seemed perfectly fine waiting on us. Don't worry about. I'm sure you're not the first person she's waited on before that she knows."

Maybe not, but it could be the first time she's waited on a guy she slept with *and* his girlfriend.

There's no way out of this. I am stuck.

Emma comes back with our drinks and starts chatting up Alli. She asks her how we met, and when Alli tells

Emma about her singing and playing guitar Emma goes into a whole spiel about how she'll have to come to a show sometime. Sitting there listening to this I want to die. Emma is messing with me, hardcore. At any moment she's gonna tell Alli the full story of how we really know each other, and Alli will be horrified and disgusted with me. Finally, Emma asks us what we want to order. Alli orders the Signature Filet Mignon, and since I've not really looked at the menu, I order the same thing.

"That is adorable, ordering the same meal. You two are just so cute," she says and heads off to put our order in.

"She's nice," Alli says when Emma's out of earshot. "I like her."

Great. What's next? Are the two of them going to become friends now?

I use the opportunity to excuse myself to the bathroom. I don't really have to go, but I have to try to speak to Emma without Alli seeing or hearing.

When I find her, she looks amused. "So, special date huh?"

"Look, I'm sorry, I didn't know you worked here. I wouldn't have—"

"Kinda young for you, eh? Younger than twenty-one, obviously. What is she? Fourteen? Fifteen? I never pegged you for a cradle snatcher."

"She's nineteen," I say. Emma just scoffs. "Look, I get it... Please just... don't... Please don't mess this up for me."

"Bloody hell, I'm not gonna sabotage your 'one-month anniversary' dinner," she says, mocking me.

"Are you sure?"

"I was just having a little fun before, that's all."

"I thought you were mad."

"What did you think I'm gonna do? Tell her I've shagged her boyfriend? Cause a big scene?"

"I don't know."

"Like I'm going to risk my job. Look, I'm not going to say anything. I never said I wanted a boyfriend, but you obviously wanted a girlfriend, so, good for you, you got one. No hard feelings. Really." She pauses, thinking something over, "But you know, if you follow me out back for a quick shag that would go a long way towards earning my silence," she says.

"Excuse me?"

"Bloody hell, Nick, I was kidding. All I ask for is a big tip."

"Consider it done."

"Kidding again. Jeez! Look, just go back to your girlfriend and let me do my job please."

I do what she says, and she doesn't say anything incriminating about me or us for the rest of evening. Despite her assurances, I was never able to be quite comfortable with her waiting on us. Even though she said she was kidding about the tip, I gave her an extra twenty bucks on top of the usual 18 percent tip as insurance.

CHAPTER 21

AFTER DINNER WE go back to Alli's apartment. I'm starting to feel normal again with that whole Emma nightmare behind, us and looking forward to perhaps taking our physical relationship to the next level... or two... or three. When *she* leads me to the couch I am suddenly confident that tonight might be *the night*. She definitely hasn't led me here so we can watch TV. As the guy I'm still expected to make the first move... and I do. After a quick bit of kissing I touch Alli through her shirt, and she does not resist. So, I reach under her shirt, and that's when she stops me. *Again.*

We've been together a month now and she's gonna tell me "not tonight" *again*?

"I'm sorry," I say. "I thought—"

"No, no... It's okay. I'm not telling you to stop."

"Oh, okay. Do we need—"

"Need what?"

"Well, I'm guessing you're not on the pill, right?"

"No, I'm not. But this isn't about protection, Nick. I mean, obviously I don't want to get pregnant at nineteen, but that's not why... Here's the thing..." Alli pauses, trying to think of the right words. "I want to... you know... keep going... I just don't want to go any further than... you know, what you wanted to do just now. Are you okay with that?"

"Yeah, of course. I told you I was okay with going slow. Everything else can wait until you're ready."

"Nick, I'm not just trying to say I want to take things slow. I'm saying that for everything else, I want to wait."

"Right," I say. "I understand."

"I don't think you do. I know you want to do certain things, and... have sex."

"Well, I—"

"It's okay that you want to. Really. It's just, I don't... want to..."

"That's okay. Whenever you're ready—"

"I don't just mean I don't want to have sex *tonight*. I'm sorry, this isn't the easiest topic for me to talk about... I mean I don't want to have sex." She winces. "I mean, I do. One day. Just, not until I'm married."

I'm taken aback by this and she notices my reaction.

"Is this... This isn't a deal breaker is it? I just want to be honest about, you know, what you should expect. It's just that you're my first boyfriend so I didn't know when the right time to tell you was. I hope I didn't mess up by not telling you sooner. I just thought I'd wait until it seemed like it might be an issue and now I can sorta see that was probably a bad idea and I really hope you're not mad, I... I'm sorry I'm rambling." She pauses to catch her breath. "I'm just really nervous. I understand if you're mad. I know most people think sex isn't a big deal. But it is to me. I think it's something very special that should only be shared between two people who are in love *and* married."

I still can't think of anything to say. So, Alli keeps talking.

"I hope this doesn't make you change your mind about being with me. I'm not saying keep your hands to yourself... We can do stuff... But when it comes to us being physical... We need to keep things *above* the waist. For... both of us. Okay, I'm talking way too much, and your silence is really making me even more nervous so please say something."

"I..." I'm not entirely sure how I feel about it. I knew we'd be taking things slow, but this is... surprising. "So, is this like a religious thing?" I ask.

"Well, not really. I mean, I guess. The Conwells took me to church, and so that's a part of it... But, it's mostly a personal decision."

"I see."

"Please tell me if you're okay with this. And be honest. I don't want to lose you, but I don't want you to be unhappy either. You've been wonderful so far. You've never complained. When I've asked you to stop, you've stopped. You don't make me feel bad or try to pressure me. I'm glad to have a boyfriend who respects my boundaries, even if he needs reminding a few times in the heat of the moment. I just realize now that we've reached a point where it's not fair for you to not know what you're really in for. Maybe my values and morals are old fashioned, but they're important to me. And I need to know if you can be happy with me."

I don't even have to think this over. I'm shocked, and, honestly, a bit disappointed, but we've been together for a month now, which is already the longest I've been in a relationship without having sex. It's tough, no question about it. But I'm happy. There's no doubt about that.

"I *am* happy with you. Happier than I've been in a long time."

"Really? You're not disappointed?"

"No, I—"

"Be honest."

"Okay, maybe a little, but, not, like—"

"Do you still want to be my boyfriend?"

"Of course, why would you even have to ask?"

"I'm under no illusions, Nick. I know the only virgin in the room here is me. And I'm okay with that. I guess. I just hope you mean it when you say *you're* okay with it. I'm sure this isn't what you signed up for, and it won't be easy for you."

"It's fine. It's..." I'm not sure what to day. I don't want her to think this is going to be a cakewalk for me, but I don't want to lie to her either.

"Nick," she says, before I have a chance to deny it. "It's okay to admit it. It's not easy for me, either."

"It's not?"

"Of course. I may be a virgin, but that doesn't mean waiting isn't difficult for me, too."

"Really?"

"Yeah, I mean, it was easier *before* I had a boyfriend, of course, but, you know, I am human."

"Okay. Well, yes. It definitely won't be easy, but, you know, you're worth it."

Alli smiles, relieved, and hugs me.

"That's so sweet. You're a great guy, you know that? I couldn't have asked for a better boyfriend."

"And I couldn't have asked for a better girlfriend."

"You really mean that?"

"Absolutely."

"I'm so glad. I always thought that when I started dating, that, you know, I'd just get dumped a lot for not putting out, you know? I always assumed that I'd just get hurt a lot before finding a boy who was, you know, understanding. I'm lucky I found you."

"So, that's why you never dated anyone before me? Because you were worried about rejection?"

"Well, no, I mean... it's more complicated than that. I was... prepared, I guess... to experience rejection. I just figured most boys wouldn't be understanding—"

She's right about that. Had I known before we started dating I probably would have had second thoughts.

"—and then you came along, and you know, something told me to give you a chance. I knew going slow wasn't easy for you. You weren't exactly a master at hiding it... but, you know, you never made me feel bad, or tried to pressure me even though you're... experienced. I'm really sorry for not telling you sooner, but I—"

"You don't need to apologize. I'm okay with this, really. I promise. I'm just sorry for assuming—"

"Don't be. It's my fault for dropping this bombshell on you now. You don't think I'm a tease, do you?"

"No, of course not. But let's keep the bombshells to a minimum, okay?"

She laughs nervously. "Okay."

"So, if there's anything else you'd like to tell me... I guess now is a good time." I'm not sure why I say this, it just comes out.

"Nope," she says quickly, almost reflexively. This reaction concerns me. Like she's hiding other stuff she doesn't want to talk about. Is it something just as big? Bigger, even? Should I be worried?

We sit in an awkward silence for a few seconds.

"So..." I start to say.

"So..." She repeats. "Anyway, I'm sorry for interrupting. Now that we're on the same page, do you... want to keep going?"

I nod. "Yes, I do."

CHAPTER 22

"YOU OKAY? YOU seem nervous." Alli asks me on the drive up to my mom's house.

Nervous doesn't quite describe what I'm feeling. I haven't exactly been looking forward to this whole overnight thing at my mom's house, and even less so about bringing Alli. I knew it was inevitable, but I was planning to put it off as long as possible. I wasn't so much worried about Alli meeting my mom as I was about her meeting Lacy. My mom can be embarrassing sometimes but she usually plays it cool. I know she'll love Alli. She already can't shut up about how "nice and sweet" she was when they briefly spoke on the phone a couple weeks ago. But Lacy... She didn't like Lauren and made that pretty obvious whenever I brought her home. And even though Lacy has no reason to dislike Alli, she may just be predisposed to hating any girl I bring home.

"I'm okay. What about you?"

"I'm a little nervous. I just want your family to like me."

"Look, you're great. You're amazing. And if they can't see that, we'll never have to see them again," I say.

"Don't say that. They're your fam—" She lets the last word hang there, unfinished, and I think I know why. She's told me that before moving here that her Dad's cousins, Dave and Christine Conwell, were her legal guardians. And that's about all I know. Any time her family comes up in conversation she gets guarded and distant. I'm guessing she doesn't have a relationship with her parents anymore, and that's why she suddenly got weird when I said we wouldn't have to see my family again. I wish I could ask for more details.

"I... sorry, got distracted," she says.

"It's okay; look, you got nothing to worry about."

"Okay, then I guess neither of us should be nervous then, huh?"

"Hey, I said you got nothing to worry about. I didn't say I didn't."

"What do *you* have to worry about?"

"We're about to go to a house full of embarrassing old photos, a mother full of embarrassing stories, and a sister who... well, she's my sister."

"Ooooh, really? Well, now I'm *really* looking forward to this trip."

"I'll turn around right now."

"Don't get any ideas."

I'm sure I'll regret this later, but I have to try to get some information out of her regarding her family. "You know," I say conspiratorially, "eventually I'll have to meet *your* family, and see your embarrassing photos, hear your embarrassing childhood stories and stuff."

Alli's jovial demeanor is suddenly gone.

"Or," I continue, "you know, your guardians, I guess. Sometime. When you want me to. We could take a trip out there. You've told them about me, right?"

"Of course. I've told them all about you."

"You just don't want me looking at old photos or your awkward early teen years, huh?"

"Not really. No."

There's something weird about the way she says this. What would normally be playful banter has her guarded and insecure.

"Why not? I'm sure they're not awkward at all. I'm sure you were a cute kid."

"I'm sure you were, too," she says.

A deflection, perhaps? I guess I better stop pressing this.

"No, I was pretty awkward."

"If you don't want me to see them I won't look at them," she says.

Even this strikes me odd, like she's trying to make a deal to avoid me seeing old family photos or something. She's visibly uncomfortable and my attempt to get some information has failed miserably.

"No, I mean, you can. Really. I was just... it's fine. You can see them. If someone brings them out. Just try not to laugh."

"Okay. I promise."

"By the way, when is your birthday?" I ask.

"My birthday?"

"Yeah, I just realized I don't know when it is. I mean, we're heading up this way for Lacy's; mine is coming up soon. You've never told me when yours is."

"Oh, I'm sorry."

"So... when is it?"

"It's not until December."

"Okay, what day?"

After a few seconds pause she says, "New Year's Eve."

New Year's Eve... the anniversary of my failed marriage proposal to Lauren—that's a crazy coincidence.

"Right. New Year's Eve," I say.

To move past the awkward turn this conversation took I turn the radio on. Alli eventually starts singing along to the music, which makes it better.

* * *

When we pull into the driveway of my mom's house neither of us move.

"You ready?" I ask.

"I think so."

"Let's leave our stuff in the car for now, we go through all the introductions and stuff first."

"Okay."

"And, you know, in case we decide to bail."

My mom opens the door before we even get a chance to open the storm door with Lacy in tow. As much as my mom has been begging me to come up for months she's far more interested in meeting Alli. She and Lacy focus all of their attention on her. When we step in the house I notice Mom and Lacy share an unspoken moment where they glance at each other. I know exactly what they're thinking: *Look how young Alli is.*

Pleasantries are exchanged and Alli wishes Lacy a happy birthday. Everyone is warm and friendly to each other and Alli's apprehension over this moment dissipates quickly. This is her first "meeting the family" moment and if it didn't go well she'd be devastated. The back and forth between Alli, Mom, and Lacy goes on for a few minutes, without contribution from me, until I interrupt to point out that we still have our things in the car.

"And, you could say hello to me too," I say to my mom and sister.

"Of course!" my mom says, hugging me. "How are you, dear?"

"I'll go get my stuff from the car," Alli says and goes back outside.

Lacy moves in for a quick hug.

"Geez, you're like such a cradle robber, aren't you?" Lacy says in my ear.

"Lacy!" My mom says.

"Oh, you thought the same thing too, don't deny it. So, come on Nick, how old is she? My age?"

"No, she's nineteen."

Lacy bursts out laughing. "That's just four year older than me."

"What difference does it make to you?"

"Enough you two. Can you behave while I take care of things in the kitchen?"

"Yeah, yeah," Lacy says. Mom leaves us, not entirely convinced.

"So, how are you doing, Cradle Robber?" Lacy asks.

"Oh, leave it alone."

"Seriously? What would you think if I was dating someone..." she thinks in her head a few seconds, working out the math, "like seven years older than me?"

"Then I'm pretty sure that would be illegal. And it would probably be my job to kill him."

"Shut up, you know what I mean. I am dating an *older man*, though."

"Is that so?"

"Yeah, but he's only *two* years older than me."

"Congratulations?"

"You are so mean. I'm just trying to have a conversation with you. And tell you about my boyfriend."

"No, you're making fun of *my* girlfriend."

"No, I'm making fun of you! There's a difference."

"Whatever, I'm gonna go get my stuff."

She grabs my arm before I can leave. "Okay, fine. Sorry. I'm just kidding around. Your girlfriend seems really cool."

"Thanks," I say. "So, is this boyfriend of yours coming out with us tonight?"

She lights up. "Yes, he's meeting us there."

"Fantastic," I say feigning excitement. "I am dying to meet him."

"Good," she says ignoring my sarcasm. "And I'm dying to get to know your girlfriend tonight." She's not kidding.

"I'm gonna get my stuff now."

"Okay, Romeo."

Alli waits for me to grab my bag from the car before heading back to the house. Lacy looks excited when we get back inside. "You brought your guitar! How cool."

"I always bring it with me. I never know when inspiration will strike. I've had songs come to me in the middle of the night before. So, I try to always have my guitar and a notebook handy."

"Very cool."

"So," mom says. "Why don't you and Alli take your stuff to your old room and—"

"Excuse me, Mrs. Walker," Alli says, her voice suddenly sounding nervous and shy. "If it's no trouble... I..."

Mom recognizes Alli is nervous. "Whatever you need, dear, just ask. You're our guest."

"I just... is there a guest bedroom I could stay in? I'm sorry, I probably should have asked Nick about that before."

Mom is taken aback by this request. Quite frankly, so am I. And now I feel stupid for assuming Alli would prefer to stay in my room and for making a big deal about that with my mom.

"Oh, well, we don't have any spare bedrooms. But there's a second bed in Lacy's room, if that's what you prefer."

"Is that okay with you Lacy?" Alli asks her. "I'm sorry to impose, especially on your birthday."

"Oh, sure, no problem at all," Lacy says, a bit too cheerfully for my liking.

"I really am sorry about this, but I just—"

"Oh, no need to explain. It's not a problem." She gazes at me. "Not at all." I can tell by the look on her face she is amused. "We are going to have a blast," she adds.

Since Lacy was like ten years old she's had two twin sized beds in her room. At the time the reasoning was it could accommodate her having sleepovers in her room, though in recent years I've been wondering if my mom is a diabolical genius and it was just part of her plan to keep my girlfriends from sharing a room with me whenever we'd stay over.

"Thank you, so much," Alli says. "Again, I'm sorry for springing this on you at the last second."

If I had known Alli was gonna do this I wouldn't have come or found some way for Alli not to come.

"Come with me, I'll show you where it is," Lacy says.

As soon as Alli and Lacy are out of earshot Mom comes over to me.

"Well, she seems like a very nice girl."

"You can certainly say that."

"She is a bit young, don't you think?"

"What I think is... I should get my stuff up to my room."

I walk away before she can push the issue anymore and carry my things upstairs. Lacy's door is shut and I can hear chatter and laughter inside. This bugs me so I just drop my stuff in my old room and go back downstairs. Mom is back in the kitchen preparing a cake for later. Alli and Lacy come down soon after, sounding like they're new best friends. Alli sits next to me on the couch and Lacy takes the seat next to her... until I give her an evil eye.

"Oh, sorry," she says sarcastically, and moves to the recliner.

We've got about an hour before we have to leave for Lacy's birthday dinner, so of course Mom and Lacy give Alli the third degree, and it goes as expected. Mom asks if she's going to college, and Alli explains that she's looking to save up some money and get established in the local music scene, before deciding if she needs to go to college. It never occurred to me to ask her why she wasn't going to college yet. I just assumed her plan has always been to be a musician and she didn't need college to do that. Lacy wants all the details about being a musician, like where she's played, or if she's ever met anyone famous. Of course, Alli also gets bombarded with a bunch of questions about how we met. Alli talks for the both of us. She tells them how we technically met at Starbucks, but that we first really met at one of her gigs. There's a lot of back and forth and follow up questions from both my mom and sister. This is the kind of intel they're not used to getting about my personal life, and Alli is the spy they've always dreamed of having.

Finally, it is time to go. We all pile into my mom's car. Lacy rushes for the backseat, clearly having devised a scheme for her and Alli to sit together for the ride while I sit up front with my mom. They talk mostly about Lacy's boyfriend, Nate. Alli gives enthusiastic replies to almost every tidbit of information Lacy offers.

Lacy's boyfriend is supposed to meet us at the restaurant but isn't here when we arrive. Lacy texts him to find out where he is. He doesn't reply until after we're seated, and it's obviously not good news because Lacy storms up from the table to call him. Before she walks out the door we hear her say "What do you mean you're not coming?"

"Well, that's not good," I say.

"Nick!" Alli whispers.

"What? Am I wrong?"

"Just, be nice," Mom says. "She was really looking forward to having him meet everyone."

So, I shut up, and when Lacy returns she informs us what we already know: Nate is not coming.

"Why not, honey?" Mom asks.

"He says he's stuck at some stupid party," she says.

"Damn, that took some balls," I say. Alli kicks me under the table. "Ow!" Alli gives me the evil eye. "Sorry," I say, but the expression on her face makes it clear she wants me to apologize to Lacy. "Sorry," I say again.

"Whatever, I don't want to talk about it." Lacy says, crossing her arms and looking down at her lap. Mom attempts to console her, but Lacy is having none of it.

"Hey, Lacy," Alli says. "Maybe you'd like your gift now?" Alli fishes out an envelope from her purse.

Lacy looks up with curiosity. There's a tear down her cheek, and she wipes it off before taking the envelope.

"It's from both of us," Alli tells her. Which reminds me that I don't even know what she got Lacy for her gift. "I also have my album for you, but that's back at the house. This is the main gift."

"What did we get her?" I whisper to Alli. She puts her hand up, signaling me to be quiet.

"Oh. My. God." Lacy is acting freaked out. "Are these for real?" She holds up two tickets in her hand.

"Uh-huh. Nick said you were a fan. I am too. I thought maybe you'd like to see her with me this summer."

In an instant, Lacy is up on her feet and running around the table. Before Alli can react, Lacy is hugging her and thanking her repeatedly. Nate's decision to abandon her on her birthday has now been totally forgotten.

"What are they, Lacy?" Mom asks.

"Two tickets to see Taylor Swift in concert at Gillette Stadium!" Lacy can barely contain her excitement, and her screams have the whole restaurant looking at us.

"That was really nice of us," I whisper to Alli.

Alli smiles. "Wasn't it?"

* * *

Back at the house more gifts are given to Lacy. We sing happy birthday and have cake. Lacy asks Alli if she'll play some songs for us, which Alli is happy to do. So, we get a private concert. She starts off with a couple of her own songs, then asks Lacy to suggest some cover songs. Everyone is having a good time. If not for Alli, this whole night would have been a major drag. Lacy, true to form, brings out an old family album for Alli to look at. Alli gives me a look, like she wants to make sure it's okay before she does. I signal that it's fine and Lacy does her best to embarrass me. Alli, to her credit, does a decent job of holding back laughter.

At 10 p.m. Alli decides to turn in and Lacy joins her, leaving me alone with my mom. I put the TV on, looking for anything to fill the silence, settling on a *Friends* rerun. Before long she tells me that Lacy was really enjoying me being here and that I really need to start spending time with her.

"And don't say she's too young to have anything in common with you," she adds. "If you can date a nineteen-year-old girl I think you can manage—"

"Mom—"

"Why don't you invite her to one of Alli's shows? They really hit it off tonight and I think she'd really like that."

"We'll see; she doesn't have many shows that are all ages."

"Just, try, please. She really had a great time with you both tonight. She doesn't have her father anymore, and she really needs a positive male role model in her life. No matter how much she teases you, she really does want to spend more time with her brother."

"Okay. I'll invite her to Alli's next all-ages show."

"Good. That's a start."

CHAPTER 23

When I wake up I half-expect to be in my apartment. Waking up in your childhood bedroom is a bizarre experience when you're nearly thirty. It's undeniably familiar but disorienting at the same time. My old furniture is all in the same place, and there are probably still clothes that fit me in the dressers and the closet that I never took with me.

I shower, get dressed, and go downstairs. As I enter the kitchen, Lacy comes in through the sliding door from the deck out back. I can hear voices out there; apparently breakfast is outside this morning.

"It's about time you made it down," she says.

"Breakfast is outside?" I ask.

"Duh."

I try to navigate around her and go outside, but she intentionally blocks me and holds up her hand, instructing me to wait until she finishes her juice. Great, she wants to grill me about something. When she finishes, she checks to make sure the sliding door is closed tight.

"Your girlfriend is awesome," she says.

"I'm glad you think so," I say.

"I still can't believe she is gonna take me to see Taylor Swift. That's the coolest gift ever! Especially from a girlfriend of *yours*."

"Thanks."

"What are you so glum about? Because your girlfriend wanted to spend the night in *my* room instead of yours?" I try to get around her to go outside without answering but she blocks me again. "Oh, come on! Don't take it out on me just because your girlfriend won't sleep with you."

"Excuse me?"

"Oh please, why else would she rather share a room with me than stay in your room with you?"

I can't think of answer, because there really isn't one.

"Exactly," she says. "So, you might as well admit it."

"Admit what?"

She whispers, "You, dear brother, are dating a virgin."

"That is none of your—"

"Does mom know? I bet she'd be so proud. I mean, that Lauren chick was no virgin. You realize I knew she used to sneak out of my room in the middle of the night so you two could screw in your bedroom, right?"

"You knew?"

"Our rooms do share a wall. I heard you guys. Totally traumatized me." She laughs. "Seriously, she was kind of a slut."

"Why would you say that?" I ask, a bit paranoid. *Does she know?*

"I—I dunno."

I get right up to her face. "Why did you call her that?"

"Chill dude. I'm sorry. I didn't mean anything by it."

"Tell me—"

"She was just mean to me."

"She was not!"

"Okay, not *mean* mean. But she used act like she was so put out by having to share my room with me. Like every time. She didn't even try to have a good time with me or be my friend. She acted like being stuck with me was the worst thing ever."

I knew Lauren wasn't exactly thrilled we couldn't share a room, but I figured she at least tried to make the best of it.

"I'm sorry," I tell her. "I didn't realize—"

"It's fine. I don't care anymore."

"Well, let's just forget about it. She's not in the picture anymore."

Lacy smiles. "That's true. So... Are you going to tell me or not?"

"Tell you what?"

"About Alli. Is she—"

"Okay... I think we're done here."

"I'm not making fun of her. If she is... you know... that's cool. I'm not making fun of you either. I'm glad you're together. I really, *really*, like her. She's awesome. It's gonna be so cool to go to the concert with her."

"Well, I'm glad you like her."

"She's actually trying to be my friend. I think that's nice for a change. I mean, come on... Lauren wouldn't have taken me to see Taylor Swift."

"Probably not," I agree. "So, let's just stop talking about her."

"Deal," she says, holding her hand out for me to shake. I shake it limply and unenthusiastically. "Are you trying to be a dick?"

"No."

"Whatever."

She sounds legitimately upset and runs upstairs without saying anything more and I feel bad because I know she was just trying to have some innocent sibling banter, and I know she really likes Alli and wasn't making fun of her. That's not what bothered me. What really bothered me was what she said about Lauren, because she has no idea what Lauren did to me—because I've never told her—but it made me self-conscious that maybe she figured it out. Did she sense something when we were here for Christmas? Did everyone but me know Lauren had cheated on me?

I go outside onto the deck, where mom and Alli are eating breakfast. When I shut the sliding door Alli turns to me and smiles. It's quiet outside. The kind of early morning quiet when the wind blows faintly, and various background noises all meld together into a peaceful white noise.

"Help yourself," my mom says, indicating the breakfast food on the table. I help myself to eggs, sausage, bagels, juice, even home fries. As I load up my plate, my mom and Alli talk, picking up where they left from an earlier conversation. When I'm done filling my plate I sit next to Alli. After a few minutes, my mom stands up and starts to collect stuff off the table.

"You two keep eating, I'll clear this stuff off and then I'm off to the gym."

"Thanks so much for breakfast," Alli tells her.

"You're welcome, dear," Mom says, and then Alli stands up and they hug.

"If you two leave before I get back, it was wonderful having you both here, come back any time."

"We will," Alli says, and smiles at me when she sits back down. My mom stacks the empty plates and bowls and brings them inside.

"So, it appears you and Lacy really hit it off last night."

"We did. I really like her."

"What did you talk about?"

"Oh, girl talk and stuff."

Again with the girl talk. First with Devon, now Lacy.

"Oh yeah? So, is she still pissed Nate bailed on her?"

All starts to say something, then stops herself. "Well she—you could ask her that yourself. I think she could use some advice."

"I can't give her relationship advice."

"And I can?"

"I'm her older brother. And, she has friends she can talk to."

"Maybe it's an older brother's advice she needs."

"Somehow I doubt she'd listen anyway."

"You'd be surprised. Seriously, you should talk with her. And spend more time together."

"I know. I know. My mom says the same thing. I said I'd work on that."

I can tell by the look on Alli's face she's worried she's upset me. "I'm sorry, I didn't mean to—"

"It's fine. I know you mean well. I just... I would much rather enjoy this moment, since it's the first moment alone we've had since we got here."

"Oh, I'm sorry. I'm being a bad girlfriend, aren't I? I haven't even seen your old room yet."

"No, I get it. You wanted Lacy to like you, and—"

"Why don't we finish breakfast and you can show me your old room?"

"Sure, okay."

When we go to my former bedroom she immediately looks the place over, picking out the details. There isn't much to see in here. Much of what I did to decorate the room (movie and band posters, photos and stuff) was taken down years ago. There are still hints of my youth in here, but mom has yet to convert this room into a guest room because, well, I'm the only guest that spends the night.

"This is nice," she says.

"Thanks."

"What's all that?" She points to a cluster of boxes in the corner.

"Music. I should bring all that back with us so I can copy everything back to my computer."

She kneels on the floor in front of and looks through them. "Yeah, you didn't have much on your laptop the last time I looked at it."

She starts with the CDs, then notices a bunch of vinyl sticking up conspicuously in a separate box and goes through that. That box has all of my Perch music. Their albums on CD, rare singles, import versions of albums with extra tracks, limited edition vinyl, live bootlegs, some on cassette even. Perhaps I was wasting my money back then, but there's a good chance I could make some money if I sold them now on eBay, which is where I got a lot of the rare stuff from to begin with. I spent a ridiculous amount of money on everything when I bought it, too. The lead singer Randall Crawley died when I was ten. It was tragic day for music. I started acquiring collectibles online a few years later. I stopped looking for stuff after I graduated from college because I didn't have the time or the money to collect that stuff anymore, and they were getting harder to find and more expensive as each year passed. Most people are impressed when I tell them about the collection. But Alli looks shocked and even a bit disappointed at the haul.

"You... were a Perch fan? I did not know that."

"Yeah, I guess you can say that. Are you a fan?"

"I—I haven't listened to them in years."

"They were kind of before your time, anyway."

She thumbs through the vinyl. "Vinyl, Nick? *Really?*"

"What?"

"Do you even have a record player?"

"That's not why—I was a super fan for a while, so I collected what I could."

"Are you still?"

"I dunno. I guess. I haven't listened to it all in a while, because my hard drive crashed last year, and my ex didn't want all this stuff cluttering up the apart—" She's quiet, and not looking at me. It's making me nervous. "You okay?"

She gets up off the floor and sits on my bed. "Nick, are you sure we're right for each other?"

"What are you talking about?" Where the hell did this come from?

"I don't know. I've just been thinking, that's all."

"What is it? What's wrong?" Alli doesn't answer. "You're not breaking up with me, are you?"

She can't look at me. She just looks at the floor, avoiding eye contact. I can see she's starting to cry. "I don't know."

"If there's something wrong, tell me, we'll talk about it. We'll work it out. Are you unhappy?"

"No Nick. That's not it. I—I've never been happier."

"I don't understand... Why then—"

"It's complicated."

"Can you be more specific?"

"Why do you like me, Nick?"

"Why do I like you?"

"I know I'm... different from other girls you've been with. Why do you still want to be with me?"

I want to tell her I love her, because I think that I do. This panic building up in me as she seems ready to break up with me is telling me this relationship is far more important to me than I expected so early in a relationship. Especially one so complicated. I can't tell her I love her now, though. If I tell her now, it will sound desperate and, I don't want this to be the moment I tell her.

"You know why," I finally say.

"Not really. I know it's not easy for you being my boyfriend. Other girls—"

"I told you I'm okay with that."

Why did I bring up Lauren and the fact we shared the apartment? I'm such an idiot.

"Why are you okay with it? I just... are you sure you're with me for the right reasons?" She asks.

"I don't understand. What are the *wrong* reasons?"

"An ulterior motive of some sort."

An ulterior motive? I'm really confused now. "Such as?"

"I can't tell you," she says.

"Well, then I don't know how I could like you for the wrong reasons. I like you completely for who you are. In fact, of all the relationships I've had, this is probably the first one I've stayed in for the *right* reasons."

"Really?"

"Yeah. I guess you could say that you're the girl I've been waiting for."

She smiles and seems visibly relieved as though whatever was bothering her isn't anymore. "That's what I needed to know."

"So, you're not breaking up with me?" I ask.

She shakes her head, and I can't even describe my relief in words.

"I should tell you that if you did, I'd fight for you. I wouldn't give up on you."

"Really?"

"You better believe it."

"That's really sweet. I never thought a boy would ever say that to me."

Perhaps now I should tell her I love her. It seems like it would be a good time. But I can still feel my heart racing, even though it's finally slowing down again, and I think there will be other, better times for that. And, if she was considering breaking up with me, maybe she doesn't feel the same way yet.

She lays her head on my chest. I think I've dodged a bullet here, and I'm glad, but I can't say I'm one hundred percent confident things are really okay. I want to talk about something, change the subject somehow, but I'm scared to say anything at this point.

"Your heart is beating really fast," she says.

"Sorry, I was just really nervous. I didn't want to lose you."

"I'm sorry. I just freaked out. I'm sorry I can't explain why, but I'm okay now. You're not losing me." She kisses me to demonstrate her point. "We're okay. I promise."

I'm so confused, and desperately wanting more of an explanation for this bizarre behavior. I should ask if this is about her family issues, but if she says things are okay now I don't want to push her. I've avoided catastrophe just now and don't want to press my luck.

"Good," I say, and lean in to kiss her. We kiss for a while, then I start to reach under her shirt, but Alli grabs my hand.

"Nick! Lacy could walk in," she whispers. "Later, okay? I promise."

So we just kiss for a while. That is until Lacy knocks on the door.

"Alli, you in there?"

Alli pulls away from me. "Yeah."

"Shower's free."

"Thank you." Alli stands up. "I'll be quick, and then we can go home and... continue."

"Be *really* quick."

Alli laughs and heads out the door, leaving me to ponder what the hell just happened. I go over everything that happened this weekend, trying to figure out what set Alli off. The more I think about it I can't see how this has to do with her secret family issues. She's never nearly broken up with me before. The only thing that makes this weekend different is her spending time with Lacy. Did Lacy tell her stuff she shouldn't have? How many girls I've brought home, or all the times she's heard me having sex with Lauren in this room? That has to be it. I know Alli says she's okay with me "having a past" but it must really bother her.

I march to Lacy's room to confront her. Her door is open, which means she's dressed, thankfully.

"What is your problem?"

"Sorry, did I interrupt a heavy make out session?" Lacy asks.

"What did you say to her last night?" Lacy looks genuinely confused. "She got all weird on me while we were in my room, what did you say to her?"

Lacy looks nervous, "We just talked about..." she stops, and crosses her arms looking angry. "It was a *private* conversation. None of your business."

"Oh really? You nearly fucking up my relationship sounds like my business."

"Wait, what? What happened?"

"Like you don't know."

"Fuck you, Nick. I didn't do anything wrong. I didn't tell her anything. We never even talked about you. What do you think I did? Do you think I told her about all the slutty girls you've brought home? Do you think I'm stupid? Do you think I want her to break up with you? I don't. I like her a lot. And believe it or not, as much as you are pissing me off right now I do want you to be happy. If something was bothering her, it wasn't—" she chokes up a bit. "I didn't... say... anything... I swear."

She's genuinely upset enough that I almost believe her. But if she didn't say anything, what set Alli off? Unable to reconcile this I just march back into my room and slam the door.

A few minutes later I hear Alli talking to Lacy in her room, and then Alli comes in my room. She's got an angry look on her face.

"Did you yell at her for what happened earlier?"

I don't answer.

"Nick, that had nothing to do with her. You know I hate lies, so please believe me. I had a brief freak out and didn't know how to handle it. I'm sorry about that."

"Okay, I'm sorry."

"Now apologize to Lacy so we can go home."

I don't argue. I walk into Lacy's room. When she sees it's me she turns away.

"We mostly talked about Nate. Okay? I just needed some advice. Things aren't... He's been—"

"Look, it's okay. I was out of line."

"You mean that, or you just saying that because she asked to you?"

"Both," I say, honestly.

She smiles faintly. "I guess I accept your apology."

I don't think I technically apologized yet, but I'll accept her accepting what I said as an apology.

"Was she helpful?" I ask.

Lacy shrugs. "She thinks I should talk to *you* about it."

"What about mom?"

"Mom? Are you kidding? Would you talk to mom about your— relationships?"

"Well, no. I'm a guy."

"Okay, your dad then?"

My dad and I don't see each other much since he remarried and moved to Florida. When we do talk, it's not about anything like relationships. It's usually perfunctory text messages, calls on birthdays, stuff like that.

"Okay, you're right," I concede. "So... did you want to... talk?"

She shakes her head. "I'm still kinda mad at you."

"Okay. Another time then. I promise I won't be a dick."

"Promise?"

"Of course."

"Everything okay in here?" Alli asks from the doorway.

"Yeah, we're fine," Lacy says. "Your boyfriend is still an asshole, but—"

"I'm working on that, trust me," Alli says.

Lacy laughs. "Good luck."

"Okay, well, I guess we should get going then," I say.

"I guess so," Alli says.

"I'll load up the car."

I carry mine and Alli's stuff to the car in one trip. When I get back in, Alli and Lacy are downstairs and Alli is all excited. "Nava just asked me if I would open for Candlepin at their CD Release Party in a few weeks! They said it was possible, but I didn't think it would actually happen!"

"That's awesome," I say.

Alli hugs me excited. "I know! This is huge!"

And so, our little trip to my childhood home ends on a high note.

CHAPTER 24

ALLI HAD NEVER expected to open for Candlepin's CD Release Party. Normally a band with a larger fan base would be chosen to help draw a bigger crowd. But she's impressed enough people that there's been a good buzz about her, and when the band that was supposed to open for Candlepin (a Philly-based band called The Portables) had to cut their northeastern club tour short due to "management issues," Nava and Blake suggested she could fill the slot. She didn't get a full hour, however. She's splitting it with a band called The Purnell Maneuver, who got the second slot, but that didn't matter to Alli. She really only plays small bars and coffeehouses that have a max capacity of eighty to a hundred people, and usually they aren't more than half-filled. The Brighton Music Hall has a capacity of three hundred and forty people, and the show is nearly sold out, so this will be the biggest crowd Alli will get to play for.

And even though she had the earliest slot, there will still be a lot of people there.

Alli is also excited because she is going to record another album with D-Line Records. She calls me after work sounding just as excited as she was when she found out about opening for Candlepin's CD Release Party. I'm excited too. Another album? How cool is that?

I'm totally psyched about the news until I remember that D-Line Records is Blake's cousin's small label. According to Alli, Blake's cousin was so impressed with the live recording Blake gave him he offered to give her some studio time on weekends and to put out the album on his label. So, of course Blake is now a hero for making it happen.

In addition to recording and producing the album, D-Line will handle getting local distribution. Alli still has to pay for production of the CDs, and she has to sell them at gigs of course, but they have a pretty good mailing list to send CDs to, including local radio stations, college stations, and local music journalists. And the album will be listed at a whole bunch of online retailers. The most important thing is that she can afford the recording sessions and mastering and all that other stuff. So, yeah, she's really excited. I know I should be too... but, the whole Blake connection really irritates me. She's going to spend *at least* three or four Sunday mornings to record the album.

Alli and I nearly got into a big fight when she told me that Blake was going to take her to the first session.

"I could take you, you know." I told her.

"I know. But it makes sense for Blake to introduce me to his cousin. Besides, I'm only going to record a scratch track for the songs during my first session. That shouldn't take too long. And then we'll record all the songs, the guitar parts first, then the vocals. So, each session should only be a few hours."

"How many songs?"

"At least eight. Ten if the recordings go smoothly. This is so exciting! It'll be so nice to have songs that are recorded in a real studio instead of by myself with a computer."

"That will be cool. But your last album did sound good."

"It's okay, but not great. Anyway, Blake thinks I can get all my recording done in three or four sessions. Then there's editing and mixing. Since it's just me and my guitar that stuff shouldn't take too long either. And then mastering. This is so exciting. I'm thinking of recording something I haven't performed yet, too."

"There's stuff I haven't heard yet?" This made me feel worse. Blake will get to hear new stuff before me? I didn't like that.

"Maybe... There could be something you've heard me practice at my place. Maybe something you haven't."

"Seriously? And you're saying I can't go?"

"I thought you had a meeting with a client?"

Shit. I'd forgotten about that. *Fuck.*

"Yeah, I do. I could ask Jay if we can postpone it. Or maybe he can handle it on his own. "

"You don't have to do that."

"If the meeting ends early enough I could come pick you up," I suggested.

"What for? Blake can—"

"It's fine, really."

"Nick, I know you don't like him and don't trust him."

"He did ask you out—"

"That was... like... nearly three months ago."

"So?"

"He's moved on, Nick. Nava says he brings different women with him to shows all the time."

"Why is she telling you that?"

"I don't know. I'm not asking about him, if that's what you're getting at." She crossed her arms angrily.

"I'm just saying that just because he's a player doesn't mean he's not still interested in you."

"I think it means he was never really interested at all. I bet he asks girls out all the time. So, I must not really be his type, and he certainly isn't mine."

"You don't think he's just trying to win you over?" I thought this was a good point. Of course, Alli didn't see it that way.

"I told him I wasn't interested and that he was too old for me—well, I said it nicer than that—but I made it clear I wasn't interested. And he understood, and I bet he barely gave me a second thought afterwards."

"Who else is going to be there?"

"Well, his cousin owns the studio, so I'm sure he'll be there too. And—what difference does it make? I'm just going to record some songs. If you trust me, it shouldn't matter who else is there."

I tried to dig myself out of the hole I'd just dug. "I— I just want to watch you record your songs."

"That's really sweet of you, but maybe I don't want you to." Her words stung me and she noticed I felt hurt. "I'm sorry I didn't mean it that way. It's just that I want to surprise you with the final product. You'll be the first person to hear it, I promise."

After Blake and his cousin, of course, I thought.

"Why do you think he's doing this for you?" I asked.

"Because he believes in my talent. And to be nice."

"Guys don't do nice things for girls to just be nice," I said, thinking she couldn't possibly be that naïve.

"Is that so? Then why do they?" she asked, now really irritated.

"Well, to get in your pants."

"Oh, I see. And that should concern you, why? Have *you* ever been in my pants?"

"No, but—"

"Then why would I let—"

"Maybe he's not the kind of guy to accept no for an answer."

This really upset her. "Nick, that's a terrible thing to say. He has always been a perfect gentleman to me. He just believes I've got talent and wants to help. There's nothing wrong with that. Can't you be supportive?"

"I'm supportive. I want you to record a new album."

"Then please, don't make me feel bad or guilty. And don't be jealous. You've got nothing to worry about. I promise. He's not interested in me. I'm *definitely* not interested in him. No one is getting in my pants. Not him, not you. No one. End of story."

And that ended that argument.

* * *

A few days later I make good on my promise to invite Lacy to an all-ages show. Alli is playing at some hole-in-the-wall coffeehouse. It's a Friday night, and late in the evening, so while our mom agreed to drive Lacy down here, Lacy has to spend the night and I have to take her back in the morning. Unfortunately, because Alli offered to host Lacy overnight and I don't have bedroom privileges with Alli I have to leave Lacy at Alli's overnight. While waiting for

Lacy to arrive I tell Alli I'm not a huge fan of this idea and propose that I stay in her room with her.

"I'm not sure that's a good idea," she says.

"Why not?"

"Well, for starters, I don't want your sister to get the wrong idea."

"Okay, but what about the other times?"

"Nick, I thought you were okay with—"

"I am okay with... that. I guess I'm just curious why, if you trust me—"

"Why you still have to sleep on the couch, and not in my room with me?"

"Right. Again, I'm not complaining, I'm just... Wondering," I add.

"I guess that's a fair question. It's not because I don't trust you. I don't want you to think that." She exhales deeply, like she's not sure she wants to tell me what she's about to tell me. "I guess it's a lot of reasons. Spending the night... in the same room... in the same *bed*... I'm not..."

"Never mind. I'm sorry for asking."

"It's okay, Nick. I'm just trying to say I'm just not ready for that. Sometimes, you know, it's not easy for me to tell you stop. I know if I ask, you will ... it's just—" The doorbell rings. Lacy is here, and the discussion is over.

* * *

There aren't many people at the coffeehouse, but of the less than twenty patrons here, a small handful have definitely come specifically to see Alli play. Lacy is impressed. When Alli goes on stage Lacy helps me run Alli's merch table.

"Your girlfriend is kinda famous, isn't she?"

"Not really."

"I know she's not *famous* famous, I just mean, you know, people have come out to see her play. So, here she kind of is."

"She's... getting there." We sit there watching Alli for a bit. "So, are you still going with that guy?"

"Nate. Yeah, I am."

"I thought maybe you were gonna dump him."

"Well, yeah. I thought I was going to. But—"

"In fairness to him, he couldn't have been too excited about dinner with your family."

"Yeah, that's basically what he said. We're passed that."

"So, things are... going well then?"

"Well, the thing is—"

A couple of college age girls come up to buy CDs. Lacy takes the cash and I hand them each a CD and a postcard with upcoming gigs on it.

"Two CDs already! Is that good?" Lacy asks.

"That's not bad. Considering the size of the crowd."

"So cool!"

"So you didn't invite Nate tonight?"

"I did. He was going to drive us down here... until I told him I was staying at Alli's overnight and he'd have to go back up to New Hampshire by himself. I think he thought we'd leave early and—"

"I can figure out the rest."

"It seems like that's all he wants—"

"Are you sure you want to talk to me about this?" I know I said I wouldn't be a jerk anymore but talking to my sister about her sex life is just really awkward.

"Why not?" she asks. "You're a guy. He's a guy. You might have some useful advice."

"Things have changed a lot since I was in high school," I say. "I'm sure things are tougher now, you know?

"Because you're so old?" She laughs.

"Yup. Pretty much."

Lacy sighs. "Well, let me ask you something. You and Alli... you're happy, right?"

"Yes. Why?"

"I mean... you guys haven't... you don't—"

"I thought we were talking about you?"

"Sorry, I just—"

Another customer comes to buy a CD. I handle the entire transaction. I try to steer the conversation with Lacy to a less awkward topic. "Things okay in school?"

"Yeah. Fine." Lacy has decided not to chat anymore and focus on Alli. She pulls her phone out and takes a picture on stage and starts posting in on social media.

"What's that?" I ask, pointing at the app on her screen that I'm not familiar with.

"Snapchat. You're not on it?"

"Nope. Not my thing."

"I knew you weren't cool."

"You just figured that out?"

Lacy laughs, and even manages a smile.

"You're not... one of those kids who sends... you know... x-rated photos on that, are you?" I ask.

"What? No! Of course not."

"Okay. Okay. I just thought I should ask. I don't want you doing anything stupid."

"Don't worry. I only send topless photos," she says. "I try to keep things tasteful."

"*Please* tell me you're joking."

"Of course I am!"

"Good."

"Thanks for caring, though," she says, sincerely.

"Thanks for not being stupid."

"Well, someone in the family has to be the smart one."

"Nice burn."

Lacy smiles with pride. "I know, right?"

A loud burst of applauses refocuses our attention on Alli's performance, so we watch her in silence as she plays her songs, and a few covers. She dedicates a Taylor Swift cover song to Lacy, a song called "Blank Space" which gets Lacy really excited. Then she plays one for me, one of her own that she explains she wrote for me called "Finding You." Lacy grabs my wrist because she's so excited. When the song ends everyone claps. Lacy leans in and whispers in my ear. "That. Was. Amazing."

"I know," I say.

"You are so going to marry her one day."

"I hope you're right."

"If you don't..." she says, pausing for dramatic effect. "I will kill you."

When Alli is done with her set she asks me what I thought of her new song. She's nervous when she asks, like she wasn't sure I'd like it.

"I loved it." I tell her. "It was, amazing and..." She hugs me and gives me a peck on the cheek.

"You were great inspiration," she says, and I can't help but blush.

Lacy is waiting in the wings to tell Alli how much fun she had, and they talk while I man the merch table, which is starting to attract some people. We sell eight more CDs, which may not sound like much, but for a room with about thirty seats available, Alli considers that a success.

I escort Alli and Lacy back to Alli's apartment. Even though Alli said I could hang out for a while, Alli has a morning shift at Starbucks tomorrow and won't stay up late, and I have to be back here to take Lacy home in the morning.

On my way home, it occurs to me that despite being with Alli for over a month now I've only managed to get Jay, Devon, and now Lacy to go to a show. Am I really lacking in friends? Am I being a bad boyfriend? I resolve to get some more friends to go to one of gigs.

* * *

The following afternoon, after I've taken Lacy back home and find myself alone and not in the mood to do work, I browse Facebook for a while, and check out my college friend Daniella's feed. It's been six weeks since I invited them to see Alli play and after spending some time checking out both of their profiles I realize I would like to hang out with them again. It would also be nice for Alli and me to hang out with another couple. We could consider it a double date. I see Daniella is online so, I message her. To my surprise she says going out together is a good idea, "we haven't seen you in ages," and all that, but it would have to be next week at the earliest. I tell her that Alli has a gig in Somerville next week, and that we can meet up for dinner there, and then they can see her play a set or two. She must like the idea because says she'll arrange for a sitter for that night.

* * *

Mike has aged terribly since I last saw him. It's quite clear to me now that he's been using a years old photo for his Facebook profile page. I don't know why people do that, it's not like people forget about your graying hair and male pattern baldness just because you're embarrassed to put a current photo of yourself on social media. He and I are the same age, but he looks ten years older. Daniella hasn't exactly aged well either. Parenthood, I guess.

Seeing the dramatic changes they've gone through makes me feel a little self-conscious about Alli's relatively young age. Seeing Mike with his thinning hair, and Daniella looking a lot more like a mother than the college student she was when I met them makes me feel like I've brought a child out to dinner with them.

Introductions are made and after just thirty seconds of small talk I can sense that they disapprove of her. When we order drinks Alli is the only one who orders a nonalcoholic drink, and I spy a look between the two of them that confirms to me they have correctly assumed she's not yet of legal drinking age. Even Daniella ordered a red wine (she explained that her doctor says the occasional glass of wine during pregnancy is okay) so it made Alli's order even more conspicuous.

To make matters worse, there's not much for the four of us to talk about. Daniella and Mike live in a completely different world from me, and Alli even more so. They're *my* friends and I'm having trouble relating to them now. To their credit, they go through the motions, asking me questions about what I'm up to (which sounds more like an interview than a bunch of friends hanging out) and then they ask Alli about being a musician, but they don't seem to really care. Daniella asks if Alli is going to college, when Alli says she didn't go to school in order to pursue a career in music, Daniella shows outward signs of disapproval. Subtle, but noticeable.

"So, you're on a gap year?" Daniella asks.

"Well, no," Alli explains. "If music doesn't work out, I'll probably go to school. But music is what I really want do."

"Alli was homeschooled," I say in her defense. "So, she is smarter than us public school students anyway."

"My mom is a public school teacher," Daniella says.

Fantastic. I can just tell they are thinking "we wasted a rare night out on this?" and if I was in their position I would totally feel the same way. There is too much effort being made by the three of us and Alli is visibly uncomfortable hanging out with people who are supposed to be my friends but are struggling to find common ground because they think I'm sowing wild oats and they think Alli is some dumb, naïve girl who is wasting her life pursuing a dumb dream of being a famous musician. They don't say this outright, but I can hear it in their voices.

It's a relief when Alli has to set up to play. Daniella and Mike whisper to each other, probably trying to figure out an exit strategy. I'm thinking they will be gone before Alli finishes her first set.

But, when Alli plays, things change completely. Daniella and Mike are mesmerized by her singing. Before long, they are genuinely enjoying themselves. When the waiter comes to take our plates, they both order more drinks. Daniella is completely floored when Alli sings her cover of "Girl on Fire."

"Wow, Nick. She is amazing," she says.

"Yeah," Mike agrees. "We had no idea."

"I told you she was."

"Believe it or not, Nick, we figured you might be just a little biased."

Daniella shushes us. "I want to listen to this."

After her first set break, Alli joins us at the table and is flooded with compliments from Daniella and Mike. When a diner interrupts us to see if Alli has any CDs to sell, they are even more impressed. Alli, realizing she's earned their approval relaxes and it almost feels like the four of us are old friends. They tell Alli some old college stories, and they're both smart enough to leave out any mention of my past girlfriends, which is a plus. And of course, they talk about parenthood. They show us pictures of their daughter on their phones. Alli and I "ooh" and "aww" at the appropriate times but it also makes me feel I have catching up to do. Of course, had things with Lauren turned out differently, I— well, I shouldn't be thinking like that because had things turned out differently with Lauren, because I wouldn't be with Alli right now. Still, seeing how Daniella and Mike's lives have had momentum where mine hit a wall stings a bit. I'm sure Alli feels out of her element again, sitting here with friends of mine from college who are already parents.

I can see why Daniella and Mike feel Alli is too young for me. Sometimes I feel that way as well. But she does make up for that in a lot of ways. She's as precocious as she is innocent. She has an incredible sense of personal responsibility—not a common trait for people her age and seems more mature than me sometimes. She's difficult to figure out. She hasn't experienced much, and so she's a tad socially awkward, and very private about her family and her past. She obviously had an unhappy childhood, but she's no helpless victim of her circumstances either. She works harder than anyone I know, I think, to prove to herself she can. Daniella and Mike don't know anything about Alli's background, but I think they see she's not a starry-eyed dreamer whose sole purpose is to become a famous musician. They see she loves music so much that she simply can't imagine not doing it.

Despite the positive shift in the evening, Danielle and Mike have to leave after Alli's second set. They have to relieve their babysitter and get back to their suburban world of parenting. I would say tonight turned out to be a success. It's clear everyone had a great time (they even buy a copy of Alli's CD) but I suspect we'll never hang out as couples with them again. I doubt *I* will hang out with them again. At least not until I'm married and have one child, because being parents is, without a doubt, the most significant thing that makes them who they are now. They've long since moved out of the city in favor of a house in the suburbs, and most of their social activities revolve around their child now. A night like tonight is a rarity, requiring advance planning and coordination with parents or babysitters. It's only ten o'clock and they're tired and ready to go home. Still, they stayed here longer than I expected, and I'm glad for that.

CHAPTER 25

WHEN ALLI HAS her second recording session at D-Line Records I offer to take her, and she again turns me down. She insists she wants me to be surprised by the songs she's chosen to record, and if I take her to the studio I'll want to stay, and that would "ruin the surprise."

"So, Blake gets to know before I do?"

This, it turns out, was the wrong thing to say.

"You really need to stop being jealous of Blake. I've told you... more than once now you have nothing to be jealous about."

"Yeah, but—"

"I'm done talking about this," she says, and she really means it.

We don't fight much, but it seems like when we do, it's about him. She refuses to believe he has ulterior motives, and she thinks I'm being a jealous idiot. She doesn't use those exact words, but that's what she means. In addition to her

Sunday recording sessions, Blake has showed up to a couple of her gigs. This bothers me the most. He has no reason to show up to these gigs unless he was planning to make a move—like I did. And he always seems disappointed that I'm there when he shows up, as if I'm not going to be with my girlfriend when she has a gig... I'm certainly not going to skip any while he's on the prowl. I try to be friendly for Alli's sake, but it's not easy making small talk with him. The only thing I can think to ask about is what brought him to Boston, but he always gives me some vague answer, like he doesn't want me to know and he seems annoyed when I ask. Then he'll bring up Alli's recording sessions, which I don't want to hear about because I hate that he gets to see them, and I don't. I'm sure he knows that it bothers me and he brings it up intentionally to make me jealous.

Thinking about Alli recording her songs with Blake around distracts me from doing my work. Jay and I have been pretty busy lately and my most productive times are while Alli is at Starbucks or evenings when we're at her place and she's focusing on her writing in her room and I'm working on the couch. Alli being busy Sundays should offer me an opportunity to be productive, but I'm just not able to concentrate today. I check my phone constantly, considering whether enough time has lapsed that she should be done.

Finally, just before 1 p.m., Alli calls me.

"Hey, Nick!"

"Hey, how's it going?"

"Really well. We got three songs done today, so we actually wrapped up early."

"Great."

"But listen, there's something I have to ask you. I just got an opportunity to open for a band called The Copper Thieves next Saturday. Is it okay if I take it?"

"Of course, it is. Why—"

"Even though it's your birthday?"

"Oh, right..." She intentionally kept her schedule free that evening so we could make plans. And that is the downside of dating a musician. Plans tend to revolve around gigs and the best gigs are Friday and Saturday nights. If something comes up last minute you take it. I know these types of gigs where she can play to larger crowds with new people are important for her. The lack of free weeknights can also be difficult too. Sometimes all you want is a quiet evening alone and the sad fact is that there are fewer of them when your girlfriend has gigs three to five nights a week.

"Did you forget?"

"No, I... just take it."

"Are you sure? I don't have to take it."

"Yes, seriously, it's a good opportunity, isn't it?"

"Yeah, they're pretty big."

"So, no sweat, your music career is more important than—"

"I feel awful though." This is hardly the first time we've had to change plans for a gig. It stinks that it has to happen on my birthday, but I certainly don't want to tell her to miss an opportunity on my account.

"Don't. Seriously. We can celebrate another night."

"You're really sure this okay?"

"Yes. Please. Take it now before you lose the chance."

"Okay. I will text them back and let them know."

"Good. So are you on your way here now?"

"Not yet. Just grabbing a late lunch with Blake."

"Oh," I say, unable to hide my disapproval.

"Nick... don't."

"Don't what?"

"We'll talk about this later okay." She's annoyed at me but is trying to not show it. I'm guessing Blake is there with her now, and she doesn't want to make it obvious we're fighting.

I know I shouldn't be worried, and it's not that I don't trust Alli, it's that I don't trust Blake. I know she doesn't see it that way. The way she sees it, I shouldn't be concerned at all if I trust her. In a perfect world it would be that simple.

* * *

Alli comes to my place about an hour later. Our little disagreement about Blake has been forgotten because she's just excited to tell me about the new gig she got, and of course to apologize for breaking our dinner date for my birthday. Apparently, a girl who was supposed to open for The Copper Thieves backed out after accidentally double booking the same night and had to go with the gig she booked first. So they needed a new opening act and they apparently opened for Candlepin the other night and mentioned their predicament, and Blake recommended Alli. Somehow, I knew Blake had a hand in it. It's like he knew it was my birthday or something.

The mention of Blake's name again irks me, but Alli doesn't notice. After her initial excitement wanes, she's extremely apologetic because she had made a point to keep that night free. To make her feel better I suggest we go out to celebrate tonight.

"Actually, can we stay in, tonight? Maybe we can just go to the gig early for your birthday dinner."

"Yeah we can do that. Is something wrong, though?" I ask, thinking maybe she really is still mad about earlier.

"No, just... I'm not feeling well."

"Everything okay?"

"Yeah, it's..." She gives me an expression like I'm supposed to be able to figure it out. She sighs. "It's that time of the month."

"Oh. Right. Sorry. Well, what a relief."

"A relief?"

"Sure. That means you're not pregnant." As soon as I make this joke, I realize it was not the best one to make. I haven't exactly been aware of her... cycle... for the obvious reasons. I expect Alli to get upset, like I'm making fun of her... But, she smiles.

"Nick, if I were pregnant... you, sir, would have a lot of explaining to do." She laughs.

"Hey, I'm not that talented."

She smiles. "You make me laugh."

"Well, I like to keep you entertained."

"You certainly do."

"Well, I'm glad you don't think I'm just immature."

"I never said I didn't," she says laughing.

"You think you're more mature than me?"

"Well, according to mother nature I've been *a woman* since I was ten years old."

"Well, I guess you're right. I was too busy playing video games to be a man when I was ten."

"Don't you still play video games at Jay's place Sunday nights?"

"Like only twice since we started dating." Alli gives me a look like I've still proven her point. "Okay, fine. I guess I'm still not a man yet."

Alli laughs. "Definitely not." She pecks me on the cheek. "But I like you anyway."

* * *

On the night of the gig we drive up early to have my birthday dinner before the show. Mom and Lacy call while we're driving up to wish me a happy birthday and see how things are going. Mom asks if I've talked to my dad today, and I tell her that we spoke earlier. Then Alli says hello and they're excited to talk to her as well, and they go back forth about what we're doing tonight and how we should come up sometimes soon when we're free and we can all celebrate my birthday. Alli commits us to a dinner "as soon as possible."

We decided in advance to save time by having dinner at the venue. This turned out to be a bad idea because a couple of guys from The Copper Thieves were there already having dinner one table over from us so unfortunately it felt like we were all having dinner together. When Alli mentions to them that it's my birthday they said they'd buy me a couple shots before the show. To their credit, they actually do, which was a nice gesture, though it didn't exactly make up for them spoiling our date.

Before long, Alli has to set up and the guys from the band have their own fans to mingle with, so I spend most of my time by myself until the show starts, when I sit at the merch table with the lead singer's girlfriend, Jessica, who is selling shirts and CDs for The Copper Thieves tonight.

About halfway through Alli's set, I go to the bar for my second drink. Jessica promises to handle any sales that might happen while I'm gone.

While I'm waiting for my Guinness I hear a voice call my name from behind. It's familiar, but I don't recognize the voice right away with all the music. I turn around and find myself face to face with Lauren. That's right, my ex-girlfriend and would-be fiancée.

"Hey," she says. "I thought that was you."

I haven't seen her in months. I'm so shocked I can't even think of anything to say in response.

"You, okay?" she asks.

The bartender comes back with my Guinness. I throw a ten-dollar bill down next to it—much more than necessary but I really wasn't expecting this encounter and would like to extricate myself from it, so I grab my beer and start to leave.

"I'm fine," I say. "Excuse me."

Lauren blocks me. "Come on, Nick. You don't have to be rude."

"I said excuse me."

"I'm trying to be friendly here."

"Okay then," I say, turning away. She's dressed to impress tonight: tight shirt, hip-hugger jeans, exposed midriff, so I hope she finds my averting my eyes to be even more insulting than I meant it to be.

"I just... I noticed you were here a second ago, and... I just wanted to wish you a happy birthday. Since you're here," she says, almost sounding hurt.

When I don't respond, she thinks of something else to get me to talk. "So, what do you think of this girl singing? She's great, isn't she?"

Oh, now this is perfect. *Yeah, she's my girlfriend, I can't wait to see your face when I tell you.* I have to play this just right. "Yeah."

"So you're here to see The Copper Thieves?" I don't answer, so she just keeps talking. "A friend of mine is dating the drummer. And they're really good. They just played at T.T. The Bear's Place last week." She looks at me like I'm supposed to respond, but I don't. "T.T.'s is closing in July; did you hear that?"

"I know," I say. Anyone connected to Boston's independent music scene heard the news a couple days ago. My connection is Alli, but Lauren doesn't know that. So, she's struggling to come up with small talk.

Now she has a curious look on her face. "So, you're here alone on your birthday?"

"I'm not."

"Oh," she looks around the room "I didn't see—"

"Thanks everyone," Alli says to the crowd. "You've been great. I'd like to thank The Copper Thieves for having me open for them tonight." The crowd cheers. "I'm gonna play a couple covers now, but before I do, I wanted to give a shout out to my boyfriend Nick. It's his birthday today, so if anyone wants to buy him a drink I'm sure he wouldn't mind!"

The look on Lauren's face when she realizes Alli is talking about me is priceless.

"Is she talking about you?"

"Yes. Yes, she is," I say, raising my glass to Alli.

"Looks like he's already got a drink, everyone," Alli says, shrugging her shoulders and smirking. "Sorry Nick, I guess I was too late. Happy birthday, anyway! You're the best!" She places a capo on the neck of her guitar.

And another priceless look from Lauren.

"Anyway," Alli says when the applause cools down. "This is a song off of Kelsea Ballerini's new album, and it's called 'Yeah Boy' and it's one of my new favorite songs."

Lauren just looks at me, then Alli, then me again. As far as encounters with your ex-girlfriend go, it doesn't get much better than this.

"Wow. Okay. So, that's your new girlfriend."

"That is my new girlfriend."

Lauren stands there, shocked, trying to process this information. "Is there anything else you want to say?"

"I—just... wasn't expecting to see you here, and—"

"Yeah, well I wasn't expecting to see you either."

"I'm sorry. I'm sure I'm the last person you wanted to see, but—"

"You think?" She only cheated on me and turned my marriage proposal into the most humiliating moment of my life.

She ignores my remark. "Anyways, I just saw you, and... I wanted to say hi... make sure, you know... doing okay. I guess you are."

"Just dandy, thanks. Can I enjoy the song now, please?" Okay, I know I'm being a dick, but I think it's justified. Lauren gives up walks away, upset. Mission accomplished. I resume my post at the merch table. No one buys me drink, but quite a few people recognize me as the guy Alli called out when they come to buy a CD.

Alli finishes her set with her song "Finding You," the song she wrote for me. I recognize the opening riff as she tells the crowd about the song. "I've got one last song to play. This is a song I wrote for my boyfriend, who is being such a great guy running my merch table tonight on his birthday. Can we give him another round of applause?" The audience obliges. I wonder if Lauren is still here and what she must be thinking right now. I can't see her while I'm sitting down at the merch table.

After the song, Alli receives enthusiastic applause. When she joins me at the merch table she asks me who I'd been talking to earlier.

"My ex," I tell her. "She's a new fan of yours, apparently."

"Why did she look upset?"

"Because," I say. Not wanting to get into details. Alli looks at me with an expression of both disappointment and anger.

"Nick. I don't know what happened between you two, and it's okay, you don't have to tell me. I have my own secrets, and you're certainly entitled to your own... But it looked to me as if she was trying to be nice to you, so, you probably should have been nice to her."

"But—why?" I say. She doesn't answer, she just grabs one of her CDs out of the box on her table and walks away. I try to follow her, but there's people waiting to buy CDs, and that is my job here. The crowd has thinned out a bit as people have gone outside to smoke or for some cool air during the break, so I can see Alli talking to Lauren.

My girlfriend is talking to my ex-girlfriend.

I don't like this one bit. I watch in shock as Alli gives her a CD! What did she do that for? I can't hear what they're saying, but I can see Lauren offering to pay Alli for the CD and Alli refusing to take her money. I can't believe what I'm seeing. They talk for a few more minutes, and then Alli heads back to the merch table and sits next to me. There's only one person left buying a CD, and when she leaves, I attempt to get some answers.

"What did you say to her?"

"I apologized for whatever you said to her, and gave her a CD."

"What did you do that for?"

"It was obvious that she was trying to be nice to you Nick. Since you weren't nice back, I had to be."

"You didn't have to do that."

"*You* didn't have to either." Why is she taking Lauren's side?

"Why would you do that for my *ex*-girlfriend?"

"I'm sorry, maybe it wasn't my place to do that, but she looked upset, and whatever happen with you two... it's in the past, isn't it?"

"Yeah, but I don't—"

"I'm sorry if I was out of line. I know I don't have an ex-boyfriend and don't know what it's like to see an ex after a long time, but forgiveness is a gift from God, Nick. I know it must be hard, and that's fine, but even if she hurt you in the past I hope you can forgive her. Not for her sake, but for yours."

I'd like to tell her that some things aren't so easily forgiven, but I won't. That would mean telling her what happened, and I don't want to do that. "Sometimes I think you're too nice."

"I'm taking that as a compliment. Look, just... if she comes back to talk to you, be friendly. You'll feel better afterwards if you do."

"You shouldn't want me talking to her at all."

"Why not? I trust you. I'm not threatened by her. I have no reason to believe you still have feelings for her."

"Fine. Just don't invite her hang out with us or anything."

Alli laughs. "Don't worry, I wasn't planning to do that."

Lauren does come back, and Alli excuses herself. Lauren holds up the CD Alli gave her and gives me a nervous smile, "Your girlfriend is very nice."

"Yeah, she is."

"May I sit down?"

"Sure."

She sits in the chair next to me.

"Look Nick, I know I probably deserve... I just... I really..." She continues to struggle to say exactly what she wants to say.

"I'm sorry," she says, finally. "About everything that happened."

I want to ask her if she thinks that a simple apology is enough. I've often thought about what I'd say to her if she ever tried to apologize. I've scripted out many versions of this encounter in my head where I say all sorts of carefully crafted lines to maximize the impact and make her feel horrible. But for some reason, it's different now. I don't have the same vengeful feelings I did in those first months after everything between us blew up. I have Alli now, for one thing, and I am happy. Happier than I think I was with Lauren. And, then there's the fact that Lauren is genuinely sorry and regretful. It hasn't occurred to me that our break-up has been difficult for her, too. That makes it harder to hate her. And regardless of Alli's request to be nice to Lauren, I feel that there's no desire for meanness on my part anymore. Lauren looks genuinely sorry, she can't even look at me when she says, "I know there's no way to fix things, or for us ever to be friends again or whatever. I just want you know—you never gave me the chance to tell you how awful I felt about everything and to say I am truly sorry. I know I must be the last person you wanted to see on your birthday but, this is the first time I've see you in... since then. So, I'll leave you alone, but I just wanted to tell you again, now that the dust has settled and all, that I'm sorry. Really sorry."

"Thanks. I appreciate that," I say. She looks at me sadly, realizing she's not gonna get any forgiveness from me tonight.

"Maybe next time I see you you'll accept my apology? Maybe even forgive me?"

"Maybe," I say.

She nods, willing to accept that answer. "I'm glad you've moved on. You two are cute together. You look happy."

"I am."

"That's great. I'm glad. I really am," she says, genuinely. "Well, I better get back to my friends now. Tell your girlfriend thanks again for the CD. She's really great."

"I'll tell her."

She smiles. "Thanks, and happy birthday." She holds her hand out for me to shake, which I do. Which feels like a very bizarre and awkward formality for two people who were once so intimate not so long ago. I can still picture her naked if I want to. I can still remember the last time we had sex and the last time we exchanged "I love yous." I don't think about those things though. Part of you thinks when you break up a person you'll do just that, but it doesn't work that way. Sure, you might *think* about how you can still picture her naked whenever you want to out of spite, but you don't, not even when she's right there in front of you because that intimate part of your history seems trivial to the emotional baggage you carry after you've broken up.

"Don't you feel better now?" Alli asks me when she comes back.

"Were you watching me?"

"Kinda. You were nice, I hope?"

"Yeah, yeah."

"Good. You earned some points for later." She smiles and kisses me on the cheek.

CHAPTER 26

THE WEEK OF Candlepin's CD release party was full of excitement.

Alli had her third recording session at D-Line Records. It took most of the day, but I didn't care since Blake is no longer able to attend her recording sessions because Candlepin has been rehearsing a lot more in anticipation of the big event. Alli believes only one or two more sessions will be needed for recording, and then there will be editing and mixing, and finally mastering. Alli explains all this to me in a lot more detail but I really don't know much about all this stuff. She's excited though, even though it will require her taking some time from working to get everything done. It feels like a long time for such a small number of songs. But Alli insists that things are moving along at a good pace because it's just her and her guitar, making set-up in the studio much quicker, and the fact that she's managed to not need too many extra takes she's expecting to get ten songs completed instead of eight.

There's been quite a bit of promotion for the CD release party, and Alli has definitely benefited from the publicity it has received. One local music journalist interviewed Alli for a very high-trafficked Boston music website. Her album got a glowing review and described her as "a rising star on the Boston music scene." Another alternative weekly paper called her "the next Taylor Swift." Alli loved that, though she doesn't really believe it. She was also included in a story about the resurgence of country music in Boston. Alli doesn't consider herself country, but she plays country songs and is definitely influenced by the genre. She is usually described as a mix of "acoustic rock" and "country pop" and she says is a fairly accurate description. Since that piece was published it has opened some doors for future gigs at venues that cater to that scene.

Alli has been busier this week than perhaps any other time since we've been dating. She even gave up some shifts at Starbucks so she could devote more time to everything she needed to do for her music. Instead of going out for dinner or making dinner at home, we've been ordering in or I've been bringing take-out to her place.

* * *

Candlepin's CD release party seemed like a lifetime away when Nava had asked Alli if she would open for them, but now we're here and Alli is split equally with feelings of excitement and nervousness. The show is sold out, meaning there will be over 300 people there.

We get to carpool to the club with the band, all thanks to Blake, who, I'm happy to say drove separately. "He's driving down with the chick he's currently fucking," Nava colorfully explains. "That's why we were able to fit you guys in."

Even without Blake and his guest we barely fit in the van because of the extra passengers, like Nava's boyfriend and the wives of Andy the bassist and Hank the drummer. So, we're squished into the van, and it isn't very comfortable, but Blake isn't here, so I don't really care.

Blake and his "guest" are waiting for us in the parking lot when we arrive. I help everyone unload the van and bring everything in through the back. The guys from The Purnell Maneuver are inside with their stuff already, and they coordinate their setup with Candlepin and Alli. After the sound checks we set up the merch table and wait for doors to open up at 7 p.m., which gives us another hour before Alli's set starts. Devon arrives somewhere during this period, and after a brief acknowledgment of our presence she disappears amongst the growing crowd, most likely on the prowl.

When Alli finally goes on stage and gets a view of the crowd I can tell she's a little overwhelmed. The stage is four feet higher than the floor, and Alli she's used to playing on a stage a single step higher. It's early, but there are at least 200 people here now. The mad rush has stopped, but people are still trickling in.

She's wearing a red dress tonight and looks stunning. Thankfully, I don't have to run Alli's merch table until after her set because I'm really going to enjoy this.

She thanks the band for supporting her and asking her to open for their CD release party. She starts up with her song "Wallflower," and the crowd warms to her immediately. By the third song, she's no longer nervous, she's enjoying herself, and a synergy has developed between her and the crowd.

She addresses the crowd again towards the end of her set. "I'm gonna play a new song tonight, I just wrote it a couple weeks ago and I've never played it before, but it will be on my new album which is currently in the works."

The crowd cheers.

"That reminds me, you can pick up my first album... right over there." She points towards to her left, at the table to the right of the stage towards the billiard room. The merch table currently being manned by Justin, Candlepin's manager and the guy Devon brought home the same night I was with Emma, who she now can't stand.

"So anyway, this one goes out to my boyfriend, who is just really awesome, everyone give him a hand, he's right here." And she points me out in the front row and the crowd does what she says. Alli laughs at the attention I'm getting. Devon sneaks up beside me gets all excited too and hoots jumps all over me like we're in a mosh pit. I don't know if she's drunk yet, but she's definitely on her way.

The last few songs of her set she reserves for songs on her first album, which she reminds the crowd is on sale at the merch table. A guy near the stage shouts at her that he wants to give her a beer. Alli laughs. "Sorry, I'm not 21 yet. But thank you. I'm sure neither of us want this place to lose their liquor license."

"Take it! Take it!" he shouts.

"Sorry," she says. "I can't."

The guy is very drunk... and offended. He keeps shouting but Alli starts to play the opening chords of her next song. This pisses the guy off, so he puts his thumb on the top, shakes it, and aims it at Alli, spraying beer all over her. He laughs like nothing in the world was so funny. Alli looks absolutely horrified. I start rushing towards him. Before sense can take over me I swing at him. I can't even remember the last time I've ever swung at anyone like that.

And I miss.

Instead of hitting him in the face with my fist, my elbow ends up connecting with his chin. The drunk guy is unfazed by the impact but looks pissed at me. I make what is certainly a pathetic attempt at a fight stance, and he looks about ready to kill me before he is grabbed from behind. I'm relieved for a brief moment, because this guy, even drunk, was going to kick my ass. But then I realize it's Blake who has grabbed him. Not only did I miss my swing, but now Blake gets to be the hero? Could this get any worse?

Blake quickly overpowers the drunk and pulls him to the front, where he is thrown out by the bouncer.

Alli's set is officially over now. She's too upset to play on, but at least she was only going to play another song or two before wrapping up her set anyway. Alli goes upstairs to change out of her dress and back into her regular clothes, and I stay downstairs selling her CDs with Devon.

"Dude, that was awesome," Devon says.

"Not really."

"Are you kidding? You punched that guy. That was hardcore. You just made yourself a hero. Alli is gonna fuck your brains out tonight."

"I missed. My elbow only grazed him."

"From where I was standing..."

"Yeah, well, Blake was the one who managed to control the guy."

"Oh, well, that sucks. I guess Alli will fuck his brains out instead."

"What the hell?" I know she doesn't know about what happened with Lauren, but that really stung.

"Just kidding, dude! Seriously, chill out."

"Don't say shit like that."

"Oh please, like that girl would ever cheat on you."

I'm unable to respond because people are forming a line buy CDs.

By the time Alli comes back down the first box is already empty, and we've cracked open another, which thrills her. When people who have bought one of her CDs notice she's returned they come back to have her autograph them. She's a little embarrassed but she obliges them all. Some even ask her about what happened and make sure she's okay. Alli tells a bunch of twenty-something girls she's fine now and the girls all agree the guy was a jerk and should have been kicked out earlier and one tells us that he even showed up at the club drunk. Alli doesn't want to talk about it anymore and changes the subject back to how they enjoyed her set. Like a bunch of schoolgirls, they are excited to tell her how much they loved it, and that they can't wait to see her play again.

I sit with Alli while The Purnell Maneuver are on stage. She's still a little shaken about what happened, but, by the time Candlepin take the stage she's in a good mood again. The guys in the band are dressed alike in bowling jerseys, and I'm pretty sure they are all wearing bowling shoes too. Nava however wears a skimpy, low-cut dress. She thrusts her hips suggestively to the beat of their opening song, flaunts her breasts and shakes her ass without any trace of self-consciousness.

Nava grabs the microphone to address the crowd. "In case you didn't know, we are... Candlepin!"

The crowd cheers.

"What the fuck was that?" Nava shouts. "You guys can do better than that!"

The crowd cheers again, even louder this time, if that was even possible.

"Fuck yeah! Okay, thank you all for coming out tonight for the release of our new album, *Steering Wheel*—" the crowd interrupts her with heavy applause, and Nava bows. "That's what I'm talking about!" She bounces around the stage and then returns to the mic. "I'd like to introduce the band... of course, you all know who I am, so I don't need to introduce myself—" the crowd cheers. "But to my left is Blake Kelly on keyboards!" The crowd cheers. Everyone except for me. "Behind me we have Hank Garcia on drums!" More applause. "And of course, we have the two Andys! Andy O'Brian on guitar and Andy Walsh on bass!" The crowd cheers. Nava does another little dance on stage. "Okay, so before we get started, I'd like to make announcement. I, Nava Ackerman... your lead singer tonight... am totally... and completely... not drunk yet!" The crowd boos. "I know, right? You know what you gotta do!" It's not long before someone approaches the stage with enough shots for the entire band. "That's what I'm talking about!" The band takes their complimentary shots and after another suggestive dance by Nava she grabs the microphone and starts to sing. She's really into her performance. When she talks to the crowd between songs, she calls out her friends when she can see them and accepts drinks from fans when they are delivered. We're all having a good time. During their second set Devon buys the band a round of shots and they make a ceremony of it. Alli and I usually leave after one set so she can go to sleep earlier for a morning shift, but tonight we're here for the whole show, and it's great. The energy in the room is amazing.

Candlepin play as long as they can before the venue manager tells them they have to stop. Within fifteen minutes half the people have left, and a few people who didn't buy a CD before the show make their purchase. Alli sells out of her second box of CDs, and most of a third box... this her biggest sales night ever.

Word of an after-party spreads quickly. Nava is telling anyone she thinks is cool enough (basically anyone she recognizes despite her inebriation) where to go. She thrusts herself in between Alli and me from behind and puts her arms around our necks. Her breath is a mélange of various alcoholic drinks she's consumed over the course of the evening. She tells us we have to go to the party.

"It sounds like fun to me," I say to Alli after Nava finds more victims to harass. I've had such a good time tonight I don't want it to end.

"Not to me. I hear all they do at these parties is get drunk and smoke pot. I don't want to be a part of that. Besides, I do have to work a morning shift tomorrow."

"Oh yeah."

"You sounded disappointed."

"No, I didn't know what goes on those things. Actually, I am kind of tired." After saying this, I realize just how true it is. While I'm no stranger to late nights, a whole evening of music and the occasional drink has taken its toll on me.

"I am too. Let me just grab my dress upstairs and we can Uber back to my place."

"I'll take that," I say, indicating the guitar case she's holding.

"Thanks," she says, and hands it to me before heading back upstairs to retrieve her dress.

Devon finds me. She's drunk, of course, and excited because she's heard about the after party from Nava. When I tell her we're not going she's pissed.

"You two can fuck each other later, come on!"

"We're not... Look we're tired, Devon. It's been a long night."

"Bullshit you are, Mr. Hero. It's an after party. How many of those have you ever been invited to?"

"I'm not a hero," I insist, and not because I'm being modest. "And we're exhausted."

"We're exhausted!" she mocks. "Don't bullshit me. You know you're going back to fuck."

"I told you—"

"Yeah, yeah, you're *tired*. As if anyone will believe that." I don't blame her for her assumption, and I wouldn't doubt that anyone else who cares that Alli and I aren't going to the party will think the same thing because why else do you pass on a perfectly good after party? "Fine, whatever dude, *I'm* going to the party."

A few minutes later Alli comes back with her beer-soaked dress on the hanger. "You ready?"

Before we can leave, Blake comes to tell us about the after-party, which Alli explains we won't be attending. But we offer to help load up the van before we go. Blake offers me the keys to the van and asks me to unlock it and back it up closer to the rear entrance of the club and suggests Alli can help pack up the audio equipment. Real smooth. Of course, he would do that to get himself alone with Alli. I know if I protest it will upset her, so I oblige without protest. We're near the front door so rather than go out the back way I walk outside to the parking lot.

As I walk by the liquor store I can't help noticing a familiar face, and that familiar face recognizes me. It's the guy who sprayed Alli with the beer, but he's with someone else now, and they're drinking out on the sidewalk. Hardly a good sign. I can tell I'm being followed.

"Yeah that's him." I hear the guy saying behind me. Something is about to happen, I know it. There will be other people in the parking lot, I assume. If not, someone will come out. As long as there's people around, I'll be fine.

I think. I hope.

He's got a bottle of something in his hand, and drinks directly from it.

"Hey! You!" I hear the guy say from behind me just as make it the parking lot. I don't see anyone back here yet.

I am screwed.

Do I pretend not hear him? Do I run? I don't even have time to decide because a hand grabs my shoulder and turns me around. I barely get a chance to look at the guy's face because all I see is the bottle in his hand coming down on me. In a split second everything goes black.

CHAPTER 27

I GRADUALLY BECOME aware that the Candlepin crew are all crouched down around me. The band, the wives, and significant others.

"He's up," says Hank. "You okay, man?"

I look around, I can hear Alli freaking out, but I can't see her because everything's a bit blurry.

"What happened?" I ask.

"A couple of guys jumped you," Hank explains. "Lucky for you that Blake showed up."

"Blake?"

Hank and Blake help me to my feet. I feel pain all over.

"Yeah, some guys were kicking the shit out of you when he came out and scared them off."

Great. Just what I need... Blake coming to my rescue.

I try to walk, but I feel a little dizzy, and brace myself against the van. Alli comes running at me and hugs me. If it wasn't for the van, she would have knocked me over. She's been crying, I can tell.

"I'm okay, I'm okay," I assure her. "Just a little dizzy."

"I'm so, so sorry," she says.

"I'm fine. Those assholes from the show just wanted the last word, I guess," I say.

"I'm so glad you're okay," she whispers, and hugs me even tighter. It hurts, but I don't care.

"Yeah, he'll be fine," Blake says, officially interrupting our moment, and probably to show off in front of Alli and the girl he brought. "Good thing I got there when I did."

Yup. Definitely showing off.

Alli breaks from our hug to give one to Blake. "Thank you, so much. If you hadn't gotten there... I mean... who knows what—"

"No problem, kid," he says like it's no big deal. And now my physical pain has become physical anger. It's bad enough that he's the one who rescued me when I was getting my ass whooped, but now she is hugging *him*, thanking *him*. Even though he's here with another girl he's managed to show me up and come to my rescue, and in both cases it makes him look like a hero to Alli. Sure, he's done me a huge favor by coming to my aid before those assholes beat me to a bloody pulp while I was unconscious, but I can't help hating him even more right now.

Once everyone is satisfied that I am okay, Alli and I Uber home. She is still so shaken up when we get back that I have to use her keys to let us in. I'm still sore and have a headache. Alli notices and guides me into her room and tells me to lie down on her bed.

"Do you need anything? Ibuprofen or—"

"Yeah, that would help. Head still hurts."

"I'll be right back."

Alli leaves me in her room. I sit up, waiting for her to return. This is the first time I've been in here, but I'm too hurt and too tired to look around. When she comes back, I take two pills and some water.

"Well, that was an interesting night," I say.

Alli starts to cry. "I'm so sorry Nick. I'm so sorry. When I saw you on the ground like that—"

"Hey, it's okay. I'm fine."

I hug her and she gradually calms down.

"You better?" I ask.

"Yes," she says, wiping the wetness from her face. "I'm sorry. I just..."

"It's okay. I understand. If you ever got hurt, it would kill me, you know?"

"That's what it felt like. I didn't know what happened or how badly hurt you were. I thought you were..."

"Hey, don't worry. I'm still here. And if I have anything to say about it, you'll never lose me. I love you, Alli."

I hadn't exactly planned to say those three words. They just came out. The last girl I ever said "I love you" to was Lauren, and the first time I did, I was nervous. I'd waited quite some time to tell her because I got myself worried that she might not say it back. She did, and everything was great... at least until things ended. I'd not expected to fall in love again so quickly. When you get hurt by someone that's usually one of the first things you promise to yourself. But I just couldn't help it with Alli. And, after I say it to her, I'm not nervous, because even if she doesn't say it back, I mean it with every fiber of my being and I'd rather her know what I feel now than put it off and risk waiting too long.

Alli looks at me, there's surprise on her face, but relief as well. So much hinges on this moment.

"You—you really love *me*?" she asks.

"Yes. I do."

"I—I love you, too, Nick. I didn't think... I never thought..." She struggles to find the right words. She gives up, flustered.

"A little... overwhelming, huh?" I ask.

She nods, and I kiss her. I don't make any other moves, I just... try to enjoy the moment while fighting back the pain I still feel from the beating I took. Eventually, I pull back, and can see she's still trying to process what's just happened between us.

"Wow, so this is what it's like. To be... *in love*. Wow."

I lean in to kiss her again, but this time Alli notices me wince from the pain.

"Oh, Nick, you should really rest."

"I'm okay."

"This is not up for debate. My house, my rules, okay?"

"Okay."

"You can stay in here. I'll be out there."

I lie back down on the bed and Alli turns off the light and shuts the door.

* * *

I wake up in the morning, having slept through the night. In addition to having slept in my clothes I slept on top of the covers of Alli's bed. My headache is gone, but I'm still sore and achy.

Alli is out in the living area, folding sheets on the couch.

"I'm sorry," I say. "I didn't mean to take your bed."

"It's okay. You needed to rest anyway." She's been up for a while. Her still wet hair and fresh clothes tell me she's had enough time to shower and get ready for her shift while I was sleeping. She's pacing around the room tidying up.

"Are you okay? You seem... distracted."

"There's something we need to talk about."

This doesn't sound good. She's regretting telling me she loved me last night and is gonna break up with me.

"You're not breaking up with me, are you?"

"No, no... of course not. I—"

"You're not... regretting what you told me last night, are you?"

"Oh, no! Not at all... definitely not." She smiles, but it's a nervous smile. She reaches her hand towards me, taking mine and leading us to the couch to sit down. She's shaking, I can feel it. She's really nervous.

"So, what's wrong?"

"Nothing, I—I just... Remember a month ago when you asked me to keep the bombshells to a minimum?"

"Yeah..."

"Well, I have another bombshell for you," Alli says.

"This doesn't sound good."

"It's not bad."

"You sure?"

"I promise."

"Okay. Is this a bigger bombshell than the last one?"

"Yes. Definitely."

"How much bigger?"

"A lot. I assure you this is the last one. I've wanted to tell you so many times, but I just didn't know how. This isn't something I can tell anybody. But we're in love, and it seems wrong to not to tell you. But it's going to change everything."

"Sounds huge."

"It is. You won't believe me when I tell you."

"I'll believe you."

"You won't, and that's okay. I wouldn't either."

"So how does this work then?"

"I'm going to tell you, and then I'm just going to have to prove to you I'm telling the truth."

"Well, you better tell me quick because I'm starting to get worried."

"Okay, well, see, you know I've been very... private about my family, and why I wasn't living with my parents before I moved here."

"Wait... This bombshell is about your family?"

"It's about my family. It's about me. It's why I'm a musician. It's why I never had a boyfriend before you. It's why I almost broke up with you at your mom's house."

"I don't understand."

"I'm rambling. I'm sorry. I'm just nervous." Alli collects herself. "Okay. Remember at the show at Revolution, when you asked if Alli was short for Allison?"

"Vaguely." I remember thinking her response was weird, but I never gave it much thought afterwards or figured it was significant in any way.

"And I said it wasn't?"

"Right."

"Well it's actually short for Calliope."

"Just like the daughter of Randall Crawley from Perch?"

"Exactly like her. See, Nick... I *am* her. I'm Calliope Crawley."

PART 3

Calliope Crawley

From Wikipedia, the free encyclopedia

Calliope Crawley is the only child of Randall Crawley (1970 - 1999) the front man for the rock band Perch, and actress Carmen Fisher (b. 1977).

Early Life and Family

Crawley was born December 31, 1995 in Las Vegas, Nevada. She was named after the Greek muse of epic poetry.

According to Randall Crawley, "Heart", the opening track and lead single from Perch's 1998 album *Odyssey* is about the birth of his daughter. The song reached number seven on the *Billboard* Top 100. Crawley has a heart-shaped birthmark on her back and shortly after her birth, Randall Crawley got a heart tattoo in the same place in her honor. Crawley and her mother, Carmen Fisher, had joined her father on tour in Europe two days before he died from a deadly combination of drugs and alcohol. It is not known when Crawley last saw her father. After the death of her father, Crawley was typically only seen in public alongside Fisher. When Crawley was eleven years old she attended the Hollywood premiere of *Harry Potter and the Order of the Phoenix* with her mother. Crawley is not known to have attended any other Hollywood events after that.

Personal Life

Between the ages of five and twelve years old, Crawley was frequently put in the care of relatives while her mother Carmen Fisher battled her own drug addiction. Following Fisher's arrest on drug-related charges in April 2008, Crawley was placed in the temporary care of her godparents Jack Hayward, former bassist for Perch, and his wife Melissa.

Crawley has been the subject of numerous tabloid articles, but Crawley has only given one official interview. In June 2009, thirteen-year-old Crawley spoke to *Rolling Stone* magazine about the ten-year anniversary of her father's death. In it she revealed she has no memory of her late father, and claimed she no longer listens to his music. "There's no reason people should think I have anything interesting to say about him. I don't remember him. I don't even listen to his music anymore. I wish everyone would stop asking me." When asked about her reportedly rocky relationship with her mother, she refused to give any details. "It's nobody's business." Crawley refused to take part in a photo shoot for the interview, which took place few months before she disappeared from the public eye. Carmen Fisher lost custody of Crawley in September 2009, but it is not known who obtained custody of Crawley as all documents relating to Crawley's new legal guardians were sealed to protect her privacy.

Crawley inherited her late father's estate, the publishing rights to his solo music catalogue, and a majority share of Perch's publishing rights on December 31, 2013, her eighteenth birthday, and has a reported net worth of $140 million. According to WhereIsCalliope.com, a website dedicated to Crawley and discussing theories on her current location, in 2014, Crawley reportedly tried to block the planned release of the 25th anniversary edition of Perch's debut album, *Lake Effect*, but Jack Hayward and former Perch drummer Rex Cobb both deny this, and the album is due for release May 2016. An unreleased Randall Crawley solo album is also rumored to exist, but neither Hayward nor Cobb claim to have any knowledge of it.

Disappearance

Crawley and Fisher reportedly became estranged while Fisher was in and out of rehab during the summer and fall 2009. Crawley's disappearance still fosters intrigue today. In 2014, she topped the *Buzzfeed* list "15 Celebrities Who Have Ditched Fame" and has appeared in similar lists on other pop culture websites. Carmen Fisher has since refused to talk about her daughter. However, various Twitter posts by Fisher suggest she and Crawley are still estranged.

CHAPTER 29

OF ALL THE things I expected to Alli to tell me, her being the daughter of my all-time favorite musician from my all-time favorite band was definitely not one of them. I figured she had an unhappy childhood. Maybe she was orphaned young, or the victim of abuse and taken away from her parents. I had no idea, but I imagined her bouncing between different foster homes before she ended up living with the Conwells permanently. Whatever she had gone through, she didn't want to be a victim of her circumstances and set out to do something she loved and work hard to sustain herself.

What can you say when your girlfriend tells you that she's the daughter of a famous deceased musician? A musician you idolized as a kid, no less.

The answer is: *nothing*. A bit fat nothing.

I'm at a loss for words and to be honest, feeling equal amounts of shock and skepticism. One of her strongest qualities is her stalwart honesty. But it's hard to wrap my head around the idea that she's Calliope Crawley, *the* Calliope Crawley. The daughter of late rock legend Randall Crawley.

How can this be possible?

I was ten when Randall Crawley was found dead in his hotel room while on Perch's European tour. I remember it well. His death shocked millions—myself included. I was glued to MTV for days. Like many fans I couldn't fathom the idea that there would be no more Perch. There have been all sorts of theories about what "really happened," whether he accidentally overdosed or if it was intentional. Some even wonder if he is really dead. Crawley was allegedly looking to start a solo career at the time he died, and some people believed he faked his death to start over. According to one theory, Randall Crawley is not only alive, but he and Calliope are living anonymously somewhere in the world making music and living off his royalties. I never questioned that he had actually died, but some people refused to believe it. I believed it, and I mourned.

Calliope Crawley was only two when he died. I do the math in my head, and Alli is at the age Calliope Crawley should be. Rumors of what happened to her are just as nutty as the ones about what really happened to Randall Crawley. Fascination regarding Calliope Crawley's whereabouts has waned over the years, but occasionally her name resurfaces, usually following some incident with Carmen Fisher. Since Calliope turned eighteen she's rumored to have tried to stop a number of planned releases like an album of B-sides and demos, or a rarities boxset. That kind of news typically rekindled interest in where she was, why she was allegedly trying stop these things, and of course, how she was even doing all this stuff off the grid. There was a list published less than a year ago of "7 Popular Theories on What Happened to Calliope Crawley." But, none of the theories listed said that Calliope Crawley's would end up living incognito here in Boston or that I'd be dating her.

Alli watches me pondering all this in silence for a while before she speaks. "You don't believe me, do you?"

"I—it's not that I don't *believe* you, I mean, I know you're an honest person and wouldn't lie... it's just—"

"Impossible? It's not. I *am* Calliope Crawley. But I can see from the look on your face that it's going to take more than me saying so to convince you."

"I—"

"Nick," she says, taking my hand. "It's okay. Really. I can't imagine anyone would believe this. And when I found out you were a fan of Perch, I knew that if I told you who I really was it would be difficult to accept without proof. I mean, I might not be a liar, but you might think I'm crazy." She tries to laugh to ease the tension, but she's still nervous.

"You're not crazy."

"Thank you. But I think it's important that I show you anyway, so there's no doubt in your mind."

"Okay."

Alli smiles and kisses me on the forehead. Then she turns her back to me and starts to pull her shirt up off her back.

"What are you doing?" I ask.

"Showing you proof."

"How—"

"You'll see. Hold on." She pulls her hair around to the front and unhooks her bra, completely exposing her back. Slowly I understand and see all that I need to see.

"Do you see it, or—"

"No, I see it." *It* is a small heart-shaped birthmark just below her right shoulder blade. She's not kidding around.

She *really* is Calliope Crawley. I find myself unable to say anything. I've seen this birthmark before, in pictures of Calliope Crawley from when she was a toddler. The sight of it now conjures up the memory and I know for sure she is Calliope Crawley.

What can I possibly say? This isn't something you normally find out about a girl you've been dating.

Alli rehooks her bra and pulls her shirt back down. "Nick are you gonna say something?"

"I'm sorry. I should have taken your word for it."

"Nick, really... I don't blame you." She leans in to hug me. "Are you okay?"

"Yeah, I think so."

"I was worried you might freak out."

"Really?"

"Yeah, you know, Mr. Perch Super Fan."

"So, that's why you nearly broke up with me at my mom's house?"

"Yeah. I just... you know... I got paranoid... I was worried I'd never know if you liked me for me, or for... you know... being Calliope."

"So, why tell me at all?"

"We're in love, and it just felt wrong to keep hiding this from you. I know it will change things, but I really hope they'll change for the better. There's so much I've had to keep bottled up inside me. So much I've wanted to share with you that I couldn't. As we got... closer, it got so difficult to dance around my past and who I am. I can only imagine what you must have thought every time I dodged questions or said 'it's complicated' or was just the vaguest girl ever when it came to her past. I was nervous telling you my birthday."

"So, what's with the new identity? Why'd you do that?"

"It's complicated—I know I keep saying that, sorry—but, you know, my relationship with my mom wasn't—still isn't—good. We haven't spoken since I was thirteen and with good reason. You probably know enough about her to know she's not the nicest person? Well, she wasn't very nice to her only daughter either. Her only interest in me seemed to be that I was the key to my dad's money. She's never said so, but I believe she got pregnant with me in the hopes he would marry her. I think she knew that her best days in Hollywood were over, since she was mostly famous for movies and sitcoms she starred in before she turned twelve. She met my dad when she was eighteen, they started dating, and before long she was pregnant with me. She used to encourage me to embrace my dad's legacy to my advantage, to give my own career a jumpstart, that I'd never make it without his legacy and money, that no one would love me without it. It was awful, Nick, to hear my own mother tell me I was worthless without my dead dad's fame and fortune."

"I... can't even imagine."

"So, yeah... we haven't talked for five years. I know this sounds awful, because she's my mother, but it's better that way. My life with her wasn't good. It was bad enough the courts agreed she wasn't fit to be my legal guardian anymore. As embarrassing as it is that my parents were never married, my dad was smart not to marry her. So, when she lost custody, I wanted to start my life over. I stayed with the Conwells while my mom was in rehab when I was seven and when I was ten. I remember being so happy staying with them, and we kept in touch when I went back to living with my mom again, or even when the courts put me somewhere else. When I was thirteen I was considered old enough to make some of my own decisions and I knew then I wanted to go back to living with the Conwells. So, I did what I had to do to make that happen. They were more than happy to adopt me. So, they did, and I changed my name, and here we are."

"Here we are," I say.

"So... are you okay with this? Nick? Are we going to be okay?"

"Yeah. I mean... I think so. This is all kinda weird and strange and unexpected... I'm still kind of... processing all this... but... yeah... I think so."

Alli looks relieved.

"So... you thought I would freak out?"

She smiles. "Yeah, I thought it was possible. I'm actually impressed at how... calm you are."

"Don't be fooled, I'm definitely... surprised and trying to process this information. I mean, it's not every day an ordinary guy like me finds out his girlfriend is famous."

"My parents are famous. I'm not. Nick, believe it or not, I'm really just an ordinary girl. I may be the daughter of Randall Crawley and Carmen Fisher, but that doesn't define me. Not anymore. I haven't done anything to be famous. I've been trying so hard to be my own person. To neither be a victim of my mother's cruelty or a beneficiary of my father's fame."

"It must be a hard secret to keep—you know, who you really are."

"Actually, not really. It was... *liberating* to have a new identity. The hardest thing was keeping it a secret from you. I've been praying and praying about it for a while now, waiting for a sign that it was the right time to tell you. When you told me you love me... I... not only knew the feeling was mutual, but that this was the moment I was waiting for... for someone to fall in love with me not knowing that

I was Randall Crawley's daughter. I guess part of me still believed my mother... you know... what she said."

"I'm sorry."

Alli wipes away a few tears. "I'm okay. Really. I'm happy."

"Me too."

She hugs me, and the pain makes me gasp.

"Oh, Nick, I'm sorry. I almost forgot! Let me get you something for—" Alli's cell phone starts vibrating. She takes it out of her pocket.

"Oh, Nick, I'm sorry, I'm supposed to go to work now."

Work? How can she possibly go to work at a time like this?

"Oh, I should go then?" I really mean it as a question, even in my state I can remember that Alli doesn't like anyone in her apartment when she's not there. Even me.

"No, I'll get some water and some ibuprofen. You can stay here and rest some more until I get back."

She goes to the kitchen to get me some water and pills, I lay down on the couch.

"You can take the bed while I'm gone... if you want," she says.

"You sure?"

"Of course." I take the pills and we go into her room. "We'll talk more when I get back, okay?"

I nod and she kisses me. "I love you," she says.

"I love you, too," I tell her.

When she leaves and closes the door, and I collapse on Alli's bed.

Calliope Crawley's bed.

I'm lying down on Calliope Crawley's bed.

Calliope Crawley is my girlfriend.

My girlfriend is Calliope Crawley.

My girlfriend is—

My phone vibrates. Jay has sent me a couple text messages about a project I should be working on. He apparently hasn't heard about what happened at the CD release party last night. I write back to let him know that I'm on it. There's a text from Devon as well. She has heard about what happened after the CD release party and is checking in to see if I'm still alive. I write back to tell her that I am very much still alive, then try to get back to resting. Of course, my brain is still on overload.

Alli is Calliope Crawley.

Calliope Crawley is my girlfriend.

My girlfriend is Calliope Crawley.

I say this to myself over and over in my head... trying to wrap my head around it.

CHAPTER 30

SOMETIME LATER THERE'S a knock at Alli's door. While my pain is getting a little better, falling to sleep seems to be impossible right now so I answer the door. It's a girl, about twelve or thirteen, with a dog who I recognize as Derby.

"Hi, is Alli here?"

"She's not, she's—"

"You're the boyfriend."

"Yeah. You must be..." I can't remember what her name is supposed to be.

"Eden. And this is Derby," she gestures towards her dog.

"Oh, I know Derby, we've met." Derby approaches me, and I pat him on the head.

"Oh yeah," she says and laughs. "Alli told me that story. That was funny."

"Yeah, it was. Did you need anything?"

"No, I was just seeing if Alli wanted to join me while I took Derby for a walk. Sometimes she joins me if she's home. I guess I'll just go by myself. Unless you want to come?"

"Me?"

"Yeah."

"Should you really be asking someone you don't know—"

"You're Alli's boyfriend."

"Maybe I'm not."

"I've seen, like, tons of you photos of you and her on her phone. I know you're her boyfriend."

"Smart."

"Thank you. So, I figure I'm safer walking with you than I am walking by myself."

"That makes sense."

"So, are you coming?"

"Sure." I suppose I could use the distraction anyway.

We walk Derby up the road, not saying much. Eventually, Eden decides to break the ice, which is good because I can't think of anything to say, and if she was waiting for me to say something, we probably wouldn't talk at all.

"So," she says. "Alli says you're a good kisser."

"Is that right?"

"Yeah, like *really* good."

"You two talk a lot about your boyfriends?"

"No. I don't have one. I'm only twelve. But we talk about you sometimes. She *really* likes you."

"I really like her, too."

"That's so cool."

"How come your dad couldn't walk with you?"

"Oh. He's fighting with my mom on the phone."

"I'm sorry."

"They're divorced. Or, in the middle of getting divorced."

"My parents are divorced too."

"Really?"

"Yeah, long time ago."

"Sucks, doesn't it?"

"Yeah, it does," I tell her, and explain how when my parents divorced it was tough for a while, but I got used to things. I tell her how my dad's work kept him traveling a lot, so he didn't try to get partial custody or anything. Just visitation. "Eventually both my parents remarried. It gets better, I promise." I don't tell her that my mother's second husband died.

"I hope so."

When we return to her house, I discover I've locked myself out of Alli's basement apartment.

"Oh, I know where the spare key is. I'll go get it," Eden tells me.

She goes up the steps, taking Derby with her. She's back in a couple minutes, without Derby, to let me in.

"I really shouldn't do this... but you were in there when I came here earlier... so... I guess it's okay."

"You were the one who invited me out, too."

"That's true." She laughs. "I guess it's my fault."

She stands there, like she doesn't want to leave.

"Ummm, can I stay here for a while? My dad and mom are still fighting on the phone. I won't bother you or anything, I'll just watch a movie on my phone."

"Has she been giving you refuge here a lot?"

"Sometimes, when she's here... and you're not." She gives me a teasing look.

"Okay, well I guess it's okay then."

So, we each take an end of the couch, Eden plugs earbuds into her phone to listen to music or watch a movie I guess, while I neglect my work responsibilities to do some research on Calliope Crawley. I'd never really given her much thought before. I may have been a Perch music fan and put some significant effort into getting high quality bootlegs and stuff like that, but I was never one of those people who would sit there thinking "I wonder what Calliope Crawley is doing right now."

The first thing I do is a Google image search. Most of the pictures are of her as a baby or a toddler with Randall Crawley. There are occasional photos of her in her preteen years, and some in her early teens, attending Hollywood events with her mother. I can see the resemblance, but her face is thinner now, and her hair is no longer blonde, but light brown. There's enough different that if you don't know who Alli really is (like I didn't) you wouldn't notice. I mean, how much do people really resemble their thirteen-year-old selves when they are nineteen?

A Google web search for "Calliope Crawley" brought me to her Wikipedia page, which was the top result over mostly gossip articles about her whereabouts and news stories about her mom's troubles with drugs and the law.

Most of the stuff I find knew already. I click through to WhereIsCalliope.com, mostly to see what was being said there about where she is. It's disturbing that such a website exists. There's a gallery page full of every known photo of her, from birth to not long before her disappearance. I check out reddit.com and find that there is a subreddit dedicated to discussing Calliope Crawley, and yes, it is still active. The theories discussed there range from the plausible but wrong, to the outright absurd. The absurd theories tend to be the popular ones.

Eden eventually gets bored watching her movie and starts asking me question about how things are going with Alli. I'm thrilled when Alli arrives to relieve me of trying to maintain this awkward conversation.

"Hi, Alli!" Eden says.

"Oh, hey Eden, I wasn't expecting to see you here."

"My parents..."

"I'm so sorry, sweetie."

"Nick walked Derby with me, too."

"That was very nice of him. Derby's not here, is he?"

"Nope, I know he's still on probation."

"Good. Listen, Eden, would you mind—"

Alli is interrupted by a muffled bang, and then yelling. We can't hear what's being said, but it's obvious that Eden's father is still fighting with her mother on the phone. Eden is not happy to hear this.

"Oh, okay. I can go."

"No, it's okay, you can stick around for a while," Alli says. She eyes me an apologetic look, but she's not going to send Eden back upstairs while her parents are still fighting.

So, the three of us watch TV together. Eden picks a movie on Netflix that I'm not particularly interested in, but about twenty minutes later, Eden determines it's safe to go back upstairs based on the lack of yelling through the ceiling, so she thanks Alli for allowing her to say, and apologizes for the intrusion.

"Anytime," she says, and they hug.

"Bye, Nick," Eden calls to me from the door. "Have fun you two." She makes an exaggerated kissing face at the two of us.

When Eden's gone Alli apologizes.

"I'm sorry about that. She's really having a hard time, I know we have... stuff to talk about... I just hated the idea of having her go back up there, when—"

"Hey, I've been there. I understand. Actually, it was really good."

"It was?"

"Yeah. I wasn't sure what it would be like now. I thought it might be weird and different, but really, sitting here watching TV with you two... the only weird part was Eden being here. But you know, it's cool."

"Good."

"She says you told her I'm a kisser."

Alli blushes. "I may have said something to that effect."

She leans toward me and kisses me. And I kiss her back, and things heat up quickly. She's unusually assertive, kissing more passionately than she usually does. Or maybe that's all in my head, I'm not sure, all I know is that before long Alli is guiding my hands to her chest. Usually, I'm the one initiating such things, and she has to stop me before I end up going further than she wants to. Today, though, I oblige briefly, then pull back to focus on just kissing her. This is unusual for me, and Alli notices. She stops and takes my hands in hers.

"What's wrong?" she asks.

"Nothing."

She looks at me like she's telling me she is not fooled.

"Come on, Nick. Usually I'm the one pushing your hands *away*. I thought you said things were okay."

"They are."

"I'm the same person as always, Nick. Maybe the context has changed a bit, but I'm still the same girl you've been dating these past couple months."

"I know," I say.

So we resume. It's a little strange at first, but after a while, I'm not thinking *Holy shit, this is Calliope Crawley*, I'm just thinking how nice it is being with her.

After she whispers to me that we better stop she looks into my eyes and smiles.

"We're going to be okay, aren't we?" It's not really a question. She knows.

"We're absolutely okay now." I tell her, smiling back.

Now that we've stopped Alli feels she wants to work on some new songs, and I gotta do work I've been putting off because of my earlier research on Calliope Crawley.

There's nothing to do on the Burnham & Modine project yet, since, in the past month and half since we got the job they've been difficult to meet with to discuss it. There's been one meeting at their office, which I made Jay go to alone because I didn't want to risk the chance of seeing Emma there. Even though she said there were no hard feelings between us, I think avoiding her is the best course of action. When I explained the situation to Jay he understood. Thankfully, we got a deposit, but we're gonna have to meet with them soon because it would be great to have something to bill them for. So, until that project is running full steam, I have some smaller projects to work on, and some final touches on the new site for Revolution, which is nearly finished.

As I work, I can hear Alli in her room. Her door is shut and she's likely working on lyrics, and melodies and chord progressions and whatever else she does to write her songs. I think it would be cool to watch her sometime, but I am sure she needs privacy during that process. She's got notebooks full of her poetry and lyrics that I've only heard about, but never seen. After a couple of hours I've basically caught up with my work, but Alli is still going strong in her room. So, I resume my earlier Googling of Calliope Crawley. The most recent news stories that mention her are stories about her mother's drug and alcohol troubles, and various attempts to reboot her career, including pitching a reality show revolving around her that never got picked up.

Most of the stories that were really about Calliope are from the months after she turned eighteen, when she reportedly tried to stop various Perch music releases.

"Whatchya reading?" Alli says from behind me.

"Oh... just about you."

"Oh yeah? Like what?"

"There are lots of people who have too much time on their hands wondering where you are."

Alli sighs. "I know. It's awful."

"You've looked?"

"I have. Once. Is there anything you wanted to ask?"

"Such as?"

"You know, 'Did you really do this?' or 'What happened with that?' That kinda stuff. If you're looking me up online you must have some things you'd like to know about."

I definitely have questions. "Okay... maybe a few... but, they're not important."

"Of course, they're not important, but you know, now that you know who I am, I'm more than happy to open that part of myself up to you and talk with you about it."

"Okay."

"So, let's have it."

"Okay, well, I guess..." I know what I want to ask but can't quite figure out how. I'd like to know why she's living in a basement apartment and juggling a job at Starbucks and her music career when she doesn't have to.

"You're wondering about the money, aren't you? Why I chose to live in a basement apartment, basically working two jobs?"

"Pretty much."

"Well, that's easy. I told you before that I'm trying to be my own person. To make it on my own. I also mentioned how my mother told me I'd never amount to anything without my relying on my father's legacy."

"So you want to prove to your mother she was wrong?"

"No, I want to prove to *myself* she was wrong. And so far, I feel like I have. I might be living in a basement, and still working a second job to support myself right now, but I'm confident I'll be able to support myself solely with my music within a year or two. If things continue to go as well as they have the past month or so, anyways."

"Makes sense."

"Is there anything else you'd like to know?"

Tons.

"Not right now," I say.

"Okay, well, don't be afraid to ask. It's nice to finally be able to talk about this stuff. I don't want to sweep it back under the rug and ignore it. It's a part of who I am, and it's been so hard keeping it from you."

* * *

The next morning Alli has another recording session at D-Line Records. So, Jay and I meet back at my place to go over our recent progress and look at some new proposals. Soon after we get our laptops set up in the living area, we hear the sounds of Devon having sex in her room. It's impossible to ignore, and not something Jay and I want to hear while we are working.

"We really should have these meetings at my place," Jay says.

"Your place is a mess."

"Hey, it's not as bad as it used to be."

"Uh huh."

"Seriously. We've cleaned."

"If you say so."

"Come over for retro gaming tonight. You'll see."

"I'm hanging out with Alli tonight."

"Bring her along."

"I doubt she'll have any fun watching us play video games."

"Pete is trying to speedrun through Super Mario Bros."

"Is that supposed to make it fun for her?"

"Seriously, he's at under seven minutes now."

"That doesn't change—"

"There will be other girls there for her to hang out with."

"Other girls are coming to watch you all play video games?"

"No, they're coming for the 80s movie night, we're watching—" Jay is interrupted by a sex scream from Devon's room. "Uh, we're doing a marathon of the *Indiana Jones* trilogy."

I know better than to point out that *Indiana Jones* isn't a trilogy anymore. After seeing the fourth one in the theatre together we agreed never to speak of it again.

"How long will that take, like six hours?"

"Almost. If we start the first one at seven we'll be done by one in the morning."

"Maybe another time."

"You chose *poorly*," Jay says.

"Yeah, well—" I start to respond but I'm interrupted by Devon coming out of her room in a T-shirt and gym shorts. The shirt is on backwards. She looks at us with faux embarrassment.

"Oh shit, I didn't realize you were both here," she says.

"Right," Jay says, doubtfully. "You knew what you were doing."

"Hey, it's not my fault the walls in this place leave little to the imagination." Devon retorts. She walks over to the kitchen and grabs a couple cans of Coke from the refrigerator. "You could have put some music on or something."

"We're working out here," I say.

"And?" The thought of us hearing what goes on in her room doesn't bother her in the slightest. "If Alli ever spends the night here, you won't hear me complain about the noise coming out of your room. Speaking of which, why doesn't Alli ever stay over? I thought she and I were cool now?"

Devon and Alli have, in fact, been "cool" ever since the incident with the guy who tried to steal Alli's tip money. But there are a number of reasons Alli spends little time here. As much as she and Devon are "cool" now, I don't think she likes to be reminded of the fact that I have a female roommate. Once Alli came over to watch a movie with me, and Devon came out of the bathroom in a towel after a shower. Rather than quietly go into her room, Devon felt it was a good idea to sit down and chat with us first for twenty minutes... in her towel. I could tell it made Alli uncomfortable.

If it's not stuff like that it's things like Devon's bras hanging on door knobs or hearing her having sex in her room that makes Alli feel awkward here. So, I don't bring her here hardly ever. And Devon has noticed.

"Yeah, you two are cool now," I explain to Devon. "But you know... she lives *alone*," I say, thinking this is a great explanation for Devon to interpret however she wants.

"See," Devon says to Jay. "Alli is totally a screamer in bed."

"Can you let us get back to work, please?" I say. "I don't have much time before Alli's show tonight."

"Whatever," she says, and amazingly, retreats to her bedroom.

"If they start up again, we're leaving," Jay says. I agree.

Jay and I finish up at Starbucks a couple hours later.

While I was working with Jay, and even when we were at my place with Devon, I wondered what they would think if they found out about Alli. I certainly wouldn't tell them, but imagining their reactions was amusing. I don't know how much either of them really like (or liked) Perch's music, but I know Devon has a faux vintage Perch t-shirt that she occasionally wears about the apartment, but for all I know it could have belonged to one of her... suitors, and not been something she purchased herself, since she was too young to even like Perch when they were active. We've never talked about it. It's been a long time since Perch ceased to exist. A lot of people may not have gotten over that, but most people I know have. Even me: I'd spent so many hours listening to Perch, collecting Perch rarities and collectibles and stuff that eventually I wore them out a bit. I still consider them my all-time favorite band, but I don't listen to them nearly as much as I used to.

CHAPTER 31

ALLI HAS AN open mic at a small coffeehouse near MIT tonight. It's small beans compared to opening for Candlepin's CD release party, and it doesn't even pay anything, but there's usually a crowd of fifteen to twenty college kids there (even on a Sunday night) and Alli likes to test out new songs to smaller, more intimate crowds. What really makes this significant is that this will be the first time I'll watch Alli play knowing who she really is. I have no idea if it will change the experience or not. Maybe it won't. But it will be amusing to think about the people watching the show who are listening and watching Calliope Crawley performing and not knowing it.

I can't help bringing this up after the gig on our way back to her place.

"Do you ever wonder what the crowd would think or do if they knew who you were when they saw you singing?"

"Sure. I used to, anyway."

"You think they'd like your music for the wrong reasons if they knew?"

"Maybe. Or the opposite. I'm not sure."

"Maybe they wouldn't care. I mean, just because they're Perch fans doesn't mean they'd care about what Calliope Crawley does."

"Nick, you've seen the websites about me, right?"

"Yeah, but you created intrigue by walking away from that life and identity."

"Maybe. But I don't think that's it. When we get back to my place I'll show you something."

Back at her apartment, she opens up Facebook on her computer.

"Look at this. Calliope Crawley has a Facebook fan page... about twenty-eight *thousand* fans... Alli Conwell has one hundred fifty-three. You see what I mean?"

"I think so."

"See, if everyone knew who I really was I wouldn't ever know if people liked my music for what it really is or if they just jumped on the bandwagon because I'm Randall Crawley's daughter. Or maybe just the opposite would happen. Maybe people would expect too much of me. I don't know. Either way, I don't want to be under my dad's shadow. I want to succeed or fail on my own. I want to do what I love doing and hope people can hear it without being biased. Me—Calliope hasn't been in the public eye for five years, and even when I was, I didn't do *anything*. Nothing to merit any interest aside from being Randall Crawley's daughter. And yet, twenty-eight *thousand* fans?"

"What do they say on there?"

"Oh, stupid stuff. And I don't just mean stupid theories about where I am. They act like they're fans of mine, like they adore and respect me. For what? I was thirteen the last time I did anything they even know about. So, all they know is that I had a famous dad who died, a mother who can't stay out of trouble and would drag me to various Hollywood events because even she knew that she was more famous as an adult for having a daughter with Randall Crawley than for anything she did in her adult career."

"That's for sure," I say. Carmen Fisher has been trying to rejuvenate her career for years, but she's never been as famous as she was when she was a child actor or Randall Crawley's girlfriend.

"It's really silly," she continues. "They'll comment on old photos and talk about the clothes I wore, as if I was making some fashion statement instead of just wearing whatever my mom made me wear to *look the part*. All they've ever seen of me is as a child who was forced into the limelight, and they think that automatically makes Calliope special? Once people know who I am... was... whatever... they will never see me as doing anything but continuing my dad's legacy. It's *my own* legacy I'm after. I want my music to mean something to people, you know? I don't want to be pre-judged because of a father I was too young to remember while he was alive. I don't even really feel like his daughter sometimes. If I'm gonna make it, I'm gonna make it on my own. Without my dad's name, or his money or his crazy fans who are desperate to find anything new connected to him be obsessed over."

"Let's just say, hypothetically, you really did make it one day. I know, I know that's not what you're setting out to do, but, you know, hypothetically, what if you make it one day, completely on your own? Would you ever reveal to the world who you are?"

"No," she says, without giving even a second to mull over.

"You're so sure of that. But you still told me. Why? You could have kept me in the dark too."

She sighs. "People do foolish things when they're young and in love." She laughs a bit, then quickly adds in more serious tone, "You know I'm kidding, right? You know why I had to tell you. Keeping the secret from you was a lot harder than keeping it from everyone else."

"I understand. I'm glad you told me," I say.

"And, you know, I figured if it was between having sex or telling you my real name, you'd prefer to know my real name." She laughs.

"I must have given you the wrong impression," I joke back.

She shrugs, holding back a laugh. "Well, now it's too late. I guess you're stuck dating a virgin."

"Well, what if I offered to tell you my middle name... what would that get me?"

"Hmm... an extra pillow for the couch?" Alli laughs hysterically.

"Deal. It's Owen."

"Well, I already knew that, so..."

We joke around for bit more, and it's nice. I imagine Alli is as relieved as I am that we can still tease each other like everything is normal and nothing's changed. Before long I remember something else I wanted to check.

"What about your dad? How many fans does he have on Facebook?" Perch ceased to exist long before Facebook was even thing, and I've never thought to check how many people still consider themselves a fan.

"Well, let's see... He's got just under two million. And... Perch has twenty-six *million*."

"Wow."

"They haven't done anything in over ten years, and they still can get twenty-six million people to call themselves a fan. I am grateful for the hundred and fifty-three that I have."

* * *

The next week we don't talk much about the whole Calliope Crawley thing. There seems to be an unspoken agreement to not dwell on it. So, things seem normal-ish. When I stay over I'm still on the couch, and when we fight we fight about the same stupid stuff as always. The most unusual thing was when Alli joined Candlepin for one of their rehearsals. She's opening for them again at the Lizard Lounge next week, but it was odd since she's never joined them for a rehearsal before. Of course, I was curious why and all she'd say was that it is a surprise.

The "surprise" happens in the middle of her set, when she puts her guitar on a stand and announces "I'm gonna do something a little different for the next couple songs," sits down at Blake's keyboards on the stage, then adjusts the microphone down to her height. The audience cheers. "Those of you who have seen me play before have only seen me play guitar, but, I also can play piano." They cheer again. "It's been a while, so I've had to practice. But I think you'll like it." Alli places her hands on the keys and plays some notes. The audience recognizes the song and starts to cheer. "I do need a little bit of help with this, so if Blake from Candlepin could kindly join me on stage I—" Alli is interrupted by cheers as Blake joins her. He takes the standing mic center stage and adjusts it higher for him. Blake is going to sing *with* Alli? What the hell is this? "Thank you, thank you," Blake says as he adjusts his microphone. When the crowd quiets down Alli speaks again. "I think most of you must know this song already, but for those that don't, this is Lady Antebellum's 'Need You Now.'" The crowd applauds, and the song begins. Everyone loves it. I may not like Blake (okay, I hate him) but I can't help thinking they sound really, really good together. They nail the harmonies perfectly. Still, I can't stand that he gets to sing with her. There's a strange intimacy on the stage (I don't know if it's because of the lyrics, or the melody, or something else I don't know about) and it pains me to realize that this is something Alli and I will never get to share since I can't sing. Instead she gets to share it with that douchebag Blake, who totally doesn't deserve to be singing a duet with Alli—Calliope Crawley for crying out loud.

Okay, he doesn't *know* that she is Calliope Crawley, but he knows damn well she is *my* girlfriend and he is singing with her on stage and looking at her in ways that just pisses me off. Alli knows I don't like him, but of all the people in the world she decides to sing with it has to be *him*? *What the fuck?* Does everybody who dates a musician experience uncontrollable jealously from their partner sharing moments on stage with other musicians of the opposite sex? It must happen all the time. How could it not? People who work in offices have affairs or even relationships with coworkers and Alli and Blake are kind of like coworkers. Working together a lot and having enough of the same interests that you chose the same line of work is certainly a good starting point for an affair.

Alli and Blake take a bow when the song is over. But they are not done, they are going to do one more song together, but this one Alli resumes her spot center stage with her guitar. Blake takes a seat at his keyboards. "This song you probably know too, it's called 'Bright' by Echosmith," Alli announces to the crowd. She's played this song at gigs before, but this time Blake performs the backing vocals. Again, the crowd digs it. What if Alli thinks it went so well that she and Blake should become a duo act? Would she do that? I can't really see it, but at the same time, listening to them I totally could... and the thought scares me.

After the set Alli asks me what I thought of the duets and my unenthusiastic response prompts her to take my hand and lead me outside. I know there's a lecture coming, but there's really nothing I can say that won't make me sound like a jealous asshole. But when we're out on the sidewalk she looks at me with a sad expression.

"I really thought you'd like it."

"You did great, really."

"But you didn't like it?"

How do I explain my distaste for Alli sharing the stage with Blake? It's not as if she had a choice between the two of us on who to sing with and I got rejected. It's just that she really seems to enjoy singing with him and music is just not something I can compete with him over. There are plenty of other things I am sure there would no contest between us. He is bigger, most certainly stronger than I am. And while I am hardly one to understand how women are attracted to men, on a superficial level I think it's safe to say he beats me on the scale of physical attractiveness. Why wouldn't Alli be drawn to him? He has musical talent and he's better looking. And now that I think about it, Alli has talked about him more than usual lately. I can't believe this. I never used to be like this. I've never been a jealous boyfriend before. I hate it, but I can't help it.

"I just prefer it when you play on your own."

"Was it me singing with someone else that bothered you, or me singing with *Blake*?"

My inability to respond right away answers the question for her.

"Come on, Nick, you shouldn't—"

"Something just rubs me the wrong way with him," I explain. "He shows up to your gigs on his nights off. He seems way too interested in helping you out. And whenever I ask him about why he moved here from California I keep getting bogus answers. It's like he's hiding something."

"I was hiding something, too."

"That's different. He's not—"

"Nick, he moved here after getting divorced."

"How do you know that?"

"He told me when we went out to lunch that time. I don't know what happened, exactly, because I didn't want to pry, and obviously I don't want him asking *me* too many questions about my past either, but I guess he took it hard and wanted to start over. He said he doesn't like to talk about it. Okay?"

"So, why did he tell you?" I ask.

"Because we're friends, I guess. I suppose he wanted to tell someone."

I'm not sure I accept this explanation, but what else can I do? Alli didn't tell me about her past until two months into our relationship, and only after I had told her I love her and she said she loved me. But her secret was huge. Blake had a rough divorce? Big deal. Something doesn't add up. I don't want to say this, so I don't say anything, and that seems to bother Alli even more.

"So, perhaps you should be a little more understanding about someone who doesn't want to talk about their past," she says.

"But—"

"Just stop. You shouldn't worry about it, and you shouldn't worry about him singing with me."

And now I'm an asshole, and not because she thinks I am, but because she was trying to impress me, and I've made her feel terrible about her attempt, despite her innocent intentions. *Why am I so stupid?*

"Nick, I know you don't like him. I didn't mean to upset you, I didn't even plan on singing with him, but he suggested it when I was rehearsing on his keyboards, and I thought it might be fun. I'm really sorry if that hurts you, but it shouldn't. I just wanted to try something different."

"I know. I'm being an idiot," I say. I don't think my jealousy is irrational, but a little self-deprecation seems like the best way to diffuse this situation.

"Yes, you are. I don't think I should have to apologize for singing with Blake. He's a nice guy trying to start his life over. Kind of like how I wanted to start my life over by coming here. I'm sorry that my singing with him makes you feel bad. I really am. And knowing it makes you feel bad makes me feel awful, like you must think I'm a bad girlfriend. "

"You're not a bad girlfriend."

"Then why do make me feel like one every time Blake does something nice for me or when—" Alli is too upset to finish her sentence. I try to hug her, but she steps back away from me.

"Don't. Okay? Look, I don't like it when you are jealous. It makes me feel terrible, like you don't trust me."

"I will. I promise I'll be better. I—"

"Let's just forget about it." She wipes the wetness from her face. "I'll be inside in just a few minutes, okay?" she says turning away, basically telling me to leave her alone. I don't really want to leave Alli outside, but I'm not about to piss her off again since I'm on thin ice right now.

Nava bombards me when I go back inside. She's looking for Alli. I tell her she's outside and Nava looks at me like she's knows something is wrong. So she goes outside to look for her. A few minutes later Alli is back inside. She's collected herself and has found me sitting at a table alone. Nava must have said something to her because she apologizes for overreacting and getting upset with me. I insist that I was in the wrong, not her, but she shakes her head and says she should have realized, knowing how I feel about him, that her singing with Blake would upset me, and she tells me it won't happen again.

Thank you, Nava!

I know the right thing to do here is to insist she can do whatever she wants, so I tell her not to not do it again on my account and I'll be okay with whatever she chooses to do. I know I won't be thrilled to see them sing together again if it happens again, but, I think I'd rather her sing with Blake again than have her still upset so I add, "You were great. And I don't want to hold you back from doing what you want to do or from doing things to help you grow as a singer."

She looks at me, pleasantly surprised, and hugs me.

"Thanks. I'm so lucky to have found you," she whispers in my ear. She so easily could stayed have been pissed at me for being a jealous asshole, and honestly, I would have deserved it. I want to apologize for every stupid thing I have done in this relationship so far and everything I will do in the future because I know that I'm bound to do or say something to make her upset with me and I could use some assurance from her that she'll not let those occasional errors in judgment lessen her opinion of me. But it's nice being out here now, I could stay right here, like this, for hours. I think Alli could too.

And then Blake decides to ruin the moment by showing up. And I hate him again.

"Great job, Alli," he says.

"Thanks, Blake."

The asshole looks at me. "What's up, Nick?"

"Not much," I say, putting my arm around Alli. I notice his eyes shift to notice what I've done with my arm.

That's right asshole. This girl you asked out and rejected you, she's with me.

"I'm looking forward to the show," I add.

"Uhh, thanks. I gotta get up there in a few, but, I just wanted to say you sounded great up there."

"Thanks," Alli says. "You too."

"We'll have to do that again sometime," Blake adds.

"Yeah, maybe," Alli says. Blake notices her noncommittal response, and so do I, but he doesn't say anything. Part of me wants to jump for joy at how deflated he must feel.

"Great, well we're about to go on. I'll see you two later."

As usual, Alli and I only planned to stick around for Candlepin's first set since Alli has to open at Starbucks in the morning. When Candlepin take the stage we take a spot upfront. Alli stands in front of me and I wrap my arms around her and she leans back into me. This is about as affectionate as she likes to get in public, but I rub her arms and even kiss her neck a couple times when I suspect we're in Blake's field of vision. At one point he makes eye contact with me.

See this, Blake? This girl is with me. Don't ever try anything with her or I'll kick your ass.

Okay, I doubt Blake is worried about any physical altercation we might have. He's a head taller than me and is obviously quite strong. I can't even say I've been in a real fight before. Alli is worth getting into a fight over, and if he tries anything, I don't care how much bigger than me he is, I am gonna... do something.

CHAPTER 32

IT'S BEEN NEARLY two weeks now since Alli told me that she's Calliope Crawley. Each day it seems like I've gotten more used to the idea. I've even forgotten about it a couple times because after the initial shock wore off I generally don't think about it unless something specific forces the thought on me, like her first gig after telling me... of course it would occur to me how bizarre it was that these people were watching Randall Crawley's daughter and not even know it. And when she sung with Blake a couple nights ago I certainly didn't think he was worthy of singing with *the* Calliope Crawley. I don't think he's worthy of singing with Alli Conwell either, for the record. Today, after realizing it's the anniversary of Randall Crawley's death, I can't help thinking about it again. I wasn't going to bring it up to Alli at all, because I just have no idea how she might still be affected by his death.

And then she brings it up while I'm at her place.

"So, do you remember what day it is?" she asks.

I tell her that I do know. Perch fans don't forget such things.

"I nearly forgot about it," she says, then thinks to herself for a few seconds. "My gosh... June 11, 1999 was sixteen years ago. I can't believe it. I wonder if people still go."

At first, I don't know what she's talking about, but then I remember that hardcore Perch fans have been making annual "pilgrimages" to Randall Crawley's grave near Buffalo, New York on the anniversary of his death. They're referred to as RandallFests. Last year being the fifteenth anniversary of his death, it was a particularly big one. I've never gone. When I was younger I used to want to go, but it just seemed like a really long way to drive. It's not like anyone famous ever attends either. So, you really just are going to hang out with a bunch of people who can't get over the death of one rock star. Don't get me wrong, I love Perch's music and all... but that's a level of dedication I just didn't have. I've read on the internet that people believe Calliope Crawley goes every year incognito, which gets me thinking.

"Have you ever been there?" I ask.

She looks down at the floor and shakes her head. "No, I haven't."

"Do you... want to go sometime?"

"When all those super fans are there? Not really."

"I'm not saying we should go to a RandallFest. I just mean in general. We could go. I'll take you. Whenever you want to go."

"Have you ever—"

"No. I may be a fan, but I always thought those fans were kind of nuts. Especially after all these years."

"Really? Honestly?"

"Well... Maybe when I was younger I thought it be cool to go."

"Well I'm glad you're not one of those people who go every year or have been even once. I'd probably have to break up with you," she jokes.

I feel like she's avoiding my question about going there sometime. "If you want to go out there sometime we could," I say. She says nothing. "No pressure or anything... just, you know... if you want to."

"We... could do that. It's a long drive though."

"That's no problem," I tell her.

"I have thought about going for years... But..."

"You know what... isn't his birthday coming up?" I pull out my phone to look it up. I know he died shortly before his twenty-ninth birthday, but can't remember the exact date.

"June twenty-first," Alli says. "That's less than two weeks away."

"Should we go?" I ask.

"Yes," she says instantly. "Let's do it."

I'm not sure who is more surprised, her or me.

* * *

Clearing my schedule to do this trip was easy. I only had to promise Jay that I'd bring my laptop in case I needed to work on anything while I was gone. Alli, on the other hand, had to request the time off from her boss at Starbucks, which, thankfully, was not a problem. She only had one gig scheduled during the time we'd be gone, and she was (eventually) able to trade slots with another singer to clear her schedule.

The plan is to drive out on Saturday, which will take eight to ten hours depending on how many stops we make. Sunday is the anniversary of Randall Crawley's death, and we will go to the cemetery. How long we will spend there, who knows? But, if we go in the morning, we'll still have a whole day to do whatever we want. Part of our cover story is that we're going to Niagara Falls, so at some point we will have to stop there, and that will be the day to do it. The next day we'll drive home. Alli doesn't have to go to work again until Tuesday evening, and we'll be back probably late Monday evening. There's also a distinct possibility plans could change. We are, after all, going to Randall Crawley's hometown. There are lots of places to go that die-hard Perch fans have made pilgrimages to. I found everything we needed without much effort thanks to Google, such as the name and location of the cemetery, even a crudely drawn map detailing where Randall Crawley's grave was, and a photo. It's crazy the things you can find on website by obsessed fans. One site even had a list of addresses of various locations in the area relevant to Randall Crawley's life. His boyhood home, bars he played at with Perch or previous bands he was in, his dorm building at the local college where he spent one semester before dropping out. It was fascinating and creepy at the same time. Alli and I haven't discussed going to any of these places yet because I was worried the idea of all that might overwhelm her, and she'd cancel the trip. And she has expressed some doubts about taking this trip a few times. So, I kept quiet about the planning, made arrangements with a hotel early on, and didn't tell her until after I made the reservation. I told her I didn't want her to be concerned with all the details; that she had enough to think about without worrying about all that. That was true, but I didn't want her to chicken out, or worry about paying for it.

Perch was always described as a band "from Buffalo, New York." Like most bands that achieve some level of fame, their hometown is usually assigned to the nearest metropolitan city to their actual hometown. Most fans of Perch, and more specifically, Randall Crawley, knew that Crawley's hometown was not the city of Buffalo but a town called Fredonia, fifty miles south of Buffalo... and there's a lot of Randall Crawley related things we can do between them.

Alli liked the idea of stopping at Niagara Falls, if for no other reason than it meant she wouldn't have to lie about what we'd be doing when she asked for time off at Starbucks or in the event someone like Devon or Lacy asked her. It was the perfect cover story and no one questioned it. It was perfectly plausible, and neither of us have been there before. I wouldn't say it was on my bucket list, but it is certainly something I thought would be cool to see.

The only issue we had was deciding who would pay for the trip. I wanted to pay for everything, but she wouldn't hear of it. Since it was her dad's grave we were going to see she said the most she'd even let me pay was half, and I knew she wouldn't budge on that so I agreed.

* * *

The drive is long and uneventful. If I were making this trip by myself I'd be listening to Perch the entire way... maybe a selection of greatest hits, or a soundboard-recorded bootleg concert, which I have several of. But Alli wouldn't want to listen to that, and I don't even bother suggesting it. She is nervous and exhausted, both emotionally and physically since she didn't sleep much last night. She ends up sleeping through the first leg of the trip and I can't blame her. So, as she sleeps I listen to music... anything but Perch.

Alli wakes up when I stop for gas, so we have lunch first, fill up and get back on the road. She's better now that she's slept, and while I wouldn't call her chatty, she's talkative for the remainder of the trip. When we finally arrive at our hotel, we check-in and get settled. We made no plans to do anything related to Randall Crawley today, just unwind from the drive. Our hotel is on Lake Erie, so we take a short walk to check things out, then go out for dinner.

We have a nice dinner at a local brewpub and Alli seems to be in good spirits about the whole trip. After dinner we go back to the hotel and take a walk near the lake again before it gets too dark. It's not a bad night at all. No gigs, no late closing at Starbucks. It seems like nights like this are rare for us and we both enjoy it a lot. I don't bring up our plans for tomorrow, and neither does Alli. Back in the room, Alli fiddles around on her guitar and writes in her notebooks on her bed, while I catch up on as much work as possible on mine. I still have work to do when Alli decides to go to sleep at 10:30. She brushes her teeth and changes in the bathroom, then kisses me goodnight before getting into her bed. So, now I'm working in the dark, with only the glow of my laptop monitor offering any light. It's a lot more difficult than it sounds so I give up and go to sleep.

* * *

I wake up to the sound of Alli drying her hair in the bathroom. She's gotten up extra early to shower and dress. After she leaves the bathroom she races around the room talking under her breath about what she needs to do get ready. She's nervous about today, that much is clear.

"You okay?" I ask. "You seem a little on edge."

"I'm sorry. I'm just nervous. I honestly don't know what this whole experience will be like for me. It all just hit me this morning when I woke up. I'm going to visit my dad's grave. I'm glad I'm here and that you're with me, but I also feel guilty I haven't been to visit him before."

"Maybe some breakfast will calm you down?"

"I don't think I can eat anything."

"I understand. If you're having second thoughts, just let me know."

"No, I want to do this. I have to, really. Take your shower and stuff and we'll go."

Alli is still nervous on the ride to the cemetery, and when I park the car and turn off the engine she doesn't move.

"You ready for this?" I ask.

"Not really."

"Do you want to come back later?"

She shakes her head.

"Do you want to—" I'm actually out of ideas as to what to do if she doesn't want to come back later. So we sit there for a few minutes before Alli summons the courage to open her door and exit the car.

"Do you want your guitar?" I ask.

Alli shakes her head. "Not yet. Let's find the grave first."

"Crap," I say. "I think I left the map of the cemetery at the hotel."

"We won't need it," Alli says with confidence. "I'm sure his grave will be covered with flowers, pictures, CDs and other stuff."

Sure enough, the grave was adorned with photos, flowers, and all sorts of memorabilia. There are also two kids sitting beside it, a guy and a girl. They both look around sixteen or so. Too young to have been fans when Randall Crawley was alive, but here anyway. One has a guitar and we could hear they were singing a Perch song, albeit not very well. I look at Alli, and she looks disheartened. She wasn't expecting anyone else to be here today. That was clearly a bad assumption on our part. "Do you want to come back later, when they're gone?" I ask.

Alli nods, and we start to walk out.

"It's about time some others showed up." The guy calls out to us. "Come on over!"

Caught, we turn around and approach them. Alli doesn't say anything, so I figure I got to speak. "Oh, is there a bunch of people supposed to be here?" I ask.

"No, actually. Most people come out here to pay their respects to Randall Crawley on the anniversary of his death. I dunno, that never seemed right to me."

"Right. We'll come back when you're done."

"No. Hey, stick around. The more the merrier, you know?"

I look at Alli. She shrugs.

"Did you bring all this stuff here?"

"Nah, it was all here when we got here. From the bigger gathering."

"Right."

"I'm Chris, that's Isabel. Iz and I been coming out here ever since I've been old enough to drive."

"Right. And how old are you?"

"I'm eighteen, Isabel is sixteen."

"Where'd you come from?"

"Pittsburgh."

"So, what do you do when you're here?" I ask.

Chris smiles. "Is this your first time out here?"

"Yeah, we're new at this," I say.

"It's great, we come out here and play his songs and hang out and stuff."

"That's it? Seems like a long way to drive just for that."

"No, we're gonna do a bunch of stuff in town, too. Besides, it's totally worth it anyway. When you think about how he's changed my life," Isabel says.

"How'd he do that?" Alli asks, her curiosity suddenly piqued.

"Well, his music really inspired me. His songs helped get me through some tough times you know?"

"We were about to leave to get something to eat when you guys showed up," Chris says. "We could wait a while if want, and all four of us could—"

"Oh, no," Alli says. "Don't let us keep you."

"Yeah, we might be a while," I say. "Since it's our first time here and all."

"Cool," he says, getting up from the ground. "We better be off then. Quite a few places to visit."

They pick up their stuff and start heading out. Alli keeps her distance from the grave until they pack their car up and leave. With them no longer sitting there we could see all of the items that have piled up around his grave. It was an interesting sight to see. He's been dead all these years, and fans still come out here. Even fans who were too young to have been fans when he was alive. It's bizarre to finally be here. With Calliope Crawley of all people.

I'm at Randall Crawley's grave with Calliope Crawley. How crazy is this?

"Unbelievable," Alli says softly.

"What?"

Alli points towards the grave at a picture of baby Calliope and her dad. I remembered the photo from years ago. It was taken as part of a photo session he did for a cover article in *Rolling Stone,* "Perch frontman Randall Crawley talks Fame and Fatherhood." I might still have a copy of that issue somewhere. If you do an image search for "Calliope Crawley" this is the picture that most commonly comes up.

She kneels down in front of the grave.

"Want me to..." I say, gesturing that I give her some private time alone.

"Thanks," she says, and I start walking away to give her some space.

"Hi, uh, Dad. It's me, Alli— err Calliope. I'm sorry I..." she starts to say before her words became unintelligible to me from the distance I've put between us. It doesn't take long before she beckons me back. There are tears down her face and she holds her hand out for me. I hold her hand and she grabs me tightly.

"This is harder than I thought," she says, wiping her face with her free hand. "I need you here."

"Sure," I say. "Anything you need."

She smiles at me, then looks back at her father's grave. "Anyway, Dad, I know this is the first time I've been out here. I hope you can forgive me for that. Things were... really messed up for a long time. I guess you haven't been lacking visitors, even after all these years... I hope you've been watching over me."

I kneel beside her and she squeezes my hand.

"This is Nick, my boyfriend. I think you'd like him. He's really great and treats me well. He was... is a fan of yours."

It's weird, but at that moment, it really did feel as though she was introducing me to Randall Crawley. Yeah, he's been dead for sixteen years, but being here... talking to his grave... the ceremonial aspect of it all just makes it feel real.

I couldn't shake the image in my head of meeting her dad, face to face. I could even see him as he might look today.

"You probably know this," Alli continues, "but I write songs and sing too. I guess I have you to thank for that. And..." she thinks for a minute... "I'm sure you must be sick of people coming here and playing your songs to you. But I thought maybe you'd like to hear one of mine." She looks at me. "Can you get my guitar out of the car?"

I get it for her. When I return, she's still talking to the grave. She looks up at me and I hand the guitar to her. "Thanks."

She sits crossed-legged in front of the grave. "This song is about you, dad. I hope you like it. I call it 'No Memory.'"

I've never heard this song before. I imagine she's written quite a few songs about her dad that she's never performed publicly and probably never will.

When the song ends, she sits there, crying softly. Then she puts her guitar down and starts frantically picking up all the clutter fans left behind. "Let's clean all this stuff away."

"How come?"

"All this stuff, it was put here by people who didn't know my dad. They think they had this deep connection with him because they loved his music. But it doesn't belong here. None of this does. It's not right that his grave has become a trash bin for all this junk from people who think they knew him. I'm his daughter. I'm the only one left who really cares. And I want to clean this up."

So, I help her pick up all the stuff that been left there. When I picked up the picture of Randall and her as a baby. She said, "Wait, can I have that?" I give it to her and she slides the picture out of the frame it was in, then reaches in her purse and takes out a marker. I watch as she writes a message on the back:

> *I love you, Dad.*
> *your daughter, Calliope*

She puts the picture back in the frame and leans it against the grave.

"Let's go now," she says.

CHAPTER 33

As we pack up my car, another car honks and pulls in behind us. It's Chris and Isabel.

"Cool, you guys are done? We just grabbed a quick bite at McDonald's and thought if you were still here you might want to come with us around town. We're doing a Crawley Crawl. Checking out his old haunts and stuff."

I look at Alli. This is totally her call. The plan was to drop off her guitar at the hotel, then drive up to Niagara Falls, but I can tell visiting her dad's grave affected her more than she expected, and we probably weren't going to do Niagara Falls today anyway. Alli had nixed the idea of visiting places connected to her dad because she thought it would be too much for her to handle.

Isabel gets out of the car. "You guys gotta come with! It's going to be epic." She approaches Alli and can tell she's been crying. "Oh, look at you." Isabel says, and gives Alli a hug. "It's really powerful, isn't it? I cried the first time I came here too. I still get choked up when I first arrive here."

"I'm fine," Alli says. If I were her, I'd be ready to tell Isabel that she couldn't possibly understand what Alli is going through being here.

"I know it's pretty heavy, but the Crawley Crawl is much easier. And it's fun, too. I promise."

Alli doesn't answer, so I start to say, "I don't think—"

"Okay," Alli interrupts. Much to my surprise.

"Yay!" Isabel says, and hugs Alli again.

"So, okay... how did you plan this tour?" I ask.

Chris hands me a piece of paper with a map on it.

"I brought an extra copy, so you can use this one."

I look at the paper closely and see it's a hand drawn map of the area, titled "The Crawley Crawl" and it's extremely detailed, with numbered stars indicating locations of importance to Randall Crawley. Each location on the map is also annotated with a brief explanation of what each star is and explains where the information came from. His family home from birth to age three is shown, as is the house he lived in from four to eighteen. His high school is also on map, and places he had summer jobs. The detail is impressive, but also kind of creepy. Locations of bars he played gigs at with earlier bands or Perch are also shown. If a bootleg recording exists of any show performed there it even says so.

"Dude, did you make this?" I ask.

"No way man, I got this online. The guys who run the fan club have compiled it over years."

"It's... thorough."

"Yeah. It really is," Isabel says.

Between the sites of significance to Randall Crawley's childhood, and all the bars and clubs, I don't see how we can do this all in a day. "Are you... going to every place on this map?" I ask.

"Well... not *every* place. We mix it up every year. But we usually visit some key bars Perch played their first gigs at. Other places from his childhood. Stuff like that. It just sucks that neither of us can drink yet but it be cool to, you know, have a beer at one of the bars he played at. But you know, it's still cool to go in, if they let us, and see if they got photos up of him playing there that we haven't seen before."

All this for a musician who has be dead for sixteen years? Damn.

"I marked all the places we plan go and numbered them in the order we plan to visit them. Your copy has the numbers on it too. So if you want to follow us that be awesome. I figure we can do everything in a few hours. "

I look at Alli to make sure she's sure she really wants to go. She nods.

"Okay," I say. "Let's do it."

"Sweet. So you'll follow us in your car?"

"Sure."

"Fucking awesome, guys. Let's do this!"

And so we follow them. We visit the two homes Randall Crawley lived in as a kid first. The houses themselves aren't remarkable at all, but Chris and Isabel are awestruck. Alli doesn't say anything. We keep a respectful distance from the homes seeing as how they belong to different families now. It's amazing just how much both these two kids are into this. Every place we've visited and will visit today has been pre-selected, meaning they're of interest to them. Even his high school. We don't spend much time there, but Chris and Isabel just had to take pictures there. They even asked me to take a photo of the two of them in front of it.

"You okay?" I ask Alli after we leave the high school grounds.

"Not really."

"Do you want to ditch this Crawley Crawl?"

"No. I *have* to do this... It's just... It's all so bizarre. I can't believe people—kids even—care this much about my dad... *Still*... that'll they'll take pictures of his high school like it's sacred ground or something."

When we visit his college campus we check out his former dorm building and known spots on campus super fans consider important. Chris and Isabel are so into it their enthusiasm never wanes, regardless of how mundane each location is. We discover a Starbucks in the student union which is open to the public, so we take a quick break and have lunch there. Alli has taken to private contemplation, but Chris and Isabel do enough talking for the four of us.

After our little break, we walk around downtown to check out a bunch of bars Randall Crawley played at... or at least their former locations, as some are no longer bars. When driving around gets old, we park at the hotel and visit the nearby pier, take a walk down the breakwater (something Randall Crawley is said to have done many times) which was the most enjoyable part of the tour just because of the view of the lake. Isabel notices Alli's discomfort and assumes that she understands what Alli is going through and tries to comfort her. I'm sure Alli appreciates the kindness but must be irritated that Isabel keeps assuming she can empathize with her. Alli often distances herself from the group, and Isabel takes one of those opportunities to ask me what's up with Alli.

"So, what's the deal with your girlfriend? Is she okay?"

"She's just really overwhelmed."

"I know, but she's been like, crying all day."

"Didn't you your first time here?"

"Well, at the cemetery, yeah, but this is the fun stuff."

I can see why she might think that it's odd for Alli to be reacting so emotionally all day, but, of course, she doesn't know the real reason why. "She'll be okay. It's a lot to take in." I explain.

"I know how she feels, it's just—"

"Trust me, you don't." Isabel looks at me like I've just insulted her. "You know, because everyone's connection to Randall Crawley is unique. I certainly can't understand what she's personally going through, and I know her better than you do."

She nods in understanding. "Yeah. You're right. That's so true."

Alli rejoins the three of us after a few minutes.

"You guys want to hang out on the beach?" Chris asks. "I was gonna grab Iz's guitar from my car and we're gonna play some Perch songs and stuff."

I'm sure Alli doesn't want to join them, so I come up with an excuse to bail. "Actually, we were just—"

"Okay," Alli says.

I'm shocked. I look at her and she just gives a what-else-are-we-going-to-do shrug.

We find a good spot on the beach and the four of us fit on the blanket Chris and Isabel provided. Isabel starts playing her guitar.

"You're out of tune," Alli says.

"I am? Oh. I'm kinda new at this and I don't know how to tune it. Do you? Can you?" She hands Alli the guitar, not giving her a chance to respond. She tunes it and hands it back.

"Do you want to play it?" Isabel asks.

"That's okay. It's your guitar, you should play it."

"I'm not that good yet. Go for it. I don't mind."

"Okay, what do you want me to play?"

"Play your favorite Perch song."

"I don't have a favorite."

"Then play 'Not Really Here'. I know it's not one of their singles, it being a hidden track and all, but I just love that one."

As far as I know, Alli has never played any Perch songs before. And Isabel has not given her an out to play anything but Perch, and she might find it strange if Alli doesn't know how to play any Perch songs. But I recognize the opening riff immediately. And she sings it perfectly. It's eerie how she captures her dad's vocal style so well. If I still needed proof that she's his daughter, right now I got it.

After the song Alli gives the guitar back to Isabel, who's a little intimidated to play now, so Alli asks her what song she'd like to learn, and Alli tries to teach her.

"Do you have a capo?" Alli asks. Isabel pulls out a pencil and rubber bands. "That works too. Put that on the second fret." It's funny to watch, at least for me it is. This girl, inspired to learn guitar by Randall Crawley, unbeknownst to her, is getting a guitar lesson from his daughter. After the lesson Isabel thanks Alli endlessly and gives her the guitar again so she play another one.

"Oh, okay, sure. What should I play?"

Isabel requests "Heart," and Alli hesitates.

"You know how to play it, don't you?" Isabel asks.

"Yeah. I know how."

"Cool. Let's hear it."

Listening to Alli play this song gives me chills. Once again, she matches her dad's singing style so well, but this time, it's extra bizarre because she's singing a song that is about her. I can see Alli close her eyes and tears running down her cheeks as she sings her dad's song about how much he loved her and would always be there for her. Chris and Isabel don't even understand the significance of what they are witnessing, though they thoroughly enjoy her performance. They don't even attempt to sing along with her. They would freak out if they knew who she really is. After the song Alli quickly returns the guitar to Isabel and wipes her eyes.

"That. Was. Awesome. You two should join us tomorrow, too," Chris says.

"No thanks," Alli says.

"You sure?"

"Yeah," I say. "We've got to head back home."

"That's too bad. Today was pretty awesome, huh? I'm glad you guys could join us. I feel like—"

"Why are you two so... into Randall Crawley?" Alli asks. "I mean, it's not like you knew him or anything."

"It feels like I did, though. When you love someone's music enough, you do know them in some weird, intimate way," Isabel says. "You know what I mean, right? I mean, that's why you're here, too, isn't it?"

Alli doesn't answer right away, the question upsets her, I can see it. "I—" Alli struggles to come up with a response. Then she suddenly stands up. "Nick, I'm not feeling too well, can we go back to the hotel?"

CHAPTER 34

ALLI STARTS HEADING towards to hotel without saying goodbye to Chris and Isabel. They're confused by her behavior, but I tell them she's just more overwhelmed by this trip than she expected. They aren't entirely convinced, but they also want our company so much they invite us to join them for dinner tonight at some restaurant Randall Crawley used to bus tables at as a teenager when he needed money to buy a new guitar. I explain that we can't because we were planning our own dinner for our three-month anniversary. It is our three-month anniversary, but we did not plan anything special for tonight. I haven't even brought it up to Alli. Still, it's a convenient excuse.

"Oh, okay. That's cool," Isabel says. "Maybe we'll bump into you tomorrow."

I catch up with Alli. She's upset, trying to hold back tears. I knew that she wasn't sick, just upset by Isabel's question about if she felt she knew Randall Crawley. We walk in silence all the way back. I'm not sure what to say to her. When Alli cries about one thing or another it's just easier for me to hug her and hope I don't have to say anything because I have no idea what the right thing to say is. Maybe it's because I know from experience that there really isn't anything comforting that can be said. When my parents got divorced I didn't want to hear anyone tell me they were sorry because them being sorry didn't help me any. It certainly didn't keep my family together. I'm not saying there's no room for sympathy in life, but I just can't verbalize it because I can't put myself in the shoes of the person listening to me. I have no way to even remotely comprehend what Alli's feeling right now. I know it's complicated enough that I am powerless to do anything to help her except be "there for her" when she wants to talk about it and just listen. What can you say to the daughter of a famous musician who has been dead for nearly twenty years?

"Oh, my guitar," Alli says through tears, realizing we've left it in my car.

"I'll get it," I say.

"Thanks."

So, Alli goes back to the room while I retrieve the guitar. She's sitting on the floor between beds when I get back to the room.

"Are you okay?" I ask.

"I don't know. I've just been thinking about a lot of stuff since we got here."

"Do you want to talk about it?"

"I guess I wasn't too sure what this trip would do for me. I didn't know if I'd feel anything at all. But I do. And I feel sad. I have no memories of my dad, but there are fans who do remember him when he was alive, or who think they really knew him because they love his music. Like Chris and Isabel. When we visited all those places today, they were just so... moved by it all. I felt like there was something wrong with me because it wasn't affecting me the same way as it did for them. It made me feel really sad because they feel something so strong for him and his music. I mean, I'm sad that I never got to know my own father, and I did feel something at his grave. It's just... it was really hard seeing them feel so much, and just because they like his music? He wasn't just a musician, he was my father. It's not fair they get to feel so much more than me. I mean, when he died I wasn't old enough to fully understand that he was really gone forever. I wish I could feel something for him like they do." She gets up off the floor and sits down next to me on my bed, "Isn't that sad, they can be moved by the death of a stranger more than I can be of my own father? He was my dad and I never knew him at all. Still don't really. I mean, I know as much as any fan of his knows, and that's it. Anything I know about him I've read about or heard about from someone else. I know he loved me, but I can't remember what that love felt like. I was too young when he died to remember anything. I know I loved him when he was alive, but I can't remember what that felt like either. I've never had to deal with the shock of realizing that my dad wouldn't see me grow up or never get to walk me down the aisle or anything, but I still can't get over how I don't have a single memory of him that just belongs to *me*."

I nod. Not sure what else to do.

Alli continues. "I love him because he was dad, but it's more like the love you feel for a grandparent who died before you were born. You may be blood, and that connects you, but you really are strangers because you never developed a genuine relationship. They're a photograph on a wall and you're told that that person is important to you, even if you don't know why. Even though you are who you are because of them, you can't feel any warmth from that because they never knew you and you never knew them. He's as distant to me now like an old black and white photograph of someone I never met." She wipes her eyes. I can't even imagine just how difficult this is for her. So much of her life has been affected by his memory but he is basically a stranger to her. "I wish I could remember something, anything about him. I don't even remember the funeral."

I do. It was televised on MTV, which was unexpected but most of us who were Perch fans assumed that Carmen Fisher just wanted to be seen as a grieving widow (even though they weren't married) and tout herself and her now fatherless daughter to the world as Randall Crawley's legacy since Carmen was hoping for a comeback with her acting career.

"I'm sorry," I say. It's all I can think of.

"It's okay. I've been dealing with this one way or another for years. It's just... it's been an avalanche today."

"Do you... want some space for a while? I could go out, grab some dinner to bring back here, or something."

"Really?"

"Sure. I know this has been a difficult day for you. I'll just take a drive and find some place I can order out from."

"Thanks. I'm sorry, I'm sure you probably wanted to do something nice for our three-month anniversary but, I'm just... I don't feel like going out."

"No sweat," I say.

She kisses me and grabs her guitar off the bed and sits back on the floor between the two beds.

* * *

About an hour and half later I come back to the hotel room. Alli is now sitting on top of her bed, in her pajamas, strumming her guitar, notebooks splayed around her.

"I hope you like Buffalo wings," I announce. "I thought it made sense to try some local fare."

"Sounds good to me," she says.

"You doing okay?" I ask.

"Yeah, I think so," she says, though she only ends up eating a few wings. After eating we sit together on my bed to watch TV for a while. We decide to turn in at 10:30 so we can get an early start tomorrow. I turn off the TV, but Alli doesn't move to go back to her bed.

"Am I a horrible daughter?"

"Of course not. How could you think that?"

"I feel like one sometimes, for distancing myself from my dad. It's not that I'm not proud of his success. I am. I just, I don't know. I made the decision to change my name and make it on my own, and I stand by that decision. I just hope wherever he is that he doesn't think that living my life the way I've chosen to is an insult to him or his memory."

"I think he'd understand."

"How could he understand?"

"Don't you see, he made his own success—just the way you are now. He was the reason his band made it big. He wrote all their songs. He *was* Perch. I think... I am sure he'd much rather look down and see you making your own success than taking advantage of his memory to achieve your own fame and fortune. You are doing more to honor his memory the way you are doing things now. I'm sure he's really proud of you."

She thinks about that for a minute. I think I made a good point and I think she's realizing that too.

She takes my hand and squeezes it. "Thanks."

Alli snuggles up close to me, rather than returning to her bed.

"This is nice," she says. "Being here with you."

"It is," I agree.

"Maybe I can sleep here... next to you?"

"You sure?" I ask.

"Just for tonight. And *just* sleep. It's just been a long, emotional day and I..." she takes my hand again. "I just want to be here next to you."

"I'd like that, too."

* * *

I wake up surprisingly early. The clock says 6:23 and I'm surprised I managed to wake up without the alarm going off. Alli is still sleeping, so I take my shower.

Alli is awake when I get out.

"Good morning," I say.

"Hey," she says groggily. "What time is it?"

"Just before seven," I tell her. "You hungry for breakfast?"

"Actually, yes. I am." She gets out of the bed and hugs me. "Thanks so much for coming here with me."

"No problem."

"We need to do something fun today."

"Sure. We can still do Niagara Falls before heading back."

"Sounds good. Okay, I'm gonna shower now. I'll be quick."

"Good. I'm starved."

She heads to the bathroom and closes the door. I can hear the shower turn on, and shortly after the sound of her getting in. She showers quickly, and she calls out to me when the shower stops.

"Nick, I just have to dry off and get dressed. I'll meet you downstairs in a few minutes, okay?"

Down in the lobby is the distinct smell of breakfast. Continental breakfasts are nothing too exciting, but somehow when you spend the night at a hotel they do the trick. I see Chris in the lobby.

"Hey man, how's it going?" he says.

"Not too bad my friend," I say.

"Your girlfriend okay? She seemed a bit weird last night."

"Yeah, she's okay. So, where's your... Isabel?"

"Putting on make-up or something. She should be here any—"

"Hey guys," I hear from behind us. We both turn. It's Isabel.

"Hey babe," Chris says.

"Where's Alli?" Isabel asks.

"Still drying her hair or something upstairs. So, you guys have a big agenda for today?"

"Yeah. Heading up to Buffalo for the rest of our Crawley Crawl. You sure you two don't want to join us?" Chris says.

It could be interesting to check out some of Randall Crawley's old haunts, but I know Alli won't be up for it. "I don't think so. I think we're heading home today."

"Oh, sure. Isabel thought she offended her or something last night."

"Did I?" Isabel asks, "I didn't mean to."

"Nah, don't worry about it. Everything is okay."

They chat lightly with each other about their upcoming Randall Crawley history tour. Before long Chris looks at his watch and announces they have to hit the road.

"You sure you two can't come?" he asks me again.

"I'm sure."

"Well, it was great meeting you guys. Maybe we'll see you here next year."

I am quite certain we won't be back here next year. But I tell him we're thinking about it, and that's enough for them. About five minutes after they leave Alli arrives in the lobby. "Sorry I took so long, I just had a short moment of inspiration and wrote some lyrics and stuff."

"It's all good. You missed Chris and Isabel."

"Oh, really?" She's not disappointed.

"Yeah, they're off on their next Randall Crawley adventure. It's like this is their Disneyland." Alli shakes her head dismissively. "Anyway, you ready for breakfast?"

"Absolutely."

While we're eating, Alli suggests a change in plans.

"I know we were gonna do something fun today, and we still can. But I don't have to work until tomorrow night, and I thought, maybe we could delay our return one day so you can meet my family?"

"The Conwells?"

"Mmhmm."

"Yeah, I'd like that."

"We can go to Niagara Falls for a few hours we can still be at their house in time for supper."

So, we check out of the hotel early and drive up to Niagara Falls. Alli calls the Conwells on the way up. And they're very excited that we're both coming. Alli's mood improves significantly when our plans are set. When we get to Niagara Falls, she's excited. The weather is nice, and we walk around the park. We get to see the falls up close, right at the point where the water goes down. We get a great view from the observatory, then we go down to do the Maid of the Mist and wait in line for a really long time.

The ride is fun though. Alli finally seems to be enjoying herself. In addition to the Maid of The Mist, there are other attractions here and on the Canadian side which look like a lot of fun, but we don't have time for since we have to get to the Conwells by dinner time. Alli, too, is disappointed at all the things we won't get to do.

"Maybe next time," she says.

Next time? Does she see us coming out this way again? I want to ask, but before I can, she is asking a tourist to take our picture with the Falls behind us, so we have proof of our visit.

"I guess it's time to go," Alli says. She's disappointed that we have to leave, but she's smiling.

CHAPTER 35

WE ARRIVE AT the Conwell's house just after six. Their house sits inconspicuously in a typical upper-middle class suburban neighborhood. Who'd ever think that the daughter of Randall Crawley was living here hiding in plain sight for so many years?

"This will be nice," Alli says. "I've never brought a boy home before." Then she looks at me concerned, "You okay? You look nervous."

"I am," I say.

"Why are you nervous? You've done this kind of thing before, haven't you?"

"Yeah, but this is… a little different," I say.

"I won't argue that, but still, you have nothing to worry about. Seriously, this is going to be great. I haven't exactly had a normal life, you know, I finally get to do something normal, like bringing a boyfriend home to get grilled by—"

"Grilled?"

Alli laughs. "I'm just kidding, Nick. Relax."

"Do they know that I know... everything?"

"Yes, of course."

"And they're... okay with that?"

"They know how serious I take keeping my identity secret. When I told them I had told you, they knew that I wasn't just some naïve infatuated girl who just decided to tell her *very first* boyfriend without a good reason. I guess what I'm saying is they trust my judgement."

"So, they haven't decided already they don't like me and will spend the entire evening making me feel uncomfortable?" I say jokingly.

"Of course not, silly."

It's obvious that she finds my nervousness "cute," like she knows that it's as big a deal for me to meet the Conwells as it is a big deal for her to introduce me to them. But this is no ordinary meeting of the parents. I wonder if I'm nervous because they know that I know who she really is. Would it be easier if they thought I had no idea about Alli's past? Because I know it definitely would be easier if I didn't know. I'm sure that even though they trust her judgement that they'll be putting me under the microscope, making sure that I really was good enough and trustworthy enough for Alli to tell me her biggest secret. I'd be skeptical too. The first guy who comes along and she spills the beans to him. That can't look too good from their perspective. I suspect that I'll have to prove myself tonight. Of course, thinking about all this makes me nervous, and I know it's showing, which doesn't help either.

"Well, I hope they like me."

"They will. They already do. I've told them all about you. Now, let's go." She gets out of the car. "I miss this place."

As we approach the front door it opens, and Mrs. Conwell greets us. She and Alli hug, and Alli introduces me, and then Mr. Conwell comes out and Alli hugs him and he looks over at me, "So, this is the notorious Nick we've heard so much about?" We shake hands and exchange pleasantries, then we all head inside. The foyer has pictures of the Conwells and Alli together like any typical family's foyer would. From in here the pictures seem to tell the story of a normal family, even though they aren't.

We all head into the living room. "Don't be nervous," Alli whispers. "You're doing fine."

The Conwells are friendly people. They tell us just how thrilled they are that we came, and excited they are that Alli *finally* got herself a boyfriend. I'm not sure who's more embarrassed, Alli or me, but I think despite the embarrassment Alli enjoys feeling normal for the first time in her life. Everyone here knows who she is, she can be herself, talk about anything, and not feel restricted by her secret identity. In the living room I notice some pictures on the mantel above the fireplace and take a look. I know Alli started living here around thirteen years old, but the only pictures with Alli in them she's older, closer to her age now, her face not so cherubic, her hair not so light—less like Calliope Crawley. I'm drawn to the last photo. It's a picture of Alli playing a piano and singing.

"That was taken at church on Christmas Eve," Alli says.

"She gave such a beautiful, moving solo performance of 'Breath of Heaven,'" Mrs. Conwell tells me. "I think the whole congregation was in tears."

"I was too," Alli says. "Since I knew I'd be leaving in a few weeks to go to Boston."

"I know you prefer the guitar, but I hope you've played on a piano since you moved," Mr. Conwell says.

"Not enough. The first time was a couple weeks ago. Well, that was a keyboard. I—" Alli pauses abruptly, no doubt because she's remembering the same thing I am, that she's talking about her duet with Blake, our last real fight. The look on her face tells me she's worried that talking about it might upset me.

"She was great," I say. "It was quite a performance."

Alli smiles, relieved. We all chat for a few minutes more, then Mrs. Conwell announces she's going to finish dinner in the kitchen and that Alli and I should get settled.

"Do you need any help with anything?" Alli asks.

"No, not at all. You just had a long drive, and tonight you're our guests, so you don't need to lift a finger."

"Thank you," Alli says, then turns to me. "Why don't we put our stuff away?"

"Your room is just as you left it, Alli," Mr. Conwell says, then turns to me. "We got the guest room here on the first floor all set for you Nick."

"Thanks," I say.

The guest room is nice. It's the kind of room you'd see in an interior design magazine. Alli joins me after taking her things to her room.

"Come with me," Alli says, "There's something I want you to hear."

"What is it?"

"You'll see." She guides me upstairs and into her room. Another magazine perfect room, though slightly more lived in. It's bright and large and beautiful.

"You're the first guest I've ever had in here, so I apologize for the mess."

The only area that comes even close to being messy is her desk area. Even her bookshelves are nice and organized. I'm sure she gave this room a major cleaning before she moved, but her apartment, while not as nice as this room, is similarly clean of clutter.

"So, what did you want to show me?"

Alli walks over to her desk. Above it is a shelf with stacks of CDs. Most of them appear to be albums from mainstream bands, but there's a big stack of CD cases on the end, all with white spines, and handwritten on each is a description of what each CD contains. She takes off the top three from the stack.

"I've been trying to think of a way to thank you for taking me to see my dad. And on the way here I thought of something." She hands me the CDs she took off the shelf. "So, my dad recorded a bunch of stuff before he died, demos and—"

"So the rumors are true?"

"They're true. You're holding the only copies in existence. Well, the original recordings are locked up. But you know what I mean. Pick one out. I'll play it. I don't mind."

I look at the discs. The first one is labeled *Demos – 5/1998* and the second *Demos 11/1998.* I open both up and review the track listings. Most of the songs I've not heard of, while there are some I recognize as Perch B-sides or songs that have only been played in concert. My heart races. Then I look at the third disc. Holy shit. It's labelled *Randall Crawley – Not Famous – 3/1999 Master.* I open the jewel case and read the track listing There are twelve songs. All of them unfamiliar to me. "Is this what I think it is?"

"The rumored solo album my dad recorded? It is."

Holy shit. I am holding in my hands proof that the rumored solo album exists. This is the Holy Grail of Perch fans everywhere. And I'm holding it in my hands.

"I can't believe this."

"Want to listen to it?"

I nod, unable to speak. I've only been wanting to hear this stuff for fifteen years.

She takes the CD case I've opened and removes the disc.

"There's more in the basement."

"Seriously? What's in the basement?" I ask, unable to hide my excitement.

She smiles. "Oh, there's all sorts of stuff. I got all the soundboard recordings from Perch's last tour—" Soundboard recordings from the last tour? Very few ever got out into the hands of bootleg traders. "You've probably heard some of those songs from the double disc live album that came out ten years ago. There's also lots of Perch recording sessions and demos, solo material, and—"

"All that is in *the basement*?"

"Uh-huh, it's all safe in a locked dry room. Don't worry about that."

"I'd love to check it out."

"If we don't have time tonight, you can check it out another time. Maybe we'll come back here some weekend." I'd love an entire week to go through it all. But this Randall Crawley solo album is more than enough for me right now.

She puts the CD in the stereo. The small LCD screen shows 01 for the first track and 5:08 for the track's total time. At first I'm so excited to be listening to this that I forget to pay attention to the songs, so I breathe deep to calm myself down, and focus on not just hearing the music, but listening to it. There isn't a chord or note that isn't processed in my brain. The fifth song, "Here and Nowhere," I'd heard before, even though I didn't recognize the song title. All of a sudden it hits me. It's on a bootleg I have under a different title and I think different lyrics. I don't have many bootlegs. Some hardcore fans tried to get their hands on every concert with a known recording. I only went after concerts that came from a soundboard recording or were significant for some reason, like a rare song was performed, or notable guest musicians joined them on stage. I got the bootleg specifically for this song. Perch soundboard recordings of full concerts are really rare, and in the basement of this very house are all the soundboard recordings from their last tour! Unbelievable! I am pretty sure there may only be a dozen or so from their entire existence that have ever surfaced among the Perch Online Bootleg Community, and only three or four from the last tour. Of the fifteen bootlegs that I own only six are from soundboard recordings.

We listen to the entire disc. I can't describe what it is like listening to it. It's just unreal. When the last song ends and the CD stops spinning Alli looks at me. There are tears in her eyes, but she's smiling.

CHAPTER 36

"Wow," I say. "That was... great; that was really awesome."

"So... it met your expectations?"

"Believe it or not, after all these years of wondering if these songs even existed I thought that there was no way they'd measure up to what I was hoping they be. But they do. They really do."

"I'm glad."

"Why don't you have his record label put this stuff out?"

"The whole world has hours of Perch music to enjoy," she says. "All their albums and singles, bootlegs, and the stuff that came out after my dad died. I can't even remember him, and at times it's like he's a total stranger. I told you before I have no memories of him. I just got the name he gave me, which I couldn't even keep, and this album. Something he created that no one else has. He was going to dedicate the album to me, and several of the songs are about me or for me. I just... I wanted something of his that could be my own." She takes *Not Famous* out of the stereo, and holds up the disc. "This is all I have that's just mine. I know it must seem selfish to want this one thing for myself, but there's a whole world out there that seems to know my father better than I do... or at least they think they do. If I let the album get released, I'd have nothing that truly belongs to me, his own daughter, that no one else has heard. The Perch music has been leaking out for years—it's not like I'm the only one with copies. But his solo work, I can't even—you know, I don't even have a guitar that belonged to him—though I probably should. If I want to see one, I'd have to go to the Rock and Roll Hall of Fame. Do you understand?"

"Yeah, I think so. But why did you let me listen?'

"Because you're my boyfriend and I love you."

I take the disc from her and put it back in the jewel case and hand it back to her.

She smiles. "You can have it."

"Really?"

She nods. "It's a copy. I trust you with it."

It occurs to me that by possessing this disc I will have something thousands, if not millions of Perch fans would kill to hear. That is a huge responsibility. I know I will never be able to rip this disc into mp3s, so I can listen to them anytime on my computer or iPhone. Hell, I won't even be able to listen to these again unless I know that no one will be around to accidentally hear me playing them. I can't risk someone asking me what it is, or recognizing Randall Crawley's voice, and putting two and two together. This disc will have to remain hidden, not only to protect the contents from being heard by the world when Alli doesn't want them to be, but also to protect her true identity. The gravity of this hits me, and I'm suddenly unable to decide if I can handle the responsibility.

"Are you *really* sure?" I ask.

"Of course."

"I will keep this safe. I will not copy the tracks to my computer or anything. I will keep it hidden except for when I want to listen to it. And I'll only—"

"I know." She puts her hand on mine and kisses me on the cheek. "Dinner should be just about ready," she says. "I better go help set the table."

* * *

"Alli, why don't you say grace?" Mrs. Conwell says to Alli when we all sit down for dinner.

"Of course," Alli says, and bows her head. Everyone follows.

"Dear God, thank you for the love that binds us, the food that nourishes us, and for your giving of your Son into our world to save us." We all say "Amen."

I can't remember the last time we ever said grace in my family.

The Conwells have pulled out all the stops for this dinner. It almost feels like Christmas dinner and that makes me feel slightly underdressed. But to them this is a special occasion I suppose. There's a turkey, wine, side dishes. They've even lit candles, and I suspect they've brought out the nice china and good silver, not their everyday plates and silver.

It's obvious the Conwells have heard plenty about me because they don't ask me questions like "So what do you do?" They know already and ask me questions about it. When Alli mentions Lacy in conversation, they don't have to ask who she is because they know already. It doesn't make me any less nervous being the center of attention, that's for sure.

Alli senses my nervousness and squeezes my hand under the table, then gives me look as if to say, "Everything's okay, see?"

And it is okay. After the Conwells are done asking me questions, they ask about our trip and how it went. And we talk to them about the experience, about Chris and Isabel, and the Crawley Crawl. Alli explains how it affected her and that even though it was initially upsetting she's glad she did it.

When dinner is over Alli offers to clear the table, but Mrs. Conwell reminds her that she's a guest in the house tonight and tells her that Alli and I can go to the family room while they clear up and get tea and dessert ready. Afterwards, Alli suggests we all play a board game. We end up playing Pictionary in teams. I was expecting that Alli and I would be a team, but Mrs. Conwell suggests that the teams be guys against girls, and Alli immediately agrees to that arrangement.

I'm surprised when I realize I'm having fun. Mr. Conwell and I make a pretty good team and we high five when we retake the lead, and cheer like a couple guys at a baseball game when we win. After playing for a while we have a late dessert in the dining room, and we all continue talking and having a good time. At ten o'clock the Conwells are ready to turn in. Alli insists on helping tidy up, and Mr. Conwell escorts me to the guest room, and shows me where the bathroom is and pointing out there's fresh towels and soap in there for me.

"Do you need any laundry done for the trip back?" he asks.

"No, thank you. I got some clean stuff for tomorrow."

"Great. You know where the kitchen is, don't hesitate to help yourself if you need a drink or get hungry in the middle of the night."

"Thanks," I say, even though I know that I won't need food or drink in the middle of the night. Still, it was nice of him to say so.

"Okay then. We'll see you in the morning."

Alli appears in the doorway.

"Goodnight, you two," Mr. Conwell says.

"Goodnight," Alli tells him, and they hug before he leaves.

"I hope you had a good time," she says to me, not moving from the doorway.

"I did."

She smiles. "I'm glad. I fun, too."

"It was great."

"It was," she says. "Okay, well, I'll see you in the morning." She quickly but quietly enters the room, kisses me, and heads back out the door. Before she closes it she whispers back to me, "I love you."

I whisper back, "I love you, too."

* * *

After breakfast the next morning it's time for us to go home. I can tell Alli is disappointed we can't stay longer, and frankly, so am I. But Alli has a shift at Starbucks this evening, and Jay will freak out if I don't get back to do some work with him. We say our goodbyes and get invited back "real soon," and told that I am "always welcome."

I really need a coffee before the drive home, and I suggest to Alli we hit up Starbucks. The closest one to us happens to be the one she worked at before she moved to Boston. She doesn't seem too thrilled by the idea, so I offer to go in myself while she waits.

"So, that's a nice Starbucks," I say when I get back to the car.

"It is," Alli agrees.

"So why didn't you want to go in? Were you not friends with your coworkers?"

"I was *friendly* with most of them. But we weren't really *friends*. We didn't hang out or anything. I think most of them thought I was just some weird girl."

"Weird? Why?"

"I guess I was a bit paranoid that people would figure me out here. Some people know that the Conwells are related to my dad. I was always worried someone would connect the dots if they knew too much about me. That's why Christine homeschooled me, too. It would have been nice to have had some friends, but I always felt I had to keep people at a distance."

"And that's why you left for Boston?"

"Yes. Sadly, in order for me to have my own life, I had to be away from Dave and Christine, too. They knew I'd have to go out on my own one day, so they were very supportive. And they're proud of me."

"I am, too," I tell her.

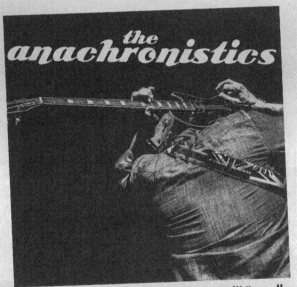

the anachronistics

with guest Alli Conwell

TUESDAY, JULY 7
@ The Nest
8 p.m.

CHAPTER 37

THE NEXT COUPLE weeks after we came back from our trip were bizarre—mostly because things just returned to normal. In fact, we barely talk about the trip anymore. It seemed like such a transformative trip at the time, but after a couple days of people asking us how our trip went, things are just business as usual. Alli's working at Starbucks and playing gigs, and I'm back to work as well.

I've only listened to *Not Famous* a few times since we've been back, too. I thought I'd be listening to it constantly, but I'm only really comfortable listening to it when I'm home alone, and lately, that's not very often. The last time I listened to it was a few days ago when Alli and Devon went out take some photos for Alli's new album and neither Alli or Devon wanted me to come along. So, I took advantage of the time I had alone and listened to it twice in a row. I keep the CD in my safe where I keep a few other valuables to make sure Devon or someone else doesn't accidentally happen upon it. I don't take the CD out of the apartment because the only other place I could listen to it is at Alli's place, and that's definitely not going to happen. I don't want the whole Calliope Crawley thing to define our relationship, so I don't bring up anything to do with Perch or Randall Crawley.

*   *   *

Right now, Alli is slightly concerned with her cash flow. This is hard to wrap my head around since technically she's a multimillionaire. But when you don't want to use that money and you're a solo musician times can be tough. Despite the recent publicity she got for opening for Candlepin this is one of those tough times. Here's the thing: even small venues have to schedule gigs weeks in advance. So the publicity she got helped her get some good paying gigs for mid-July through August, but June ended up being light because she's been focusing more energy on the new album. She's hoping to not have to request more hours at Starbucks, so I've been helping her a lot more than usual with sending out CDs and making better posters and trying to increase her social media following because I've been worried about her blaming our relationship on losing her focus on her music. Another issue is that not enough people are coming to see her play at some of these smaller venues. If she's not drawing enough customers the owners will often cut her pay or not pay her at all.

Alli was also supposed to open for The Purnell Maneuver with a five-song set at a beach party the night before Independence Day, but that fell through last minute, so we ended up going back up to New Hampshire for a pre-Independence Day barbecue with my mom and Lacy, then we drove back down early the next morning so Alli could work a shift at Starbucks for time and a half pay.

Some good news came when The Anachronistics had to cancel their gig at a small club in Harvard Square. Alli was supposed to open for them, but after the lead singer got laryngitis she was offered the chance to play their full three-hour slot. It's a Tuesday night show, so it's not going to be huge, but a longer set means larger pay.

Alli was really happy about the opportunity and I was in a good mood, too. That is, until Blake showed up. Seriously, this guy manages to show up at the worst possible times. Of course, any time is the worst time as far as I'm concerned. As usual, he's come here by himself. Every time I see him at a Candlepin gig he's got a different girl with him, but when he shows up to one of Alli's gigs he's solo. That has to be intentional.

Alli is already on stage when he shows up, which I hope means she wasn't expecting him and that there's no plan for him to join her on stage. I have no desire to watch the show with him, but the club isn't very big, so he finds me at Alli's merch table quickly and tries to chat me up like we're buddies... which we are not. I know Alli might notice us together, so I try to appear friendly. I ask about the album Alli is recording, and he starts talking in a lot of musician jargon about things, which means I only grasp about half of what he's saying. Instead of faking interest in anything else he has to say we just watch her in silence, except to cheer between songs.

During her set break Alli joins us and he asks about how she thinks her recording sessions are going, and tells us how his cousin thinks with proper marketing her new album could do very well. This excites Alli so much that she doesn't even notice I've become an observer, not a participant in the conversation. If people were watching us, she and Blake would look like the couple, and me the third wheel. And I hate it. The best part of the evening comes during Alli's second set when Blake recognizes someone who comes in, and I can watch Alli in peace. When her set is over, I want to pack up and run while Blake is pre-occupied in conversation. I watch him like a hawk, hoping he doesn't try to flank Alli after she talks to the owner about getting paid so we can sneak out of here without him seeing us. He doesn't, but when Alli gets back from talking to the manager of the club, she looks disappointed. The owner has decided he can't pay her because attendance was too low. This infuriates me, but Alli grabs me when I try to go talk to him.

"Just forget it, Nick. It happens. Since The Anachronistics cancelled the club didn't get a lot of people tonight, and—"

"I'm gonna talk to him," I tell her.

"Nick, it's okay, really. I sold some CDs tonight. That's better than—"

"You were promised payment. You should get it. It shouldn't matter that the headliner cancelled. You played. You did your part."

I walk off before she can protest to tell the manager that he's obliged to pay Alli. He sees me approaching and knows exactly why I am coming over. He raises his hands in some mollifying gesture.

"There's nothing I can do kid. I just didn't pull in enough tonight."

"You had an agreement," I say, though, with less authority than I wanted to project. Instead of sounding like the pissed off boyfriend trying to do right by his girlfriend, I came across as some kid complaining about things not being fair.

"I know. It sucks. Look, I'd like to pay your girlfriend for playing tonight. I would. But people come to see the headliner and when the headliner cancels and no one shows up I don't make enough money to—"

"What's going on?" Blake asks. He saw me arguing and decided to butt in.

"Nothing," I say. "I'm taking care of it," I say.

"I'd like to pay the girl for playing tonight," the manager explains. "But I can't. Shit happens, ya know?"

Blake looks at me. "I got this, chief."

"No, I—"

"Just let me talk to him."

"Fine. Whatever. Good luck." I stomp back over to Alli. I don't know what he thinks he can do that I couldn't, so I pick up her guitar case, and a box of her CDs. "Let's go," I say.

"Don't be so mad, Nick. Gosh, you're angrier than I am," she says. "It happens to everyone. We don't like it, but it happens. They could have told me not to play at all. But I did, and I sold some CDs. So, the way I see it, it wasn't all that bad of—"

"Got your money," Blake says, holding up a small wad of cash. "It's only half what you were supposed to get but that's the best I could do."

"Excuse me?" I ask.

"I've had my fair share of club owners try to stiff me over the years. After a while, you figure out how to get something," he hands Alli the cash.

Alli, who just seconds ago was telling me the money was no big deal, is elated over getting the cash from Blake. She hugs him, thanks him repeatedly, and I couldn't feel any smaller.

"Okay well," I turn to Alli, "You ready to Uber out of here?"

"You guys want a ride?" Blake asks.

I really have no interest in Blake taking us back to Alli's apartment. I really don't want him knowing where she lives. So, I gotta nip this in the bud right away. "No thanks man, we're goo—"

"Really? You don't mind?" Alli asks, a little too excitedly, like he's just offered her the second half of the money she was supposed to get tonight.

"It's no problem at all," he assures her.

Could this night get any worse?

So, Blake takes us back to Alli's place, and he even offers to help bring in her stuff. It's bad enough he's already emasculated me tonight and now knows where Alli lives. If he came in, he'd find some way to stick around.

"I got this," I assure him. "Thanks." I add, trying my hardest to sound sincere and not like I want to punch him in the face.

"Alright, cool," he says. "If you ever need a ride to a gig or something, instead of using Uber you can always give me a shout—"

"She's all set. I got it covered, *chief*," I say.

"Nick!" Alli shouts, disapprovingly. "Don't be rude."

Of course, I'm not done talking. "Besides, don't you have your own gigs and rehearsals—"

"Nick!"

"What?"

"I'm sorry, Blake," Alli says, ignoring me. "It's very nice of you to offer."

"Don't worry about it. And yes, I'll probably be busy, but you're always welcome to try."

"I appreciate the offer. If Nick is ever unavailable, I'll let you know."

Well, I'm gonna make sure I'm always available to take her to gigs.

Once we're inside, Alli tells me she's disappointed in my behavior. As much I know I should just apologize I can't help myself.

"It wasn't his place to come to your rescue."

"Come on Nick, what's the big deal? He wanted to help, and it turns out he could. Why does that bother you?"

"I'm your boyfriend. I was supposed to fix it."

"And I told you it was okay and not to bother in the first place. And so it worked out in the end. Okay? But it doesn't matter who got my money anyway. My boyfriend or my friend. Doesn't matter. It doesn't reflect poorly on you. You have absolutely no reason to feel threatened."

"He's also offering to take you to gigs? What's that all about?"

"He's being nice."

"Guys aren't just nice to be nice."

"I find that hard to believe."

"It's true."

"Nick..." Alli says, obviously exhausted by having this argument again. "I've told you he's not interested in me and I'm not interested in him. I'm with *you*. I love *you*. You really need to get over this."

Alli is upset enough with me that she doesn't want me to stay over tonight. So, I go home, even more pissed that because of Blake I have to take the T back to my place after midnight.

CHAPTER 38

THE NEXT MORNING Alli calls me to apologize for getting upset with me. Even though she's apologized, she tells me she doesn't want what happened last night to happen again, and of course reminds me, for the millionth time, that I have nothing to worry about, that he's just a friend who recognizes her talent and is only trying to help her... the usual speech. I apologize as well even though I'm not convinced Blake isn't still interested in her; I don't care how many other girls he's been with since she rejected him. I know he's still into her. It's obvious to me. She is, after all, a beautiful, talented girl. What's not to like? Besides, it's not like other guys don't notice her when she's on stage or at Starbucks or even when we go out on a date. But the only guy who's given me any reason for concern is Blake.

* * *

About a week later Alli comes with me to Jay's place for Retro Gaming and 80's Movie Night. I didn't think she would. I don't really believe she wanted to, but I suppose coming with me to watch a bunch of geeks play old video games and then watch a movie or two isn't as bad as being home alone. For the record, I'm not a gamer. Compared to Jay and his roommates, I'm terrible at vintage video games—and contemporary ones. These guys have several original gaming systems like Nintendo, Super Nintendo, Sega Genesis, Atari 2600, ColecoVision, and others I've never played or heard of before, and I'd guess most of the newer ones, too. How they have enough money to buy all these different systems and games is a question I dare not ask.

There are quite a few people here tonight. In addition to our hosts, Jay, Dan, Mark and Pete, we have Dan's girlfriend Jenna, Mark's girlfriend Roselyn, and a bunch of their friends, some of whom I've met at previous Retro Gaming and 80's Movie Nights but can't remember their names.

The gaming part of the evening doesn't end up lasting very long. Pete is currently on a mission to break the speedrun record for *Super Mario Bros*. He was at just under seven minutes a month and a half ago and has only trimmed about 15 seconds off his time since then. The world record is just short of five minutes. Tonight's performance, while impressive, falls short as a misjump in world 8-1 get him killed by a piranha plant. Pete is so pissed by the error that he storms off to his room.

"So, this is what you do for fun?" Alli asks.

"Well, it's kinda cool how fast he can play the game."

Alli rolls her eyes at me.

"It's certainly not my thing, but—"

"But you'll come here to play video games sometimes."

"Not much. Certainly not as much as I did before we started dating."

"I'm sorry, I'm not making fun of you. But I'm glad being with me is more fun than playing video games."

"Well, some video games." Alli smacks me in the arm.

We hang out a while waiting for a few more people to show up. There's some pizzas and other junk food in the kitchen, so we go in there before inevitable debate about which movie (or movies) to watch from their large collection of 80s and even some early 90s DVDs to watch. Soon after we start eating, a guy and a girl come in the side door. I recognize them, they both have been here before, they are friends of Dan's girlfriend Jenna, but their names escape me. I do remember that the girl, who is wearing a faded Pac-Man t-shirt, is *really* into retro video games. Her boyfriend's shirt grabs my attention immediately. He usually wears faux vintage band t-shirts, and tonight he chose to wear a Perch shirt. Which explains why Alli looks uncomfortable.

"Yo, Ken!" Mark says. "What's up?"

Ken! Now I remember. And his girlfriend's name is Courtney.

"How'd he do?" Ken asks, referring to Pete.

"Ehh, it was a bust. Don't say anything, he's kinda pissed."

"Gotcha."

Ken and Courtney make their way to the kitchen table for some pizza and soda. Ken shakes my hand when he sees me, and Courtney gives me a wave.

Ken notices Alli in the corner of the kitchen while he's drinking some soda.

"I know you. You're..."

"Alli," Alli says, shyly.

"Right... hi," he says, but something tells me he's just pretending that he couldn't remember who she is. I don't even know how or why Alli knows who he is. He looks over again at me, and back at her.

"How are you?" Alli asks.

"Good. Good."

"Hi, I'm Courtney," Courtney says, approaching Alli to shake her hand. "We haven't met."

"I'm... here with Nick."

"Ohhh, this is the infamous girl you've been seeing. The reason you never come here anymore," Courtney says to me.

"Indeed, she is," I say.

"The singer."

"Right."

"Very cool, very cool." She turns to Dan. "So, what are we watching tonight?"

"Haven't decided yet."

"It better not be *The Adventures of Buckaroo Banzai Across the* Fucking *8th Dimension.*"

"What's wrong with *Buckaroo Banzai*?"

"Are you serious? I hated that movie," she says.

"It's a classic!" Dan insists.

"Jenna? Am I right or what?"

"Hey, leave me out of this!" Jenna says. She grabs her drink off the table and starts to head towards the living room.

"Did you like it or not?" Courtney asks.

"It... grows on you," Jenna says.

"You both suck. Whatever. We're still not watching it."

"How about a *Back to The Future* marathon?" Ken suggests.

"I thought we were saving that for *Back to The Future Day* in October?" Mark asks. There are big plans for a *Back to The Future* party at Jay's apartment on October 21, 2015, the day in the future Marty and Doc Brown visit in *Back to The Future Part II*. All three movies have been embargoed during the calendar year of 2015 until that date.

"Oh yeah, good point."

"Well, it's too late to start a three-movie marathon anyway. Some of us have jobs to get to in the morning." Jenna points out.

"Fine, let's go pick something," Mark suggests.

Everyone takes that as a cue to go into the living room. Everyone but Alli and me.

"Did I miss something?" I ask Alli once they're all gone and out of earshot. "How do you know Ken?"

"He saw me at one of my first open mics after I moved here and asked me out afterwards."

"Ahh, another one," I say. "So, why did you turn him down?"

"Wanna guess?"

Suddenly I know.

"He was wearing the Perch shirt that night, wasn't he?"

Alli nods. "Uh huh. I think he wants to be in Perch tribute band, or is in a Perch tribute band... I don't remember. But that's not the only reason. He was hitting on a bunch of girls that night. He must have met his girlfriend soon after."

"So, if you had you known I was a fan of Perch from the beginning, you probably would have rejected me?"

"I don't know. Maybe. I'm not sure. But I liked you when I met you, I never liked him."

"I guess I was lucky."

"Well yeah, of course you were," she laughs, "but I was too."

"So, do you not want to stay? You looked kind of uncomfortable before."

"No, it's fine."

So, we join the rest of the crew in the other room. Mark and Ken play some *Space Invaders* on the Atari 2600. Courtney has also decided that Alli is her best friend for the evening and has taken to asking Alli all sorts of questions about being a musician and almost anything related to that. I can't tell if she knows that Alli turned Ken down once or not, so she might be genuinely curious about Alli's musical ambitions. But then she tells both of us about how Ken plays bass in a Perch tribute band, (which, of course is the last thing Alli wants to talk about) and seems to be making a point to talk Ken up as a musician. Courtney can sense that Alli isn't having a great time here tonight and suggests the two of them play a game together next, Alli feebly attempts to resist to no avail, as Courtney announces they got next turn.

When it's their turn to play, it's clear which one is the experienced gamer, and which one isn't. Courtney looks the part, with her *Pac-Man* shirt and her thick, dark framed glasses, she screams geeky gamer girl. Alli, doesn't look like a gamer, and as her game play shows, she has no idea what she's doing, despite the quick crash course from Courtney on how to play the game. Alli gets killed frequently, but Courtney is having fun anyway playing with her. After a second game, Alli seems ready to give up.

"I'm sorry," Alli says to Courtney. "I just don't play video games."

"You weren't that bad for someone who never played before," Courtney assures her. "You should come when they play Rock Band. I bet you'd have fun playing that."

"Rock Band sucks," Ken says.

"You're just saying that because there aren't any Perch songs on it." Jenna says.

"So? It's bullshit. No one can use their songs for anything."

"Why not?" Mark asks.

"I dunno, Randall Crawley's daughter—wherever the fuck she is—has control over the use of the songs and won't let them get used for anything," Ken replies.

"Well, maybe that's a good thing, the last thing we need is for you to have another outlet for your Perch obsession," says one of Dan's friends I don't know well.

Everyone laughs. Except for Alli and me.

Ken is not amused. "Fuck you man, you like them, too."

"Whatever."

"Come on, you know it's bullshit. I heard somewhere that all of the surviving members of the band wanted to let Rock Band use a bunch of songs, but that she wouldn't give them permission. Wanted a lot more money or something."

"Wouldn't surprise me," Courtney says, "I'm sure she's money-grubbing whore like her mother."

I never expected Alli and Courtney to become good friends, but I'm pretty sure any rapport they might have developed tonight has vanished. I look at Alli to see how she's reacting. I catch her eye and I she can tell know that I'm on the verge of saying something, because she discreetly mouths "don't," but I can see the hurt in her eyes and I can't help myself.

"How can you possibly know that?" I ask. "Do you realize how stupid that sounds?"

"Come on, what other reason could there be?" Ken asks.

"I'm with Ken on this one," Mark says. Others in the room express agreement with him as well. "And it's not just the whole Rock Band thing. There's a ton of music she ain't releasing either. That's bullshit, too. Fucking bitch. Stop holding out for more money and give the fans what they want!"

Under different circumstances, if they'd been talking about unreleased Randall Crawley music, I'd have found it amusing and even felt a bit pompous because I have heard the very music they wish they could. But right now that doesn't even matter. I know the truth, and they've besmirched my girlfriend... or at least a version of my girlfriend... and right in front of her. I'm sure she expects most people will have some negative opinion about why she keeps her dad's unreleased music under lock and key, but I can't imagine it's ever happened in front of her face before. I'm sure it doesn't feel good, and I can't help but defend her—err, Calliope.

"Maybe she doesn't want her dad's music exploited or something," I say. Nobody seems to think that explanation makes sense. "If money had anything to do with it, she would have—"

"Does anybody else want this?" Alli says, holding up her controller, deliberately interrupting the conversation.

Jenna reaches for Alli's controller, and Alli stands up and hands it to her, then walks out of the room.

She doesn't come back right away, so I go look for her. I hear the faucet running in the bathroom and knock.

"Alli, are you in there?" I call through the door.

The knob turns and the door creaks open. Alli is at the sink, having just washed her face, to hide that she'd been crying.

"You okay?" I ask.

"I just... That was the first time I've had to sit there and listen to people say such horrible things about... me." She wipes her face off with a towel and closes the door, shutting us in. "You shouldn't have said anything," she whispers.

"I'm sorry, but how am I supposed to sit there and not say anything when they're all ragging on my girlfriend?"

"But your girlfriend isn't Calliope Crawley, it's Alli Conwell." Did I just make a major mistake by not showing that I considered Calliope and Alli two different people? In general, I think I've managed to separate the two, but really, knowing what I know, how can I not have said something. I'm not sure what to think about this. I don't know how I am supposed to separate her from her past life when she couldn't even handle what just happened like it was nothing?

"I know you had good intentions, and it's really sweet that you wanted to defend me—or who I used to be, but the old me doesn't need a defender. I'm a different person now and—"

"Then, why are you upset?"

"You're right. I shouldn't be. I just am... or was... I don't know."

"I had to say something for the same reason you feel upset."

"I know. And, I know this will sound mean, but I don't want you to take it that way, I don't need you to protect Calliope Crawley's reputation. I'm sure if you didn't know the truth you'd probably have joined in with them."

"I—not necessarily."

Alli scoffs. "Come on Nick. You would have. It's okay. Everyone thought you were nuts out there. Even I did."

"Okay, probably, but—"

"But nothing. If you didn't know the truth, you'd believe the rumors, because, how could you possibly know better?"

"Do you want to go back out there?" I ask.

"Can we go home? I don't really feel like being here anymore. Tell them whatever you want. I just want to go."

She waits outside, and I tell everyone that Alli isn't feeling well, and that I'm taking her back to her apartment.

"For real?" Courtney asks. "We're either going to watch *Sixteen Candles* or *Say Anything.*"

"Yeah, maybe we'll come back another time," I say, knowing very well that's not going to happen any time soon.

CHAPTER 39

JAY CALLS THE next day. I thought I was going hear him complain that we left early, but instead he tells me that he's not surprised, and that it was obvious that Alli wasn't having a good time. He didn't buy the excuse that she wasn't feeling well.

"I told you she wouldn't enjoy it," I say.

"Hey, there were other girls there. Other geeky girls she could relate to."

"You think Alli is a geek?"

"I mean that as a compliment. I just mean, you know, a bit socially awkward, smart and, umm…"

"I get it."

"I mean, everyone there last night is a geek in some way. Well, maybe not Jenna. But Roselyn and Courtney… classic geek girls. But they're both cool and even kinda hot."

"I told you, I get it."

"She's not into gaming or anything, but you know, she's really into music and shit."

"So, like a band geek?" I ask.

"Kinda." I get what he's saying. There's a reason why Alli and I don't hang out with groups of people often. She's usually uncomfortable in social situations and is usually more relaxed with smaller groups. "And I mean that in a good way." Jay adds.

"I know. I get it."

We talk shop for a while, planning out the next few weeks of work, discussing outstanding invoices and such. The Burnham & Modine project is supposed to start full steam next month. It's still moving slowly because it's been difficult to set up meetings with them. But we've got plenty of other work to keep us busy until then.

Alli is also busy. This month has been pretty nice for regular gigs, especially after her June drought. Blake hasn't showed up for any of them either because Candlepin is on the road doing a little mini club tour that is taking them to clubs as far down as D.C and various places between there and here. They'll be back in time to play one of the last shows at the T.T. The Bears club before it shuts down for good. That is also the weekend of the Taylor Swift concert at Gillette Stadium that Alli got tickets to see with Lacy.

* * *

When the highly anticipated Taylor Swift concert finally comes, I have the "pleasure" of being their chauffeur for the evening. Not exactly an ideal evening for me, especially since Alli's gig and work schedule has been so hectic it's been a while since we've even had a night out or even a relaxing night in. But I have no interest in the concert, and

Alli only got two tickets anyway, so being the driver at least gives me the opportunity to spend some time with Alli.

Because the concert tickets were a gift to Lacy from both Alli and me, we go down early so all three of us can have dinner together first. I didn't expect to be included for dinner, and I thought it would be good for just two of them to hang out together without me. So that helped make the evening a little better.

Hanging out with Lacy is a lot easier with Alli. She's like a bridge that helps connect us. Maybe that's not the best metaphor, but it's the best I can come up with. In any case, Alli and I don't often hang out with other people. Hanging out with friends of mine clearly isn't working and she doesn't really have any friends that she hangs out with. She's friendly with her coworkers at Starbucks, but we've never hung out with them. She doesn't see any of her musician friends outside of gigs either. The only person I've known her to hang out with besides me is her landlord's daughter Eden, and I would say she doesn't even count. So, I'm actually glad that Alli has found a friendship with Lacy.

I finally leave them to themselves after dinner. They're both really excited about the show. Neither has been to a Taylor Swift concert before, and they both anticipate it being a "magical experience" or something like that. So, I go home to do some work. Not exactly the most exciting Saturday night ever.

When I pick them up after the concert, they look like they've had the time of their lives. It's pretty late but they're both pumped up on adrenaline, reliving the concert, talking about the songs Taylor performed, things she said to the crowd. They don't stop talking about it for the entire drive back to Alli's place. After bringing Lacy's stuff down into Alli's apartment I decide to head back home rather than stick around since they're still having so much fun. Lacy hugs me goodbye and thanks us both for the millionth time for getting the concert tickets. Alli walks me back to my car and then gives me a long, deep kiss.

"Thanks for driving tonight," she says. "You're the best."

"It was no problem. I'm glad you had fun tonight."

"Yeah, it was great. And it really meant a lot to Lacy. I'm glad you're okay with me and her being friends. You are okay with that, right?"

"Yeah. Of course."

"We get along really well, and I don't really have a lot of friends here."

"I understand. I'm cool with it, really. I know I wasn't exactly thrilled about you two being all buddy-buddy at first, but, you know, it was nice to see you enjoy yourself tonight. You don't really have many nights off."

"I know. I'm sorry about being so busy lately. We'll do something fun tomorrow night after I get off work, okay?"

"Absolutely. What did you have in mind?"

"I was thinking of putting a movie on and *not* watching it," she says smiling.

"That sounds great to me."

"I thought it would." She smiles and kisses me again. "I... better get back to Lacy, now."

"Okay," I say. "I'll see you tomorrow."

"I can't wait."

CHAPTER 40

ALLI PLAYS AT Bell in Hand Tavern a couple nights later. I sell a bunch of her CDs and from talking to people at the merch table it sounds as though there's a real buzz developing about her music.

"She opened for Candlepin once, right?" asks one buyer.

"She's opened for them a few times," I say.

"I thought so. Well, cool, yeah, she's good, I'll buy a CD."

Another person, some college chick, already has Alli's current album and asks about a new one.

"I bought this CD at Hennessy's a while back. I love it. Does she have anything new?"

"It's in the works," I explain. "She's recorded a new album, I think it will be ready soon."

"Awesome!"

I hear from a couple other people who have seen her play at some small coffeehouses who saw on Facebook that she was playing here tonight and came out to see her play. That doesn't make her famous by even local music standards, but it's still cool. One couple asks me all sorts of questions.

"Are you her manager?"

"Nope, I'm the boyfriend."

"Well, lucky you. Don't let this one go, she's going places."

"Trust me," I tell me. "I'm not letting her go."

* * *

The next night Jay and I have a meeting at Burnham & Modine to discuss their website and go over what we've done so far (which isn't much) and hopefully get another check (which will hopefully be big). We have a list of things for them to provide us, like the company history, bios of the owners, and stuff like that which will go on the new site. None of this stuff is needed any time soon, but Jay and I agreed that at the rate things have been moving so far we need to get them started on it now so we'll have something to put into the design when it's ready.

I'm only attending this meeting because it's after business hours and Emma shouldn't be there. She's not, but a bunch of other employees are, and they don't look too happy about it either. The meeting lasts a ridiculous two and a half hours, which means I missed an open mic Alli was going to play at. It wasn't the worst thing in the world, she only was going to play for a half hour, but this meeting would have been a lot shorter had we not needed to explain things multiple times, or if they had given us the information we had asked for via email the past couple months. Alli's cool about it when I text her to explain the meeting is going longer than expected and tells me I can just meet her back at her place when we're done. When the meeting is finally over even Jay is none too pleased with how long it took, and our usual post-meeting pow-wow is postponed until tomorrow. So, I hop on the Red Line at South Station to Park Street, switch to the Green Line and wait for a C-Train to go to Coolidge Corner. I'm already in a bad mood because of this stupid meeting, and the subway ride was no help. I'm hoping the walk to Alli's place will afford me enough time to blow off steam. As I walk up the street towards the house, I notice a familiar car parked in front. It's not the landlord's car—he parks in the driveway—but, I figure he must have a visitor or something until I notice the Candlepin bumper sticker on the back of the car. All of a suddenly I know why the car is familiar.

It's Blake's car.

Why would he be here after 9 o'clock on a weeknight? Why would he be here, period? I'm panicking because I don't know what to do. My heart is racing, and I am torn between running up to the house to Alli's apartment and find out exactly who's there and what's going on or getting a closer look at the car and hopefully discover I was mistaken, that it's not Blake's at all. I'm not sure why I'm not rushing to Alli's place, but some part of me is terrified. I know I'm torturing myself, but I can't help it. In my head, I want to work out a situation where it's anyone but Blake in Alli's apartment with her.

And that's when I see Blake walking towards the car from the house. It's dark out, so I hide behind a tree so he doesn't notice me. I'm so angry right now I can't even describe it. He walks to his car, leans against the back, and pulls something out of his pocket. It's a pack of cigarettes. He takes one out and lights it. Then he pulls out his phone and looks at the screen while he smokes. Before long he's had enough, and tosses the cigarette on the ground, gets in and drives off.

Blake was at Alli's apartment. Blake was at Alli's apartment. That asshole was at Alli's apartment.

What the hell was that asshole doing at Alli's apartment?

Alli's door is locked so I start pounding on it. There's a small voice in the back of my head warning me not to jump to conclusions and I know I'm being unreasonable, that Alli wouldn't cheat on me, but I can't help myself. It's like all the rage and betrayal and hurt I've been carrying around ever since Lauren cheated on me is flared up inside me, taking me over and I can't stop. Alli comes to the door instantly and smiles when she sees me.

"Hey Nick, what's wrong? How was the—"

"What was Blake doing here?"

Alli's smile disappears. "Excuse me?"

"I saw him leave here. I know he was here. What was he doing here?" I want to stop yelling and accusing, but it's like my mouth is totally disconnected from my brain.

"Oh my gosh, Nick. I can't believe you."

"I just want to know—"

"So, let me get this straight. Despite the *countless* times I've told you not to worry about him, or that you know I hate lies and would never lie to you, or be unfaithful, the first thing you think when you see him leave here was..." She can't say the words. She's in tears. And I can't say anything because there's a fierce burning in my stomach preventing me from talking. "You really think I would... that I would do that to you? After everything..."

"Then why—"

"You know something, Nick. I've tried really hard to make you trust me. When you got upset about Blake and me singing together, I decided not to do it again. For *you*." She's really angry now. "You know the biggest secret I have, and you still don't trust me. How can I reconcile that? I've prayed and prayed that you would finally realize that you could trust me. How could you even for a second think that would be unfaithful to you? That really hurts you know? You give your heart to someone and then..."

The look on her faces turns cold, really cold. "You want to know what he was doing here? I'll show you." She heads over to her coffee table and picks up a CD in a jewel case. "He came to bring me this." She lifts up the disc to show me. "It's a rough mix of my new album. He even brought two copies because I asked him to make an extra one... for *you*. He was here for no more than five minutes. I was even waiting until you got here to listen to it." She wipes her eyes with the back of her hand. "I was so excited to listen to this with you... and you just ruined it."

My anger over what I thought had happened here tonight turns to fear over what's happening right now.

"I just thought—"

Alli chucks the CD towards the wall in anger. The jewel case explodes on impact, and the disc bounces off the wall and onto the floor. "You thought what? What exactly did you think was going on here?"

"I don't know, I mean, I see... *him*—"

"You're such an asshole," she says in a barely audible whisper. I've never heard her curse before, and I'm so shocked when I hear it that it takes me a few extra seconds to grasp that she's called *me* asshole. *Me.* And I really feel like one now. I will never forget the pain in her voice when she said that. Curses have been in my vocabulary for as long as I can remember. But when *she* curses, it's just different. Her aversion to profanity is such that even when she plays cover songs with curses she changes the lyrics to make them radio friendly. I feel guilty, not just for coming to the wrong conclusion tonight but also because I feel as though I've corrupted her.

"You need to leave now," she says. In the past thirty seconds she's cursed at me and asked me to leave. This is really bad. I know I'm as deep into this hole as I'm going to get, but there is still a part of me that hopes that she really doesn't want me to go, but merely wants me to leave before she says something else she'll regret.

"Wait, let me—"

"I don't know what else I could have done to assure you. To make you trust me. I've tried. I've tried really hard... and what good has it done? I can't do this anymore. I'm sorry."

"What do you mean?"

"This... us... I can't... I can't do this anymore."

She's breaking up with me. I can't believe it.

"Don't say that," I tell her. "Look, I'm sorry, I just..." I draw a blank. I know there's nothing I can say right that that will repair the damage I've done. I know that the best thing for me to do is leave and let her cool off. But I don't want to leave her like this, and I can't seem to move. She looks at me frustrated and goes over to the door and opens it. I stand there like an idiot. She tries to say something but is too upset to get the words out. She holds the door open, waiting for me to leave. I don't see any other choice now, the longer I stay the more pissed off she'll get. It takes an incredible amount of effort to walk through the door. She can't even look at me as I walk by her. As I walk up the stairs she closes the door behind me. She doesn't slam it shut, which I want to believe is a good sign, but I know it really doesn't matter.

I have no idea what to do or where to go, so I just head back to towards Beacon Street. I'm dizzy. What the hell just happened? Can I fix this? I'm so disoriented I nearly trip twice, so I stop in the first bar that I come across. I need a drink anyway.

How do I fix this?

I order a Guinness. Part of me hopes the bartender will ask me what is bothering me (because I must look bothered, how can I not?) but the bartender is a girl about my age and is more interested in working a big tip from a group of three guys on the other side of the bar from where I've sat. I guess it doesn't matter. What could she tell me, anyway? Since when does being able to mix and pour drinks qualify you as a surrogate therapist anyway?

So, it's just me and my thoughts. I down my beer quickly, hoping it will make me feel better.

It doesn't.

How could we have broken up? After everything we've been through? After all that she told me? I know who she really is, for crying out loud. I've got to fix this somehow.

"Another Guinness?" the bartender asks. I'm sure she can tell I'm not in a great mood, but she still doesn't ask me about my troubles. It shouldn't matter, but it bothers me she's not even making an effort.

"No thanks," I say, and she leaves me to my thoughts again. I give her a shitty tip and leave sober.

CHAPTER 41

I WAKE UP the following morning trying to convince myself I had a nightmare. I didn't, unfortunately. I also crashed on the couch for some reason. I feel like hell even though I'm not hungover. A soft giggling sound comes from Devon's room, and I know she's not in there alone. So, I put the TV on to drown out the noise. Before long Devon pops her head out.

"What the fuck are you doing here?" she asks.

"I just am," I say.

Devon gives me a suspicious look. "You okay? You look like shit."

I don't answer. Devon recognizes something is wrong. "Hold on a second." She closes her door, and I can hear her barking orders at whoever is in her room with her. In less than a minute the door opens and she's pushing some shirtless guy out of her room and towards the door. "—that was fun, blah-blah, we should do it again sometime, yada-

yada-yada, say hello to my roommate, etc. etc., you got my number, see ya." She opens the door and escorts him out.

"Not a keeper, is he?"

"Dude shut up. What's up with you? You were supposed to stay at Alli's last night... but I don't think you did. And you look like death." I don't answer. "Something is up. I can tell. You haven't looked like this since..." She pauses, and I can tell she's figuring it out. "You better tell me, because I have a feeling I know what it is."

"You are probably right."

"No fucking way. Alli broke up with you?"

I nod.

"What. The fuck. Did you do?"

"I don't want to talk about it."

Devon sits next to me couch.

"Talk to me. You can tell me you know. I know I give you shit all the time... and her... but, I liked you two together. Seriously. She made you a human again."

"Yeah, well, so much for that."

"What happened? Tell me."

"Uggh, fine. I went to her place last night and Blake was there."

"Blake?"

"From Candlepin."

"So? Wait, did you think she was cheating on you or something?"

"He asked her out before we met."

"And she rejected him?"

"Yeah, but, he's been showing up to some of her gigs, and showing me up... and he got her the opportunity to record another album."

"That's all very interesting," Devon says sarcastically. "Seriously, did you really think that girl would cheat on you?"

"I don't know. It's not that I didn't trust her, it's—"

"Yeah, yeah, you didn't trust *him*. You're still an idiot."

"Thanks."

"Hey, I said you could talk to me about this, I didn't say I was gonna sugar coat anything."

"Well, I appreciate it."

"If it helps, I think you'll get through this."

"What do you mean?"

"I mean, I think you'll work this out."

"You mean that, or are you saying that to make me feel better?"

"I told you I don't sugarcoat shit. I mean it. She's mad because you got the wrong end of the stick. But she's crazy about you, and she wouldn't throw that away just because you let some stupid jealousy cloud your judgment."

"I think it's more complicated than that."

"Just give her a little space for a while. You'll work it out. Look, I gotta do some project photography for Burnham & Modine, you can come with me if you want. Clear your mind."

"I think I'll just stay here and be miserable."

"You're not going to call her or go to her place or nothing, are you? Because that's the last thing you should do."

"No."

"Seriously, don't be stupid. Give her some space, she'll cool off eventually."

That's easier said than done. For the rest of the day I constantly check my phone, hoping Alli will call or text.

She doesn't.

* * *

It's now been a few days since Alli and I spoke. We haven't gone this long without talking since we started dating. It feels like what a smoker must feel when they try to quit. Every time my phone rings I get that nervous boiling sensation in my gut because I don't know whether to hope it's her calling me or not. She could call and tell me everything is okay again and we can pick up where we left off. Every day she doesn't call leads me to believe it's truly over. Is it better to know bad news, or to be a complete basket case with no idea? I go back forth. Sometimes I just want to know so I can stop torturing myself. Sometimes I am grateful that I've made it through another day without getting bad news.

More than once I've considered going to the Starbucks she works at to see if she's there, or even to one of her gigs. I did go to her Facebook page to see if I could find anything out there. I find out she cancelled her gig a couple nights ago. For Alli, cancelling a gig is a big deal, and she's obviously still upset over our fight... break up... whatever. Is that a good thing or a bad thing? It appears she did go to her gig last night, but whether that means anything I have no idea, because Friday night gigs are a bigger deal.

I'm driving myself crazy Facebook-stalking Alli. So, I decide the best thing to do is leave the apartment. I haven't had any coffee yet this morning, and between that and this whole break up situation, I have a really bad headache. Some fresh air and caffeine should help. So, I decide to go to Starbucks. Not Alli's Starbucks, of course, a different one.

I almost expect to see her at the register or behind the espresso machine when I come in. She's not here and I'm not sure if I'm disappointed or relieved.

I didn't bring my laptop, because I have no desire to work, so all there is for me to do here is sit, drink my coffee and wait for the caffeine to relieve my headache. After a couple hours of obsessively checking my phone, waiting for a call or text I hear a familiar voice call my name. I look up to see Lauren. The sight of her surprises me. She's got one earbud in and one dangling down her sweatshirt.

"What are you doing here?" she asks.

"Having coffee," I say.

"By yourself?"

"Yeah," I say.

She hesitates before pointing to the free chair at my table, "Mind if I sit here?"

I'm in no mood to protest. "Sure." She takes the seat and sips from her drink, some flavor of Frappuccino, and places her iPhone on the table.

"Are you okay?" she asks, concerned, pulling the other earbud out. She hasn't stopped playing the music she was listening to because I can hear something familiar coming faintly out of her earbuds.

"Not really," I tell her. There's really no point in hiding it.

I pick up her iPhone off the table and look at the screen. What I see floors me.

"I know, is that weird? Me listening to your girlfriend's album. I can't help it. I love it. And, she was so nice to me that night, and—" She looks at me curiously. "What's wrong?"

"She's not... my girlfriend anymore."

Lauren is taken aback by this. "Oh, no. What happened?"

"It's a long story."

"You can talk to me about it if you'd like I know I'm probably the last person you'd want to discuss it with, but, I don't know maybe I can help?"

"I'm not sure that you can."

"Try me."

So, I tell her the story. I tell her about Blake's behavior the past few months, Alli's multiple warnings for me to knock off the jealousy, and the *coup de grâce* that ended the relationship last week. Lauren's reaction is surprising. She covers her mouth with her hand and gasps, then buries her face in her hands like she's upset at herself.

"I'm sorry," she says. "This is my fault."

"What? How is it your fault?"

"Nick, we were together a long time. You are not the jealous type. You never were. If I hadn't... you know..."

"If you hadn't we'd be planning a wedding right now."

Lauren looks down at the table, sullen. "I know. I know. And I don't blame you for breaking up with me. But I still feel responsible. I may not know her, but I am sure she wouldn't cheat on you. She's just so sweet and... well, you know... But obviously what happened with us made you paranoid. I'm so sorry, Nick. I feel so awful. Maybe there's something I can do to help?"

"I don't think so."

"I could talk to her. I wouldn't mind, I—"

"Why would you even want to do this for me?" I ask.

"I know I screwed up big time with us. I'll always regret that. It broke my heart to hurt you that way. But I really do want you to be happy. And you two... you looked very happy together. If we had just broken up for some other reason you'd still be with Alli now, I know you would be. I know I can't fix us, but maybe I can make it up to you by fixing things with you and Alli."

"I appreciate that but—" my phone vibrates in my pocket and I take it out. My heart races, thinking it's Alli calling. But according to the caller ID it's Lacy. I ignore the call. "—just my sister calling," I say.

"Oh, how is she?"

"She's... good, I guess."

"That's good. Listen, I'm supposed to meet some of my friends later, so I need to get going."

I look at my phone and see it's already 7:30. "Wow, I didn't realize how late it was."

"Yeah. Listen, I know I've already said this, but I really am so sorry about everything. About us. About you and Alli. I hope you two can work things out."

"Thanks," I say.

Lauren stands up and prepares to leave and waits to see what I plan to do. Are we supposed to hug now? I don't know. Is that even possible, given how things ended with us? Can we be friends after having been a couple for so long? I've never considered that a possibility, and such a situation only happens in movies or in television. Of course, Lauren and I dated for years, lived together, and had a horrible breakup. How could a post-relationship friendship even work? I'm not sure it can, but her offer to help me with Alli has me seeing her very differently now. She genuinely wants to see me happy again, even if that means me being happy with someone else. I want to hug her to thank her for the offer, but all I can do is stand like I'm ready to leave.

"I'll see you around?" she asks awkwardly.

"Sure." Lauren hesitates before walking away.

"Listen," I say. "Before you go..."

She turns to face me.

"I'm sorry about what happened… with us. I was… a bit harsh completely cutting you off. I know you felt bad about it and I guess what I'm trying to say is… I—I forgive you."

Next thing I know she's hugging me. It's bizarre after hating her for so many months to be hugging her again, but it also feels familiar and reassuring. When we pullback from each other I can see a huge weight has been lifted from her.

"Thank you," she says.

CHAPTER 42

On the way back home I ignore another call from Lacy. I just can't deal with her right now. She'll ask about Alli and I won't know what to tell her. She'll be devastated, and I can't deal with comforting her while I'm still trying to accept the situation. Unfortunately, I don't know what to do with myself now that I'm alone. It occurs to me I haven't listened to *Not Famous* in a while, but somehow listening to it now, while Alli and I are broken up, just seems wrong. Thinking about that makes me remember that I had I not jumped to incorrect conclusions a week ago that I'd also have a copy of the rough cut of Alli's new album. Instead, when I get home I'll put on the recording of her performance at Revolution from the night we first really met. That seems like so long ago now.

Before I can hop on the train my phone vibrates again. It must be Lacy. I'm not sure why she keeps pestering me tonight, but I figure if I don't tell her to knock it off it won't stop. My heart nearly skips a beat when I see it's not Lacy calling, but Alli.

"Hello?" I say, my voice cracking from nerves.

"You need to come up to Hennessy's. Right away."

There's panic in her voice. Something's wrong.

"Huh?"

"It's Lacy. She's here. She's... just come, please."

"I'm on my way."

* * *

Alli and Lacy are in the small alley outside Hennessy's when I arrive. Lacy looks upset, and Alli is comforting her.

"What's wrong? What happened?" I ask, then look at Lacy.

Alli takes me aside and whispers to me. "I don't know what happened to her, but don't say anything about... us... Okay? She's hysterical enough."

"Okay," I say.

"Lacy," Alli says. "Can you tell us what's wrong? What happened tonight?"

"And why are you down here in Boston?" I add.

Lacy collects herself. "I was at a party."

"Okay," I say. "Can you give us more than that?"

"I was with Nate." It takes me a second to remember that Nate is her boyfriend. Though, I suspect he isn't anymore.

"Did something happen with Nate?" Alli asks.

"He ditched me at the party." Lacy starts to cry hard, and Alli tries to comfort her.

"It's okay, Lacy. Everything will be fine. I know it hurts now, but—"

"I think I'm pregnant," Lacy blurts out.

"Oh geez," I say.

"Oh, Lacy..." Alli says, and starts to cry.

"I'm sorry! I'm sorry! I'm so stupid! I..."

"So, you told him you think you're pregnant and that's when he ditched you?" I ask.

Lacy nods and tells us how she and Nate had gone to a party at his cousin's house, where everyone was hooking up and having sex. When she overheard some girl complain she was on her period Lacy suddenly realized she was a week late. She freaked out and told Nate, who went nuts and claimed it wasn't his. That's when he ditched her and she tried calling me. When I didn't answer she looked up Alli's gig schedule, found out where she was playing tonight and figured out how to take the train here.

"What am I going to do? What if I'm pregnant, Nick?"

"Have you taken a test yet?"

Lacy shakes her head.

"Okay, well, maybe you should take a test and see if you're really pregnant," Alli suggests. "There must be a pharmacy somewhere nearby Nick can take you to."

"Yeah, there's one close by," I say.

"Okay, I have to set up for my gig. Get a test, and you can take it in the bathroom inside, okay?" Lacy nods. "I'll see you soon, okay?"

So, Lacy and I walk to the nearest CVS.

"You must think I'm such an idiot," she says.

"Nahh."

"Oh, come on. *I* think I'm an idiot. I know I shouldn't have slept with him. He always made me feel like shit for saying no. And then the asshole ditches me at a party."

"That's pretty rough."

"Worst break up ever, I'm sure."

"My break up with Lauren was pretty bad, too."

"Really?"

"There's a reason I've never told anyone what happened with her."

"Tell me."

Given her situation, I figure telling her my story might make her feel better, or at least distract her until she takes the pregnancy test. So, I explain how I had proposed to Lauren, how she broke down and told me she'd cheated on me. Everything.

"Omigod, Nick, that's horrible. Why didn't you say anything?"

"I've never told anyone. It was literally the worst and most humiliating moment in life."

"That must have been awful. You could have told me. I would have been there for you."

I almost want to tell her about Alli and me, but Alli did tell me not to say anything, and I know it wouldn't go over well, so I decide to keep quiet. "Yeah, well, I just wanted to move on and forget about it."

"I guess we both have been through some bad shit when it comes to relationships, huh?"

"Must be genetic," I say and Lacy laughs. Then I remember something I'd nearly forgotten after all these months. "I still have the ring, too."

"You do? Why?"

"Remember that part about it being the most humiliating moment in my life? Well, returning the engagement ring can't be much fun either. I'll return it or sell it or something if I'm ever in need of a lot of cash. So, I keep it in the back of my safe right now." The safe that also holds my copy of *Not Famous*.

When we reach the CVS Pharmacy I offer Lacy some money, but she is too embarrassed to buy a pregnancy test on her own, so I have to buy it for her and we head back to the pub. Alli is done setting up when we arrive, and she shows Lacy where the bathroom is.

"Omigod, I'm so nervous. What if it's positive?" Lacy starts to cry again.

"If you're really pregnant, we'll all be there for you. Me, Nick, your mom. We'll all help you through it," Alli assures her.

"Really?"

"Of course. I know you're scared, but if this baby is really coming, you'll love him or her with all your heart, and even though it won't be easy, we'll there for you and eventually you'll won't be able to imagine not having that precious little soul in your life. And if you're not pregnant, it wasn't meant to be, and that's okay, too."

Lacy nods, holding back tears.

"Now, go on, we'll wait for you out here, okay?"

"'kay."

Alli hugs her again before Lacy takes the test in the bag from me and goes into the bathroom.

After a few minutes of Alli and I standing in silence, I say something. "I'm sorry if this is, you know, messing up your evening."

"It's okay, Nick."

"I didn't tell her—"

"Thank you. I just... she doesn't need to deal with that, too. Not right now."

"Well, maybe she doesn't have to at all."

"Nick—"

"What? Why can't we try to work things out?"

"I—"

"I'm sorry. I was stupid. I don't see why we can't talk things out."

"Nick, this has been... so hard for me... I can't deal with this now, I—"

"I screwed up. I was a jealous ass, I know that. But that's no reason—"

"You know it was more than that, Nick. You know how important it is... *was* that you trusted me. You know how much it hurt that no matter how many times I told you not to worry about Blake or that I wasn't interested that you still couldn't find it in yourself to trust me to be faithful to you? I love you. You were my first boyfriend. You know *everything* about me. I trusted *you*. But you still couldn't trust me. Do you realize how much that hurt? And still hurts? It still hurts me to think you couldn't trust me. I've had to cry myself to sleep at night every night this past week."

"It's been hard for me, too. I—"

"I can't do this now, Nick. I need to figure things out. Maybe... I dunno... maybe I'm really not ready for a boyfriend. Maybe I just need more time. I don't know. All I know is that you hurt me really bad, and I can't—" Alli chokes up a bit. "I'm sorry, I can't... When Lacy's done taking the test, you're going to have to leave. This is too hard for me right now, I—"

"What's going on?" It's Lacy. She's returned from the bathroom without us noticing.

Oh, shit.

"Hey, did you take the test?" I ask, hoping to change the subject.

"I'm *not* pregnant," she says like it wasn't the huge deal it was just five minutes ago. "But why are you two fighting? What's all this 'get back together' stuff?"

"Lacy, I—" Alli starts to say.

"Did you two break up?"

"Lacy, I'm sorry," Alli says.

"Omigod, when? When did this happen?"

"Last week, we..." Alli starts to say, but Lacy isn't listening anymore. She plows in between us and marches out the door. Alli runs after her and I follow. When I get outside, Alli is hugging Lacy, who is sobbing uncontrollably. She tries to console her but is barraged with questions that Alli can't or doesn't want to answer.

"This is literally the worst night ever," Lacy says.

"I'm sorry Lacy, I know this is tough. It's tough for me too... and Nick... We... just had some issues we couldn't work out, we—"

"Alli, you're on," says a voice from the door, someone who works at the pub.

"Okay, thanks. I'll be right there," she says, and then looks back at Lacy. "Okay, why don't you have a chat with your brother and calm down, okay? We'll talk later, I promise." Alli looks at me as if to say, "you got this," and leaves me alone with Lacy.

"You going to be okay?" I ask.

"What happened? Why did you two break up?" she asks.

"I was stupid."

"You're gonna work things out with her, right?"

"I'm trying."

"Good."

"But listen. I'm sorry about what happened to you tonight."

"It's not your fault," she says.

"Yeah it is. You've been wanting my advice, and I... I should have been a better brother. I'm sorry."

"It's okay. I forgive you. I know I can be a pain in the ass, too. Let's just promise to be nicer to each other in the future."

"Deal," I say, offering her my hand to shake.

"Just hug me, you idiot," she says. And we hug.

"So, what do you want to do now?"

"Can we watch Alli's set?"

"Sure."

"Then maybe I can... crash at your place? I told mom I was staying over a friend's house, and... you know..."

"Sure. And, your secret is safe with me, okay?" I tell her.

"Thanks," she says, relieved. "Okay, let's go in."

We go in and Alli is on stage singing. We take a spot as far from the stage as we can, since my being here might be a bit of a distraction for her. It's a decent sized crowd for a Tuesday night. Alli's merch table is vacant and it feels weird not to be manning it. The crowd cheers when Alli finishes her song, one of her own, and while she's visibly grateful for the response, she still looks sad, and I feel awful that my being here can't be making her performance any easier.

"We should leave after this first set, okay?" I tell Lacy. "Hopefully she didn't notice us coming back in."

"Okay," Lacy says.

Alli adjusts the tuning on her guitar and speaks to crowd. "Thanks so much for coming out here tonight. I'll be selling CDs during the set break." The crowd cheers. "Thanks. So... I normally wouldn't play this song for this crowd, but, a friend of mine is here tonight, and—" Well, I guess she noticed us come back in. The crowd applauds again. "—so, my friend has had a rough night tonight, and I wanted to play this song for her." She starts to play the opening chords of a song. Lacy recognizes the song immediately and gasps. I look at her confused, but she doesn't say anything.

"This song is by Taylor Swift and it's called 'Fifteen.'"

A few people clap, and Lacy is at full attention as Alli starts to sing. Within a minute, Lacy is crying again. She moves closer to the stage, and I follow her. Up close, I can see that Alli also has tears coming down her face, too. When the song is over Lacy rushes up the stage to hug her. While they are hugging Alli and I make eye contact, and the hurt is her eyes just stabs me. When Lacy gets off stage I tell her it's time to leave.

"But why?"

"I have to go. I can't stay anymore. She doesn't want me here."

"Should I tell her we're leaving?"

"No. She's about to start her next song. She'll see us leaving."

"I'll just—"

"I'm leaving," I say, and walk out.

About a minute later, Lacy joins me outside. "I'm sorry," she says.

"About what?"

"I wasn't thinking that staying here would be so difficult for you."

"It's okay. Let's just go back to my place."

We start walking towards Government Center station. We don't talk much, but eventually she asks me again what broke Alli and me up, and I give her an abridged version of the story. Lacy considers the details I've shared and concludes Alli will eventually take me back.

"What makes you think that?"

"You were jealous? Big deal, all that means is that you were... I don't know... protective... of your relationship. It's not like you knocked her up and ditched her at a party or anything. She'll come around."

"It's more complicated than that."

"How?"

I can't explain *how* to her. I can't tell her about how Alli is really Calliope Crawley, and despite her need to keep that a secret from the world she told me... and yet I didn't have enough faith in her to keep things platonic with Blake.

"Trust me," I say.

"Whatever. I still think you'll work things out."

It's barely passed ten o'clock we get back to my place, so Lacy tries to find a movie on Netflix for us to watch. She searches for a while before giving up and deciding she's tired anyway.

"You can crash in my room if you like," I tell her. "I'll take the couch"

Lacy thinks this over. "Have you had sex on that bed?"

"Not *recently*."

"Ever?"

"Yeah, of course."

"I'll take the couch," she says without hesitating. I don't tell her that Lauren and I had sex on the couch plenty of times, and I'm sure Devon has more recently, too.

CHAPTER 43

WHEN I WAKE up Lacy is still sleeping. I hear a knock from the balcony door. Devon is out there, and she beckons me to join her. I join her on the balcony and close the door behind me. Devon is tinkering with her camera and smoking a cigarette. She's also wearing her Gadsden flag shirt and nothing else.

"Dude, maybe it's none of my business, I know you're depressed again and all, but that girl is way too young for you. What is she, twelve?"

"First of all, that's my sister, Lacy."

"Oh, sorry. And second of all?"

"Can you put on some pants please?"

"I'm wearing underwear."

"For a change."

"Exactly, so don't be such a prude. Anyway, second of all?"

"She's fifteen, not twelve."

Devon points her camera out and adjusts the zoom before taking a few pictures. "So why is she here? You never brought her here before."

"She... Well... She had a situation last night. So, she crashed here."

"Anything serious?"

"Dumped by her boyfriend."

"She's pregnant, isn't she?"

"She thought she was. She told him. He ditched her. She took a test and thankfully she's not pregnant."

"So she came running to you? That seems odd. From what I know you two aren't exactly tight."

"She tracked down Alli at her gig."

Devon perks up and adjusts in her seat to give me her full attention.

"Well now this story got a whole lot more interesting."

"My fifteen-year-old sister thinking she might be pregnant and getting dumped wasn't exciting enough for you?"

"Shit, sorry. No. That sucks for her. I just mean... You know... You saw Alli then? What happened? Did you two talk?"

"She didn't want to talk. She basically told me I had to leave because she couldn't deal with me being there."

"That sucks."

"Yup."

"Give it time. She'll come around," she says, then extinguishes her cigarette. "So, your little sister's been laid more recently than you, huh?"

"Excuse me?"

"Oh, please Nick, it's pretty obvious that Alli hasn't let anyone, even you, in her panties."

"If you say so."

"I am willing to bet my half of next month's rent that I'm right."

"Okay, fine, you're right. How did you know?"

"Well, for one thing, she told me she was a virgin that night we all went to dinner and she ran off into the bathroom after flipping out on me. And I haven't seen anything to make me think you've gotten laid since she told me. So, I'm quite confident she still hasn't given up the goods."

"Well, congratulations, Sherlock."

"Look, I'm not trying to be a bitch. Honestly."

"Sure. Whatever."

"Listen, I'm not the most eloquent person, especially when it comes to relationship stuff. And I know you must think I'm a real slut—"

"No, I..."

"But I think what you two have is really... awesome."

"For real?"

"Of course. Think about it. How many boyfriends have I had since you've known me?"

"I don't know... too many to count."

"Zero."

"Bullshit. You've been with a bunch of guys—"

"Oh, I've *slept with* a bunch of guys. I haven't *dated* any of them." She puts a new cigarette in her mouth and lights it. "I am not 'dating material.' I may not be the biggest slut in Boston, but I have a reputation. If I made a guy wait more than one or two dates they would move on. They wouldn't waste their time because I'm an easy lay."

"So, what's your point?"

"My point, Einstein, is that despite my reputation, deep down I do think you have something incredibly... special with Alli and—"

"Had," I say. "*Had* something special."

"Dude, you been with her for months without popping her cherry. How many guys would have bailed after five seconds?"

"I dunno."

"Most. Trust me. You two had something special. You love that girl. And she loves you. I like sex as much as the next person, but damn, I'd be pretty psyched if some guy felt the way about me the way you do about her."

"So, what are you trying to say?"

"I'm saying don't sit around here feeling sorry for yourself. If she was worth waiting for, she's also worth fighting for. Go to her next gig. Try to talk to her. If she pushes you away, go to the next one. Fight. Win her back."

"I thought you said—"

"You've given her enough space now. If you don't go see her now she'll assume you gave up on your relationship."

"I dunno. I'll think about—"

There's a knock on the sliding door. It's Lacy. She's slides the door open.

"Hi," she says to us.

"Hi, you must be Lacy! I'm Devon, your brother's roommate."

Lacy looks at me confused. "I didn't know you had a girl for a roommate."

* * *

Later, after taking Lacy home, I look up Alli's gig schedule on her Facebook page. I've decided to take Devon's advice and see Alli again at one of her gigs. She's opening for The Copper Thieves tonight at the Lizard Lounge... but I think I need to give her a little bit of space before trying again.

Sunday night she's opening for Bullhorne at Revolution, which is perfect. It's four days away, which gives her plenty of time to cool off, and gives me time to figure out what to say. It's also the place I first saw her perform. It must be a sign that's the place to go to clean this mess up.

In the meantime, I don't know what to do with myself. Waiting for Sunday seems like torture. Then I notice the crate of Perch CDs in the corner of my room. That makes me think about the copy of *Not Famous* in my safe. I still haven't listened to it since Alli broke up with me. Evening having it seems wrong. Since Alli is playing at the Lizard Lounge tonight I can deliver the CD to her apartment without running into her.

So, I grab the CD out of my safe, write a note in it telling her I'm sorry about everything and that she should have the CD back, then seal it in a manila envelope. Taking it on the subway makes me a bit paranoid, so I keep it hidden from view until I reach the stop for Alli's apartment.

While I'm walking up the street towards Alli's place I hear a dog bark, followed by a girl yelling. It's Derby and Eden. I guess Derby noticed me and started running to me, causing Eden to drop the leash. When he reaches me, I kneel down and grab his collar.

"Hey Derby, how you doin' boy?" He jumps up trying to lick my face.

Eden soon reaches us, panting from chasing Derby. "Thank so much for catching him, I—" she pauses when she realizes who I am. "Oh, it's you." Eden looks at me nervously, like she's not sure she should be talking to me.

"Yeah. It's me." I offer her Derby's leash. She puts her hand through the loop and puts a firm grip on it.

"Thanks," she says. "Alli's not home, she—"

"I know. I just wanted to drop something off for her."

"I can't... umm... you know... unlock the door for you now. I... I'm sorry."

"I understand."

"I can bring it to her when she's back."

If it were anything else besides this CD, I would leave the envelope with her, but I can't.

"That's okay. I'll just put it through the mail slot."

"Oh, okay. Come on Derby, let's go." She tugs on the leash and starts to walk Derby down the road, but stops, and turns back to me. "What did you do?"

"Do?"

"Why did she break up with you?"

"She didn't tell you?"

"No. She's really sad. Can't you say you're sorry?"

"I have. But..."

"Do you love her?"

"Yes."

"I think she should get back together with you."

"Do you think she would?" I'm not sure why I am asking this twelve-year-old about my relationship with Alli but it's all I got.

"I don't know. Maybe."

"I guess that counts for something."

"Do you want to walk Derby with me?"

"Even though I'm not Alli's boyfriend anymore?" Derby pulls on the leash, anxious to get moving again. "Okay, sure. I guess it's safer to walk with me than to walk alone, right?"

"Right!" Eden says, smiling.

So, we walk Derby for a while in silence, and then I escort them back to the house. Eden says goodbye and goes in the house through the front, while I got around back and down the steps to her apartment, open the storm door and drop the envelope with the disc through the mail slot.

I half expect Alli to call me the next day, but she doesn't. I don't even get a thank you text message. I'm not saying I returned the CD in the hopes she'd reach out to me, but I'd be lying if I said the thought hadn't crossed my mind. So, I spend the next couple of days questioning whether the note I put with the CD was good enough, if I should have written something else, what that something else should have been. Self-doubt is brutal.

CHAPTER 44

LACY CALLS ME on Friday to ask me if I've spoken to Alli since the other night. I tell her about my plan to go to her gig on Sunday.

"Want me to come too?"

"I... don't think so."

"Come on. Maybe she'll be... more receptive if I'm there. Like, she won't yell at you if I'm there."

She might have a point. Alli was much more aggressive while we were alone than when Lacy was with us. But something tells me I need to do this by myself.

"Tell you what, if this attempt doesn't work, I'll bring you next time."

"Yay! Well, hopefully that won't be necessary."

"Yeah, hopefully. So... how are you doing?"

"Things could be worse," she says.

"Yeah, you could be pregnant."

Lacy laughs. "Don't remind me. By the way, I got my period yesterday."

"Okay... too much information, and congratulations."

"Just thought you'd want to know that the test was accurate."

"Well, good."

* * *

Lacy calls me again on Sunday to wish me luck and to ask me what I plan to say. I have to admit that after four days of thinking about it I still have no idea. Lacy assures me that I will know what to say when I see Alli. I hope she's right.

Alli is supposed to start at 8 p.m., which means she'll probably play an hour-long set. My intention is to show up close to when her set is almost over, go inside from the rear entrance off the alley (which is usually unlocked so staff can go in and out easily) and go undetected upstairs to the little band lounge on the second floor and wait for her to come up to get her stuff. I don't really like the idea of ambushing her, but what else do I have? Waiting for her to come around and talk to me isn't working.

I get to Revolution about a half hour into Alli's set. Slipping in through the back entrance is easy, and no one notices me. Alli is on stage but can't see me.

I scan the room from a distance to see if there's anyone here who might recognize me. There are several familiar faces, people who are either regulars here, or that I've seen at another venue. I catch Nava with, I assume, some of her friends, but by the looks of things she's drunk or just enjoying the show too much to be able to notice me in the back hall. So, I figure it is safe to watch Alli for a bit. I miss seeing her play, but it sucks having such a shitty view.

Seeing Nava makes me wonder why Blake isn't here. If she's here, Candlepin doesn't have a gig or a rehearsal. Maybe Blake has other plans? It's while I'm considering this that I finally see him coming in through the front door. He tosses a cigarette out on the ground before entering. Seeing him makes me panic, because he could have seen me as he walked in. Just in case, I rush upstairs to the band lounge.

Shit, this was stupid.

I'm not really sure what to do now but wait. So, I sit on the couch, trying to calm my nerves. The sound of Alli's performance downstairs is muffled, but I can tell when she's played her last song, said her thank yous, and received her last big round of applause. I don't hear her coming up the stairs right away. Of course, she has to run her merch table. So, that'll be another ten minutes or so. I close the door to the lounge and wait.

The wait is torture. What am I going to say? What is she going to say? I'm still pondering a script when I finally hear footsteps and voices.

Alli's and *Blake's*.

Fuck.

Without thinking, I hide in the bathroom. There is literally nowhere else to go, except out the window. There is a fire escape, but they'd no doubt catch me going out the window, so I take my chances in this tiny little bathroom and hope neither of them comes in here. I shut the door and lock it. That should help.

With nothing else to do but wait until they leave, I try to listen to their conversation. But between the closed door and the sound of wind coming through the ancient exhaust vent in the ceiling it's really difficult to hear most of it. The first voice I hear is Alli's.

"Thanks for coming out tonight, I ..." she speaks another few words that are unintelligible to me.

"No problem, I always like to..." I hear Blake start to say, before his words become inaudible. He must be heading towards the door to leave. That's good.

"Why are you... door?" Alli says, the middle of her question I can't hear due to a gust of wind coming through the vent.

Running water in the pipes in the wall (probably from the adjacent staff bathroom) makes it difficult to hear Blake's response, but I'm pretty sure I hear something like "... after everything I've done to help you."

"I appreciate your help, Blake, but I told you..." Alli's words become muffled. She's moving around.

"Are you kidding me?" he asks. I can hear that part clearly, he's yelling, now and very angry. I'm momentarily paralyzed, unable to process what must be happening beyond the door. My heart is beating fast and my stomach burns in fear. Rage is building up. I know something is wrong. I hear running footsteps, and the doorknob turn, but since I've locked the door it doesn't open. There's a loud noise, and the door bounces on its hinges. I'm pretty sure Blake has pushed Alli and pinned her against the door.

"Blake, stop it. I told you, I—" her voice trails off, she's apparently gotten away from him and is heading towards the other door now. I unlock the door, hoping she'll try to come in here again, and then Blake will find me in here, and I can... well, I'm not sure what I'll do. He's bigger and stronger than me, but I'm filled with rage and adrenaline. If she can make in here safely, the element of surprise might give me enough of advantage to take him down.

Just in case, I look around the bathroom for something... anything. It would be nice if there was a baseball bat in here, so I can bash Blake's head in, but there's nothing remotely close. I hear Alli struggle with the door to the lounge so hard that I know that Blake has locked it. She must be too terrified to process how to get it unlocked. "Stop it. I mean it!" she says, much more panicked than before. There's another noise, like a thud against a wall or the floor.

She's not making it back here.

I lose all sense of fear. Anger overwhelms me, and I plow through the door to see Alli pinned against the wall by Blake, like he's trying to kiss her. Her face is turned away from me, so neither notices me. On a normal day, I wouldn't mess with someone like Blake, but this is not a normal day. Every bad thing I have felt about him before is nothing compared to the hate I feel for him now, and I barely think about what I'm doing when I charge at him with a closed fist. It's a direct hit to his face, which stuns him a bit, and he turns to face me directly, whipping his arm towards me knocking me to the floor. He recovers from my punch quickly and lifts me effortlessly off the ground and slams me against the wall opposite where he had Alli pinned. Alli is frozen stiff.

"I am going to kick your fucking ass," Blake says, with his big fucking hand on my neck.

"Bring it on, asshole," I say.

I'm sure later on I'll think of many better, more menacing replies I could have made. I am too angry to think, and it's quite obvious he is not appreciative of my interruption and plans to show me just how much he doesn't appreciate it. He punches me in the gut, knocking the wind out of me. It's taken him mere seconds to recover from my pathetic punch and turn my advantage of surprise around and take control of me like a sock puppet. As long as it gives Alli a chance to get out I don't care.

Adrenaline does the job of keeping me from feeling any significant pain, but the superhuman strength I was counting on before never makes an appearance, so I am a human punching bag, and there's not much I can do about it. You imagine having fights like this and you think that you'll achieve ninja skills or something when you are in the middle of it. You think, "I'll be able to block every punch." Well, if anyone can swear to it happening to them, I can't.

I am getting my ass kicked.

I focus on all the reasons I hate him, trying to muster the strength to break free of him and gain some leverage to pin him down or something. All wishful thinking let's be honest. Then, I notice shadows moving behind him. There's a blur, a crunch, and then Blake lets go of me and crashes to the floor. He's out cold. I slide down the wall, my legs giving out under me.

Alli stands there, her guitar in hand. Or at least what's left of it. The body of her guitar is now a broken mess, detached from the neck. Only the strings hold the two together now.

I look up at her, and we make eye contact. She looks horrified, but I'm not sure if it's because of what happened with Blake, what happened to her guitar, or my presence here. Something tells me it's all of the above.

She opens her mouth to say something. But no words come out. I start to feel all the pain of being pummeled by Blake and I taste blood in my mouth. Alli is shaking. Things start to get blurry, but it looks like he didn't hurt her badly.

"I'm sorry," I say. "But I—" I'm interrupted by the sound of Alli's guitar, which she has dropped to the floor.

"Omigosh," she says, her voice still sounding terrified. She runs towards the door, and tries to get out, but it's still locked. She manages this time to unlock it and run out.

I stand up, and it hurts like hell. Alli must be rushing to get help. I'm not sure why, but I don't want to be here when help comes. There's only two ways out of here though, the way Alli left, or the fire escape.

I choose the fire escape.

I already regret leaving her behind. I should be with her now. But she's not mine to comfort anymore. She'll go back there, grab Nava or someone else, tell them what happened, and Alli won't need me.

People look at me on the train ride back home. Based on my reflection, Blake got me a few times in my face, leaving a couple bruises and a swollen eye. I just look away and don't say anything. My whole body aches. I reach for my phone in my pocket and discover that it got damaged somehow while Blake was beating the shit out of me. It's not working anymore.

Devon is photographing a wedding tonight, so she's not home when I arrive. Because it's a Sunday night she said she expected it to end early, but she'll probably find a groomsman or someone else to spend the rest of the evening with.

I don't even make it to my room. I just fall flat on the couch and pass out.

CHAPTER 45

DEVON WAKES ME in the morning by shaking me on the couch.

"Hey, what happened last night, did you see Alli or did you—holy shit what happened to your face?"

"Does it look bad?"

"Oh no, it looks amazing. Of course, it looks bad! What happened? Did Alli beat the shit out of you?"

"No, Blake did."

"Oh, shit. You gotta tell me what happened."

I tell her the whole story.

"Why would he do that to her? It doesn't make any sense," Devon says. "I'll be right back."

"Where are you going?"

"I'm calling Justin. I think I still have his number."

Devon rushes off to her room and shuts the door. I can tell by the sound of her voice she's gotten a hold of him and she's giving him the third degree about Blake. She listens with the occasional response of "holy shit!" and "no fucking way!" before thanking him and hanging up.

"Did you know Blake was married before he lived here?" Devon asks when she returns.

"Yeah, Alli mentioned it."

"She knew?"

"She said he told her he was divorced, and I guess he took it hard and moved out here to start over or something."

"Is that what he said? Well, he's a fucking liar. Apparently, he used to beat up his ex-wife."

"Oh shit."

"Yeah, the dude's a total scumbag. His ex-wife never pressed charges or anything, which is complete bullshit, but that's why he left California. Good news, though. They kicked him out of Candlepin, obviously."

"Is that supposed to make me feel better?"

"Of course not. I mean do you realize what would have happened if—"

"Don't say it."

"Well, he wasn't trying to feed her grapes. He's a violent asshole who thought he could take advantage of some innocent chick. Shit, Alli must be a fucking wreck right now." Devon thinks for a moment. "This. Changes. Everything. You need to go see her."

"She won't want to—"

"Don't tell me she won't want to see you. You saved her from being violated, man."

"I got my ass kicked and *she* took him out with her guitar. Shit, her guitar."

"What about it?"

"It's destroyed."

"So the fuck what? She'll get a new one. I think under the circumstances—where are you going?"

"I'm gonna take a hot shower and go take care of something."

If feel much better after the hot shower, and I even look a little better too. I get dressed and do an online search for guitars. Alli has... or had a Gibson acoustic electric guitar. I don't know much more than that but the closest thing I can find to what she had is a lot more expensive than I thought. I thought it might be a few hundred dollars. But it turns out it's closer to $2,000. I don't have that kind of money sitting around, and if I did—wait a second. I still have Lauren's engagement ring in my safe. If I return it I can get more than enough to cover a new guitar for Alli and get myself a new iPhone.

First thing I do is bring the ring back where I bought it. Unfortunately, I'm way beyond the time frame of the return policy, and the man I speak with is not about to make an exception for me. After pleading with him, he tells me there are plenty of jewelers who will buy the diamond, and discreetly recommends a few for me to consider. Two offer me a lot less than I paid for it, but the third one appraises it more fairly, and offers to buy it for quite a bit less than I paid for it, but still enough for me to accomplish what I need to do today. After getting paid for the diamond, I deposit the check at my bank, and then go to an Apple store for a new phone. I don't get back home until early evening. I activate my new iPhone and sync it up with my iTunes. An avalanche of notifications comes in. At least two dozen from Lacy. I call her as soon as my phone is synced up.

"Oh. My. God." Where have you been?" she asks when she picks up the phone. I tell her the whole story of what happened last night.

"I can't believe it. Is she okay?"

"I think so."

"You *think* so?"

"Well, I left."

"Nick, you have to go see her. *Today*. This changes everything. Does she have a gig tonight?"

"How can she? Her guitar is busted."

"So, go to her place."

"You really think I—"

"Yes! Go! Then tell me what happened!"

* * *

When I get to Alli's apartment she isn't home. She must be working, so I go to her Starbucks.

She's not working there either. I ask one of the baristas and I'm told she was supposed to work this morning but asked to take a sick day. I sit down and look on her Facebook page on my phone to see if she has a gig scheduled tonight. There is a bunch of talk on her page. The top post is about tonight's gig at Forge, a coffeehouse in Cambridge she's played at a few times before. It has over a hundred comments. I scroll through them and it's clear that word has gotten out about what happened last night at Revolution. People ask if Alli is okay, if she's still playing tonight, what's going on with Candlepin now... Nava reports that Blake has been kicked out of Candlepin, and that their gig tonight is cancelled, but their show tomorrow night at House of Blues is still on. The keyboardist for Bullhorne will fill in for Blake until they find someone permanent. She also reported that Andy, Candlepin's guitarist, offered Alli the use of one of his acoustic guitars so she can still do her gig tonight. Comments from Alli are curiously absent until about two-thirds of the way down, with a single comment "I'm still performing tonight." That comment received a ton of likes and responses. Further down there are more questions about what really happened last night, what Blake did, which Nava handled personally, telling everyone "let's just say he's lucky I didn't personally castrate him." I keep scrolling for more comments from Alli, but there aren't any.

So, she's playing tonight. By now she's already started, so I jump on the T and make my way to the coffeehouse. On the way, Lacy texts me to ask if there's anything to report. I write back that there isn't, but I'll let her know.

The coffeehouse is crowded. It's not filled to capacity, but it's definitely got more people than Alli's usual draw here. I look inside through the storefront windows and watch for a bit. I walk in between songs while everyone is clapping, staying hidden in the back of the crowd. Alli looks overwhelmed, probably surprised that so many people have come just to see her on a Monday evening. She asks the crowd if they mind if she plays a cover song, and the cheer their approval. "Thank you. This is a song... well, I've been listening to it a lot recently and wanted to play it tonight. Now seem like a good time." She starts playing the song. The emotion in her voice is intense, and she seems near tears by the end of it. The crowd is ecstatic.

"Thank you," she says when the cheering subsides. "Thanks so much. So... Thank you all for coming out tonight," she says before wiping her eyes. "I really appreciate all your support. It was kind of a rough day today." The crowd cheers and hoots, and Alli smiles with gratitude. "Thanks. Thank you all so much. I wasn't sure if I was gonna make it here tonight, I—" Alli notices me in the crowd, pausing abruptly. "So, umm... this is a song... a new one... I... I wrote it this past week. One that has been hard for me to write, cuz..." She chokes up again, and steps back from the microphone to collect herself. She wipes her eyes and comes back to the front of the stage. "Sorry. I, uh, went through a break up recently and it's been a rough couple of weeks and... and so I haven't played it before so I—"

"Don't cry, we love you!" some random girl in the crowd shouts, and everyone else cheers and Alli smiles nervously.

Ali forces a smile and a chuckle, but tears are visible down her face. "Thanks." She wipes her face. "So, this is a song about a boy that I... it's called 'Missing Pieces'... I hope you all like it."

I suddenly feel nervous, my heart beats really fast and there's that burning sensation in my gut again. It's a beautifully sad song, and the fact that she's singing through tears just adds to the effect. She struggles on occasion to finish verses, but the crowd claps, letting her know they don't care that's she's messed up. Hearing the song, listening to the lyrics, it's like she's speaking directly to me about how I hurt her and how difficult things have been for her. I knew this already, but hearing her sing about it, hearing how she took all her feelings and condensed them all into this heart-wrenching breakup song... it brings all my guilt and self-loathing to boil because I know I'm responsible for all that the pain. It's so difficult to listen to that it takes all my strength to wait for the song to be over before bolting towards the door to get some air. Alli gasps from the effort it took her to finish song, and crowd claps and cheers and I even notice a few people stand up from their chairs to give her a standing ovation. Just as I open the door to leave I hear Alli say, "Well, I think I'll need a break after that one," and the crowd cheers even louder.

The air is cooler outside, which is exactly what I need. I sit down on the curb, feeling like the world's most awful person, wondering if coming here was a mistake, and if the best thing is to just leave Alli alone for good. I watch cars go by, and for the next few minutes, try to clear my mind.

"Hey," says a voice behind me. Alli's voice. She points to the space on the curb next to me. "Mind if I—"

"Sure." She sits down close to me. I don't look at her, but I can see out of the corner my eye that she's wiping her eyes, but she doesn't say anything. We watch the passing cars for a few minutes in silence. She fidgets with her hands like she's working up the courage to say something. Finally, she speaks.

"So... you were right... about Blake."

"Yeah," I say. "I, uh... I just want to say, before anything else, that I didn't come down here tonight to say, 'I told you so,' or anything. I just... I wanted to see you, to make sure you were okay."

"I know. Thanks."

"And last night," I add. "I came just to talk to you. I didn't know he was going to be there... I wasn't—"

"It's okay. I didn't either."

"So, you're... okay?"

"I will be... eventually. My arm is still a little sore, but he never—" She starts to cry. "Last night... it was just the scariest moment of my life, Nick, I can't even begin to..." She wipes her eyes again. I so badly want to comfort her, to tell her everything will be okay. But I can't yet. I just look out at the passing cars, hoping that I won't break down myself. Alli takes a few deep breaths. "I thought he was just trying to be a friend. To help me. I feel so stupid."

"You're not stupid," I tell her.

"I... and you just sorta left. I never got to thank you. I tried to call you after..."

"I'm sorry. I didn't know. My phone got destroyed last night," I explain.

"Oh, I'm sorry."

Another brief and awkward moment of silence.

"Thank you for the CD, but it was yours. You didn't have to—"

"I didn't feel right keeping it. I just... I wanted you know that no matter what, I'd always keep your secret."

"I never doubted that."

"I just..." I notice Alli's eyes tear up again.

"Nick, if you weren't there last night..."

"I know," I say, before she has to say the words.

"I... am so grateful. I really can't express that enough. Thank you."

"You're welcome," I say.

Neither of us speak for a while.

"You really nailed him good," I say, breaking the silence. "You knocked him out cold."

Alli smiles. "Thanks."

"I'm sorry about your guitar."

"Don't be sorry."

"Well," I say, reaching in my pocket. "About the guitar. I... this ought to cover the cost of a new one," I say, handing her a check I wrote. Her eyes widen.

"Nick, I... Where did you—"

"I never told you... or anyone this before. My ex... Lauren... I..."

"I know what happened between you two."

"You do?"

Alli nods. "Last week, she was at the Copper Thieves show. She told me everything. We had a long talk."

"I'm sorry I never told you."

"Me too. If I had known... I wish you'd told me."

"I was too humiliated to tell anyone... or even return the ring. I did today though. That's where I got the money. I want you to use it to get a new guitar, I—" Alli rips up the check. "Why did you..."

"It's not your fault, Nick. If you weren't there I'd have bigger problems than a destroyed guitar."

"But if I had been... I dunno, stronger or if I'd—"

"Nick, don't. Besides, you know how I feel about you paying for stuff."

"You let me when we were dating."

Alli sighs. "And, if we were dating, I still wouldn't let you pay for it."

Her words sting, like she's just told me not to expect reconciliation. I obviously failed miserably to hide the disappointment in my face because she looks at me horrified. "Oh, Nick, I'm sorry. I didn't mean it like that."

"How did you mean it?"

"I... I just meant... I'm sorry. I don't know what to say. The past couple weeks have been so hard and confusing. I've never broken up with someone before, and no matter what I do, I'm miserable, and I cry, like, all the time... and I'm so sad and I miss you like crazy, and it just gets worse every day instead of better, and I still love you and I just want—"

"I love you, too," I tell her. "I always will."

Alli leans her head on my shoulder, and offers me her open hand, which I take. I feel the wetness from her face through my shirt. We sit there in silence, holding hands, watching traffic.

"So, what do we do?" she finally asks. "What happens now?"

"I'm thinking we should get back together," I say. She doesn't answer. "I mean, if you want to."

She still doesn't say anything.

"Do, you *want* to get back together?" I ask, unable to hide the nervousness in my voice.

Alli wipes her eyes with her free arm and stands up. She doesn't let go of my hand, so I stand up with her. This is not the reaction I was expecting, but she's got a subtle smile on her face.

"Can I give you answer after my last set?"

"After your—" I start to say, before remembering we've had this conversation before, months ago, when I first asked her out. I smile too. "You're really going to make me wait that long to tell me?"

"Of course, I am." She has a much bigger smile on her face now. "I figure it gives you a reason to stay until the end." She squeezes my hand. "Come on, let's go back inside," she says, and leads me away from the street and back into the coffeehouse.

The End.

A MESSAGE FROM THE AUTHOR

Thanks so much for reading *Not Famous*. I really hope you enjoyed reading it. Reviews are incredibly important to self-published authors like myself, and I would be grateful if you took the time to post a review on Amazon, Goodreads, etc., to help spread the word.

Your review can help this book get noticed!

ABOUT THE AUTHOR

Matthew Hanover has been reading books all his life and is now writing his own. He hopes to one day be able to quit his day job and write full time. *Not Famous* is his debut novel.

Connect with Matthew Hanover

Facebook: facebook.com/matthanoverfiction
Twitter: @matthewhanover
Instagram: instagram.com/matthanoverfiction
Book Bub: bookbub.com/authors/matthew-hanover
Amazon: amazon.com/author/matthewhanover
Website: matthewhanover.com

5502R00233

Made in the USA
Lexington, KY
20 February 2019